EATING FIRE AND DRINKING WATER

D0375771

ARLENE J. CHAI

Fawcett Columbine
The Ballantine Publishing Group • New York

A Fawcett Columbine Book
Published by The Ballantine Publishing Group

http://www.randomhouse.com

Library of Congress Cataloging-in-Publication Data
Chai, Arlene J.
Eating fire and drinking water / Arlene J. Chai
p.   cm.
ISBN 0-449-91143-8 (alk. paper)
I. Title.
PR9619.3.C417E28   1998
823–dc21   98-10090
CIP

Cover design by Min Choi
Cover illustration by Julie Quinlivan
Text design by Jie Yang

Manufactured in the United States of America

First American Edition: May 1998

10 9 8 7 6 5 4 3 2 1

To Adrianne

Acknowledgments

MANY THANKS TO my publisher Jane Palfreyman and, most specially, to my editor Julia Stiles, whose patience and words of encouragement kept me going and whose insight helped shape this book.

Yvonne Ellis, Cheryl Wong-Horne, and my sister Adrianne for reading through my drafts.

Julie Quinlivan, good friend and gifted artist, who has once more created a work of art for my cover.

Suzanne Mercier, Kathie Dixon, and Alan Barry, who helped me keep my sanity over the last three years as I worked on this manuscript.

And to Bryce Courtenay, who continues to be a source of encouragement and inspiration.

Contents

List *of* Characters

THE JUDICIARY
Judge Romero Jimenez—head of the commission investigating military violence; "the Hanging Judge"

THE PALACE CIRCLE
El Presidente
Madam
Maia—daughter of the First Couple, bride-to-be of Iñigo Pellicer
Chief of Staff (Raul)
Press Secretary
Ding Sarmiento—Madam's jeweler

THE HACIENDA ESPERANZA CIRCLE
Don Miguel Pellicer—the sugar baron known as "The Don"
Marina Pellicer—wife of the don
Iñigo Pellicer—son of the don, bridegroom-to-be of the First Couple's daughter
Doña Carmela Pellicer—the don's mother
Zenaida Ysmael—the don's old flame

"EL TORO" AND COMPANY
Sixto Mijares—notorious senator known as "El Toro"
Lorena Zamora-Mijares—the senator's wife
Ana—the senator's mistress

THE CONVENT OF SANTA CLARA CIRCLE
Mother Superior (Sister Socorro)
Sister Luisa
Pepito Mariano—solicitor

SMOKY MOUNTAIN
Mang Serio—Philosopher of the Mount

SEISMOLOGICAL STUDY CENTER
Armando Cruz—head of the SSC

Prologue

I only have to close my eyes and I am in that blackened street once more, amidst the smoky ruins of what had once been the homes of people who now walk about with unseeing eyes, citizens of a world suddenly grown unfamiliar.

I only have to close my eyes to smell the heavy tainted air and to feel the onslaught of heat on my face and to see the charred remains of the fire's only victim being lifted from the pyre that had been his store.

How was I to know that this dead stranger would appear in my life again? That he had been there right from the beginning, holding the secret to who I was so that the very mysteries of my own life would find their answers at last. How was I to know that this fire in a street I had never been to would somehow eat away at my life's invisible boundaries so that into it would come rushing names and faces which until then were unknown to me?

I only have to close my eyes to return to the beginning of it all, to the precise moment when I ceased to be just a reporter of events, becoming instead a part of them.

To say that I am someone who went looking for a story only to find herself caught in one would not be too far from the truth.

On the Monday morning that Calle de Leon went up in flames, I was sent by my paper to gather facts, which I did without wasting time. I found what I needed then left to file my report.

Had this been just another day, I would have forgotten the fire and its victim as quickly as the compositors set my story back at the *Chronicle*. But there was to be no walking away, no forgetting that day.

Much has happened since. Twists and turns that no one could have foreseen. And many people, too, have come and gone from my life. Like Luis Bayani, whose last words to me before he disappeared never to be seen again were: "Who knows, Clara, you may write about this one day."

But Luis is not here to read this, and this will always be the deepest regret of my life.

Enough hours and days have passed to allow for some understanding of all that has happened, and for me to join together the separate moments that make up this tale—those moments I lived through and those recounted to me by others. Where there were gaps I have filled them with my imagined truth. This is a writer's privilege.

I sought to find a pattern, a deeper purpose, for, at the time, the events I am about to recount seemed random and arbitrary. The reporter in me, you see, insisted there is order in the universe. And my own life attests to this. Besides, to deny the existence of order means to believe in a world of permanent chaos. And I find such a concept unacceptable.

So if there is a message to be found in this tale, it is this: there is sense . . . a plan behind everything that happens.

PART I

1

There Is No Such Thing
As a Small Story

On the morning it all began, I was in the middle of Lacson Bridge, in a crowded jeepney with ten other passengers, caught in the peak-hour traffic jam that seemed to occur at this very spot every morning.

I was a twenty-three-year-old reporter. My name—Clara Perez. And I worked for a small metropolitan daily called the *Chronicle*.

I was someone hungry for stories; more specifically, I was someone who craved after facts. It is easy now to see where this hunger came from and how it determined my choice of profession. I was, you see, at the start of this tale, a person with no history. I had no story of my own. Lacking this, I developed a curiosity about other people's lives. I filled my life with the facts that framed the human dramas which unfolded in my city, and which I reported faithfully.

On that particular morning, on the way to work, as I sat in the jeepney breathing in the oppressive smell that rose from the river, I heard the unmistakable wail of fire engines. I scanned the skies for the telltale pillar of smoke. It was rising in the distance to the west and I tried to guess which suburb lay in that direction.

But my thoughts were soon interrupted as the old wooden bridge shook under the weight of the fire engines thundering past in the opposite lane. The deafening pitch of their sirens and the sweep of air on my back marked their urgent passing. I became thankful then that I was stuck where I was and not at the *Chronicle*.

I knew Torres, the news editor, too well. This fire was just the sort of thing he would assign to me.

Eighteen months at the paper had not elevated me in any way in the news editor's eyes. I was still the reporter who copped the fires and floods and all other forms of natural disasters, as well as incidents of domestic violence, road accidents, and epidemics; not to mention every boring social event in town, such as the fashion show at the Hilton I was scheduled to cover at noon that day.

Once, unable to contain my frustration at yet another of these assignments, I said to him, "Not another robbery!"

As soon as I spoke I regretted it, for I saw how much my words irked him. "No, Clara," he said, "it is *not* just another robbery."

Torres was of the opinion that there was no such thing as a small story. I didn't agree and argued that some stories were simply fodder.

He countered by saying that the problem with me was that I viewed things with too much objectivity. Although he never said so, I think Torres sent me out on these assignments to shake me up, to see if I would shed some of my so-called detachment.

He kept the stories I wanted from me. Every day it was to some other reporter that he gave the palace stories, the stories of military exploits, the stories involving the powerful names that determined the fate of this city and the nation.

And that Monday was no different.

"There's been another riot," Torres announced as he charged out of his cubicle.

I caught his words just as I set foot in the newsroom, late and looking somewhat frazzled from dashing to the building from the jeepney stop across the road.

Like everyone else, I took out my pad and pen, ready to jot down the details of my assignment.

Torres filled us in on what he knew, delivering his words with barely concealed excitement. Like the true newshound he was, Torres spoke in headlines. The students of the Loyola University, led by the charismatic student leader Luis Bayani, had been fired at by the military. The peaceful sit-in organized to protest the tragic

June 6 incident, which saw eight students brutally clubbed and gunned down, had deteriorated into another violent confrontation. Now a student and a soldier fought for their lives at Santo Cristo Hospital, with many others badly injured; and at the camp, some forty students were being detained for questioning. The palace was due to make an announcement.

Hearing this, Joey, the staff photographer, let out a long soft whistle, then said, "I'd like to see him get out of this one." By him, Joey meant El Presidente, whose sixteen-year regime was being challenged at last by a growing radical student movement.

For the next three minutes, Torres broke the story down into sub-stories. "Danny, write about the riot and get an interview with Bayani and the military commander—Reyes, I think, yes that's right, Commander Reyes—see if you can get some witness accounts from the residents in the university area. I want every angle covered. Max, take the palace conference at eleven. Joey, go with Max and get a photo of El Presidente. Then I want you to head for the hospital, see if you can take some shots of the soldier and the student. Mel, a quick call to the hospital should do, you don't have to go, just talk to the doctor in charge. This way you can interview that pest from the SSC."

Then turning toward me and holding my gaze, Torres said, "Perez, I want you at Calle de Leon."

I had never heard of this street before, didn't know where it was or what was there.

"It's near the Loyola. There's been a fire." Still holding my gaze, Torres handed me a sheet of paper with directions on it.

I fought to keep my expression neutral as I turned and walked out of the room. But once out of Torres's sight, I felt, to my horror, tears of frustration forming in my eyes.

The others were waiting by the lift when I got to the foyer. As I made to join them, Joey, sharp-eyed as usual, noticed my overbright eyes and tried to lighten the moment.

"Now, Clara," he said, "get that frown off your face before you grow more white hairs."

With his photographer's eye for detail, Joey had been the first to notice the narrow streak of white that had started growing near my right temple some six months ago.

He asked me back then, "Does it run in your family?" I could only shrug in reply. Personal questions always embarrassed me. How was I to know where that white streak came from when there was no one to tell me?

To divert Joey then, I had said, "It's Torres's fault. He's causing me to age prematurely." Since then Joey always referred to that streak in relation to my work at the *Chronicle*. He knew I hated the stories Torres assigned to me.

Now, standing by the lift, I felt Max, the senior reporter, nudge me with his elbow. He grinned his boyish grin. "C'mon, Clara, the fire's not as bad as Mel's assignment. Why, she's got to talk to some crazy guy from the Seismological Study Center who insists we're about to get badly shaken up!"

That made me smile but it wasn't enough to rid me of the depression that was beginning to take hold of me. My life was growing as predictable as the stories Torres assigned me. But I could not have been more wrong.

Torres, you see, had unknowingly handed me the biggest story of my life. Of all the stories out there, this was the one I was destined to write.

In sending me to cover that same fire I had watched earlier from the bridge, I was to learn the truth in the news editor's words at last: there is no such thing as a small story.

2

Just Another Day

*F*ate, no doubt, had a hand in it.

Even before I reached the bridge that morning, fate had already been at work, carefully positioning the players of this tale so that each would be at the right place at the right time to enact his or her role. It seems to me that while people are caught up in the living of their individual lives, they are often unaware that their separate pursuits are not that separate after all. They are constantly hurtling toward some intersection where they are about to join others in stepping into a tale.

The morning I speak of, one such player was a simple man named Charlie.

There was no way Charlie could have known he was about to die.

When Charlie the Chinaman woke that Monday morning at his usual time just before dawn, his killer—a soldier of the 22nd Infantry—lay in his army bunk at Campo Diaz, talking in his sleep.

I imagine Charlie on his last morning rising from his cot and going through his usual rituals. That like all the other mornings of his life, he sits down once more to a simple breakfast in his sparsely furnished room. The room itself is not really a room but a section formed by a two-meter-high timber panel which separates it from the front of the single-story house that served as Charlie's store. In this windowless enclosure, Charlie sleeps, cooks, and eats his meals.

Now he is drinking the *oolong* tea he loves, in between mouthfuls of hot *pan de sal*. And perhaps his eyes wander to the photographs stuck on his wall. There are five of them, all featuring a child. The same child at different ages—from toddler to perhaps age five, maybe six. A fair-skinned girl with dark hair and serious eyes. He smiles on seeing these images and I imagine him reaching out and gently running a finger over the faded prints.

Who is this child? How is she related to him? Surely she must be dear to him or her pictures wouldn't be in this room. No one can tell her place in the Chinaman's life, for other than Charlie, no one has ever seen her pictures on the wall.

He is private by nature, not by design.

Although Charlie has lived in Calle de Leon for thirty years now, no one knows anything of significance about him except that he came from China in his youth. He is a friend to everyone, listening to the tales they bring to him, the secrets they whisper through his window. But of himself he says little.

He is an enigma to his neighbors. They can't help wondering at his solitary state. No one ever visits him, none of his neighbors can recall seeing Charlie with a friend; and he never speaks of family, of connections.

But every fourth Sunday of the month, Charlie dresses in his best clothes, shedding his usual gray slacks and white *camiso de tsino*, and heads off somewhere just as the sun sets behind the row of *accessorias* that line the street. And always Charlie takes with him a bag of goods, obviously a present for someone. So there, the neighbors say to themselves, the Chinaman can't be as lonely as we thought.

Right now, as he pours himself another cup of *oolong* tea, Charlie hears the faint sounds of the world outside. He sits and listens to the swishing of the street sweeper's broom, the coughing of a cold engine, the barking of the neighborhood dogs.

Every now and then he checks the time.

Charlie, a creature of habit, always slides open his window panels at precisely seven A.M. and, with the exception of Sundays when he closes two hours earlier, he slides them shut at precisely eight P.M. Only on two occasions has he failed to open for business at the usual time, but this is not the place to talk about those momentous two days in Charlie's life.

He is almost ready for another day of business. And Charlie expects today to be like all the others.

Three doors down from Charlie the Chinaman's store, Consuelo Lamuerta wakes to the crowing of Istanbul, Mang Lino's fighting cock. His loud, crackling cry abruptly cutting the strands that connect her to her dream. She pulls frantically at the gossamer images that are quickly losing their definition, but in a matter of seconds, they are gone. Was there a fire? A crowd forming a snakelike queue? And the figure of a sleeping woman? All Consuelo is left with are disjointed images she can make no sense of.

Flinging her blanket aside, she rises to make her bed and almost loses her balance. She attempts to steady herself and for a brief moment shuts her eyes and experiences the strangest sensation.

In her words to me later, this was how she described the moment: "I felt the world shifting, riding on a wave."

She remembers which day it was: "It was the Monday of the fire."

When this strange sensation passes, Consuelo straightens up and makes her way to the small shower room downstairs, where she washes before changing into a black dress. Consuelo only ever wears black. She is a widow.

Consuelo Lamuerta arrived at Calle de Leon over two decades ago. Those who remember her from those days still speak of her beauty. And how, of the many men that would have offered for her, none summoned up the courage to express what lay in their heart, for Consuelo's eternal grief made them keep their distance.

As for the young husband she tragically lost soon after her marriage, Consuelo never speaks his name.

Looking at her now, she is still beautiful, her face almost untouched by time. And where grief was once visible, now all one sees is calm. Her prayers, they say, have dispelled her sorrow.

But whatever you hear about Consuelo, remember this: she is not all she appears to be.

Here, in Calle de Leon, she is known for her candles. All day and all night, she burns two candles in a small room she has turned into an altar room. When in the beginning her neighbors expressed their fears of a fire starting, she quietly but surely replied, "No fire will touch my home," and they let her be.

In light of what is about to happen, Consuelo's words, spoken long ago, will take on a new meaning.

Consuelo genuflects by the doorway; she makes the sign of the cross, enters her altar room, and kneels in front of Our Lady, whose meter-high statue stands at the center of the altar. Our Lady has a benevolent face framed by a white veil; and next to her is the Santo Niño, the crowned figure of the Infant Jesus with a red-and-gold cape, scepter in one hand and globe in the other.

Consuelo begins to pray.

Laslo Jimenez stretches his aching limbs, swearing softly under his breath, his body sore and cramped. The hard concrete steps of the administration building have robbed him of sleep for the third night in a row.

Since the first evening of the campus sit-in, he has wished for the comfort of his bed, except going home is out of the question. They're in this together, right? They're here to show solidarity. Besides, he can't go off and leave Sophia.

He glances toward her sleeping figure next to him, her body twisted at an angle, her head on the crook of her arm. She doesn't look too comfortable but at least she is sleeping. He gently pulls the coat more securely over her shoulders, and for a second thinks of pushing her long hair away from her face, but he stops himself, not wanting to wake her.

Still thinking of his bed at home, he yawns, exhausted. And the thought of home reminds him of his father. It isn't just Sophia that has kept him from leaving. His father is reason enough. Nothing in the world could have induced Laslo to give his father the satisfaction of seeing him return.

Laslo is the son of Romero Jimenez, the Hanging Judge, a man who in his thirty years in court has sent thirteen men to fry in the electric chair, and two to die by firing squad. Just as well that Laslo does not have to stand before him now. The judge disapproves of student activism and Laslo's involvement in the university sit-in has done nothing to improve their already strained relationship. It hasn't helped either that the judge has pronounced his son as spoiled, immature, and irresponsible, which carries a grain of truth with regard to the Laslo of this fateful morning.

The Laslo that you find here is different from the Laslo I would later encounter by the river when I was searching for the spirit of a dead friend. That Laslo had lost all innocence and wore the look of someone haunted by all the horrors he had seen. But I am leaping too far ahead in time. The journey to the river will be a long while yet.

Right now, Laslo longs for sleep the way men in a desert long for water. But his thoughts prevent sleep from coming. Laslo cannot help thinking of the coming morning. And this makes him nervous.

Laslo joined the sit-in because of Sophia. He is her shadow, going where she goes, doing as she does. In fact, he joined the Youth for Reform Movement not because of any heartfelt commitment to the cause but simply because he wished to be near her. Sure, he had heard of YRM before he met Sophia. Everyone had, in the same way that everyone knew who Luis Bayani was. But he had no desire to join YRM until Sophia came along. He was drawn to her like a magnet is drawn to steel.

Although Laslo is a reluctant participant, he has to admit that there have been moments when he has felt himself swept along by the passionate tide created by tens of thousands of demonstrating students. One such moment occurred last year when the controversial manifesto calling for political reform was drawn up by YRM and signed by over thirty thousand students from various colleges and universities, then handed over to a representative of Congress.

There was much euphoria on this occasion. Laslo remembers glancing at Sophia and seeing her eyes brim with tears. He felt his eyes water, too. He cannot explain the fervor and pride he felt, but he felt them just the same.

The students soon realized, however, that the government considered the manifesto no more valuable than the sheets of paper on which it was written. So they took to the streets in greater numbers. Laslo among them.

Finally, El Presidente decided to act.

In a show of force, the military was sent in to intimidate the students, but instead of being cowed by the sight of armed soldiers, the students fought back. Twenty-two of them were injured and the press had a field day. This was the first violent showdown. More followed. And Laslo became a veteran of these violent encounters.

Then on June 6, eight students were killed as soldiers opened fire in the middle of a rally on Plaza Cendaña.

It was concern for Sophia's safety that had saved Laslo's neck that day.

When the first shots were fired, Laslo froze momentarily in fear, but the need to get Sophia away had spurred him to move; as it turned out, not a second too soon. As he ran in her direction, he missed a bullet speeding toward him. That bullet found another target, embedding itself in the neck of the student standing right behind Laslo. After his narrow escape, Laslo managed to drag Sophia to safety.

Except now they are both here. Both at risk again.

He wonders if this cause she so believes in is worth dying for. Such thoughts are, of course, to be kept secret. Not only because of Sophia's certain disapproval, but also because of Luis Bayani. Laslo values the student leader's opinion, is in awe of him.

Laslo searches for Luis Bayani's figure. He catches sight of him at the top of the steps: tall, lean, and still, a pensive air about him. It occurs to Laslo he is not the only one who has not slept. Bayani has had more to keep him awake, he bears the greatest responsibility in the coming confrontation.

Thinking of sleep makes Laslo yawn again, and this time, with less than an hour of darkness left, it comes to him at last.

But all too soon the sun is out and morning light bathes the university grounds. Laslo opens his eyes, automatically looking around for Sophia. He finds her gazing down at him. He only has to meet her eyes to know the time has come.

"Get ready, Laslo," she says.

Laslo rises to his feet and his nervousness returns with such force that he feels nauseated. He swallows hard. Then reaches into his pockets, finding reassurance in the hardness of his secret hoard of rocks. Luis Bayani has insisted on a weapons-free sit-in, but Laslo knows that many of his companions have gone in search of something to arm themselves with. No one trusts the palace or the soldiers. Nothing is being left to chance.

Just then Laslo catches sight of the two students running toward the administration building, shouting, "They're coming! The pigs are coming!"

The students take up their positions.

The orders come through just before midnight.

The soldiers hurry out of the room, a disorderly lot muttering to themselves as they head for the briefing room in Block 12 just what could be so important that they have had to be wakened?

Rogelio Campos, surrounded by his bleary-eyed companions, has a few ideas of his own. He has, after all, been following the news since Friday. All matters that involve the military interest him. More than any other member of the 22nd Infantry, Rogelio is a dedicated soldier. To him, being a soldier is more than just a job. It is a whole new life, one so different from his old one.

Rogelio has a secret, you see, one he guards carefully, one he has never confided to anyone, not even to his friend Dario. Rogelio Campos is an escaped *sacada*.

Before joining the army, Rogelio, like his father and brothers, was an itinerant worker contracted to cut sugarcane in the biggest plantation in the south. Rogelio hated the life, the poverty and the injustice of it, and so he stole away one night, taking with him a well-worn change of clothes and a book that was his most cherished possession. And he made his way to the city and into the army.

That was three years ago.

In the briefing room, Rogelio Campos takes a seat next to Dario just as Commander Reyes makes his way to the front to address the members of the 22nd Infantry. As soon as he speaks, Rogelio knows that his hunch is right. They are being sent to the Loyola University.

"Five hundred students have taken over the campus since Friday night. They have camped out on the front steps of the administration building. They are insisting that the university administration join them in denouncing the government's role in the June 6 incident. The students need to be dispersed before the start of classes in the morning.

"At a quarter to six, twenty trucks will depart from here to take you to the corner of Remedios and Generoso. You will disembark and march into the campus grounds. You will arrive there at approximately six-thirty. The students must be escorted out of the grounds no later than seven. No one must be allowed to remain in the administration building.

"One more thing: El Presidente does not want a repeat of the June 6 incident. Do not use force, do not fire your weapons, there are two of you to every student. And remember, the media will be watching."

The men walk out of the room, grumbling to each other about the orders they have just received. Banned from using their weapons, the soldiers are stripped of the only effective way of enforcing order. Back in their quarters, the discussion continues and grows more heated until someone turns off the lights. For the next hour Rogelio can hear the tossing and turning of his companions and the occasional whisper in the dark.

Until finally only Rogelio remains awake.

His mind is filled with thoughts of tomorrow. The violence the military has engaged in lately has disturbed him, yet tomorrow perhaps he and his fellow soldiers will have an opportunity to right that. But good intentions are not enough. Under pressure there is no predicting how anyone will act.

With all these thoughts churning inside him, sleep is slow in coming. After a while, he turns on his side as if to dislodge his worries. It is then that he hears a familiar voice call out, *"Sige . . . bilisan mo ang takbo!"*

His friend Dario, the new recruit from the south, is dreaming of horses again. Dario, who has a knack for guessing the winning horse, though he has continually refused to place bets on the San Lazaro Sunday races. "Then it'll be for real and I'll be nervous and that drives the luck away," he explained. So they bet on paper and check the results every Monday morning. So far, Dario has had three firsts and five placings out of twelve races.

Now Rogelio wants to go to his friend and shake him awake. He wants Dario to reassure him, Dario with his ability to foretell things. He wants to tell his friend, "Stop dreaming of horses, dream of the coming morning instead."

Two hours before waking time, Rogelio finally falls into a restless sleep and does something he has never done before. Like his friend Dario, he talks in his sleep.

In the morning, a fellow soldier asks him what he has been dreaming of, for he spoke the following words: "Did you read about me?"

How long has he been napping? The room with its drawn curtains lets no light in. He can't see the time. He reaches for the light switch, groping along the curves of the alabaster lamp base. His fingers make out the familiar shape of the smooth flat belly, the pair of small firm breasts, the head sensuously tilted to one side to reveal a graceful neck, until he finds the switch hidden at the nape.

The light filters through the silk lampshade. This can't be right, he thinks, looking at his watch. Five to six. So much for his plan to have a catnap.

Senator Sixto Mijares, notorious member of the Upper House, rises from the bed and strides to the armchair where his clothes are draped. He dresses quickly, then checks his watch again.

Five past six.

He shoves his feet into his shoes and walks back to the lamp to switch it off. He hears the rustle of sheets, and pauses. Glancing down, he sees a long white arm emerge. For a while he fears Ana will wake and talk to him, delaying him further. But the figure simply shifts, and the silk sheet remolds itself around her body. Had not the strange rumbling sound, like an insistent murmur, roused him from the spell Ana is beginning to cast on him, he would have reached out to touch her.

Instead, he turns, leaves the room, and runs down the stairs, where Sushi, the Japanese spitz, yelps at him as he lets himself out of the front door. It is already light outside. He notes that his car, a vintage Lincoln Continental with government plates, is clearly visible. He gets in quickly, starts the engine, and drives away.

He turns into Remedios Street and heads toward the T-intersection with Generoso. He likes driving along this wide road, for it takes him past his alma mater, the Loyola University, where he was an economics major and served as student-council president in his senior year. But this morning he only gives it a cursory look. There is no time to spare.

What the unsuspecting senator does not know is that it is not chance that brings him to this vicinity at this hour. He, too, has a role to play; one he rejects at first, which is hardly surprising. Everything I had ever heard said of him until this moment concerned his preoccupation with the pleasures of the flesh. And it was just like him to describe this turning point in his life as "bad timing."

As he approaches the intersection, the strange rumbling sound he heard earlier grows louder. It sounds like the thundering of large trucks or lorries. But he knows there is a ban on them until ten in the morning, so it has to be something else. Before he can think of another explanation, Senator Sixto Mijares finds himself slamming hard on his brakes as he comes face-to-face with the military convoy bearing the 22nd Infantry. The trucks come to an abrupt halt across the top of Remedios Street, their tires screeching. Seconds later the thousand-strong 22nd Infantry pours into the barricaded street.

The senator, shaken but not speechless, steps out of his vehicle and is about to abuse the commander of the infantry and to demand the trucks clear out of his way when a member of a television news crew emerges out of nowhere and aims his camera at the senator. The video footage will show the senator with his finger pointing at the commander, and his face half-turned toward the camera, contorted with rage.

It is precisely fifteen past six and it will be a while before Senator Sixto Mijares, also known as El Toro, can make his way home to his wife.

And so, with each player in place, this tale of mine began.

3

Death of a Chinaman

*L*aslo made for the topmost step of the administration building. But even from this vantage point Remedios Street remained concealed. The tall acacias that grew along the perimeter of the university fence and the main driveway leading to the building blocked the view. Laslo was impatient for the soldiers to arrive. He wished to face the enemy. That frightening prospect was preferable to this endless waiting.

He made his way down to where Sophia stood, and in a low voice told her, "I'll be next to you, just stay close, okay?" She returned his gaze but said nothing.

Then the soldiers arrived.

From where Laslo and the students waited, the synchronized marching of the soldiers grew more and more audible. The place suddenly seemed charged with a high voltage. Slice through the air and you could have heard it crackle. Laslo shifted on his feet and shook his arms. He needed to loosen his muscles before his mounting fear took command of his body.

"Whatever happens, stand your ground," Luis Bayani called out from the front row. Before he finished speaking, the screeching sound of rusty hinges was heard. The heavy chain used to secure the gate fell to the ground. The campus was not built to be impregnable.

Moments later, the 22nd Infantry entered the university grounds at last.

Laslo and his companions were not alone in watching the soldiers' approach. The residents of Remedios Street, who had been woken by the sound of rumbling trucks, now stuck their heads out of their windows, while the more adventurous spilled out of their front doors to gape with awestruck expectation at the neat columns of advancing soldiers.

As the soldiers made their way up the main approach to the administration building, slowly closing the distance between them and the students, an explosion of abuse greeted them. Amidst the loud whistling and booing, a baritone voice shouted out, "Pigs and puppets!" Immediately, Laslo and the rest took up the taunting cry.

Overhead, birds burst from the trees, taking flight in a confusion of wings, scattering in the air.

For the first time since entering the campus, Commander Reyes spoke into his megaphone, his voice booming loud and clear. "You are being requested to leave the campus. . . . Disperse now or you will be arrested."

Sophia, cupping her hands over her mouth, shouted back: "*You* go home . . . go home to your camp!"

The five hundred students chanted, "Go home . . . go home . . . go home. . . ."

"I repeat . . . disperse now before you get arrested!" ordered the commander.

"Go home . . . go home. . . ."

The soldiers were now just twenty meters away from the students, and filming their approach was a cameraman from one of the networks.

A minute later, the soldiers came to a halt. The air was still as the two groups came face-to-face. Between them, like some mediator, stood the bronze statue of the Great Benefactor of the Loyola University.

The infantry commander called out once more to the students, directing them to disband and clear out of the campus, to which Luis Bayani, speaking for the first time, replied that the students were exercising their constitutional right to assemble and that this was a nonviolent protest, so no law was being broken.

Commander Reyes, in a stern voice, countered with an ultimatum: "You have five minutes to organize yourselves, then you will be escorted out of here. Listen carefully, you have five minutes."

It was at this point that Laslo left Sophia's side.

"Where are you going?"

Laslo heard her urgent question, but he refused to look back, to reconsider his action.

Laslo had had enough of the commander's words. The sight of the soldiers with their bullying faces, and their threatening weapons slung over their arms, made his blood boil. He would pay them back for all the beatings he had received from them, all the bruises and cuts he had suffered, and most of all, for the bullet that had narrowly missed his neck.

When his eyes took in the bronze sculpture of the Great Benefactor, the idea quickly took shape in his mind.

Perfect. It was just perfect.

All eyes followed Laslo.

Luis Bayani cursed the distance which prevented him from reaching out and restraining him. What was the reckless fool up to? Luis had always sensed Laslo's unpredictable, headstrong nature. But he had said nothing, for Sophia believed in him.

The student leader had a sickening feeling that Laslo was about to jeopardize his plans. Didn't he know everything was so tightly balanced that one wrong move could throw them into another bloody confrontation?

With growing apprehension Luis watched as Laslo, looking disheveled, took a deep breath and with a supreme effort hoisted himself onto the pedestal of the Great Benefactor. He watched as Laslo, who now towered over the crowd, turned and faced the soldiers; watched as a snaky smile appeared on his handsome, unshaven face, as he slowly unzipped his fly, whipped out his manhood, and pointed it insolently at the soldiers below; watched him as he released a stream of golden piss onto their upturned faces, in full view of the network cameraman, who recorded this public display for the evening news.

It was a few seconds before the soldiers realized what had come their way. They raised their hands to shield their faces but by then the urine had seeped into their apparel, forming dark patches, the smell of which would stay even after the stains had dried.

The students cheered and applauded this unexpected performance by the judge's rebellious son. And Laslo, enjoying the attention, grinned, then bowed with flourish to the crowd, all the while precariously perched on the pedestal.

Luis, heart thumping, expected at any moment to hear the exploding sound of weapons firing. "Laslo, get down!" he ordered, his voice a blend of fury and panic as he watched with horror as the soldiers reached for their weapons.

Just then the infantry commander shouted urgently to his men: "Don't fire!" and Luis knew that only the commander's loud cry had stopped the angry men from blasting Laslo into a bloody pulp.

Only after Laslo jumped down to join a scowling Sophia did Luis breathe a slow, painful sigh of relief. The Hanging Judge's son had come so close to dying and he didn't even realize it. How Luis longed to wipe the self-satisfied smile off the brazen idiot's face as Laslo zipped up his pants. And it didn't improve his mood that the students greeted Laslo's act of stupidity with yet another round of applause.

Just then Luis Bayani had the uncomfortable feeling that he was being watched. He turned around and scanned the faces of the soldiers. There he saw someone staring at him with such penetrating intensity he could only interpret it as hate.

It was him. It could be no other. He recognized him.

Luis Bayani.

LB.

Rogelio made the connection at last.

LB were the initials in the book he had carried with him from his old life. That he should meet the giver of the book again—its original owner—astounded him. What twist of fate, what luck had brought the two of them to this place at this moment?

It had never occurred to Rogelio that he would set eyes on the student's face again, although he had thought of him often enough in the past three years. He had wished to tell him that he had made a new life for himself, that he was a soldier now, not some poor suffering *sacada*.

Later, in the quiet of his cell, when his life seemed devoid of hope and all he had left was time to think his endless thoughts, Rogelio would realize that it was only natural that the young man he met three summers ago, who had been instrumental in his escape to freedom, should turn out to be the controversial student leader Luis Bayani.

But during that moment of recognition as he stood facing Luis at the Loyola University, Rogelio's reaction, which had been one of surprise and disbelief, quickly gave way to confusion. How was he to reconcile the fact that he and this man whom he admired now stood on opposite sides? He wanted to call to him, to catch Luis Bayani's attention, but he didn't know how. And even if he succeeded, what was he to say? The last person Luis Bayani would welcome as a friend was a soldier.

Just then his thoughts were interrupted by the sound of Luis Bayani issuing his bold command.

"Forward!" Luis Bayani ordered.

Sensing the situation could quickly deteriorate into a bloody riot, Luis decided it was time to act. His dark longish hair framing his intense face, he took a step forward and the soldier facing him instantly took a step back. He repeated this once more and the soldier retreated another step. Watching him, his companions learned at last his plan. The simplicity of it surprised them: Luis Bayani intended to drive the soldiers off the campus grounds. He would do it by making them retrace their steps all the way to the main gate.

Soon all five hundred students followed suit. Taking a step forward, forcing the soldiers facing them to take a step back. And so began an ignominious military retreat with the soldiers falling back against each other as though engaged in some strange haphazard pantomime.

"Hold your line . . . hold your line!" Luis heard the infantry commander cry. But the students could not be stopped now in their bold single-minded advance. The soldiers continued to lose ground as the student leader and his followers increased their pace.

The retreat may have been completed without incident had not a pimply youth with long curly hair hurled himself forward and spat on a soldier's face twice in a row.

The students' offensive came to a sudden halt and all sound ceased, so that only the whirring of the news camera was audible.

On video is captured the stunned expression of the soldier, his body immobile, frozen in disbelief; while around him both students and soldiers watch with fascination the spit, which hangs over his lashes, travel down his cheek like a tear. The soldier blinks once. Twice. Meanwhile, facing him, the cocky youth pools more saliva to spit in his face.

Luis Bayani, fighting the inertia of those around him, forced his way through the crowd. And just as the student made to release a third volley of saliva, yanked him hard by the arm, but he was too late.

The shot reverberated in the air, a rude, ripping sound that tore at the silence. It seemed to distort time, so that seconds stretched into eternity and Luis caught every nuance of the drama that unfolded before him: the student staring at the soldier then down at his shirt at the crimson spot that slowly appeared, gradually turning blue cotton into a gruesome red; the student clutching his middle, his soft groan before slowly crumpling like paper to the ground.

And as he knelt next to the bleeding student, struggling to halt the eager flow of blood, Luis Bayani knew that there was no staving off disaster now. This was no nightmare happening in someone else's dream, this was happening here and now. And he felt that in some way he was the author of this scene. He was responsible for the angry cursing and shouting of his companions, the Molotov cocktail going off, the shower of rocks, the swinging of chains, bats, and metal pipes, the smashing of bottles, the savage exchange of blows.

Then he heard the first volley and knew that the firing of

weapons was no longer an isolated aberration. It had become a mass action. He heard all this, but most of all, he heard the question he repeatedly asked himself: why did you fail to see this coming?

From where he stood, Rogelio could see the fallen student. Then he swung around to look at the soldier who had fired his weapon. What he saw horrified him. Dario. It was his friend Dario.

A meter away from him, Dario stood stock-still, staring at his smoking weapon, unwilling to believe that he had fired it. Then from the corner of his eye Rogelio caught sight of the attacking student. Rogelio shouted Dario's name but Dario failed to move in time.

Thirty seconds after firing the shot that ripped through the guts of a nameless student, Dario, the recruit from the south, member of the 22nd Infantry sent to disband the demonstrators, fell from a savage kick to the head by a burly student nicknamed "Bulldog" who captained the university's soccer team.

Rogelio heard a loud crack, like brittle wood snapping—a sound he would never forget—as the student's foot came into contact with Dario's head. He saw Dario's head jerk sideways as the force of it sent him sprawling to the ground. Rogelio ran toward his friend but found his way blocked by an entanglement of arms and legs. Almost lost in all the shouting and scuffling, he heard Commander Reyes's frantic and futile cry: "Don't fire! Don't fire!"

Meanwhile, a student wearing a baseball cap swung his bat at Rogelio, missing him by a centimeter as he ducked to the right to avoid the blow. It was a miracle that he had escaped getting his skull smashed. Then the student who had pissed on the soldiers charged toward Rogelio, calling to those nearby to follow.

And so the hunt began.

And Rogelio Campos, who would find himself lost in Calle de Leon in another eleven minutes, raced for his life.

On Remedios, the curious onlookers lining the street scattered, rushed into their homes, and bolted their doors. Rogelio, thinking he would find refuge in some open doorway, ran across the main street and rounded the nearest corner. At an old apartment block, he pounded on the doors but no matter how hard he banged he found no refuge. He broke into a run once more.

A rock flew past him, hitting a street sign with a loud clang before bouncing onto his shoulder. He flinched but kept running. He made no effort to look back. The urgent clinking of heavy chain reached him. He ran, expecting a blow to the back or head at any second. The students were armed to the teeth, while all he had were his feet. It didn't occur to him to use his weapon. Not yet anyway.

They were closer now. The sound of their obscenities louder. His eyes darted around, searching for an escape route. But subterfuge was impossible at this time of day. The light betrayed him. So wherever he turned, they turned. Even the scent of his fear gave him away. His only hope was speed. He picked up his pace, his feet pounding on the asphalt surface; he rounded another corner, disturbing a group of dogs gathered around a garbage bin, sidestepping rotting ends of vegetables on the way. As he ran, overgrown shrubs and hedges reached out to whip and slash at his face, but desperation drove him on.

His shirt clung to his skin, glued by his sweat, which mingled with the tang of urine. Streams of perspiration flowed down his head and hung over his lids, blurring his vision.

As Rogelio ran toward the place fate had chosen for his brief and unfortunate encounter with the man chosen to be his victim, something inexplicable happened. Everything around him vanished and he found himself running in a vacuum, neither hearing his pursuers nor seeing the passing scenes of houses, vehicles, men, women, and children.

It was not surprising then that when, in another minute, Rogelio Campos found himself standing in Calle de Leon, a sense of disorientation came over him. He looked around in confusion. Where was he? He could not distinguish between what was real and what was unreal. Heart beating wildly, he heard a loud scraping sound from behind him. His panicked brain registering this, Rogelio Campos reached for his weapon and, turning his body, fired blindly in the direction of the unseen enemy. The bullet released from its chamber whizzed through the air, gathering speed as it traveled toward its target.

In my mind's eye, I see Charlie the Chinaman reaching for his tobacco tin; he flicks this open, pinches some of the aromatic leaves between his fingers, and sprinkles them on a square piece of cigarette paper before carefully rolling it.

It is his only vice. The one act of indulgence that precedes each day of business. He takes a puff and inhales deeply. He feels the smoke travel down his chest, then back up again, where he releases it through his mouth in a curl of smoke whose progress he follows on its way toward the ceiling. For the next few minutes, Charlie sits and enjoys his cigarette.

I imagine that Charlie checked the time once more, after which he set his cigarette on the glass ashtray on the counter. Then he got up from his stool and reached for the first of the timber panels that covered his shop window. Perhaps he heard the sound of scuffling feet from outside and imagined it to be the sound of people now up and about.

His hands are on either side of the heavy wooden panel and slowly he slides this along the groove, wincing a little at the loud scraping sound it always makes. Suddenly morning light rushes into the room and Charlie welcomes it with a smile. He loves feeling it on his sun-starved skin. Its warmth has the feel of life.

The light suffuses Charlie's face, blinding him as he looks straight into it. But perhaps even without this light, he would still fail to see what is happening before him.

If Charlie could play back the last image he saw, would it be that of a man with his back to him suddenly turning in his direction, pointing at him? Would Charlie's mind have registered that the man was a soldier or that he was holding a gun? And would he have had the time to associate the loud echoing sound as coming from it?

The bullet takes Charlie by surprise, the bullet that travels toward him, passing through the space between the iron bars of his shop-front, finally entering between his eyes. It is a strange sensation, this hot searing object tunneling through his head, slicing a clean, narrow path into his brain before exploding.

In the frozen instant when the bullet bores into him, Charlie's eyes widen with surprise, then slowly he feels his life seep out of him. Perhaps it is in an effort to stop his life force from escaping through the shattered walls of his skull that Charlie lifts a hand to his head. Oh, the effort it takes to move that hand.

Within minutes of Charlie slumping to the floor, his cigarette rolls off the counter, landing next to an old plastic container of kerosene which Charlie keeps for emergencies. Still alive, he sees the first flame come to life but cannot move from where he is lying. And soon the store in the corner of Calle de Leon becomes a flaming memorial to the man who has lived in it for the last thirty years.

It is precisely seven A.M.

At the exact moment the bullet entered between Charlie the Chinaman's eyes, Consuelo Lamuerta gasped at the sudden stab of pain she felt, dropping her rosary as she reached up to touch her palm against her forehead, where a hot, burning feeling made her moan and her eyes brim with tears. Then just as quickly as it had come, the pain disappeared.

Her sense of peace, however, could not be restored. The sounds of banging doors and loud screaming penetrated the walls of her home. And she heard a familiar voice calling her name. Consuelo Lamuerta, picking up her rosary, rose from her kneeling position in front of the altar and opened the window, where a blast of hot air blew over her face.

"Sunog! Consuelo . . . may sunog!"

Consuelo gazed down at her neighbor, Trina, still in her sleeping clothes with her long hair uncombed, frantically waving to her. Consuelo turned in the direction of the flames. The fire was only three doors away from her now. Farther up the road where the fire must have started, she saw a red-and-orange curtain of flame around what had once been Charlie's store. The store's rusty tin roof had curled up in the heat. She searched for Charlie through the billowing smoke but failed to catch sight of him. She noticed, though, that a fight had broken out in the street but the heat and licking flames made it impossible to see clearly.

"Run . . . Consuelo . . . are you mad?" Trina's hysterical voice reached her.

Consuelo looked at her neighbor and the scene of confusion below. And a sense of detachment descended on her. As the flames continued to eat at the walls of the *accessorias*, Consuelo Lamuerta gave the street below one last look, then shut her window. She approached her altar and got down on her knees again. Unknown to Consuelo, she was about to begin a journey that would take longer than a prayer.

"Oh Mother, intercede with your Son. . . ."

As Consuelo prayed, a pall of smoke became visible in the city skies. In the taxi on my way to this burning street, it was like a signpost. Impossible to miss, it guided me to where I needed to be.

4

Stepping into a Tale

So I finally arrived at Calle de Leon and stepped into this tale. And I must say now that I arrived expecting nothing out of the ordinary.

Just another fire.

When my taxi turned into the street, the fire trucks positioned in front of the block of *accessorias* were already getting ready to leave. The men had done what they could and now it was left to the residents to get their lives back in order.

The heat greeted me as I stepped out of the cab. Calle de Leon smelled of smoke, the air itself was colored a dark gray, and I recoiled at having to breathe it. From all around me rose a babble of voices as people scurried about, carrying bundles and setting them down again because no one knew where to go or what to do.

From where I stood, my eyes were drawn to the blackened and partly melted galvanized metal sheet being lifted by a group of men. On the footpath lay a burned sign on which the only word discernible was STORE.

I learned three things in the time I was there: one, the fire had started at the neighborhood store owned by a Chinese man called Charlie who had perished in the fire. Two, the fire had spread to the row of *accessorias*, claiming three apartment units in a matter of minutes. The residents said the structures were so old and the wood so dry the flames just gobbled them up. The third thing I learned was that a woman called Consuelo Lamuerta had collapsed from excessive smoke inhalation and had hurt herself.

You must understand that nothing was said at the time about the nature of Consuelo Lamuerta's wounds or I would have pursued the matter immediately. But as things stood, I didn't dwell on her. In fact, I'll admit to listening only with minimal interest to the bedraggled-looking housewife who informed me that Consuelo Lamuerta had refused to leave her home. And how it was a lucky thing that the fire had been put out in time. Consuelo Lamuerta's *accessoria* was the fourth one in the row of apartment units and would have been next to go up in flames.

My attention soon transferred itself to the landlady—the owner of the burned *accessorias*—who arrived some fifteen minutes after me. A short, plump, matronly woman who looked as though she spent her days sitting in beauty salons getting her hair coiffed and her nails manicured, trying to counter the effects of time.

She emerged from her car and inspected the damage to her property. Shaking her head, she said, "That stupid Chinaman is to blame . . . but he's dead now and I can't make him pay." She bemoaned the fact that the insurance money would not be enough to pay for the building of new apartment units. She quoted a figure that I promptly wrote down on my notepad.

As I stood listening to her, a man carrying a black doctor's bag hurried by in the company of an elderly lady. They stopped in front of the *accessoria* of the woman called Consuelo Lamuerta. Knocking urgently, they waited for the door to open. After a few seconds, a priest appeared. The two entered quickly and as he was about to shut the door the priest looked my way. His eyes on meeting mine widened in surprise. The landlady had, at this point, moved on to the subject of rebuilding and its attendant problems. As she spoke, I was aware of the priest coming toward me.

"I didn't know someone had come to see her. . . ." he said as his hand motioned toward the *accessoria*.

Before I could reply, he spoke again, saying: "Have you been waiting long? She's—"

Excusing myself, I turned from the landlady and spoke to the priest: "Oh no, I'm not a relative. I'm a reporter. Clara Perez from the *Chronicle*."

"Clara Per— oh, you must excuse me, I thought for a while that . . ." Then the priest shook his head, frowning slightly as he continued to gaze at me. Finally he said, "Never mind, it was a mistake. And she . . . you can say she hurt herself on falling."

After this, when the priest returned to the *accessoria*, I resumed my exploration of the street and thought no more about our brief exchange. As I walked, I gazed at the lucky ones whose homes had escaped being destroyed. They were busy moving their possessions back to their apartments; meanwhile the ones who had been rendered homeless walked about in a daze, mumbling to themselves. The street itself was strewn with all manner of things that lay like spilled innards for all to see. A boy of three, still in his pajamas, sat in the middle of the street on his potty, sucking his thumb.

I listened to the confusing accounts of the morning's disaster: how they had been dressing, getting ready to go to work, when the store at the corner went up in flames; how they had rushed about in an effort to save their belongings. After a while, the discussion turned to the poor store owner and the women shook their heads sadly.

"*Ang malas naman . . . kawawang Charlie.*"

A large crowd had gathered in front of the burned-down store. I walked back and stood in their midst, watching three ambulance men retrieve the charred remains of the store owner. Several policemen stood by to keep the onlookers away. The men lifted the body and laid it on the center of a large black plastic sheet. When they had covered it completely, they lifted their burden once more and walked toward the waiting van. As they passed, the aroma of burned flesh reached me.

Because the Chinaman was the sole fatality of the fire, I focused my attention on him. I started asking about the victim. Did the store owner have any family? I asked the man next to me. No, the man said, Charlie lived alone. Did you know him well? Oh yes, the man replied, been here thirty years, moved into the neighborhood about the same time as myself. Where had the store owner lived before coming to Calle de Leon? The man shrugged. Did he have friends? Did anyone come to visit him? Can't help you there, don't know much about Charlie. But didn't you say you've known him for a while? The man scratched his head and said yes, but Charlie never said much.

The man turned his attention back to the scene before him, and thinking he was just being unhelpful, I approached two elderly women. But I was faced with the same lack of knowledge. It was as though they had never known the store owner. And yet they had dealt with him every day for thirty years, stood by his shop front and gossiped with him. How was it that they could not detail his life?

Can a person have no past? Is it possible for a man to live in a place for all of thirty years and for no one to know him any better than they had the day he first arrived? Is it possible for a man to keep his life so secret that no one knew anything about him beyond his name? Or was it that no one was interested enough to ask even the most ordinary questions? When were you born? Where did you come from? What do you believe in? What do you think? How do you feel?

If Torres had been aware of the questions I was asking myself about this dead stranger, he would have smiled with satisfaction. Some of what he had been drumming into my head had finally sunk in.

The store owner's death wasn't what concerned me but the lack of facts about him. Everyone I knew had a history that defined them in space and time, so it intrigued me that there was this person who seemed to have no past. This man puzzled me and I would have dwelled on him longer as I stood in that street had I not learned something that would divert my attention from him, so that when I finally addressed his missing history once more, the world and my life as I knew them would be changed beyond recognition.

I had decided to leave, you see, for I had all the facts I needed to write my story. I didn't think there was anything else that I would unearth in this place to make it more interesting reading. After all, this wasn't a case of arson. Before leaving to hail a cab, I stopped and spoke to the fire inspector. I made arrangements to call him later that morning to confirm the cause of the fire.

"Oh, I can tell you now," he said, "it's definitely the container of kerosene we found on the scene, old plastic container, probably leaking, must have been ignited by accident. But the death of the store owner is another matter. It may have been a bullet."

That was when I learned about the fighting that had broken out in front of the corner store. How twelve students had been arrested as they beat up a lone soldier. When the police were summoned by the residents, the students accused the soldier of firing at the store owner. They told of how, shortly after his weapon went off, the store burst into flames. Soon after this, a military van arrived and all twelve students and the injured soldier were herded into it.

"Where were they taken?" I asked.

"Campo Diaz, I presume. He was one of the soldiers sent to the Loyola this morning to end the sit-in. Claimed the students chased him from the university all the way here. Also insisted he had fired in self-defense, hitting the store owner by accident."

As the taxi made its way across the city from Calle de Leon, my mind turned over the matter of the soldier and the man he had allegedly shot. To me, the soldier's presence was of more importance than the fire itself because it was unexpected. You see, I was still several days from realizing the significance of that fire, and how all the things that happened that day, and in the subsequent days, were somehow connected. It never occurred to me that I would soon be returning to this street, brought back by circumstances I could not foresee.

What was clear to me was that I had come to this smoking street expecting nothing out of the ordinary. But by the time I left, I knew I had stumbled upon something. What, I wasn't sure of yet.

5

Seers and Prophecies

I asked the taxi driver to take the Lacson Bridge route.

From Calle de Leon, this was not the shortest way to get to the *Chronicle*, but I had a sudden urge to be near the palace. I hoped my proximity to it would bring some understanding of the morning's events.

The soldier's presence at the scene of the fire was, to my mind, a sign that the problems that had beset the palace were now much greater than ever before. And I wondered if its occupants were even capable of reading the situation clearly.

There are two ways to see the palace. Both of them difficult. The first is via the main approach, Loreto Avenue, from which the Lacson Bridge rises. The palace lies at the end of the avenue and is obscured from view by an ornate iron gate and the tall trees growing on either side of it.

The other way to see the palace is via the river which flows past it. But there is no disembarking from the ferries that go past. The palace is off-limits to the public. Its interior forever a mystery to the average citizen.

I believe this problem of visibility works two ways. The palace is a place that cannot be seen. It is also a place from which it is impossible to see out. And so the palace is blind to what is happening around it.

Its present occupant moved in sixteen years ago. At no time in the archipelago's history had anyone ruled this long or wielded this much power. At the National Press Club downtown where Mel and I sometimes went after work, it was a well-known joke that the only way El Presidente would leave would be in a horizontal position. This cynicism toward him did not always exist, certainly not in the beginning.

I was seven years old when El Presidente came into power, riding on a wave of hope. I still remember the euphoria that greeted his election. The teachers at school spoke of nothing else for days. They said he would bring changes the country had long waited for. That we must remember this moment.

What I remember with clarity to this day is his inaugural ceremony. Watching and listening to him, my seven-year-old mind labeled him a hero, not only because of the many medals he had earned in the war but also because of the way he carried himself. He stood rigid and straight and I took this to be a reflection of his character. The extent to which appearances can deceive us is amazing.

El Presidente was a master of deception who had hidden his desire to rule forever. Or perhaps this desire was absent in the beginning, coming into being only after he had grown attached to his power and feared himself diminished without it. But the past sixteen years had revealed to us his true nature. So whereas his presence was once warmly welcomed, his demise was now much awaited.

The city is full of rumors of his fall.

There is even a prophecy concerning the end of his long reign. I first heard of it from Mel Magay at the *Chronicle*. Mel possessed a big heart, a big laugh, and the largest store of gossip. She also had a knack for coming upon the quirkiest tales. She collected them the way other people collected odd-shaped bottles, first-issue stamps, or out-of-circulation coins. In the eighteen months that I had worked with her, I had heard her recount some real gems.

One night, as Mel and I stayed back to work on a feature about the current wedding preparations—El Presidente and Madam's daughter was about to marry the Pellicer heir—we spent some time speculating about the implications of this high-powered match. The

Pellicers were as close to royalty as we would ever have. As for El Presidente and Madam, they were the powers that resided in the palace.

"Not for long. There's the prophecy, you know. . . ." said Mel, her voice dropping to a mere whisper.

I looked across to where she sat, then decided to give in and swallow the bait, but not before exclaiming, "Not another prophecy, Mel!"

"It's *not* just another prophecy!"

"You sound like Torres," I said, glancing toward the news editor's office.

According to Mel, Madam was rumored to consult regularly with an old seer in the town of Isidro. When, thanks to the student radicals, the government became the subject of much public criticism, Madam had the seer summoned to the palace. The seer arrived and asked to roam the palace grounds.

He was reported to have circled the palace three times, each time pausing in front of the river.

"He gazed into it, they said, as if seeing things in it. His head was cocked to one side, as if listening to something. Then he did something strange. He got down and put his ear to the ground; after a while, he rose and walked toward the river and dipped his hand in the water," said Mel.

The seer, watched from a distance by Madam and her aide, made his way to where she stood. He proceeded to speak at last. But if she expected to hear reassuring words, he spoke only of misfortune.

"He foretold the downfall of the regime and that three things would occur to signal its end," Mel said dramatically.

The man told Madam that a river would sing and its song would be heard by those who slept and by those who were awake. Then he said a church that has stood for centuries would return to the earth and no trace of it would be seen again. And lastly he said a bridge would be crossed and that when this came to pass, there would be a change of power in the palace and that those who ruled there would be no more.

"His words displeased Madam so much that she had him removed from her presence immediately. But not before she made sure he got paid. It is not wise to refuse to pay a seer," said Mel on concluding her tale.

Skeptic that I was, I told her, "It makes a good story, Mel, but rivers don't sing. Churches don't just disappear. And as for bridges, they're made for crossing."

Mel simply shrugged. "You never know, Clara, stranger things have happened. As for making sense of it, who knows what seers mean when they speak, they always speak in riddles."

Now, as the taxi crossed Lacson Bridge, I gazed down toward the river whose waters gave off a less-than-pleasant smell. I wondered if this was the river referred to in the prophecy, not that I believed there was any substance to such tales.

The view from the bridge was a study in extremes, for the north bank was picturesque and the south bank an eyesore. The river divided the city into rich and poor.

As for the river itself, it must have been postcard pretty at one time. But I have never seen it so. As far back as I could remember, its waters had been murky. Even the pink, white, and yellow waterlilies which grew in it failed to hide its ugliness or mask its pervasive odor. The river had to be dredged twice a year because it carried more than just human traffic—it had become a catchment area for both human and industrial waste. And sometimes the river coughed up the unexpected. It was often used as a dumping site for the bodies of the victims of gang wars and political killings. Earlier in the year, I had seen one such victim fished out of the river, face blue and bloated, eyes bulging. "Salvaging" was the operative term for such executions.

To me, this was a sorry river that reflected the sorry soul of my city.

As I looked out of the window at the length of water that was visible from the bridge, I thought how the river, touching the ground on which the palace stood, had the power to tell truth from lies. Of anyone in the city, it alone knew what went on within the palace walls.

This reminded me of my decision to chase after a bit of information myself, partly to complete my report and partly out of curiosity. On reaching the *Chronicle*, I rang Campo Diaz and asked for the name of the soldier found in the vicinity of Calle de Leon. But the information office refused to divulge his name. I tried another department and drew a blank once more.

Finally, I decided to wait for Mel. She had been on the phone when I got back from covering the fire. The phone interview with a man from the Seismological Study Center was proving a waste of time. I could see her trying to finish off their conversation. She rolled her eyes at me. From where I sat I could hear the man's voice, although I couldn't make out his words. And Mel was saying, "Well, no, Mr. Cruz, unfortunately I can't write about a coming earthquake based on conjecture. I need facts." Her voice dripped with impatience.

Then, with a sigh of relief, she put the phone down. I quickly explained my problem then asked her to call the camp for me, just in case my voice gave me away as the caller who had been pestering them in the last half an hour. But Mel, too, failed to get the soldier's name.

"Sorry, Clara, no luck. Makes you wonder what they're up to," she said, replacing the receiver.

Then Max returned from covering the palace press conference and told me everything I wanted to know.

"The soldier's name is Rogelio Campos and, yes, he did fire his weapon."

The soldier had been suspended from duty and was now under investigation.

"There's no chance he'll get off, you know," Max said, before casually dropping in the most interesting bit.

The Hanging Judge was heading the commission.

6

In the Palace by the River

How the soldier Rogelio Campos came to be at the mercy of the dreaded Hanging Judge was the result of much devious scheming at the palace. It began soon after the news of the shooting at the Loyola reached El Presidente's ears. The first bearer of bad news—there would be two that morning—was the Defense Minister.

The Defense Minister was a gaunt-looking man with a sunken, cadaverous face. And his photographs during this period show the progressive deepening of his worry lines with each military debacle.

I imagine his face wore an even grayer pallor that morning as he paced about in El Presidente's office waiting for him to arrive. With the Defense Minister was the Chief of Staff, whose face wore the same serious expression. For one man was the bearer of bad news, the other was there to pick up the pieces. Both knew El Presidente well enough to know an explosion was inevitable.

The Chief of Staff glanced at his watch. There was time to make another phone call. He might as well get things organized in view of what had transpired. He had been through many crises before, though admittedly nothing of the kind that seemed to be besetting El Presidente lately.

Just as he expected, El Presidente walked into his office at eight-thirty sharp. As his superior took his seat, the Chief of Staff noted his wan appearance and the watery quality which his eyes had recently acquired. Only last week he had convinced El Presidente to see the doctor. El Presidente complained about waking up tired every morning, as if he had not slept at all. The doctor recommended shorter hours, a slower pace, and earlier nights. But there were too many matters needing his attention—the insurgency problem down south, the forthcoming wedding of his daughter Maia, and of course, the crisis brought about by the demonstrating students—so the doctor's advice had gone unheeded.

"Good morning, sir," both men said.

El Presidente looked up, noticing the presence of the Defense Minister for the first time. El Presidente was a small man of solid build. His eyes were his most dominant feature. They were small and slanted, betraying an Oriental strain in his blood. Depending on his mood, they either wore a steely look or took on a cunning expression. The look he gave the Defense Minister was sharp, the message unmistakable. It said: "How have you blundered this time?"

Clearing his throat, the Defense Minister began his nervous recital. His carefully rehearsed speech coming out in a rushed monotone. As he spoke, El Presidente's face hardened, his lips pressed into a thin line, and his eyes glinted dangerously. Finally, what he and the Chief of Staff had been expecting came.

"Imbecile!"

El Presidente's voice reverberated in the room as he slammed his fist down on the mahogany desk, sending his pen rolling to the edge. The Chief of Staff caught the pen in the palm of his hand and carefully replaced it on the desk.

"A simple operation! It was a simple operation! And it gets bungled. Whoever fired the shot, I want him charged!"

El Presidente rose, pushing his seat back violently.

"And Reyes, that incompetent fool, suspend him. I want an investigation into this affair. You are not listening to me!" Pointing at the Defense Minister, El Presidente said, "I want an investigation. Find a culprit. Nothing short of that will satisfy the press!"

Then he swung around to face the Chief of Staff.

"What is it with these people? Tell me, Raul, why is it they can't follow instructions? I said no shooting. Any moron could have understood that. These fools have nothing but sap between their ears!"

For the next few minutes, El Presidente ranted on, face black with rage, hands gesturing, and only when he took an armchair by the glass doors and leaned his head back did the Chief of Staff speak. In a calm voice he said, "It was unfortunate it happened, sir. I've made the necessary arrangements to deal with this. The staff has been informed that a meeting is forthcoming, at your convenience of course. There have been calls from the press."

"The press! Hah! Of course they'd be the first to smell blood. Well, call them in, the vermin!"

"I've set a press conference for eleven, sir," said the Chief of Staff, his voice designed to soothe. "And, sir, I thought it prudent to arrange a visit to the wounded student."

"Waste my time on a rabble-rousing student!"

With a quick, apologetic glance at the Defense Minister, the Chief of Staff explained. "It would distance you, sir, from the military."

El Presidente weighed what the Chief of Staff said, then nodded to show his grudging agreement. When he finally spoke, his anger had subsided. "Ask Madam to make time for it. It might as well be this afternoon."

The Chief of Staff turned to go but El Presidente spoke once more, saying, "Raul, I do not wish to be disturbed for the next hour." Then turning to the Defense Minister, he said, "Stay. We need to decide what to say."

The Chief of Staff stepped out of the office and left the two men to thrash out the details for the press conference. As he made his way toward Madam's office in the opposite wing, a presidential aide called to him, "Call on Line Three from the SSC for El Presidente, should I put it through?"

"From where?"

"Seismological Study Center . . . some urgent message about—"

The Chief of Staff shook his head and waved his hand, saying, "El Presidente is not to be disturbed for the next hour. The SCS—"

"SSC."

"Whatever! They can wait."

Ignoring the protest of the caller, the presidential aide requested him to ring another day.

While the staff in the east wing mobilized themselves for the press conference, the staff in the west wing attended to matters of a different nature. The west wing of the palace was, after all, a different world. It smelled of the fragrance of roses, jasmine, lavender . . . exotic perfumes that signaled that a woman reigned here.

The wife of El Presidente is a statuesque woman, nearly half a head taller than her husband, and she walks with the bearing of a queen. Given to sweeping, grand gestures, she is elegant in appearance, with a face that still hints at her earlier beauty. It is no secret that she wields equal power with El Presidente, whom she helped put on the thronelike seat in the ceremonial hall.

Back then, with her by his side, El Presidente had stormed the remotest *barrios* of the archipelago, knocking on doors, shaking hands with the lowliest citizen, kissing babies, talking, selling, and dazzling the simple folk with his fiery oratory. While he delivered his speeches, she sang the people love songs. She courted them, made love to them, until they paved the way to the palace for El Presidente and herself. Now, sixteen years later, she still sings the same songs to them, but not as often, and as for herself, she is no longer the same.

At the *Chronicle*'s photo library there are shots of her that go back to the beginning of her rise to power. Looking through them recently, I remarked to Mel that one could see the history of change on her face. To which Mel tartly replied, "Well, she was never who she claimed anyway."

Mel has collected many stories about Madam. True or false? Who knows? After all, who can tell where truth ends and a lie begins?

If Mel's tales are to be believed, then Madam is a witch. She rewrites the past and changes the future, and her present state is illusory. She has created and re-created herself, has written many versions of her life, all of them true and all of them false.

An old woman in a town down south where Madam was born claims she knows the truth about her, from the time when she had not yet tarted up, gilded, and bedecked herself with jewels; re-shaped, revised, restructured, and reinvented her past. She knows of the one that existed in the beginning.

The old woman is a shriveled, dark, bent creature from the town of Macopa, a place named after the tree that bears plump pink fruits which promise sweetness but taste of nothing. She says she knew Madam as a child when she and her brother and her ailing mother lived in the garage of the family home. Her mother was the second wife of a wastrel with wealthy connections. The children from his first wife lived in the big house.

When Madam was fourteen, the old woman said, her sickly mother died. Motherless and cursed with a useless father, her future looked as dismal as her surroundings. But her spirit could not be dampened; the worse things looked for her, the more she grew in beauty: she was meant to shine.

Her father's brother, a wealthy astute politician, saw the value of his niece's unusual beauty. She could be married off to a powerful man, thus augmenting her family's influence. He brought her to the city and raised her as one of his own. She stepped into her new life with eagerness. As to her humble beginning, she shed this the way a butterfly emerges from its chrysalis. She left it all behind.

That is, until the old woman's tale somehow traveled from the small town of Macopa to the big city, where it was told and retold, contradicting the official version of Madam's life story which was released in the form of a biography some ten years after she and El Presidente moved into the palace. In the official palace version, Madam's life was that of a princess living a fairy tale, and so the old woman's tale was denounced as a lie. By the time a reporter set out to find the old woman in the town of Macopa, she could not be found. So which version is true and which one false will never be known.

And if you asked the three men who now sit waiting to be summoned to Madam's presence, not one of them would dare question the palace's version. More to the point, each of them believes that Madam's past is irrelevant, for Madam in the present is what matters.

They have served her many times and know she is capable of

many things. Had someone told them she could raise the dead the way Lazarus was raised by Jesus, they would believe it. You had to believe in a woman who could order the reclaiming of land from the sea, build a sprawling center for the performing arts in a hundred days, and a film center resembling the Parthenon in twenty-eight weeks. There was power in her words and in every wave of her hand. Let there be light. And there was light. These men believed in the power she wielded in the present; her past was of no concern to them.

They were the architect, the banquet manager, and the jeweler. All handpicked to help put together the grandest wedding the country would ever see.

The door opened and Madam's secretary stepped into the room where the men waited. She called the architect's name first. He rose from his seat and walked to the door, aware of the look of irritation that appeared on the banquet manager's face and the renewed surge of sweat on the jeweler's body. They were being made to wait while he met with Madam first.

Madam's office was ornately furnished with antiques. In an alcove was a round teak table on which stood a porcelain figure of a soldier on a warhorse, a Tang piece purchased from Sotheby's. A tapestry, which once graced the hall of an Italian palazzo, hung from a wall. The chandelier was of Venetian glass and had been imported on the occasion of the third refurbishing of the room some six years ago.

The architect found her sitting on a claw-footed settee in the heart of the capacious room. He bowed to her and they exchanged polite pleasantries. After a while, she got down to business, saying, "Well, Trillo, can you finish everything on time?"

The architect nodded, choosing to start with the cathedral.

For the wedding of the presidential couple's daughter, Maia, a suitable church had to be found. But Madam's requirements were difficult to meet. She wanted a big church—a cathedral—yet refused to consider the historic one in the old part of the city. Everyone, she said, who thought they were someone got married there. She wanted something like the old stone cathedrals in Europe that exuded history.

There was, Mel believed, another reason for Madam's insistence on an old church. "Can't you see? By restoring an old church she would counter one of the things mentioned in the prophecy—that a church which has stood for centuries would disappear." This at least was Mel's theory.

So the search for an old church that could pass for a cathedral began. Armed with video cameras, teams of researchers were sent all over the archipelago but none of the churches they proposed pleased Madam. In the end, it was El Presidente who came up with the answer to their dilemma.

"In the outskirts of the town I was born in stands a big church you may want to look at."

Madam said, "It has to be a cathedral."

"Call it a cathedral, then! The Cathedral of the North. There! Who would dare question you? It is old . . . sixteenth century most likely and enormous. In my youth, it was already a decrepit old church, it may be too old even for your purpose."

The condition of the baroque church built with coral blocks would have discouraged anyone, for time and nature had inflicted much damage, but not Madam. She was a creature of grand visions, and more importantly, she had direct access to the national treasury. So it was not surprising when she announced that it was exactly what she wanted.

Then she sent for the architect Trillo.

That was many months ago; now Juan Trillo laid out the photographs showing the last stages of his work on the Cathedral of the North. "As you can see," he said, "all the timber beams on the ceiling that needed replacing have been replaced. Now, here is a shot of an original beam and here is one of a replacement beam. No one can tell the difference."

Madam had wanted the church restored while keeping its centuries-old look. So every part that was replaced was made to look like the original. Light fittings were installed. New ones fashioned like old ones. The altar was refurbished. And a decorator with a team of painters trained in the art of antique finishes was flown in from Paris to work on the walls. The walls were cleaned of their age-old dust, soot, and grime, and with the clever use of special pigments, intricate brush strokes, sea sponges, rags, and tinted varnishes, were made to look old again.

Next, the architect displayed the photographs showing the work that had been done on the house where El Presidente was born. It had been restored and enlarged to make it the most imposing structure on the street. "Wings" were built on either side of the original house to be used for displaying El Presidente's famous war medals and hundreds of paraphernalia related to his life. But when the so-called wings were erected, only a meter separated the house from the neighboring houses. A handsome offer was made to the owners of these properties, which were then demolished to make room for flowering shrubs and palm trees.

To house the two thousand expected guests, Madam built a hotel in the sprawling Spanish hacienda style. Twelve kilometers away from the Cathedral of the North, it was adjacent to a beach and rose unexpectedly from the graceful folds of the sand dunes. But Madam, who had a propensity to put things together in ways that defied logic, found the presence of these sand dunes offensive. So twenty-two tons of garden soil went on top of them, followed by a carpet of Bermuda grass.

The Madam announced that she disliked the color of the sand on the beach. So seventy tons of white sand were flown in from Australia's Queensland coastline and spread over the area. Seeing the contrast between sand and turf in the architect's photographs, Madam made it known that she was pleased.

As the architect stepped out of the room, he gave the two waiting men a brief nod then quickly made his way toward the grand staircase. Before he made his way down, he looked toward the east wing, where he caught sight of the Press Secretary hurrying toward El Presidente's office.

For the second time that morning, bad news reached the palace.

This time the bearer of the news was the beady-eyed paunchy Press Secretary, who ten minutes earlier had received a call from a journalist asking him what El Presidente had to say regarding the coming protest march.

"What protest march?" had been his shocked reply.

Now sitting opposite El Presidente, his short legs stretched out before him, the Press Secretary reported what he had learned.

"Sir, the whole student body of the Loyola University has gathered in front of the administration building to protest against this morning's incident. The Dean has addressed the assembly saying he is demanding an apology from the government, compensation for the families of the wounded students, the immediate release of the arrested demonstrators, and a full-scale investigation into the incident. After he spoke, Luis Bayani went before the assembly to announce a mass protest to be held Friday next week. They are marching to Campo Diaz, and the other universities have announced they will join the march as a sympathy gesture."

The Press Secretary paused before turning to the Defense Minister to say, "We'll need more soldiers this time."

"No, that's the last thing we need," argued the Defense Minister. With the students marching toward the military camp, the soldiers could not be seen to be defending the camp. It would draw attention once more to the issue of military violence. "What I think is best," he continued, "is to call in the constabulary or send the riot police in. The last thing we need to show is a soldier wielding a gun."

"Look, whatever we do, they'll still say the government is protecting the military," the Press Secretary countered.

"They'll stop all talk of that when you give them their man," said El Presidente, addressing the Defense Minister.

"He's in a coma."

"Find someone."

"Well, they're looking into the fire at Calle de Leon. There might be something there. The students say a soldier started it or killed someone, it's all pretty muddled at the moment."

"Get it straightened out. If not, give them Reyes. He's been suspended, hasn't he?"

"From what I gathered, sir, he ordered his men not to fire," said the Defense Minister in an attempt to save the commander, whom he liked.

"But he failed. So if you can't find anyone else, it'll have to be him."

The Defense Minister said no more about the matter. He would try to save Reyes's neck by looking for someone else who could take the heat. At least there were two other possibilities: the soldier who lay in a coma and the one under detention pending further investigation. If one of them came through, Reyes would be off the hook.

The Press Secretary spoke again. "Sir, instead of just handing them a soldier, why not create a commission, an independent commission to look into the matter of military violence?"

The Defense Minister was about to protest this when El Presidente said, "It's not a bad idea, we could make an announcement to the press, and it would defuse the situation some." Hearing this, the Press Secretary beamed, quickly stealing a glance at the silent Chief of Staff. He had bested him this time.

"Who?" asked the Defense Minister. "Who will head the commission? No matter who you choose, he'll be considered a palace appointee. It may be the intention to sacrifice someone from the military"—the Defense Minister said this with distaste—"but you don't want to be obvious, the public would reject a token sacrifice."

A long discussion followed as names of possible candidates for the position were proffered by the men in the room. The pros and cons were weighed and one after another, the names were rejected. Just when it seemed there was no one else to consider, the Chief of Staff, who until then had not said a word, finally spoke.

"Jimenez. How about Jimenez?" he suggested in his calm, quiet voice.

A long silence followed. Then, after what seemed like an age, El Presidente nodded, and for the first time that morning, his eyes glinted with life.

"It's a devious idea, Raul, a very clever one. More so because you've been keeping it to yourself while allowing us to argue it out!"

On hearing El Presidente's words, the Press Secretary, who could not abide the Chief of Staff, felt a green wave of displeasure shoot through him. But he made an effort to smile and nod his head, too, which of course did little to deceive the Chief of Staff.

El Presidente continued to speak. "It is no secret that the judge is against his son's involvement with YRM and disapproves of student radicalism. The students and the public think he will rule in favor of the military but he does the opposite. He rules against a soldier whom we intend to sacrifice anyway. The public, however, will believe that justice has been carried out, for Jimenez has passed judgment."

"Will Jimenez cooperate, sir? He's always been unpredictable. Perhaps you should have a word with him first," suggested the Defense Minister.

"That's the last thing I should do," replied El Presidente. "Jimenez must act out of a sense of justice. Unimpeded. Our hand in this affair must not be visible to him."

"But what you're saying, sir, is that you're sure he'll rule against the military," said the Press Secretary.

"He will. Jimenez is only capable of seeing in black or white. Which is why there is no need to ask for his cooperation. His very nature will work for us. All Jimenez will see is the fact that a soldier fired his weapon, and as a result, violence broke out. Or if we take the case of the soldier in the fire, all Jimenez will see is, once more, a soldier used his weapon, killing an innocent man and causing a fire to break out. Jimenez is our man, all right, but he musn't know this."

While El Presidente and his advisers finalized the details for the press conference, the jeweler sitting in the west wing lifted the Nehru collar of his shirt, which was beginning to stick to his skin with perspiration. In spite of the coolness in the air-conditioned room, he sweated profusely. It was not just his nervousness that made him sweat. Ding Sarmiento suffered from a weight problem. Tipping the scale at a hundred and thirty-five kilos, he was sensitive to even the slightest rise in temperature, and now his problem was further compounded by the long wait that gave rise to many terrible thoughts.

To be third and last! The shame of it all! Sitting in abject misery, the jeweler wondered how he had offended Madam. What had he said?

What had he done? Nervously his mind flicked through the past, but he could not recall having been guilty of any indiscretion against Madam. On the contrary, he had done everything to please her.

Had he ever said anything when he had been summoned in the middle of the night to open his shop for her and her friends? Had he not graciously served them on many such midnight jaunts? Had he not bought many a magnificent piece of jewelry for her from overseas?

So why was he the last to be called now? As he fretted, he kept touching the leather briefcase that rested against his chair. Surely whatever had caused Madam to be displeased with him would disappear once she laid eyes on what he had to show her. Oh yes, he would surely find himself in favor once more. He derived some comfort from this thought.

Fifteen minutes later, the reed-thin figure of the banquet coordinator emerged through the door. He nodded to the fat jeweler as he walked past. The jeweler straightened up and quickly checked his shirt for embarrassing wet patches.

A minute later, Madam's personal secretary escorted him to her office and he entered with hesitant steps, eyes darting quickly to Madam's face as he approached her. Did she look pleased or annoyed? The jeweler could not tell until she spoke.

"Oh Ding, I am so sorry to have kept you waiting. But you know how these meetings are, they just go on."

Ding Sarmiento sighed and said a silent prayer of thanks. She was not upset with him. He was still in the magic circle, a person blessed, one of the chosen.

So it was with great flourish that he unveiled his surprise for her. On seeing it, Madam lifted it from its silk-lined case, turned it around slowly, and said, "Ahh . . . my tiara."

The light that filtered through the glass doors formed a halo around the stones, giving each pearl a milky translucent glow and the diamonds a brilliant sharpness. "The pearls have a thickness about them and a luster that is hard to match. They all have the same hue, the same quality of whiteness. The diamonds, of course, are perfect," explained the jeweler.

Madam simply nodded, but her eyes betrayed her pleasure. Emboldened by this knowledge, he said, "I am pleased that it meets with your approval, Madam. It is the best piece I have ever created and I am very honored to have been asked to design it. Why, the honor alone would be enough reward for me."

Madam's eyes gleamed on hearing the jeweler's words. Giving him a calculating glance, the meaning of which he failed to read, she said, "Really, Ding?"

In his rush to flatter her and ingratiate himself further, the jeweler did not weigh his words before speaking. "Oh yes, Madam, the honor alone is enough!"

Later, he would come to regret his extravagant words. But now, flushed with success, he could only beam with pride as his patroness smiled at him indulgently, saying, "Why, I am most pleased to hear that."

Gracefully, she extended her hand to the jeweler, who jumped out of his seat, almost knocking it over as he took her hand and kissed it. Then, expressing his best wishes on the occasion of her daughter's forthcoming wedding, he made his final bow and took his leave.

Ding Sarmiento left the palace in high spirits. That night, while most of the city watched the drama-filled evening news, the jeweler was busy feasting, his doctor's words of caution forgotten in a mood of celebration. He dined on a plate of caviar and smoked salmon followed by a sumptuous steak of prime beef with a rich sauce, then cheese and berries, which he downed with a bottle of red wine. As he savored his food, his mind filled with images of Madam walking down the aisle of the Cathedral of the North, wearing the Sarmiento Tiara.

The jeweler had another reason to celebrate. Tomorrow he was due to open his new store at the luxurious, five-star Maharlika Hotel, another addition to his growing chain of jewelry outlets. Things were looking up for Ding Sarmiento. So much so that he could be forgiven for thinking that all that transpired in the city that day paled in comparison with his personal glory.

7

The Evening News

If Mel and Joey had had their way that night, I would have gone to the Press Club with them after work to hear what reporters call the real news behind the news.

But I begged off. I didn't particularly care for an evening of rumor-mongering, which pretty much summed up what went on in the crumbling two-story building a few blocks away from the *Chronicle*. I was as exhausted as the day that had just come to an end.

"I'll have an early night, Mel," I said, then to appease her added, "but I'll join you tomorrow."

Mel was five years older than me and ten times more gregarious. I liked Mel but I was unlike her. The bigger the crowd, the happier she was, while I tended to clam up. Mel's life was an open book. I, on the other hand, guarded my privacy jealously. She accepted all this about me and when in my company suppressed her reporter's tendency to dig and pry. She was aware of my aversion to questions, and even kept Joey at bay.

"You could be out having fun with me, imagine what you'll miss!" Then, arching his brows, Joey said: "What's at home anyway, Clara?"

"Time away from you, that's what," was Mel's quick reply. "C'mon, Romeo, or I'm leaving you!"

I waved good-bye to them and watched as Mel dragged Joey away. Then I crossed the street and waited for a ride home.

Home was a rambling mansion in Vito Cruz which had seen better days. I moved into it soon after joining the *Chronicle* a year and a half ago. Although strictly speaking my personal space was no more than the room I paid for, I had the house, the lower part of it anyway, pretty much to myself.

The house belonged to an old lady in her sixties who had fallen on hard times. She lived upstairs and rented out the two ground-floor bedrooms to make ends meet. The living areas, bathroom, and kitchen were considered common space. The other tenant was a quiet, spinsterish schoolteacher who seldom ventured out of her room, which suited me just fine.

My room was tucked in the back of the house. To get there meant going through a mazelike passageway. But I didn't mind. The room had a northeast aspect, so I always woke seeing the morning sun. The large bedroom window overlooked an overgrown garden. The old lady could no longer afford a caretaker. So whenever I could I went out and raked the leaves. Overgrown as it was, there was something tranquil and beautiful about its tall leafy trees, unmowed lawn, and leaf-strewn ground. Its many shadowy nooks reminded me of another garden I knew, the one I played in as a child.

For what I paid every month I got a lot of room in return. My bedroom was of such generous proportions that I had comfortably fitted in it all the pieces of furniture I had slowly acquired—my bed, the large scarred study desk and chair I bought from a secondhand furniture dealer, a tall shelf filled with books, a big plump armchair with its embarrassing green velour upholstery, a pinewood wardrobe, and at the corner of the room, the tall mirror that had once been a wardrobe door.

The objects of my life.

While others defined their life by their relationships, I defined mine by the things around me. Not that I was materialistic by nature, my upbringing alone would have been enough to preclude such an inclination. It was just that what lay in my room symbolized the life I'd built.

Slowly, slowly, I was creating myself.

I arrived home wanting only the peace and quiet of my room. A night of reading. I decided to have an early dinner. Without bothering to change or even take off my shoes, I left my room again and headed for the kitchen.

It was empty. The only sound came from my own footfalls on the tiled floor as I moved around making my dinner. With my plate in hand I made for the lounge room. Might as well watch the evening news. I switched on the old black-and-white.

The evening report on Channel 4 began. As to be expected, headlining the news that night was the Loyola University shooting. But despite the seriousness of the subject, the news footage caught me by surprise and soon I was chuckling to myself.

Judge Romero Jimenez's mood, on the other hand, grew darker as he watched the campus drama unfold on his screen. Although the image was unclear, the judge knew with unshakable certainty that the student hoisting himself up on the pedestal of a bronze statue was his son. The insolent public pisser was Laslo himself. Just as well then that Laslo was locked up in Campo Diaz, where he would remain safe from his father.

Judge Romero Jimenez had not earned his title the Hanging Judge for nothing. A man with a stern demeanor, he resembled a squat pugnacious boxer. But where boxers are said to be affectionate dogs in spite of their appearance, the judge was exactly as he looked.

He was a man who practiced an antiquated form of justice. The last man he had sentenced to death was a notorious drug dealer whom he had ordered executed by firing squad. The judge's critics said the era of the Spanish Inquisition would have suited him better. When two decades ago capital punishment came under attack by human-rights lobbyists, the judge's lone but vocal defense of death by hanging, electric chair, or firing squad was enough to keep the law in effect. So he became known to his critics and the public as the Hanging Judge.

His son could not have agreed more with his father's detractors. It was common knowledge in court circles that the judge who ruled harshly over others failed to rule over his only son. Laslo Jimenez found his father's dictatorial ways and uncompromising attitude a heavy cross to bear, but he was no silent martyr. He had the ability to rile the judge, which gave him perverse pleasure; while on the judge's part, his son's rebellious nature made him even more determined to bend him to his will. So theirs was a combative relationship, with father and son engaged in constant feuding.

The judge had yet to forgive Laslo for taking to the streets with the members of the Youth for Reform Movement. It must be said, though, that his anger at Laslo was equal to his fear for his safety. The bumps and bruises his son came home with convinced the judge that worse could happen to him. Laslo's eyes had to be opened somehow, his reckless nature tempered.

Now, watching Laslo's latest antics on television, the judge absolved himself of the guilt he felt for refusing to secure Laslo's early release from Campo Diaz.

Earlier in the day, the judge had received two phone calls in his court chambers. The first was from a friend whom he seldom saw, but who kept in touch whenever the need arose. His friend rang to alert him to the fact that Laslo was among the students arrested in the Loyola riot. His friend offered to get him out. But the judge replied, "I don't wish it." When told that Laslo could be detained for as long as three days, the judge did not soften. He hoped that a stay in the camp would cure Laslo of his silly notions.

When the report came to an end, the judge turned to his silent wife and said, "Hah! Let's see if your son even dares ask to go for a piss in the camp!"

The judge found himself the subject of the next news report, reminding him of the second disturbing phone call he had received that day.

On the surface, his talk with El Presidente had been straightforward enough, but there was something not quite right, thought the judge, something he was not seeing and hearing. In his work, he had learned that it was the things that were left unsaid that revealed the most.

The only directive he received was to conclude the investigation before the wedding. Judge Romero Jimenez knew that there was something that El Presidente had withheld from him. And it had to do with Laslo and the student activists. There was a connection somewhere, only he could not see it yet. He found this intolerable. The judge's rigid nature demanded everything in his world be clear. And that was the crux of his problem: he possessed no understanding of what lay before him.

What was it that El Presidente wanted from him? How did he want the judge to rule? The judge shook his head, appalled at his train of thought. "My God! You are trying to make a ruling without even hearing the case, Romero!" he chided himself. Was he becoming like all the shady characters that served in this government?

Although he had no illusions about the government he served, he had managed to see justice done on his terms.

Yes. His terms.

He realized then that this was how he should approach his role in the commission. It was the only way he would maintain his ability to pass judgment wisely. He resolved to play it his way.

As his attention returned to the screen, the judge found himself looking at the furious face of Senator Sixto Mijares. It puzzled him as to what business the senator had at that time of morning in the vicinity of the university.

The senator's wife could have told him the answer: a woman.

Lorena Zamora-Mijares watched the stormy look on her errant husband's face and felt a part of her threaten to boil over. How dare he humiliate her in this public manner! It had taken all her control to stop herself from telling him this morning that she knew where he had spent the night.

Lorena was the daughter of Senate Speaker Emilio Zamora and the jewelry heiress Elsa Piñon. As a matrimonial candidate she had offered both wealth and power. Six years ago when her father broached the subject of a possible match with the controversial congressman Sixto Mijares—dubbed El Toro by the press for his many sexual exploits—Lorena's heart did a somersault. Who, after all, did not know of the dark and sensually attractive politician?

In a city made up of three kinds of people—those who created gossip, those who were gossiped about, and those who believed in the gossip—the many stories about El Toro were always welcome in the exclusive bars and restaurants and country clubs. There was an amusing tale that made the rounds at the National Press Club, about how El Toro was the cause of an enduring feud between two women who belonged to the palace circle.

It began on the evening both ladies flirted with him at an official function in honor of the new French ambassador. One lady had the luck of sitting next to him, while the other found herself strategically placed across from the notorious gentleman. As the dinner progressed, the one next to him, the young wife of a fellow congressman, had laughed at his teasing, spanking his hand playfully, while being watched enviously by every other woman around the table.

Unknown to her, he was also being entertained from another quarter. The older, more mature woman, the wife of a senator from the south, had surreptitiously extended her silk-stockinged foot under the table and rested this between his thighs. He gave a slight start, then decided to sit back and enjoy himself.

After a while, a somewhat dazed look came over his face, and the lady next to him said, "You must not look at me like that."

"Then you must stop doing what you're doing," he replied in a whisper loud enough to be heard across the table.

At the end of the evening, the suave Sixto Mijares said to El Presidente and Madam, "Thank you for a most stimulating evening, I have enjoyed myself in more ways than one."

Standing nearby, the women heard his parting words; the younger one blushed, the older one wore a Mona Lisa smile.

The phone lines burned across the city as both ladies boasted to their friends of their escapade. Finally, of course, the two women became aware of the other's tale and the cold war between them began. Just for the record, it was agreed by the women in their circle that the older woman had done better than the younger one. Not that El Toro bothered to maintain any contact. He was a prize catch but a hard one to hold.

His future wife learned this soon enough.

Lorena Zamora-Mijares needed little convincing to agree to the match. El Toro's animal magnetism was impossible to resist. An intelligent woman, she recognized that he was trouble with a capital T. But like many women in love, she fell into the trap of believing she could change him. He, on the other hand, appreciated the political advantages that marriage to Lorena would bring him. So a date was set and the knot was tied.

For their honeymoon, the couple traveled to Greece, where the congressman was most attentive toward his bride. Lorena believed marriage had turned him into a new man. Foolish Lorena.

On their return home, her husband quickly reverted to his old ways. It must be said, though, that he had the best intentions but his libido was stronger than his will. The fact that he was now married made him a greater challenge than ever before. Women sought to prove he could be made to stray, and he proved them right.

Lorena took stock of her situation and chose to handle it with a show of indifference. Her pride demanded it. She quickly cultivated the art of appearing cool and distant, and her demeanor soon earned her the title of Ice Princess. With time she convinced herself she had the ability to postpone happiness, perhaps even live without it.

The Senate Speaker, aware of the state of his daughter's marriage, spoke to his son-in-law. "Discretion is the issue here, Sixto, not sainthood. I was never a saint but I never shamed my wife. Lorena deserves as much." So Sixto Mijares conducted his affairs with discretion. And for this he was rewarded. With the Senate Speaker's support, he ran in the senatorial race and won.

The years passed with the couple living under the same roof while going about their separate lives, sleeping in separate rooms. There were times when Lorena found herself thinking wistfully of what might have been, but these occasions were rare. She was not one to waste her time pining.

But acceptance of her situation did not mean ignorance of her husband's affairs. It would have surprised the senator to learn that his wife knew of each mistress he had kept over the last six years. Lorena knew all but did nothing as long as the senator kept his side

of the bargain. But last night he had broken their unspoken agreement. And for that she would make him and his mistress pay.

Lost in her vengeful thoughts, Lorena Zamora-Mijares paid little
notice to the next news report. A quirky tale about some miracle in
an unheard of city street.

But the tale had the power to capture my attention more than
any piece of news, no matter how important, that evening. For it
was set in a street I had walked on that very morning, and was about
a woman whose name I had written on my pad and mentioned in
my report.

Calle de Leon reclaimed my mind.

8

The Miracle of Calle de Leon

The street had transformed itself. Within hours of my leaving it that morning, Calle de Leon had given up its decades of anonymity. By a twist of fate, it had become the miracle street of the archipelago. And in another few hours, it would be the site of a mass pilgrimage as the sick, the poor, and the hopeful descended on it in the hope of a miracle to change their lives. At the heart of its fame was the woman called Consuelo Lamuerta.

Consuelo Lamuerta had not opened her eyes or spoken a word since they found her soon after the fire. It was strange that fire. It began at the corner store and spread within minutes, eating away at the old, brittle timber frames of the apartment houses that stood side by side, their common walls making it easy for the fire to devour everything in its path. Then, as if an invisible wall had suddenly been erected, the fire stopped. It came to a halt right before Consuelo Lamuerta's *accessoria*.

They found her in her altar room, prostrate on the floor. Arms extending out. Feet together. The shape of a fallen cross. They lifted her up and carried her to the bedroom, where they laid her on the bed. Padre Luis came soon after.

Then the local doctor was called in. The woman who had come running to his house had told him about the unconscious Consuelo Lamuerta, but not about her wounds. Consuelo Lamuerta's wounds would come as a surprise to him.

When Padre Luis ushered him into the bedroom, the doctor found her on the bed, one hand over the other as they rested on her chest. She looked serene. He took her hand to check her pulse. Only then did he notice the wound on the inside of her palm. He thought she had somehow hurt herself. He lifted the bleeding hand and then saw that her other one wore a similar wound. A savage wound. As if someone had driven a nail through the flesh.

He felt a quivering sensation inside him, a dipping sensation as though he had driven up the crest of a hill and careered down at a frightening speed. Then he forced himself to look at her exposed feet, where he knew he would find gaping wounds, like bleeding eyes that dared him to look away.

The air rushed out of his lungs and the hairs on his arms stood on end. He raised his right hand and made the sign of the cross. He felt out of his depth, lost in a world so primeval and alien to his rational mind.

The doctor felt something was expected of him. He had been summoned here for his healing skills, but how could he heal these wounds that left him in so much confusion and terror? How can a man of science explain the wounds of Christ? He stole a glance at the padre, hoping the man would give him some direction, but when the priest finally returned his gaze it was only to nod his head, a sign that the doctor must speak his mind.

He cleared his throat and said, "I . . . I don't know what to make of this. I can only give you a medical opinion, Padre Luis. She has been traumatized by the fire and has retreated into a state of unconsciousness. I suggest she be brought to a hospital where her condition can be monitored."

Padre Luis shook his head. "I do not think it wise to let her condition, her wounds, become public knowledge. Not yet anyway."

So it was agreed that the doctor would check on Consuelo again later in the day. Meanwhile, the priest would consult with the cardinal. The doctor left soon after, understanding that silence was expected of him.

His silence, however, was a futile one, for in a neighborhood such as this, everything one did, from sneezing to scratching, was soon known to all. The first sign that Consuelo's wounds were public knowledge came from his own wife that very same day.

"Is it true what they say about the wounds on her hands and feet? Is it really a case of the stigmata? They say it is a miracle. The padre, I hear, is conferring with the cardinal. People are saying she will be made into a saint."

"A saint? To be a saint one needs to have performed a miracle."

"She stopped the fire, didn't she?"

Before the day was over, rumors about the miracle of Calle de Leon had become national news.

Watching television in the lounge room of the house in Vito Cruz, I felt my world had changed orientation. I couldn't explain why this particular news item should affect me so. All I knew was I wanted to visit that street again. Not just in my mind. I wanted to be there, actually walk on it, to stand in front of Consuelo Lamuerta's door. I wished to see her.

I told myself a follow-up story wouldn't be a bad idea at all. After all, it was I who had covered the fire. I was curious about this woman who could stop a fire, who wore Christ's bleeding wounds, who performed miracles in an age where miracles no longer occurred.

When I think about it now, I realize that a part of me must have been wishing for a miracle in my own life, one that would dispel the feeling that I was always holding my breath, waiting for something to happen, for life to begin.

As I got up to switch off the set, I promised myself that as soon as I could—maybe even tomorrow—I would go back to Calle de Leon, to the street where mysteries and miracles could be found.

I was not the only one who heard it call.

The screen went black and the man sat back and stared at it. Then he rose and slowly walked toward the window, where he pushed aside the drapes.

He was a tall distinguished-looking gentleman of fifty, with an aquiline nose and cold piercing gray eyes. Standing feet slightly apart, his hands clasped behind him, he peered at the shadowy scene outside. The sun had set a good hour ago.

Out here in the country, darkness came quickly but it was a darkness of many shades and tones. In the black of night he made out the shapes that formed the landscape. He could make them out even with his eyes shut, for he knew this land and its never-changing vistas by heart.

Twenty-four long years ago he had accepted this land as his destiny. His inheritance. He had given in to its demands. Taken the path it offered him, knowing he could never look back. But the past is populated with ghosts, and a few minutes ago one such ghost had breached the walls that separated past from present, demanding that he look at it, at her, once more.

It had to be her.

When he heard the news reader say her name, he felt a coldness come over him, climbing up his spine to tingle in his head. And in the center of him, he felt a hand grip tight, cutting off his breath. He wanted it to be her and wanted it not to be her.

Consuelo Lamuerta. How many would carry such a name? He knew it was her.

He, Don Miguel Pellicer, the lord of Hacienda Esperanza, Sugar Baron of the South, on hearing her name again felt the walls he had built around his life begin to crumble to dust. He felt a hope growing in him and yet what was there to hope for after all these years? Had he not turned his back on her and she on him? Consuelo the heartless. Consuelo of the traitorous heart. Consuelo his dark deceiving Madonna. Schemer. Liar. Opportunist. The folly of his youth. The bane of his life. The poisonous memory that stuck to him like a leech, sucking him of his capacity for joy. He had banished her long ago, exiled her in the land of black hate, and yet her being had persisted, had returned once more. And now he must go to her.

But there was much that demanded his attention for Iñigo's wedding. How he wished the affair were over, for the whole business was distasteful to him. He was nevertheless aware of its importance and implications. He knew he should feel honored. His many friends and associates had repeated often enough how fortunate he was that Iñigo was taking such a bride. But he secretly shuddered at the prospect of his name, his blood, being tied to the family of Iñigo's future bride. He felt sullied.

His wife had been party to it all along. Marina had promoted the match. She and Madam. They had seen it as the perfect union.

When Marina had come to him with the news that Madam had thought it would benefit both families, he had told her, "We do not need that sort of connection. We have enough land, enough money, and an old name. The little that could be gained would not be worth the price we have to pay."

"What can you be talking about? There is everything to gain. Miguel, this is the First Family. They will give us power!" She had been impatient with him, irritated by his lack of enthusiasm.

"There is enough power behind our fortune."

"But not enough to protect it," was her brisk retort.

"And you think they can protect it?"

"Yes, because of who they are!" she exclaimed.

"Marina, they will not be the last First Family in this land."

"After sixteen years he is in no hurry to go," she said, adding, "Why, even the Constitution has been changed to accommodate his desire to rule forever. Any fool can see he intends to establish a dynasty. So we might as well benefit from it."

He held his tongue, unwilling to be drawn into a contentious discussion with her. She had the ability to tire him. And if truth be known, he was tired of her. In the early years of their union, he had judged her an attractive woman of aristocratic bearing, properly raised to become the partner of a powerful man like himself. Marina had been chosen by the don's mother.

"Find me a woman you approve of and I will marry her!" were the words he had flung at his mother long ago.

His mother had found him Marina. Now he judged his wife harshly, the years having worn away his tolerance. He recognized in her sharp calculating eyes, high cheekbones, and pointed chin the look of the predator. He recoiled at her grasping nature. Her insatiable appetite for wealth and power. And yet she was his other half, the woman who carried his name and had carried his child. That child was now a grown man but he had not grown into the don's image. Iñigo was his mother all over, monster child in the image of his monster mother, sharing her ambition, seeing life with myopic eyes.

It was futile trying to explain to Marina that El Presidente's days were numbered. Could she not tell how the wind was blowing? So his wife Marina had pushed their son Iñigo. And mother and son, kindred spirits, saw to it that the match was made. Iñigo, his only son, the heir to a legendary fortune built over several generations, was to use power acquired through marriage to further the family's wealth. In exchange, Madam would gain a lasting tie to one of the country's oldest, wealthiest, and most respected names.

But wedding or no wedding, the don would go and see her. The news said she was in a coma. Perhaps she would not wake and he would not be able to speak to her at all; but he would go just the same, for at least he would go to his grave knowing he had tried to find the answers to the questions he had long wanted answered. Why had she done what she did? Did she set out to deceive him right from the start? Had she rendered him blind so that he had failed to see her motives?

In the middle of his thoughts, he heard the tinkling of a bell. Somewhere in the house a servant was being summoned. Dinner was to be served soon. He drew the curtains and made for the study door. On his way down to the dining room he decided to inform his family that he would be leaving for the city within a few days. That he had business to attend to.

Unknown to his wife and son, the great don was about to embark on a secret pilgrimage. For from his mansion in the verdant hills of Esperanza, he was hearing the call of Calle de Leon. The time to face the past had come.

9

Milagros Is Marching

As it turned out, the following day took me everywhere in the city except where I wanted to be. On arriving at the *Chronicle*, Torres quickly sent me out to the slum district of Milagros near the docks.

While the rest of the city slept the night away, the members of two rival gangs had spent the small hours of the morning in a brutal fight, slicing at each other and staining a dark alley with their blood.

There is, I believe, something in man that finds the proximity of others intolerable. And so Milagros was a natural breeding ground for violence. No other place in the city was as desperately congested as Milagros. This place is, to me, the most blatant expression of social inequality, the most shameful example of too little for too many that seems to characterize life for the majority of those who live in this city of mine. It even has a famous monument to poverty, a giant rubbish tip several stories high called Smoky Mountain.

On a map, the district is difficult to find. It takes up a small triangular area, easy for the eye to miss. It is bordered on one side by the south bank of the river, by the docks on the other, and by Calle Real, which separates it from the suburb of San Ignacio, on its land side.

In this meager space is the highest concentration of the city's poor. Here they have been herded together and kept from view. The exact population is anyone's guess. Life here is as marginalized as the living space allotted to each person. My room in Vito Cruz could have easily accommodated three households. It amazes me how a place like this could sustain life in such large numbers.

I first came here when I was a high-school student at La Consolacion. The purpose of the trip being to open our eyes to how the other half lived. What I came away with was a definition for the word "possible." It was possible to cram a family of seven, even ten, into a room half the size of a classroom. It was possible to live on near to nothing.

The impossible was possible in Milagros.

Time had not changed Milagros for the better. If anything, the place seemed to be even more congested that Tuesday morning. That is, until I realized that the great number of people I was seeing were rushing to some gathering a few streets away from where I was heading.

After hesitating a second, I decided to follow the crowd part of the way. They were converging on a square. From where I stood I could make out a makeshift stand. And then I heard the painful high-pitched screech of a microphone pierce the air.

I turned to a man next to me and asked, "What's happening?"

The man looked me up and down. "Why do you want to know?" His tone distrustful.

I decided to come clean. "I'm a reporter."

"Find out for yourself." He moved away and I found myself the recipient of more hostile glances from those around me.

This was a place that did not welcome strangers. Danny at the *Chronicle* told me once that slum dwellers functioned like a giant clique, united in their distrust of the world at large. I was obviously an outsider.

I started to make my way through the crowd that had gathered behind me, and after much pushing and shoving, I reached the street I had come from earlier. I glanced back briefly and from that distance, I caught sight of something I had missed before. A streamer read: YRM.

I recalled then something about a YRM-operated community center here in Milagros. Danny had mentioned it once, saying, "If

YRM can win the slum dwellers over to its side, it'll become a force
to contend with. But it's near impossible to do. The poor of Milagros
are true nonbelievers, they have seen too many promises broken.
They're not just token cynics, Clara, these people have lost the
ability to trust. Bayani has his job cut out for him."

So, I had accidentally come upon a YRM meeting. I wondered
whether anyone at the paper knew about it, whether there was
someone from the *Chronicle* in the crowd. My curiosity, which
had been dampened by the unfriendly residents, was back. I wanted
to know if Luis Bayani was speaking at Milagros that morning.
I wanted to see him in person, see if all that I had read and heard
about him was true. Whether he was as impressive a figure as
the media made him out to be or whether his larger-than-life image
was something people of my profession created for the sake of a
headline.

As I turned a corner, I passed a group of young men and women
whom I knew instantly to be the YRM delegation. They had the
look of Loyolans about them. Elitist. Confident. And yet they were
clearly welcomed in this place as the people quickly made way for
them. Danny would have been astounded to see this. Bayani and
YRM had obviously gained a foothold here. But I couldn't make out
if Bayani himself was with the group. Besides, I had only ever seen
photos of him. And people seldom resemble their photos.

Realizing how long I had been lingering in that place, I reluctantly moved on. Torres would not appreciate my returning without
the story he wanted. So I went in search of my bloodstained alley.
I found it only after losing my way several times. Milagros with
its narrow lanes and closely packed shanties can confuse you with its
impression of sameness. But after a few wrong turns, I found the
place and interviewed the residents, learning yet another tale of
brutal and meaningless bloodletting.

Then I moved on to my next assignment, which took me across
town to the Ministry of Cultural Minorities. A controversy was fast
developing around the construction of a dam down south which
would result in the destruction of an ancient tribal burial ground.

This assignment took up the rest of the morning and gave me just enough time to make it to the Maharlika Hotel at noon, where the jeweler Ding Sarmiento was opening his newest store.

At the hotel I found a phone and called through my stories for the morning. Then I made my way to the arcade, where a throng of expensively dressed bejeweled women with their well-groomed escorts milled about drinking champagne. The opening party was in full swing. I bumped into a magazine reporter I knew, one I secretly thought of as a repository for social trivia. She has yet to disappoint me.

As soon as she reached my side, she whispered into my ear, "Guess who's here?"

I waited for her to tell me.

"El Toro himself. And guess what else?"

I waited once more.

"He bought a South Sea pearl pendant . . . this big," then she named a ridiculous price. I nodded, trying to look impressed. Before she walked off, she said with a giggle, "And no one, of course, believes it's for his wife!"

I made my way into the shop and inspected the glass-and-chrome decor and the pricey baubles laid out on the gleaming counters. At the center of the room, half a head taller than the rest of the crowd, stood the senator, impeccably dressed as usual, a smile on his sensual lips. I had seen him on two previous occasions and had been struck by his aura of snaky sexuality. It was no hard task understanding why wherever he went he left a trail of female hearts behind.

The jeweler was easy enough to spot. His enormous bulk would have been difficult to hide in any place. I introduced myself and asked him a couple of questions for the paper's social pages. He was a businessman who appreciated the value of publicity and so was very obliging. As we spoke, he reached out every time a waiter walked past with a tray of hors d'oeuvres.

I left forty-five minutes later, refusing to dally any longer than necessary with the guests. Social functions always left me feeling out of place, and I often failed to see the sense in them. But as Mel explained to me once, "You can't imagine how many people out there read only the social pages." I told myself I was doing my bit to keep the paper in business.

A surprise awaited me when I arrived back at the *Chronicle*. By mistake, someone had left the front-page galley on my desk.

In boldface, the headline read: MILAGROS IS MARCHING.

I felt goose bumps on my flesh. I grabbed the sheet and quickly scanned Danny's article, learning then that Luis Bayani had indeed been at Milagros that morning. He had stood in front of a throng of thousands, had spoken to them, and most importantly, had convinced them to take part in the coming protest march.

Danny walked in as I put the galley on his table.

"Well, he's done it," was all he said.

"What now?" I asked.

Danny merely shrugged. He, too, must have felt the same sense of excitement and apprehension I did. It was as though someone had thrown the whole pack of cards into the air and watching them fall, we could make no sense of them. We sat in silence, I on Danny's desk and he in his chair, both of us pondering the matter carefully. To me it was a momentous thing that the poor of Milagros were marching. By drawing them out in their great numbers, Luis Bayani had shifted the dynamics. With Milagros behind him, he now had the power to make the palace listen. And that evening, the palace's attention was irrevocably focused on him.

10

❦

The Stone Moves On

The image of Luis Bayani filled the screen.

Sitting in an armchair in his private study, El Presidente stared at the student leader and let out a sigh. It was a sound that carried with it all the problems of the long day that had just been. News of Milagros's participation in the protest march had reached the palace by mid-afternoon. And since then the whole place had been in an uproar. To add to the sense of disorder, Madam, on hearing of the Milagros development, had flown into a rage.

"How dare these people compromise the government's position at this crucial time!" What concerned Madam was the bad press the march would generate. She feared it would mar the coming wedding celebrations.

Not that there had never been bad days at the palace before. It was just the atmosphere this day was different. The Chief of Staff, in describing the problem to me later, said: "We were not the ones pulling the strings."

The Chief of Staff understood that power was about retaining control. And somehow El Presidente and those around him had lost their grip. They were merely reacting. And this young man who stared out of the TV screen had become, in El Presidente's mind, the harbinger of disaster. Only the Chief of Staff understood that

Luis Bayani was simply a part of the flow of things. And unfortunately the tide had turned against his superior.

He stole a glance at El Presidente. In the face of the man he had served for sixteen years he now saw the erosion of power. He had seen him at the height of his popularity, had admired him, believed in him and supported him, had continued to do so in spite of his gradual transformation from a ruler with power to one who was corrupted by it. He knew he was witnessing El Presidente's decline. Perhaps the man had it in him to weather this storm; the Chief of Staff hoped so, but in his heart doubted it.

I wonder if the Chief of Staff knew of the things whispered about El Presidente's true source of power; and if so, did he, too, think that the stone had moved on?

Have you heard what they say about El Presidente?

In a country given to the telling of tales, strange stories grow in abundance, although this tale admittedly is stranger than most. They say El Presidente's power comes from a stone as old as time itself. A small stone coughed up from the core of the earth many millenniums ago when the earth shuddered and opened its mouth, bringing forth molten rocks and rivers of boiling mud. No one walked the earth then, no one resembling humans. In this regurgitated mass was one small stone that glowed red from the fire that burned in the earth's heart, and it continued to glow for a long time, until it finally contained its power and became in appearance like all the lesser rocks and stones around it. In this way it remained undisturbed for thousands of years.

They say it was first touched by human hands five hundred years ago. The first to find it was a young nobleman, the son of a powerful rajah. He saw the stone while fishing with his friends along the north bank of the river that ran through his father's land. It lay in the shallows of the riverbed, visible in the clear water. It was quite unremarkable in appearance, except for a red hue that became discernible in the light. While the lad sat on a rock fishing that morning, his gaze returned to the stone again and again. Finally, he reached for it.

The water was cold. It made him shiver. But when his fingers curled around the stone, he found to his surprise that it was warm to the touch. He drew it out of the water and discovered another surprise. The stone whose weight and heat he felt in the palm of his hand was nowhere in sight. It had, however, left in the center of his palm a red mark, the exact shape of the missing stone, and this would stay on his palm for many years.

He was the first of the chosen.

The stone changed his life and time seemed to quicken. In that year, the rajah, who had been nothing but strong and hale, suddenly grew frail and thin, while his son grew more imposing by the day. Then the old rajah died and his son stepped into his father's shoes.

Under his guidance, the clan prospered, its fortune grew tenfold, and its landholdings increased, reaching all the way to the harbor. To protect his people he built a military stockade, an imposing structure designed to put fear in the heart of his enemies. Many believed he would be the greatest rajah of all time. But how long can good fortune hold out when the wheel of life continuously turns?

The rajah's decline began the day the conquistadores landed on the shores of the island.

On hearing that a powerful rajah owned all the land that lay before them, they chose to employ diplomacy instead of arms. The visitors sought an audience with the ruler. On being received by him, the head of the delegation made the rajah a proposition: "In exchange for all your land, we make you this wondrous offering."

Before the rajah was placed a brilliant ceremonial platter of pure gold.

The rajah desired that which was placed before him. Lifting it, he was impressed by its solid gold weight, and on turning it in the light noticed how it shone as nothing had ever shone before his eyes. He coveted it with all his heart, questioning neither its value nor its usefulness. Its resemblance to the sun made him think it was magical and so he agreed to the exchange.

Carrying his precious new possession in his arms, he and his people departed from the land that had been their birthright since as far as they could remember. Where they moved to is unknown. And soon after their departure, the mark on the rajah's hand faded, and his fame rapidly declined until his name was mentioned no more.

More than three hundred years passed before the stone was found again. This time by a youth of twelve called Jose, who lived in a small town that was two moons away from the city. Walking to school one day, he saw it glinting on the road. Being curious by nature, he picked it up and took a closer look at it, noticing its red hue. He liked the feel of it. It felt like a part of him. The boy Jose put the stone in his pocket, and on returning home from school that day, made a small pouch for it. From that day on, he carried the stone with him wherever he went.

The stone gave him a different kind of power. According to his heart's desire, it gave him the power to heal. He grew up to become a doctor who healed people's ailing bodies, even restoring his mother's eyesight. He also became a man of letters, one whose words began to heal the spirit of his people. Through his writings he planted the seed of independent thought in his countrymen's minds. He exhorted them to shed the shackles of the colonial powers and to be proud of the color of their skin.

He continued to carry the stone even as an adult. When asked once by a friend why he still had this souvenir from his youth, he replied, "It is a reminder to me that I must keep to my youthful ideals, never to give in to cynicism or to lose hope, for in the end my dreams are the one thing I can truly own."

The man Jose never lost his dreams. A few years later he was branded a subversive and sentenced to death by the Spanish authorities. As the guard assigned to escort him out to the execution ground began to tie his hands behind him, he asked that he be allowed to clutch the small stone he had kept with him throughout his imprisonment. The guard agreed for he was used to strange requests from men on their way to death. A few minutes later, the condemned man was led out into the open field where the Spanish authorities had ruled that he be shot in the back like a coward.

When the soldiers fired their muskets, the man Jose tightly

clutched the stone in his hand and he felt it blaze hot in his palm. The stone granted him his last wish. Instead of falling with his face to the ground, it gave him the strength to turn around so that he fell looking up at the sky.

Today he is called a hero, with many streets and even a famous library named after him but, more importantly, his writings are read by every student in the nation. His words continue to inspire. He did not die in vain.

Less than ten years after this man's death, the stone came into the possession of another young man, a simple provincial sort. It was given to him by an old woman he met on a road one evening. She told him that it had come from a *duende* who told her that on the third night after the full moon—which was that very night—she should wait on that road and give it to the first man she met. So the stone must be given to him. For some strange reason, the man found himself desiring it, so he promised to do whatever the old woman asked of him. She ordered him to put it in his mouth and swallow it, which he did, and then he promised that before his death, he would pass it on to his son, who must do the same. He asked how he could retrieve the stone he had swallowed but the old woman said that the stone knew its business and would take care of that when the time came.

The man's fortunes changed. He not only prospered financially but also became a respected figure in his town. The stone opened many doors for him and for his children. His eldest son would go on to become a lawyer and much more.

With time, the man forgot the presence of the stone. For as he grew more worldly in his ways, he stopped thinking of his beginnings. Until the evening he celebrated his fiftieth birthday. He felt a sudden shock of pain hit him in the chest. His sons quickly took him to his bed while a servant ran for the doctor.

Meanwhile, he felt something in his chest, a lump, like a small stone. He remembered it then and realized his time had come. He called for his eldest son and, gripping his hand, said, "You must obey me, do you hear? What I ask of you is my last wish, you must obey me."

His son nodded, bewildered by his father's words. The man, to the horror of his son, began to choke. As his wife wept and his daughters wailed, his son struggled to raise him by supporting his back. The man gasped out the following words: "You must swallow this." A small stone, glowing red, warm to the touch, came out of his mouth.

His son took the stone, revulsion written on his face, but he had made a promise, so when his father ordered him once more, saying, "Swallow it!" he put the stone in his mouth and swallowed it. It was coated with the bitter bile from his father's body and he was thankful that it slipped down his throat easily. He felt it travel down to the center of his being, marking a path with its heat. The sensation passed and the stone became a part of him.

His father squeezed his hand so tight that he winced. Looking into his eyes, he heard him gasp out these words: "It is a stone of power, it will give you power." Those were the last words his father spoke.

And this is how they say El Presidente came upon the stone that has enabled him to stay on in the palace for so long. The people who believe this tale have one more thing to add: "The bearer is only a temporary vessel, the stone always moves on."

Perhaps the stone finally moved on the night Luis Bayani spoke on television, his rise to prominence marking the decline of El Presidente's power, like one taking from another. And yet looking at Luis Bayani, the Chief of Staff was surprised at what he did not see. The student leader did not have the appearance of one who could topple a regime and its leader.

What the Chief of Staff saw was a dark-haired young man with a lean build who was indistinguishable from any other young man of his generation. Until you met his eyes. Behind his spectacles, those dark pools glinted with intelligence, hinting at a mind old beyond his years. He exuded a firmness of purpose, a controlled passion tempered by reason. And he had a great capacity for stillness.

So when he spoke, you listened.

Of what Bayani said that night, the Chief of Staff would find himself later asking this question: had the student leader known the impact his words would have on the course of his life, would he have chosen to speak differently? Perhaps not. For who among us can tell what each will reap from day to day? The vision one holds of one's life is so limited, reduced in scope to a moment, so that each person can make choices only within that narrowed reality.

Addressing the nation, this is what he said. "Milagros is marching. The poor of this land are calling for change, they are joining the protest march and I call on you to do the same.

"By marching you are making yourself heard. You have been silent far too long, and your silence cannot change things.

"The right to rule is a mandate given by the people to those they elect. It must follow then that a government which has ceased to be of the people—like ours has—must lose its right to govern. It is our right to revoke this mandate. This is one of the fundamental aspects of democracy, and El Presidente says we are a democracy.

"The protest march we are staging next Friday is an opportunity for you to make our leaders listen. We ask you to join us, to take action, to be responsible at last.

"All the injustices we cry about, all the problems that sixteen years of misgovernment have given rise to, are as much our creation as the government's. In failing to speak out and act, we have contributed to the sorry state of our country, we have been irresponsible, but now we have the chance to be responsible once more."

Looking back to this moment, the Chief of Staff would say, "This was when the decision was made. This was when the end began." What he meant was that if at any time El Presidente had believed Luis Bayani was a passing problem, he changed his mind the night Bayani spoke. And so he took what, the Chief of Staff believed, was a fatal step.

Without waiting for the news broadcast to finish, El Presidente rose from his seat and walked to the door. He had come to a decision. In a tired voice he said to the Chief of Staff, "Tomorrow, Raul, have Aure recalled from the south."

A look of surprise came over the Chief of Staff's face. But before he could speak, El Presidente had walked out of the room. The matter would have to wait then. Tomorrow, he promised himself, tomorrow he would appeal this decision. For Aure was not the answer to their problems. Aure was more a danger to them than a solution. He must make El Presidente see this before it was too late.

It was his turn to sigh now. It had been a long day and he, too, wished to be gone. Walking toward the television set, he caught sight of a man he did not recognize who was babbling on about an earthquake.

"Up north, the main fault line is up north!" the man was saying in an emphatic tone.

The Chief of Staff flicked the off button and the man was gone. A second later he emerged from the study and made his way through the empty outer office, noting the eerie silence around him. For a brief moment he believed himself to be in a deserted palace.

11

We May Read About You

*I*n his cell at Campo Diaz, the soldier Rogelio Campos longed for escape. But there was nowhere his mind could flee to. The future was filled with frightening vistas, the present with confusion.

Since his detention on Monday morning, he had spent countless hours trying to make sense of his plight. He understood that he was charged with killing an innocent man, a fact that he had yet to come to terms with. What he could not understand was what they wanted from him. He had been interrogated over and over, had told them over and over exactly what had happened, but they kept calling him in for more questioning.

He did not know his interrogators, which only added to his fears. The army, which had been home to him the last three years now, showed him its unfriendly face, so that Rogelio began to dwell on the dark things said about the detention center.

Prisoners, he knew, were brought here before being transferred to other detention camps on the outskirts of the city. He knew, too, of the unspeakable things said to happen to them during their stay. Many, it was rumored, were never seen again, erased from sight if not from memory.

There were vehicles that arrived at night, though he had not seen them himself. They were loaded with bags, the contents of which could only be guessed at, then driven away before light, a journey to some unknown place.

What Rogelio wished to do was talk to a lawyer. Surely the army would defend one of their own. When he had spoken to the officer in charge about the matter, the man had looked at him with disdain and merely said it was not up to him to decide such matters. Rogelio then asked to see Commander Reyes. It distressed him that his superior had made no effort to see him. Only then did he learn that Commander Reyes was himself under investigation. Rogelio's sense of isolation deepened.

He longed to have someone to speak to. He missed Dario and wondered how he was doing. All he knew was that Dario was still in hospital. Other than that there was no news about him.

Then on Wednesday, his third day under detention, he was brought to the interrogation room, where a man in a suit sat waiting for him. A lawyer at last. But whatever stirring of hope Rogelio felt quickly disappeared.

The lawyer flatly informed him, "Self-defense is when someone attacks you, or threatens to, and you react in defense of your life. This store owner did nothing to you. What the Hanging Judge will see is that you shot an innocent man with no provocation whatsoever."

When Rogelio protested, saying that he was being chased by a pack of students, the lawyer briskly replied, "They had no firearms, only sticks and stones; you had a weapon."

The lawyer then picked up the papers on the table and tapped them into a neat pile. Then he paused. He looked up and held Rogelio's eyes and said to him, "You know, if you want to get out of here sooner, you really need to . . . cooperate."

"But I have told you everything that happened."

Leaning closer to Rogelio so that he could watch his every expression, the lawyer told him, "I can tell you what to say and if you say it, it will facilitate matters for you and you will be . . . rewarded."

Rogelio drew back with shock on hearing the lawyer's words. His mind raced and he told himself he was mistaken. He had misunderstood the man. But the truth could not be denied. Rogelio may be a lowly fieldworker's son, but he was no fool.

With an innocence bordering on ignorance, he replied, "But I am cooperating, sir, I have told you the truth, all of it."

The lawyer leaned back, his eyes narrowing. "Then I'm afraid I cannot do much for you. The hearing, by the way, starts on Monday."

At the door, the lawyer stopped and opened his briefcase; reaching into it, he pulled out the day's newspaper. "Here, you may want to read about yourself."

The lawyer left the camp soon after but not before deciding to inform his superiors that this soldier, being simple and untutored in the ways of the world, could be easily dealt with. His cooperation would not even be necessary. For, unknown to the soldier, the lawyer knew his secret, knew where he came from. Creating a case against him was the easiest thing he had come across in his twenty years of practice. Rogelio was the best kind of victim—an unsuspecting one.

He could not have been more wrong, though. For as Rogelio was led back to his cell, he carried with him the knowledge that he was truly on his own. Although Rogelio did not understand the exact game the man was playing, he knew that it was not his interests he had in mind.

Ironically, the soldier now felt that his only hope was the Hanging Judge. A harsh man, true, but a just one. He remembered the lawyer's words about the judge, and how he would see the case. But Rogelio prayed that the judge was discerning enough to see the truth. That to him matters were not simply black or white. He took comfort in the thought of a wise judge, but his comfort deserted him easily. With each step he took, Rogelio swung from hope to despair and back again.

Back in his cell, he stared at the paper in his hand, reluctant to read it. When the words came into focus, they struck him like a blow to the chest. The headline read: SOLDIER IN COMA DIES. And there staring at him was a grainy photograph of Dario. His eyes watered as he thought of his friend who would never dream of horses again. He tried to read on but the words were a meaningless series of strokes and dots and lines. He shut his eyes to rest them. Then opened them again. Once more he let them travel down the columns until he saw what he was looking for.

His name.

Rogelio felt his stomach lurch. Unable to quell his fears, he vomited into the paper, as if somehow this would smear the type and erase his name from view. He stretched out on his cot and shut his eyes and remembered.

The sweet sickening smell of molasses invaded Rogelio's small airless cell. It was the smell of a world he thought he had escaped from long ago. A smell carried by the wind from the sugar central to the fields where the men hacked at soaring walls of sugarcane in the plantation known as Hacienda Esperanza.

Hacienda Esperanza employed hundreds of *sacadas* every harvest season, itinerant sugarcane fieldworkers who came from the neighboring provinces, traveling where work could be found, like flocks of migrating birds in search of food and warm weather.

Life in the sugarcane plantation was measured in seasons—wet and dry—and in cycles of planting, cultivating, and harvesting. It was the last that Rogelio found the hardest. For when the canes were deemed mature, the backbreaking work truly began.

Rogelio, along with his father and brothers, would rise at three-thirty in the morning and by five would have left the cramped *cuartel* where the workers lived. They would trudge barefoot to the cane fields a kilometer away. Once there, the cutting would begin the day.

Lying in his cot, Rogelio winced with remembered pain. He could feel the *espading* in his hand and the calluses it had left on his palm. His body remembered the motions of cutting. The bending of the entire body. The endless monotonous action of cutting the tops and bottoms of the canes with strong strokes; the grasping and pulling of the canes with the other hand, canes that were twice the height of a man. The removal of the leaves which always drew blood.

By mid-morning the process took its toll on the body. As the sun climbed higher in the sky, the work became more punishing with each passing hour; but Rogelio never let this slow him down. He had to cut one and a half tons of sugarcane each day.

The day did not end with the cutting. When this was done, he needed to find some hidden reserve of strength to carry his pile of canes to the railroad tracks and dump them in the *vagon*. If the cut cane was not loaded, he did not get paid.

The *sacadas* were condemned to live under a system of exploitation. At the top stood the *hacendero*, the wealthy and often absent sugar baron. In Rogelio's case, he had never even met the man. He only knew his name—Don Miguel Pellicer.

The man that Rogelio and his fellow workers dealt with was the hated *contratista*. Bloodsucker. Exploiter. Parasite. He was the middleman whom *hacenderos* like the don depended on to hire laborers. His position allowed him to exploit the *sacadas*, charging them exorbitant interest rates for the advances they made, forcing them to buy overpriced goods from the *cantina* which he owned and operated, and taking a big cut out of their meager pay.

Once Rogelio asked why they didn't just go and complain to the don, but his father admonished him, saying, "What makes you think these things happen without the don's knowledge? He knows but he doesn't care. As long as this man gets the cane cut and milled on time, it doesn't matter what the *contratista* does to us."

Shaking his head at his father's words, Rogelio replied: "Surely there is a better life."

His Kuya Hermano listened to his words of frustration and understood his sense of desperation but refrained from encouraging him. If Rogelio left before paying off his account with the *contratista*, as his brother's guarantor, he would have to pay it off for him.

There was simply no escaping their miserable life. Unless one was a dreamer like Rogelio. Often, while the rest of the men numbed their bodies and quieted their minds with drink at night, Rogelio would sit and read by the waning light.

Rogelio's father watched him with growing concern. To his eldest son Hermano, he said, "What use is all this learning? It will only make your brother more dissatisfied; he is restless enough as it is."

When Rogelio was eighteen and had been cutting cane for three seasons, a priest from the big city came to stay at Hacienda Esperanza for the summer, accompanied by a group of university students. They were housed in the *cuartel* adjacent to the one Rogelio's family lived in.

The workers looked upon these visitors with suspicion. They doubted their sincerity in wanting to help the *sacadas* by learning more about their plight. So it surprised them when, at dawn of the following day and every day after, the visitors rose and walked to the fields, working side by side with them. Soon the workers warmed to them and began looking forward to the end of each long day so they could all gather around a fire and talk late into the night.

All except Rogelio, whose shyness—and pride—condemned him to watch from a distance. But he watched closely the one called Luis, who seemed to possess a keener mind and who, when he spoke, displayed a depth of understanding which Rogelio admired.

One night as Rogelio sat reading by the fading light, the student walked up to him, saying, "What are you reading?"

Rogelio shrugged and clutched tightly at his *komiks*, embarrassed to let the student see what he was reading. But the student simply leaned closer and took a look at what Rogelio held in his hand. He gazed into Rogelio's eyes and smiled at him: "I have a book you might like to read . . . *Noli Me Tangere* by Rizal." Even Rogelio, with his limited schooling, knew of the national hero and his writings.

The student continued to speak in an easy friendly manner. "It is one of my favorite books. I read it in high school along with *El Fili-busterismo*, Rizal's second novel. Every now and then I reread them both but it is only the *Noli* I have with me now. I will give it to you when we leave in two weeks." Having said this, the student said good night and walked off to join the others.

Two weeks later, on a Friday, the students and the priest left before dawn. Rogelio watched them head for the main road while he and the other workers made their way to the fields. As he watched their retreating backs, he felt that he had missed an opportunity, that somehow a new world could have opened to him had he shared some moments with them, especially with the one called Luis. He regretted not accepting his overtures of friendship.

That evening they sat and ate their meal in silence. The departure of their friends had left them all feeling deflated and despondent. But shortly after the washing-up was done, one of the women came to him and said, "I have something for you. Luis told me to give this to the young man who is always reading. Who else could that be but you!"

She handed him the book and Rogelio took it, hands trembling, unable to believe that the student had meant what he said. Then he opened the book and on the upper right-hand corner of the title page saw the letters LB. Slowly, he turned the page and began to read Rizal's story.

The more he read, the more restless he became.

Late one evening, his eldest brother asked him, "What will you do if you leave here? You are not trained for anything but harvest work."

Without hesitation, Rogelio replied, "Join the army. Soldiers don't need a lot of education, as long as I know how to read and write I will have a good chance of getting in. Why, even Pedring was accepted into the army!"

Rogelio's Kuya Hermano realized that Rogelio had given the matter some thought. So when some months passed and Rogelio's discontentment did not ease but instead deepened into a brooding silence, he told him, "Go! Go to the city. Leave this place. You do not have to tell our father, I will tell him after you leave."

"But *Kuya*, you are my guarantor!" cried Rogelio.

"So what? If I worked for the rest of my life, I will not be able to clear my account with the *contratista*. It makes little difference then if I take yours on as well."

"That is not how you should look at it."

"Rogelio, stop raving about things you cannot change. Go. At least going will change something. You leave with my blessing."

Late one night at the end of the harvest season when the moon was just a sliver in the sky, Rogelio packed his meager possessions. As he and his Kuya Hermano stood before each other, unshed tears in their eyes, the last thing his eldest brother said to him was: "We may read about you yet, eh, Rogelio?"

Now lying in his cell recalling his brother's words, Rogelio took some comfort in the knowledge that news from the city traveled slowly, if at all, to the fields of Hacienda Esperanza. His desperate plight would remain unknown, and perhaps his fate, if it proved unfortunate, would also remain his secret.

12

Tears for a Chinaman

Thursday came and brought with it a sweltering heat. We'd been having hot days followed by sudden downpours. Danny called in sick and Mel said it was probably influenza. There was a lot of it going around. Torres reshuffled our assignments and split up Danny's between Max, Mel, and the others. I ended up with my usual workload as well as Mel's.

It was not a day to be out and about. My skin felt uncomfortably clammy and I had an unquenchable thirst as I went from one end of the city to another. At midday I found myself standing in the median strip of the highway leading to the airport, watching eighty palm trees being stuck in the ground by a brigade of workmen. It was part of Madam's instant beautification project. Another one of her quick fixes designed to dress up the city for the wedding guests due to arrive in less than three weeks. Although the celebration was to be held up north in the town of Salinas, the foreign dignitaries and celebrities would be stopping in the city before and after the wedding.

Back at the *Chronicle* that afternoon Mel, who was big on wedding gossip, rattled off the names of the guests to me. I knew for a fact that she wanted to cover the event but Torres was still undecided as to which reporter to send.

"You just want to go on a junket, Mel," I said, teasing her.

"Well, what's wrong with that? It's not as if a celebration like this happens every day. Wonder who's footing the bill, you know, for the feast and all?"

"The palace, I suppose."

"Well, the don can well afford it, too."

Having said this, Mel leafed through the stack of photographs on her desk marked *Wedding File*. The palace had supplied all the publications with official shots of the two families. She picked one out and said, "He really is quite impressive looking, forbidding though. I saw him once in person, he's rather tall, too. Pity about the son, he's good-looking enough in that *mestizo* way but he lacks the father's presence, takes after the mother."

I reached out and Mel passed me the photograph. It was of the don and his family. I gazed at it carefully. At the don's face. At the imperious gaze, the aristocratic nose, the lips that seemed to hold back words, the stubborn chin. It was too distant and cold a face to be described as good-looking. But it certainly suggested strength and breeding.

Taking the photo back, Mel said, "He's the type you'd want on your side; he'd make a formidable ally."

"Or a formidable enemy. I wouldn't want to get on the wrong side of him."

Mel and I began clearing our desks.

"Home, is it?" she asked, looking hopefully at me. I steeled myself against giving in. I'd already kept my word and gone to the club with her on Tuesday night. So I said, "It's a bit late to go now." I explained to Mel my curiosity about Calle de Leon and that I wanted to do a follow-up story.

"Not worth it, Clara, just about every paper's run something on it, everyone knows about it by now."

"Well, it's definitely home for me then."

But Mel was wrong. There were places in the city where news took an eternity to travel. I was to learn with surprise that it was not until late Thursday of that week that news of the fire finally reached the Convent of Santa Clara.

On that Thursday afternoon I speak of, the new novice at the Convent of Santa Clara knocked on the door of Mother Superior's office. There was a man waiting to see her, she informed the nun. On hearing that it was Pepito Mariano, Mother Superior smiled and went out to meet him.

"Pepito!" she called to him as he stood gazing out the window in the foyer. He turned quickly and approached the old nun, noticing her warm welcoming smile.

Mother Superior, now in her late sixties, had been a young nun when he had first met her many years ago. Hers was the first face he had seen when he opened his eyes after having lain unconscious from a fall for several minutes. He had been a boy of eight then and had scaled the convent walls to pick some ripe mangoes that hung temptingly from a low-hanging tree branch. But before he could pluck himself a fruit, a cat sitting on the branch of the tree had clawed at his hand. He lost his footing and fell from the wall. As his head hit the ground with a loud thud, he lost consciousness. Sister Socorro had been one of two people to find him.

Now she was known as Mother Superior. With the years, she had gained stature and wisdom but these had not robbed her of her natural warmth and kindness. He could see these in her eyes. She exuded a quiet kind of happiness even now, which puzzled him.

"Sister Soc . . . I mean, Mother Superior," he quickly corrected himself.

The old nun chuckled. "Aaay . . . I am still Sister Socorro to you and to tell you the truth, you will always be little Pepito to me even if you are now a head taller than myself."

The boy Pepito had not only grown taller but had become a successful lawyer. Attorney Pepito Mariano had stayed in touch with the sisters of the Convent of Santa Clara who had cared for him long ago. He made it a point to see to their comfort, sending them sacks of rice and other foodstuffs with which to fill their pantry. And when he came to visit, the nuns always welcomed him with open arms.

But he expected today to be different.

This visit was proving more difficult than he had expected.

Looking at the old nun, it was obvious to him that she did not know what had brought him to the convent. He had not expected to be the one to break the news to her. He had been away when the tragedy happened and had not learned of it himself until his return to the city that morning. He had searched for the legal papers and had come straight to the convent. He wished now that he had phoned first. It would have prepared him for the task ahead.

How to begin.

But Mother Superior was not insensitive to his mood. Seeing the pensive look on his face, she realized something was troubling him. She touched his coat sleeve and said, "Come to my office, Pepito, we can talk in peace there."

He nodded and followed her, their steps echoing in the hollow hallway. Once inside her office, she showed him to one of two cane chairs, then took the other.

"Now, tell me what is bothering you, for I can see something has unsettled you."

Pepito Mariano hesitated, then leaned forward and took her hands. In a voice that was gentle yet firm told her, "Mother Superior, it's about Charlie. I didn't know you were unaware of this. I myself just found out—"

"Charlie . . . Oh my goodness! Is he ill? I must go and—"

The attorney shook his head. "Charlie is dead."

As the old nun stared uncomprehendingly at him, he very carefully explained what had happened. He watched her face closely. And gradually he saw understanding winning over shock. Grief, he knew, would come later.

Listening to him, Mother Superior found herself thinking how Charlie had been dead for four days and she had not known at all. Had had no inkling. What was she doing four days ago? She tried to remember. Why had nothing happened to make her feel Charlie was in trouble? To think it had been in the news and still she had not known. They led such quiet sheltered lives in the convent. Knowing Charlie, he would not have told anyone in his neighborhood of his connection with the Convent of Santa Clara, so no one had come to inform her of his death.

"I am sorry that you should find out in this manner." Pepito Mariano's voice broke through her thoughts.

Mother Superior let out a deep sigh. The lawyer looked down at his hands, giving the old nun time to compose herself. But when she finally spoke, it was with a steadiness that reassured him. "And Charlie, where is he, where is the body?"

"I'm sorry. . . . It was badly burned."

She sighed once more before continuing, "We must give him a proper burial. I will speak to the other sisters. He had no one but us. We will make a resting place for him here. He was never baptized, you know, but I shall speak to the cardinal myself about letting Charlie rest here."

"This may distress you more but you must know now that his body cannot be released yet. It is being held by the people involved in the investigation."

"How long?"

"There is no telling. All we can do is wait. In the meantime I must see to this other matter, Mother Superior."

He reached into his coat and from an inside pocket drew out a white envelope. He cleared his throat and explained, "This is Charlie's will, drawn seven years ago. Charlie always lived simply, and thirty years of frugal living have allowed him to accumulate quite a substantial sum."

Pepito Mariano named a figure which made the old nun look at him in surprise. "And he has willed half of this to the convent for use in whatever manner you see fit." Before the nun could say anything, he continued, "And the other half he leaves to the child. . . ."

"The child . . . the child, he has never forgotten her. You know of her?"

"A little. But I don't know the details. He never spoke of the situation and I did not feel it my position to ask." Unable to suppress his curiosity, he asked, "Does she know about him?"

The old nun shook her head. "But I will tell her everything, surely now he would understand she must be told."

Pepito Mariano rose from his seat, saying he would be in touch to finalize the details of the estate and that she should not hesitate to call him in case she had any questions or needed any assistance. The old nun with her white habit swishing about her accompanied him down the hallway to the reception area and opened the front door for him, thanking him for his visit.

On returning to her office, she sat and thought about the news she needed to break to the nuns. No. She couldn't face telling them about Charlie yet. She would wait till tomorrow morning.

She walked to the corner table where the kettle stood. She turned it on then reached into the cupboard under the table, taking out two teacups. As she made the tea, she resolved to undertake two things: tomorrow she would go to Calle de Leon, to Charlie's store, then she would send for the child.

Taking one cup, she put this near the chair Charlie always sat in when he came to visit. Then she raised the other cup to her lips and spoke to the absent Charlie: "Be patient, my dear, we will bring you home soon."

The tea tasted salty, like the sea that flowed down her lined cheeks. And so the first tears for Charlie the Chinaman were finally shed.

In her room at Calle de Leon, Consuelo Lamuerta looked around her then slowly rose to a sitting position at the edge of the bed, wincing at the throbbing pain in her palms and feet, the cause of which she could not determine. She stood and walked to the old wardrobe with the mirror on its door. As she gazed into it, she caught sight of another image of herself, the one that remained lying on the bed, a tube taped to her hand, feeding her with fluid from a bottle.

Puzzled, she turned and made her way back to her bed, each punishing step bringing tears to her eyes, until at last she came to stand over her sleeping self. Someone had brushed her hair out. She was surprised at how long it was. She reached out to touch it with her aching hand, she laid her palm on her head and was surprised at what she felt. Her face did not have the coldness of stone. She was not dead.

Consuelo bent closer to her body and her gaze fell on her bleeding hands. The source of her pain. She looked down at her feet and found that they, too, carried the same wounds. When recognition finally came and she was able to put a name to her wounds, she found herself frightened and confused.

How was it that all her prayers all these years should come to this? She prayed for healing, for her fragmented soul to be whole again. Now she had been given these wounds to wear. What did they mean?

She longed for the comfort of prayer. She turned and made her way out of the room.

In the hallway, she stood looking down at the woman who sat on a chair by her bedroom door. She recognized her as one of the ladies from the morning novena group. The lady had fallen asleep; beads of perspiration sat on her forehead, giving it a shiny look.

Consuelo entered her altar room and found that someone had kept two candles burning. She made to get down on her knees and the pressure on her feet brought her pain back with renewed force, but Consuelo bore it all. For the next few minutes, she lost herself in her prayers.

But loud footfalls disturbed her and she heard a familiar voice say, "How is she today?"

"The same, Padre Luis: she continues to sleep."

Consuelo came out to stand in the hallway as the woman said, "If she stays like this much longer, the doctor said she will need to be taken to a hospital. They will stick more needles into her to keep her alive."

"Hush now. The doctor only knows so much; there are things even the medical books cannot explain."

"Like this, Padre; it is a miracle, is it not?"

Padre Luis refrained from answering.

In the silence of the room, the sounds from the street could be heard. A low murmuring sometimes interrupted by a high-pitched voice or the wails of a child, cars pulling up, doors opening and slamming shut.

"I can hear them arrive," the woman said.

"Yes, there was already a large group gathered outside when I came in. But they let me through quickly."

Padre Luis frowned at the memory of the women calling to him, only their respect for a man of the cloth stopping them from tugging harder at his sleeves. "Pray to her, Father. Please ask her to help me!"

What had disconcerted him most was a woman holding out a white handkerchief, begging him to take it. "Touch it to her wounds for me please, Padre, please, her blood will heal my child. . . ."

Padre Luis walked to the window with the woman and opened the shutters a little. As they gazed down at the crowd below, Consuelo Lamuerta, unseen by both, joined them. She, too, looked out and saw the queue of people waiting there, the street hawkers, the cars, the souvenir stalls. It was the first time she had seen her street transformed. The size of the crowd, the clamoring of the people frightened her. She wanted to escape, to be far away from here.

In the middle of the street, Consuelo caught sight of an old nun speaking to a man selling *sampaguita* leis, her eyes drawn to the white billowing habit brilliant against the gray of the street. She saw the nun jerk her head up to gaze at the window where Consuelo Lamuerta stood. The nun raised her hand and made the sign of the cross.

Mother Superior had left the convent early that morning.

She broken the news of Charlie's death soon after morning mass as the nuns gathered in the dining room for breakfast. Sister Corazon, the oldest nun in the convent, had bowed her head and wept. Mother Superior had quickly signaled to one of the novices to help the frail nun to her room. Breakfast was left untouched as the nuns headed back to the chapel to pray. Mother Superior left soon after to escape the collective grieving.

She had refused to be accompanied by anyone, insisting she could manage on her own. They knew better than to argue with her. She had walked out to the main road and boarded a jeepney then got off and changed to another jeepney until she arrived at the intersection leading to Calle de Leon.

She had been here once long ago, in the first year that Charlie had opened his corner store. She had come one day without warning. It was one of the rare trips she had made, for the nuns at Santa Clara seldom ventured outside the convent walls.

She remembered standing a distance away, looking at him, her Charlie, as he served his customers. She watched him as he listened to a housewife chatter on, while passing her child a piece of candy. When they had finally walked away, she had approached the shop, saying, "Be careful, Charlie, that you don't give all your wares away for nothing."

"Sister Socorro!"

She had laughed at his expression. The pleasure in his face and his big smile left her in no doubt of her welcome. Charlie rushed to welcome her. As he ushered her in, he apologized for the smallness of the place but she had reassured him it was a very good spot to have a business.

Speaking in his usual respectful way, he showed her the small room where he slept. It was painted white to offset the lack of light, for the room, being a forced partition, had no proper window. Once the shop was closed, she imagined it would be dark and warm inside. Charlie said the heat didn't bother him, for he had bought a small electric fan. He showed it to her, a gleaming new fan that sat on a little table against a wall.

"Do you eat well, Charlie?"

He nodded, saying, "Yes, yes . . . I take care of myself."

"And do you go out at all? Have you made friends, Charlie?"

"No need to go out . . . many people come here and talk to me," he replied; then, with the corners of his eyes crinkling, he leaned closer to say, "I know about everyone. They treat me like Father Mathias, like a father confessor." Charlie said there was little time for going out. He explained that Monday to Sunday he opened the store at seven in the morning and closed it at eight in the evening.

It was then she told him, "Sunday is a day of rest. God rested on the seventh day, remember, Charlie? So you must rest, too. Open the store at the same hour but close earlier on Sunday. One Sunday a month, you choose which Sunday, come to the convent and spend time with the sisters. Everyone misses you. I will tell them I saw you and that you will come one Sunday each month. I know you must get back early but at least stay an hour; better still, stay for dinner. We will expect you."

Charlie had served her a cold drink, which she drank while he got up every now and then to serve a customer. Before she left, it was agreed between them that he would visit every fourth Sunday of the month.

"And I will tell everyone about your store, Charlie, I will describe it to the sisters. They will want to know how you go."

That was thirty years ago, and now the store was no more.

Mother Superior stood and gazed at the charred black empty space. She took in a deep breath and slowly let it out to ease the pain that had gathered there. Only then did she become aware of the bustling street.

"*Sampaguita . . . tatlong piso lang . . . ang bango . . .*"

A *sampaguita* vendor came by, flogging leis of fragrant white blooms. He extended one toward her so she smelled its sweet jasmine fragrance. "Will you buy a lei for three pesos, Sister? Make an offering to the saint?"

A woman carrying a sickly-looking child took the lei the vendor had been offering the old nun.

"Here, three pesos. It is all I have left, for I have come all the way from the province, but I will make an offering. Maybe she will cure my daughter, who has fits. See, I let her bite my finger, better my finger than her own tongue. I will pray for a miracle and perhaps the saint will cure her."

It was then that Mother Superior first learned of the Miracle of Calle de Leon. She looked closely at the crowd and noticed they were gathered in front of one of the *accessorias*. The flower vendor spoke once more. "They say her hands and feet still bleed as she sleeps. It is truly a miracle, don't you think, Sister?"

The nun made no comment and the vendor took this as an invitation to continue. "I say she will perform miracles. Is not the stopping of the fire a miracle? She will heal the sick, I am sure. And perhaps change the government, too; now, that will really need a miracle!"

Mother Superior smiled at the man and asked, "What is her name, do you know?"

The flower vendor, a puzzled look on his face, said, "You mean, you don't know? But everyone knows! Consuelo Lamuerta!"

For what seemed an eternity, Mother Superior felt her heart had stopped. The man continued to speak. "Why, already they call her Santa Consuelo. They will make her a saint."

Looking up toward the window, Mother Superior made the sign of the cross and the vendor heard her softly say, "She is here . . . she is still here."

"But that is what I told you."

The old nun, a distant look in her eyes, thanked him and instead of making her way to the apartment, hailed a passing Jeep and quickly boarded it. The lei vendor shrugged his shoulders and approached another lot of pilgrims. As he made to cross the street, a chauffeur-driven dark blue Mercedes-Benz cut in front of him and drew to a stop. The rear window rolled down and an aristocratic gentleman leaned forward to gaze up at the apartment window while the people stared at him with unconcealed curiosity. After a few seconds, the window rolled back up and the automobile moved forward once more, its progress impeded by the movement of pedestrians and street hawkers, until it reached the corner, where it turned, gathered speed, and disappeared from view.

13

The Hands of Aure

Danny's illness brought me a story I would not have missed for anything in the world. It was worth giving up Saturday for. Weekends off were rare for people in the news business. Ours were strictly rostered by Torres. And that Saturday I was due to have mine off. But Danny had still to recover, so I was told by Torres to report for work.

Torres, of course, apologized for the inconvenience, but I suspected that he secretly thought weekend work was no great sacrifice for me, or even for Mel, as we had no family obligations.

What I didn't know then was that I needed to be somewhere myself on Saturday, but even had I known, I would still have agreed to work. My business, whatever it was, could wait. It's not every day that I was given one of Danny's stories. That Saturday, my assignment took me to the domestic airport, where Colonel Santiago Aure was due to arrive from the south.

Perhaps like me you share the belief that a person's nature can be read in his face, that what lies inside us never stays hidden for long because we betray our motives and our passions with our speech, our mannerisms, and the very way we live our life. As a general rule this is a valid one, as shown in the case of the senator, a man of strong appetites whose appearance betrayed his carnal pursuits. But as with anything, there are exceptions.

The law of appearances does not apply to the colonel.

When I learned on Friday that Torres wanted me to cover the return of Colonel Santiago Aure, I already had a notion of how he would look and sound. Who, after all, hadn't heard of the colonel and the things whispered about him? When I finally saw him, I was surprised and somewhat mystified by the fact that the picture I had painted of him in my mind bore no resemblance to the man whatsoever.

I arrived at the domestic airport building in the afternoon to find myself in the midst of hundreds of waiting people. Domestic flights were often late in leaving and late in arriving, so there was always a big, confused, and impatient crowd waiting. I looked around for my own kind and found them easily enough. They are not hard to spot.

The return of the colonel was important news because of the problems down south. The communist-influenced rebels had long been a thorn on the government's side. And the colonel had achieved the status of a hero because of his role in the fight against the rebels, who called themselves the People's Army.

Now let me tell you about the colonel's reputation: he was a legend at escaping death. He had survived thirteen ambushes which claimed the lives of a total of three hundred and eighteen soldiers.

When one afternoon at the start of the rainy season he and his men trudged up a winding path on their way to the village of San Simeon, where it was reported that rebels were hiding, a grenade exploded three meters away from him; he was flung by the force of the explosion and landed behind a boulder while eight of his men were instantly killed. Seconds later, the rebels swooped down from the hill and the wounded were quickly finished off and stripped of their M16s. In their rush to leave the scene of carnage, the rebels missed the colonel, who had been knocked unconscious a short distance away.

Another time, unable to sleep in the hut he and his men had been using as a temporary shelter, the colonel took his bedroll and slept out in the open in a small clearing about a hundred meters away. Thus he escaped a midnight ambush by rebels who had crawled into the hut, slitting the throats of the sleeping soldiers.

While they bled to death, the colonel slept soundly, unaware of the fate that had befallen his men.

He woke earlier than usual, a few minutes after dawn, the soft light from the morning sun just rising on the horizon touching his face. He rolled up his sleeping bag, slung this over his shoulder, and made his way back to the hut.

Easing the thatched door open a little, he peered inside. It was dark and the men did not stir. Then he smelled a familiar smell, the heavy metallic scent he always associated with blood. The colonel flung the door wide open and the sight that greeted him made him swear vengeance.

Two nights later, the colonel retaliated. With the stealth of those used to moving in the dark, he and ten soldiers surrounded a small farmhouse where a leader of the People's Army sat talking with farmers and simple folk, conducting an indoctrination session the topic of which happened to be land reform. The colonel, hidden in the shadows, listened to the man tell the farmers that they must take up arms and fight, that they must have balls and stand up for their rights.

Suddenly, the leader's body gave a jolt and he jerked about spasmodically, arms and limbs all over the place, his torso writhing to the rhythm of the blasting anger of gunfire. His men fell next to him along with many unfortunate farmworkers who the colonel felt should be punished for listening to a member of the enemy. As everyone who had failed to escape from the farmhouse lay dead or dying on the dirt floor, the colonel took out the small fine dagger he always carried with him and approached the leader, who lay in a pool of blood.

The man was still breathing, though weakening rapidly from his gushing wounds, but was not so weak that he failed to give one long, loud, anguished moan when the colonel, after ripping his trousers open, proceeded with a few deft strokes to cut his balls off and stuff these in his mouth.

The colonel would survive many more ambushes and battles at the same time that he initiated his own share of violent carnage; and in time his reputation for dodging death grew. It was natural that many individuals—the less informed—attributed his good fortune to God's blessing, saying that the powers in heaven were protecting one of their own. The colonel, after all, was a brave man who risked his life in the service of his country, fighting the vicious insurgents who terrorized the farmers down south. He was simply reaping the rewards of his good deeds.

But those that were more informed, those belonging to the inner circle, those who had access to privileged information, said it wasn't divine providence that preserved the colonel's life, but the devil himself. To them, he was an artist of suffering whose canvas was the human body. His methods appalled them.

As one story goes, during a "practicum," the colonel had sat and watched one of his pupils at work. When the man had finished with his subject, the colonel, looking at the mass of tissue, tendons, and organs, had declared with disapproval, "You are too messy, even butchers do a cleaner job."

The colonel then gave one of his most quoted lectures.

"A carefully placed incision will do the job. The subject remains conscious. And like you, he can watch what is happening to his body. He is alert. And that alone is enough to cause him concern. The instruments you are to use are before him. You pick one up— like this long, fine, sharp point—you place it upon his flesh, then slowly turn, gently twirling it between your two fingers so it becomes gradually embedded in his wrist. Or you take this razor-thin blade and take it to his flesh. It is so fine that it takes several seconds, an eternity it seems to him who must wait for the evidence of the violence done to him, an eternity before he sees the beads of blood form in the cut. He feels his arm go slack as a tendon is cut loose. He sees, feels, and is aware of everything. Every cut and prick is done cleanly. There is no bruising. And the blood flows slowly. The process moves at a graceful pace.

"When you have finished and the subject is cleaned, there is little or no mess. That is art. Even the finest, most experienced surgeon cannot do better than this. This is what you must strive for. When you are capable of this, you have learned a valuable discipline. It is called control. To hack, to saw, to stab, to cut without thought is undisciplined. You are no better than a butcher. Discipline and self-control form the foundation of our art."

It was very likely that tales like this were invented by those jealous of the colonel's achievements and of his special status. It was known to all that he was one of El Presidente's favorites, and in the government, jealousy is a permanent state of mind. For these tales to gain credibility, it would require the testimony of a victim, but none could be found.

Nevertheless, the tales conjured up an image of the man. So as I waited for him to make an appearance in a cordoned-off section of the arrival lounge at the airport, I expected to see a man whose face hinted at brutality, a rough, bullish face with a down-turned mouth, hard eyes, and a solid build. What I saw walking into the lounge was a man of medium height with a lean almost slight build, a surprisingly ascetic appearance. But what struck me as the most jarring thing about him, the part of him that was most mystifying, was his hands.

I noticed the hands of the colonel when we swarmed toward him, firing one question after another. The colonel raised his hand as if to tell us to slow down; one question at a time, please, those hands said to us. Those hands that belonged to someone else. Had he cut them from one of his victims, I wondered, and sewn them to his wrists? If so, he would have had to do the same for every part of his body. Everything about him did not fit his reputation.

Colonel Santiago Aure did not resemble a man who could defy death. Certainly not one who was reputed to have a hundred lives, and his hands seemed incapable of hurting another living thing. If anything, they defined him in the way he himself did: as an artist.

His fingers were long and straight, hinting at a tender sensitive nature. They were not made for holding a gun or a dagger or the many other instruments he was supposedly familiar with. Rather, these were hands one could easily imagine on a piano. They could just as likely hold a paintbrush or shape cool soft clay to capture the grace of a woman.

As you can see, my impression of the colonel contradicted everything I had ever heard of him. A case of cognitive dissonance. But then that may be because we are visually driven beings; we tend to make conclusions from appearances. Or perhaps my inability to see him for what he truly was lay in my lack of experience with chameleons.

There are other ways of seeing, I would learn this soon enough, that one's eyes are the most unreliable means of judging the world and humans. And it would be Laslo Jimenez who would reveal to me the true nature of this man. Laslo whose nightmares were filled with the hands of Aure.

Meanwhile, I managed to shout out my question to the colonel. "Can you tell us why you have been recalled from the south?" His answer, given to me in that measured and even tone of his, would later dawn on me as being so like the man: it could not be taken at face value.

I would not be allowed to forget the colonel.

It seemed to me that in these past few days, beginning with Charlie the Chinaman, my life was being crammed with people who had the ability to claim my thoughts even after I had committed their stories to paper. They refused to pass out of my life. News writers are objective creatures. We report and there our job ends; we do not maintain a relationship with the cast of characters that populate the events we cover every day.

But the colonel, as I said, would stay in my mind. He would return to my life; but not just yet, for when I arrived at the house in Vito Cruz late that Saturday afternoon, I was to find a note under my door.

I was expected at the Convent of Santa Clara.

PART II

14

The Convent of Santa Clara

So now we come to my story.

I arrived at the Convent of Santa Clara mid-morning on Sunday. As I walked up the familiar path to the main building, my eyes took in the pale sun-bleached lawn and the shrubs that lined the driveway, remembering the times I had hidden behind them in some child's play.

Here lies, you see, my known beginning.

As the story the nuns told me goes, I was a few weeks old when a novice found me early one morning by the convent's front steps. I was asleep inside an old shopping basket, oblivious to the strange twist my life had taken. I was a child with no name, no history; and no matter how many times the novice looked in the folds of the blanket wrapped around my tiny body, she found no clue to my identity.

Perhaps whoever left me there wished for me to have a fresh start; perhaps she believed that when you don't know who you are, you can truly begin again. And that was what the nuns did, they started from scratch and what they invented is what I am today. They named me Clara after the Convent of Santa Clara. Saint Clare, as you probably know, was a devout woman who loved and admired Saint Francis of Assisi. In seeking to emulate him, she founded the Poor Clares, a religious order for women which became the counterpart of the Franciscans. I was named after a saint and I believe this was more than just a case of expediency, that the nuns felt I needed extra guidance and protection, that having no roots in this world, I could do with a heavenly connection.

But even a waif needs a name, so I became Clara Perez; the Perez was bestowed upon me by the then-Mother Superior of the convent whose family name it was. That Mother Superior has passed away and Sister Socorro became the new head of the convent in her place. It was she who called for me today.

I no longer live here, having left soon after graduating from university. The nuns had asked me to stay on, saying I would always have a home with them, but I had turned down their kind offer. If I had taken vows, it would have been a different story, but having no desire to become a nun, I felt my place lay outside these convent walls. I realized, too, that the convent with its generous grounds and solid walls was only a minuscule part of a greater universe of which I had no knowledge. So I ventured out, beyond the margins and safety of the only world I had ever known, but I always returned.

Of my history prior to my arrival here I have long given up hope of discovering. The stones and mortar of this place, if they remember the face of the person who left me on the convent's front steps, have never divulged her name.

So everything I know of myself lies here. And of the years I spent in the Convent of Santa Clara I can tell you much. There is time. Mother Superior is not expecting me for a while yet.

The stone angel peeped out from the overgrown hibiscus, and seeing how wild it had grown, I wished for my gardening shears, itching to prune the offending shoots. This had been my job when I lived here, a self-assigned chore, because I had always been drawn to this little cemetery in its secluded corner by the convent's west wall. The wall itself was in a state of disrepair; the roots of the mango tree had long ago undermined the structure, lifting it from the base, so that the pressure had caused a wide fissure to form, wide enough for someone to slip through.

As a child, I often stuck my head through the crack in the wall to gaze at the street outside. But the quiet of the cemetery held more magic to me than any street scene, so I spent hours on the stone bench under the tree. This was no morbid choice, for having grown up in a convent, I had acquired a different view of life and death. When looking at cemeteries, I see them more as a testimony to life; the silent headstones whose etched letters I traced with my fingers were proof of lives lived.

On hot humid days I would often come and sit under the shade of the tree. Sometimes I would climb its branches and pluck green mangoes, which I would peel and slice then dip in *bagoong*, a sauce so tasty I forgave it its fishy smell.

Yes, there are many memories here, and if I jump about in recounting them, you must forgive me. There is little order in memories. They do not come in sequence, following some strict chronology; rather they surge forward, several at a time, as though having been confined in a recess of the mind for so long, they are in a hurry to escape into the present, rushing in great numbers through the little opening the act of remembering offers them.

My earliest memory is of the refuge. A block away from the convent is a home for abandoned or orphaned children run by the nuns. I spent my early years there and through it all I nurtured the hope that my mother would come back for me. It happened sometimes that a woman, in a moment of panic and desperation, left her child at the convent or at the refuge late at night; then, after a few days, sometimes weeks, returned for her.

Mine never did.

In this sense I was no different from most of the children: most of them were never reclaimed. They, however, found new homes but I stayed on. Although the women who came to the refuge always played with me, asked my name and my age, they invariably chose some other child, which taught me not to put too much importance on the attention people paid me. Perhaps it was because of the child I was: serious, full of questions. I don't know. It could also have been the way I looked. I was lighter-skinned than most, so perhaps the women felt I could never pass as one of their own.

At five, I was the oldest child in the refuge, too old to stay on, so the nuns moved me to the convent. It was Mother Superior herself who showed me to my room, saying, "I hope you like this room, Clara. It is not big but I think it is the best room in the whole convent; it faces east and my mother used to say young girls must have a room facing east, for that is where the sun rises. So when you wake, Clara, the sun will be there to give you the blessings of a new day."

It lightened my heart hearing her say those words; otherwise, the day I moved in with the nuns was the saddest day of my life. To me it meant I would never be part of a family and this had always been my secret longing. Sometimes this longing would creep up on me and I would go off and sit on this very bench, forlornly gazing out over the gravestones. It was during one of these moments that Mother Superior found me one day. When she asked me why I had such a serious face, I told her it was because I couldn't understand why my life had turned out the way it had.

She sat next to me and said, "There are some things we cannot change, things that are meant to be, although we cannot see the reason why. It is understandable that you ask these questions but it is wiser to dwell on today, because who your parents are and how different your life could have been are not as important as asking what you want to be, and how you can become what you are meant to be." This Mother Superior who gave me her name had a directness about her that often drove away my darker moods.

I attended the parochial school during the day and when I came home to the convent, the process of learning continued. I found in the nuns many teachers. There was Sister Luisa, who taught me about gardening. On weekends, I would spend the morning tending the small vegetable patch near the kitchen.

"It is older than you, Clara; it was begun by someone special who came to stay with us for a while."

"A sister?"

"No, not a nun, just a special woman who cooked very well. She prepared us the most delicious meals while she was here."

"Where is she now?"

"I'm not sure, sometimes we lose touch with people." Sister Luisa stopped and gazed at me for a moment in silence, then reached out and ruffled my hair before continuing to speak. "But all is not lost, Clara; why, you are here with me today to keep me company."

I enjoyed working the soil and watching the progress the eggplant made on the trellis. And I took much delight in seeing the cabbage, spinach, onions, and tomatoes grow in neat rows.

Underneath the kitchen window grew a row of rosebushes. And once a week, on Sundays, I would cut some flowers and arrange them in a vase then take them to the chapel. This was a task I liked doing, for the convent garden had a profusion of fragrant gardenias, *ylang-ylang*, and *sampaguitas*, and several brilliant red hibiscus shrubs.

On weekends, I was also responsible for bringing in the eggs that arrived at the convent. Santa Clara was the saint people prayed to for fair weather. When the day of a special event or celebration approached, people would make an offering of fresh eggs, leaving these by the convent's front door. Though clear skies were never guaranteed, the eggs were always welcome at the breakfast table.

At the convent I learned to sew with Sister Matilda.

"There are fifty-two stitches, and every young lady should know them all. First, the running stitch. Second, the chain stitch. Third, the cross-stitch . . ."

From Sister Teresa I learned to love books. In the convent, television viewing was something we seldom engaged in. So while my school friends were fed a steady diet of cartoons, comedies, and dramas, I was fed stories by Sister Teresa. She conducted catechism classes on weekends and I sat in and listened to her tell Bible stories. With the years, my desire to hear stories was transformed into a passion for writing my own tales. And so I scribbled away on a ruled exercise book and read my tales out to the nuns.

Time passed without much to disrupt life in the convent. Perhaps because the nuns vowed to pray all their life, God shielded them from the daily trials and tribulations that beset most people. And living with them, I shared their calm existence.

When I finished at the parochial school, I took the entrance exam for La Consolacion and won a high-school scholarship. And when I completed this, I went on to the State University to study journalism, intent on being a writer. Before I knew it, I had completed my education and, armed with my degree, went out into the world.

As I said, I chose to leave. There had been a time when I believed I was expected to join the nuns because they had taken me in. The thought brought me little happiness. One day, while pulling out the exhausted tomato plants from the ground, I broached the subject of becoming a novice with Sister Luisa. She looked at me in surprise and a frown formed on her face. After a while, she spoke.

"This ring, Clara, this ring that I wear is a wedding ring, for I am wedded to Christ, a decision I made in response to my calling. You have to hear it. This calling. Don't feel that just because we raised you . . . you have to embrace our life."

"Don't you want me here, Sister?"

"This is not about wanting you. It is about what you want to be."

"But I don't know what it is I want."

"What gives you joy, Clara, what gives you the greatest pleasure, there lies your calling."

"I think I want to be a writer but I'm not sure, I may never find out."

She smiled and, brushing off the soil from her hands, said, "Clara . . . Clara of such little faith. You must trust that you will find out. Why, inside his little chrysalis, the grub knows there is a purpose to his life and so becomes a butterfly. You, too, will sprout wings. And if at the end of the day you are indeed meant for a life of prayer, you will bring so much more to our community when you come to us enriched by your experience of the world."

With her words, Sister Luisa released me from the pressures that sprang from obligation and gratitude, but my freedom frightened me and I told her so.

"Oh that! That is not fear you are feeling, it is excitement!" she exclaimed, adding, "I often confuse the two myself."

So I went out into the world, chasing after stories to write, capturing with words the brutality of accidents and murders, the sense of rootlessness that resulted from the destructive forces of nature, the pain of dying, the anguish of loss, and those very rare moments of euphoria when the human spirit triumphed. I worked at the *Chronicle*, taking the stories Torres handed me, hoping that one day he would give me a big one, only to discover that the story that would outweigh all the others was to be found right here, within the walls of the convent I once called home.

I heard the sound of dried leaves crunching and I looked up to see the familiar face of Mother Superior. I watched her push open the rickety gate that led to the cemetery. As she came up the pebbled path, she greeted me with a warm smile and said, "I had a feeling you'd come by here first. You always liked this spot . . . just like Charlie."

And so it was that I came upon the story of Charlie the Chinaman.

15

❦

The Missing History

"He was called by another name," was how Mother Superior began her tale.

Before he became Charlie the Chinaman, he was Chen Lu Pin, the only child of a young farming couple in the south of China.

At a young age, he was used to hearing his mother say, "Ahh, Lu Pin, look, you have turned-out ears. They are the ears of a traveler and they mean you will not die in the land of your birth."

He would feel the turned-out fold of each ear and he would shake his head and say to his mother, "I am not going away, Mother, I will live here with you and Father." His mother would smile at him, reach out and straighten his collar, and send him out to play.

Life on the farm went by peacefully, with one day flowing into the next. He played with the young farmhands, and sometimes was allowed to accompany his father out into the fields. He liked playing in the open where he could feel the wind on his face and would have gone with the men every day if his mother had not insisted that he learn to read and write. So he studied to please her and to make the studying pleasant, she stayed close by. While he read, she worked in the kitchen, kneading dough to make tasty dumplings, singing him little tunes she knew he loved.

Sometimes he would look out the window and say out loud, "It's more fun outside."

And she would answer, "You don't want to be a farmer all your life, so you must study."

"But Father is a farmer," was his reply.

"Yes, I have not forgotten," said his mother.

The young boy did not understand the meaning of her words, not until his fifth year when his father fell ill of a disease of the lung, and within three months was laid to rest.

Their lives changed, for with no man to farm the land, it passed out of their hands. The things in their little home were sold off one by one. And one day, his mother dressed him in his best clothes and together they traveled the long journey into town, with only one carryall between them containing the few pieces of clothing they owned.

"Where are we going, Mother?"

"Home," she replied.

He asked no more, although her answer puzzled him.

At the hottest hour of a summer day, they entered a large busy town and continued along the main road before turning right into a private lane. Then his mother, who walked a few steps in front of him, came to a stop. The boy stopped, too, and looked up and found himself in front of the imposing gates of a high-walled town mansion.

He glanced at his mother and saw her straighten her back and lift her shoulders the way people do when they are in need of courage. The boy soon discovered through the angry words flung as a greeting that this was his mother's home before her marriage. That she had left in disgrace, having eloped with one of her family's farm tenants.

His mother pulled him next to her and pressed him down by the shoulders so that his knees bent and together they knelt and begged for a place in the family home. She begged for a roof over their heads and for food. She begged in a strained, tearful voice as her eldest brother, who now headed the clan, looked at her with disgust, while his wife, his children, and his servants looked on.

His mother's brother grudgingly gave them a home. But they were never made to feel welcome. He treated them the same way he did his servants. And his servants treated them as though they were even lower than the lowliest serving wench. And on every occasion his uncle could find, he reminded them they were there only on sufferance.

Two years of living in her brother's home robbed the boy's mother of her spirit. She no longer sang the pretty tunes he loved, she no longer smiled. His young mother, who was once beautiful but now wore a sad face, began to say to him over and over, "You will leave here, Lu Pin, you must promise me that when there is nothing left to keep you here, you will leave."

The boy was too young to understand what she meant, so he insisted that he would do no such thing. He insisted that he would always stay by her side and take care of her; she needed a protector and he would protect her.

One night, as his mother said good night to him, he noted the sad look on her face and so said to her, "When I grow up, I will take you away from here and you will never be sad again." Two tears rolled down her cheeks and he lifted his hand and brushed them away, begging her not to cry.

She smiled at him and replied, "After tonight, Lu Pin, I will no longer cry."

On hearing her say this, he believed she was reassured and he soon fell asleep.

That night, his mother disappeared and her absence was not discovered until the following day. At first it was believed she had run away but they were soon disabused of this thought when a servant who had gone to draw water from the well discovered her body. The well was too narrow and the poor widow, on jumping down, had not reached the bottom. Instead, she had been wedged in the passage and died after suffering much bruising and bleeding and exposure to the cold air that rose from the well.

The act did not raise any grief in her brother's heart, instead it raised his ire. Purple with rage, he shouted at his dead sister. "Worthless woman! Worthless in life! Causing trouble even in death!"

When the servants finally managed to pull her body out of the well, the boy's angry uncle pushed him forward, shouting, "Look! Look at your ungrateful, useless mother."

The boy Lu Pin refused to cry; he clenched his fists and bit his lips.

He would take with him the memory of that bruised face. And its tragic eyes would follow him into his dreams. For a long time after, he would wake from his sleep, screaming, drenched in sweat and soaking in his own urine.

To add to his uncle's displeasure, the water in the well became undrinkable. It lost all its sweetness. The servants, speaking in whispers, believed that although the dead woman's body had not touched the water, her spirit had. They said that in the moment of death, she had released all her sorrows with her last breath, tainting the water so that when one drank from it, one tasted her bitterness and regrets.

Lu Pin was seven when his mother died. And in his child's heart he believed that had he been aware of the depth of her unhappiness, he might have done something to change the course of her life. Her death and his inability to prevent it became a weight he carried in his heart. This sense of failure stayed with him, so that on reaching adulthood, he constantly watched for signs of unhappiness in others, and perpetually sought ways to alleviate their pain.

For another eight years he remained in his uncle's house, doing chores like one of his servants. Then one night he packed his belongings and disappeared, never to return again.

He was the first of his clan to leave the ancestral home, the all-too-familiar town where the name of his family has been inscribed in the temple books for many generations. He was a lad of fifteen when he first boarded a trading vessel that took him from the south of China to the tropical land often spoken of by his countrymen. On board the ship he worked as a deckhand. He helped the crew, cleaned up the mess everyone made, and in this way earned his passage.

The boat, after several weeks at sea, docked in a huge thriving port late one afternoon. And as everyone rushed about, dragging boxes and trying to be first off the vessel, Lu Pin found himself standing on the deck, gazing in awe at what unfolded before him. He had never seen a sun that took an eternity to set. He was last to disembark.

With his small bundle of belongings under his arm, he walked the streets. And as he walked he spoke to his absent mother. "I have left and I have arrived just as you foretold."

He was at last in the strange bustling city of his mother's wishing, the city of a thousand tales. The streets, he found, were not paved with gold but the people were friendly, even if some of them did stare at him as he wandered around in clothes that marked him as a stranger. But no one bothered him. His kind was not new to this land: men from China had traveled to these shores centuries ago in search of fortune.

On his first day, he walked around with no particular destination in mind. He trusted his feet to take him wherever he should go. He told the time by the rumbling of his stomach but kept walking until his feet could carry him no more. He paused for a moment and searched for a place to rest. He espied a crack in a thick stone wall and found himself drawn to it. He peered in and saw the leaf-covered ground and the inviting bench under a tree. He squeezed through easily, for the crack was generous, and only then did he see the scattered headstones.

He had found his way into an old convent and he lived, undiscovered, in the grounds for a week, venturing out early in the morning, passing through the crack in the wall, stepping out into the street to start a day of exploration. With each day, he widened his field of exploration, shedding his timidity the more he saw.

At dusk he would make his way back to the secluded section of the cemetery and in a shaded nook, hidden by the scarred trunk of the mango tree, he would make his bed and sleep the night away. For days, he ate one sweet juicy mango after another until a rash began to form on his arms and his chest. He remembered his mother's words then: "Too much heat, mangoes have too much heat, bad for the skin." But still, he ate them. They were free.

In those lonely nights, all he had for company was the stray cat he spotted peering at him through the leaves of the tree. She had adopted him, letting him cuddle her while he slept.

One night, sadness descended on him and he longed for the familiar taste of steamed dumplings, the sight of rice fields, even the smell of rich manure in freshly turned soil. But he knew there could be no going back. No one would be waiting for him. Besides, the thought of spending weeks at sea was enough to make his stomach turn and his head swim. No, he could not face it again. He would wait and see, he said to himself, something might turn up the following morning.

That something turned out to be an eight-year-old boy who scaled the cemetery wall late one afternoon to pick one of the mangoes dangling from a low branch. The boy balanced himself at the top of the wall, stretched his arm out to pluck a fruit visible through the thick foliage when suddenly a clawed foot scratched his hand. The boy gave out a sharp yelp, took a step back, and lost his footing. The world blacked out as his head hit the ground. The little mango thief had failed to see the young Chinaman who found him seconds later as he lay unconscious with a gash on his head.

It was then, too, that Mother Superior—still Sister Socorro then—strolled into the cemetery. Seeing the strange youth struggling to carry the unconscious boy, she ran to his aid. Together they carried the boy to the convent, where the other nuns came running with towels and warm water. They washed the gash on the boy's head and bandaged it. When he regained consciousness and was well enough to speak, the little boy told them his name: Pepito Mariano.

Mother Superior, accompanied by Lu Pin, took the boy Pepito home to his parents, Armando and Rafaela Mariano. As it turned out, the boy's father owned a stall in the city's wet market, where he and his wife sold chickens and fresh eggs. Grateful for the lad's help in rescuing their son, they befriended him and offered him a job. They were, in fact, the ones who named him Charlie. His real name they found too difficult to remember, so Charlie he became from that day on.

On realizing that Charlie had been living in the cemetery, the nuns offered him the shed on the convent grounds which the old caretaker had vacated. So this became his first home. In exchange for his lodgings, he did odd jobs in the convent, raking the leaves in the cemetery and the rest of the convent grounds, cleaning the floors, and wiping down the seats in the little chapel during his free time.

The diligent and cheery way in which he approached his work was much appreciated and one of the nuns took it upon herself to teach him the native tongue. With time, he learned to understand the speech of his new country.

Every day at dawn, he left to go to work in the market with the Marianos. In this place, the blood of generations of astute merchants and businessmen stirred inside him. He began to see opportunities for his own future. He worked for the kind couple and lived with the nuns for ten years. He saved every peso he could until one day he announced his plans to set up his own business—a variety store in a street called Calle de Leon.

So Charlie moved on. But he did not lose touch with his old friends. He visited the Marianos every Christmas, bringing baskets of fruit, expensive ham, and canned goods to their home. Despite the age difference between their son Pepito and Charlie, the two became friends; and when Pepito became a lawyer, Charlie shared in his parents' joy. He also continued to visit the convent regularly, bringing gifts to the nuns, his gratitude never-ending.

"The fifteen-year-old lad we helped became our benefactor," Mother Superior said with a smile, then she grew silent and I thought she had come to the end of her tale. After a while, I made to rise from the bench but she reached out and grasped my hand. I turned to look at her and she said to me, "Many years later, Clara, he asked for our help once more. He asked us to open our door to a friend of his . . . a woman."

"My mother. He brought my mother here?"

Mother Superior nodded slowly.

"Who was she?"

So I received another surprise that afternoon. I learned my mother's name. It was a name that shook me in ways I cannot begin to tell you, for I had no trouble placing it. Consuelo Lamuerta, the woman of the fire, of Calle de Leon.

Hands in my pockets because I couldn't stop them shaking, the same way I couldn't still the pounding of my heart, I stood up and paced about. I paced and stared at the sky the way the confused often do, hoping to find answers written in some bold heavenly script.

I learned something about myself that afternoon. That I was a master of self-deception. For many years now, I had convinced myself that if I never discovered my true history, it would make little difference to me. Nothing could have been further from the truth.

"She was a beautiful woman," I heard Mother Superior say, her words cutting through my turmoil. I stopped pacing. She continued, "Your mother was very quiet and detached, but underneath her calm exterior I sensed her fear and sadness, and most disturbing of all, I glimpsed the depth of her anger."

I said nothing to this, choosing to absorb this piece of information quietly. Then I asked about Charlie, for I had an inkling as to who he was, but Mother Superior's answer neither confirmed nor denied my suspicion.

"His role was never clear to us, except that he was a friend. Perhaps he was more than that. Charlie did not say much and we did not ask. We knew he had his reasons and she hers. So we helped without asking."

I was bursting with questions. Why did she leave me here? Why was she so angry? And at whom? At Charlie? It didn't make sense for he was the one who brought her here. How were these two people connected? Was Charlie my father? I am fair-skinned, you know. If so, why didn't he just marry her? So many questions, and my reporter's mind kept coming up with more. It was strange covering my own story, keeping my feelings at bay as my objective eye examined the situation. As to the questions I raised, I knew that the only person who could answer them was in no state to do so. But I refused to let this be a barrier. I would dig up the facts, no matter what. I realized at that moment that nothing short of the whole truth would give me peace. I had to know everything.

"I am going to her," I announced to Mother Superior.

I left the Convent of Santa Clara just before dusk, robbed of whatever peace I had come with. I swore that tomorrow I would return to Calle de Leon to see my mother, who hid her secrets in her sleep.

16

Heat Wave

From here on, writing this tale grows more difficult. I am inclined to focus on my story, to give it precedence over every other event. But much as I wish to tell you of my encounter with my mother, I must postpone doing so. For in the scheme of things it is only part of a greater tale. And to dwell on it to the exclusion of other events would give it an importance beyond the personal. It is so easy to lose one's perspective.

If there is anything being a reporter has taught me, it is that human vanity often leads to the perception that the world revolves around us. But in reality, the rest of the world often remains unmoved or unaware of the great upheavals in our life.

So I must first report to you the other events which occurred during that momentous week when I found my mother. I mention them now, for they will have much bearing on the future.

That Monday was to be the hottest day of the decade.

For once I was thankful that Torres had kept me in. The ride to work had been a test of patience and endurance. The traffic was worse than usual and the hellish temperature had left me feeling like the wilting fern that sat on Mel's cluttered desk.

When Torres handed me the pile of press releases to rehash, I almost thanked him. To think that reporters often found this part of the job boring. Polishing up the press and photo releases sent in by various government departments and private companies was enough to send anyone to sleep. But although these filler stories were low on news value, they did serve a purpose. They earned us the goodwill of the companies whose stories we printed. And that Monday morning they gave me an excuse to stay in the air-conditioned premises of the *Chronicle*.

It was a quiet morning with just myself and two other staff reporters in the office—Sandro, who worked on the foreign-news section, and Ramirez, who handled the business page. We hardly spoke. Even the phones rarely rang. But still I made little progress with my work, for thoughts of Consuelo Lamuerta and the mystery surrounding her kept distracting me. I was impatient for the day to be over.

At ten Danny walked in, still pale and his movements slow.

"God, it's hot out there," he announced in a flat enervated voice as he pulled his chair out and slumped into it.

"You should have stayed home another day. You don't look too well," I said to him.

"Got bored. Too quiet at home. Mila left for work and the boys for school, and I got sick of reading magazines," he replied. "At least here I'll know what's happening."

He checked the time. "It should be starting any minute now. Who's there, Clara?"

"What?"

"Who's at the judiciary?"

"Oh . . . Max, I think, I'm not sure."

Only then did I remember that it was the day the Jimenez Commission was due to convene.

In the old judiciary building downtown, the thermometer near the stairwell read six degrees above average at eight in the morning. By ten, when the central door to Court 2A was flung open to let the people in, the temperature had risen by another three degrees.

Court 2A was the designated venue for the investigation. And within minutes of the public being admitted, every seat was taken.

Near the back wall, those who lost in the race for seats stood squeezed against one another. While up in the gallery brawny guards were busy turning scores of people away as this, too, had quickly filled to capacity. Standing was prohibited. The building administrator had raised the possibility of the structure collapsing.

Outside, several hundred demonstrators had also gathered. Placards denouncing the military were raised here and there. But how long the demonstrators would last before surrendering to the merciless sun was uncertain.

Back in Court 2A the tension was palpable, not that this was surprising considering the opposing wills that filled the room. Everyone was there and there was no shortage of opinions: the students, their parents, the educators, the witnesses, and the military all had something to say. As for the members of the media, they were on the alert for any new controversy.

What about the head of the commission himself, the feared Judge Romero Jimenez? The judge wore a stormy face, brows bristling over blazing eyes as news footage of the riot was replayed in the courtroom. When the segment showing Laslo's impudent act appeared on the video monitor, the crowd snickered and the judge's displeasure grew. All those present knew the identify of the public pisser.

Many, in fact, harbored the wish that Laslo had been present that morning, for the potential of a showdown between him and the judge would have added a few more sparks to the already volatile situation. Many also wondered what had passed between the judge and his son and they would have been surprised to learn that the judge had still to set eyes on Laslo. Since his release from Campo Diaz the previous week, Laslo had not returned home. So the judge had not yet had the satisfaction of giving his son a piece of his mind.

Laslo had expected a hero's welcome.

On leaving Campo Diaz, Laslo headed directly for YRM's unofficial headquarters, the printing room of the Loyola University where the campus newspaper was churned out every month. Emboldened by his newly gained notoriety, he sauntered into the room expecting to hear a barrage of greetings and receive a couple of congratulatory pats on the back. But instead, he was the recipient of some hesitant smiles and many sidelong glances.

"What's the matter?" he asked one of the students bundling up piles of pamphlets announcing the protest march. Laslo watched him shrug then look toward the partitioned meeting room. Laslo followed his gaze and caught sight of Luis Bayani, who had just emerged from it. Just then Luis Bayani looked up and their eyes locked. He stopped and with a slight nod of his head indicated to Laslo he wished to speak to him. Laslo followed the student leader into the meeting room. He was in Luis's bad books. And he didn't need to guess what it was that had displeased him.

"Did your mother not toilet-train you, Laslo?" began Luis Bayani.

"You could have been shot," Luis continued in a voice that left no doubt as to the extent of his disapproval. He didn't raise his voice. The gravity of his expression and the evenness of his tone were enough. "Under similar provocation, Laslo, *you* would have shot someone."

Laslo, feeling he had to say something to defend his action, protested. "They killed eight of our people! And shot one more!"

To which Bayani briskly replied, "And you wanted to be the ninth! Was that it? The purpose, Laslo, was to make yourself heard, not to get yourself killed. Did you forget that there were others with you and that they may not have been as eager to die as you? If you must get yourself killed, for Christ's sake, do it for a better reason."

Laslo made to speak but changed his mind. There was no point arguing with Luis Bayani. Not when deep down he himself realized the foolishness of his actions and felt a growing anger for exposing himself to censure. Coming from Luis Bayani, the words of disapproval brought him acute embarrassment. Had the ground opened up there and then, he would have gladly jumped in.

He was thankful that Sophia was not around to witness his humiliation. But he was sure that she knew of Luis's displeasure, the same way the students outside did. It explained their embarrassment on seeing him earlier.

Trying to salvage what little there was left of his pride, Laslo's arrogance reasserted itself.

"If you're through," he said in a defiant tone, "I'm leaving." To hell with YRM, Laslo thought. He would explain things to Sophia later. He'd make it up to her some other way. He didn't have to stay where he wasn't wanted. He turned on his heels and headed for the door. But before he could push it open, Luis Bayani's words stopped him.

"No, Laslo, I'm not through with you yet."

Laslo swung around as Luis Bayani said, "We're marching next Friday. I need you to help with the placards. Or have you given up, Laslo?"

For what seemed like an eternity, Laslo weighted Luis Bayani's words and what they meant. Luis was displeased with him, true, but he had just made it clear that he needed him. So the judge's son reconsidered his decision to leave. Without saying a word, he looked at Luis Bayani and nodded, then let himself out of the room.

As the door shut behind Laslo, Luis Bayani let out a sigh. Laslo had succeeded in stretching his patience to the limit. It was seldom that anyone had the ability to exasperate him so. When Laslo made to leave the room, Luis understood that it was unlikely he would ever see him again. Admittedly, the prospect had appealed to him. But Luis had never given up on anyone yet. So he had called Laslo back. He hoped he would not live to regret his decision. Laslo with his unpredictable nature could easily upset the most well-laid plans.

Thinking of the plans he needed to make, Luis Bayani was reminded of the fact that there were many things now beyond his control. The June 6 massacre had taught him this, and the disastrous Loyola sit-in had served as painful reminder. And now there was the protest march to plan for, a bigger gathering with a greater potential for danger.

He walked to the window and looked out at the campus grounds. He raised his hand and ran it over the glass. The dust covered the pane on the exterior, forming a dull gray film which made seeing difficult.

Underneath his window Luis Bayani could make out a lorry parked in front of the building entrance. Several men were unloading steel pipes from its rear. The construction of the annex had begun the week before. Peering into the distance to the open field used for football practice, he watched groups of students strolling across on their way to the language center.

As he gazed at this scene, he thought about the problem with the city council. The council, under instructions from the palace, had refused to grant the marchers an assembly permit and declined to close off the camp road to traffic. This made it impossible to set up a platform and a public sound system. Without these, there would be no focal point for the marchers.

Luis had considered appealing to the council once more, but he knew this would only be a waste of time. Then he had thought of building a stage in defiance of the ruling. But this, too, came with many attendant problems. It would take at least a day to do and they couldn't just leave it in front of the camp. The structure would immediately be destroyed or taken away. There had to be another way. Quick and fail-safe.

Looking through the dirt-covered pane of his makeshift office out across the campus grounds, he pondered this problem. He noticed the shapes that stood out from the rolling green space. The cluster of trees. The jutting rocks where the ground dipped before leveling off to form a playing field. He also noticed two figures clambering up the platform that stood on the west end of the field. As he contemplated this scene, he heard the lorry engine start up. He glanced down and saw it reversing out of the driveway. He followed its progress, then his eyes returned to the field beyond. After a while, a hint of a smile formed on his lips. A solution had been staring him in the eye all along.

No clear answer presented itself to Judge Romero Jimenez, however.

In fact, the judge, who had started the investigation in a clear frame of mind, on the second day of the investigation found himself most confused. And nothing could have angered and frustrated him more.

The cause of his confusion was the soldier Rogelio Campos.

Reports submitted to the committee and the testimony of other witnesses identified Rogelio Campos as the man responsible for the death of an innocent store owner, and for causing the fire at Calle de Leon. So far, all was clear.

The case against the soldier was further strengthened when on Friday of the previous week a confidential report prepared by the military was turned over to the commission members. It stated certain disturbing facts about the soldier under investigation, facts the military itself had not been aware of until two days ago. One, Rogelio Campos came from a family of *sacadas*, whom everyone knew to be disgruntled laborers. He was, in fact, an escaped *sacada*. Two, he was the close friend of the soldier who had fired at a student during the Loyola campus riot. And three, both men originated from the south, where people were sympathetic to the insurgents' cause.

The report raised the following questions: did the two soldiers have an ax to grind against the upper class as represented by the university students? Or, of graver import, were they misguided individuals whose sympathy lay with the rebels down south, their actions part of a bigger plot designed to discredit the government?

Recalling these points, the judge believed he had before him an open-and-shut case—until the soldier Rogelio Campos was led into the courtroom.

On seeing him, the students sprang to their feet and began shouting, "Murderer!" The soldier froze mid-step and the four guards quickly closed in to shield him.

Meanwhile, the back doors were flung open and a dozen armed guards charged into the room and dragged the unruly protesters out. Just when things seemed under control, a bottle came crashing down on the aisle, splintering to pieces, missing the soldier by a few centimeters. A brief scuffle in the gallery ensued as the guilty party was escorted out.

All the while, the judge pounded with his gavel. When all was quiet once more, he turned his attention to the soldier, who had visibly paled by the time he took his seat.

The judge watched him carefully, sizing him up, taking note of everything, even the way he clasped his hands on the table in front of him. He was Laslo's age but without Laslo's cockiness. What the soldier had was a seriousness of manner, and a nervousness which was to be expected of someone in his precarious position. Then Rogelio Campos looked up and met the judge's piercing gaze, fixing on it. Few men had managed to do this, for the judge was one who saw through subterfuge. What the judge read in the soldier's eyes was an openness whose message was unmistakable: the man had nothing to hide.

This set the judge thinking. Was this man, then, not fearful of admitting to his premeditated deeds or was his look of honesty the result of his innocence? The judge told himself he would learn this soon enough.

As the soldier swore to tell the truth, the judge leaned forward, listening keenly in the hope that the man's character would be further revealed by the quality of his speech.

The questions came one after another as the members of the commission tested the soldier's story for consistency. They rephrased their questions many times, hoping to catch him out on his version of what transpired at the Loyola University. He repeated his statements over and over, always consistent with the original telling, and he answered with conviction.

Judge Romero Jimenez came to the conclusion that the soldier Rogelio Campos was either a brilliant liar and a gifted actor or he was simply what he appeared to be: a man who had been in the wrong place at the wrong time.

What became obvious to the judge was that the case had more to it than had appeared at first glance. He was determined to get at the truth.

He was also determined to thwart Friday's protest march.

As the second day's proceedings ended, the judge had the court clerk announce the schedule of testimonies for the rest of the week.

When the crowd heard that Luis Bayani was being summoned to testify on the day of the march, they sprang from their seats and began to stamp their feet. The judge banged his gavel but the rhythmic stamping drowned out all other sound in the room.

Contrary to what everyone thought, Judge Romero Jimenez was not out to prevent the march for the military's sake. He was on a rescue mission.

Like many others in the past week, the judge had heard Luis Bayani speak on television. He was surprised by the lucidity of the young man's thinking, and moved by his earnestness. He remembered his reaction, was still amazed by it. He wanted to reach into the screen and grab Bayani by the shoulders and tell him, "Slow down. There is time for all you want but you must slow down."

The judge had encountered idealists before. They had one thing in common: a willingness to sacrifice their lives for a cause. He recognized this quality in Luis Bayani and he wished to save him. But he understood that Luis Bayani was beyond saving. As the student leader called on the public to join the protest march, what the judge saw was a man journeying down the road to martyrdom.

While most of the city followed the progress of the Jimenez Commission, the jeweler Ding Sarmiento paid little attention to the twists and turns of the various testimonies aired in Court 2A of the judiciary building. Not only was it a sham—he had summarily labeled it as such—it also had nothing to do with his business, having no effect on the price of precious stones, gold, silver, and platinum or the cost of labor. So he ignored it.

On Friday of the week I am writing of, Ding Sarmiento was still in a celebrating mood, still blatantly ignoring his doctor's orders and continuing his gastronomic binge. He was in fact at the Maharlika Hotel, where he had gone to check on his new shop, after which he decided to dine at the hotel's poolside restaurant. And here he came across something that was worthy of his attention.

Ding Sarmiento pushed open the double glass doors and stepped out into the sun. He made his way down the steps to the linen-covered tables by the pool. His progress was slow. The effort of moving showed on his face, suffusing it with color. He was short of breath.

A solicitous waiter greeted him. "Dining outside for a change, Mr. Sarmiento?"

"Yes. I'd like a table with an umbrella."

The waiter led him to a table and pulled the chair out for him. Ding Sarmiento eased himself into his seat and asked for his favorite fruit drink. A health tonic was how he thought of it.

"A Four Seasons for me with lots of ice. Actually, make that two."

"Yes, sir, it is a warm day. Two Four Seasons coming up."

While he waited for his drinks to arrive, he fanned himself with the wine list. He wished he had brought his Panama hat. It was a hot and humid day and the pool bobbed with people, mostly foreigners staying at the hotel.

Then the waiter arrived with two tall glasses of a tropical concoction of watermelon, pineapple, mango, and cantaloupe juice. Ding Sarmiento sucked the liquid through a long plastic drinking straw and finished it in less than a minute. He was thirsty as a desert. As he reached for his second glass, his attention was drawn by the strange behavior of the waiters. They were nudging each other and ogling someone in the distance.

He followed their gaze. Coming toward him was a woman in a thin-strapped satin dress that clung to her body, leaving little to the imagination. She sauntered past the pool area, indifferent to the stares of the men and the cocked brows of the women. She had about her the air of a woman aware yet careless of her beauty.

As she passed his table, the jeweler eyed her appraisingly. He admired the way she carried herself but not as much as he admired the piece of jewelry she wore around her neck.

How interesting.

It was a priceless South Sea pearl, one he recognized immediately. It was one of his. It gave him great pleasure to see the piece had been given to someone whose looks matched its rare beauty. The jeweler smiled to himself, thinking that whatever else his faults may be, Senator Sixto Mijares had excellent taste in women.

* * *

The Cowrie at the Maharlika Hotel was famous for its seafood and named after the seven thousand one hundred shells strung together and hung from the ceiling to cover its walls. The interior decorator explained that he had taken his inspiration from the archipelago's many islands. But whether or not there were in fact that many shells cannot be ascertained, because in the dimly lit interior an accurate count was simply impossible. It was, in fact, almost impossible to see anything clearly and this was the reason Senator Sixto "El Toro" Mijares had chosen The Cowrie for a rendezvous with Ana.

Ana had arrived earlier and sat waiting for him in a secluded corner. In her burnished copper satin dress—yes, it would pass for a dress—that left much of her creamy skin exposed, she had caused quite a stir on entering the restaurant. It was naughty to have worn it really, a fact which was quickly confirmed by the senator, who recognized it the moment he set eyes on her.

"My God, Ana! Why in heaven's name are you wearing that?" the senator whispered to his mistress.

"You gave it to me."

"To be worn in bed!"

Ana shrugged, not bothering to reply.

The senator eyed his mistress and decided to let the matter drop. She was a free spirit who cared little for the rules of polite society. And it was this quality of hers, after all, that drew him to her.

Early on, the senator realized Ana was rare among women. The way she had first engaged his attention attested to this. Theirs was an interesting beginning. He had first seen Ana—an image of her—at an exhibition opening at the Metro Gallery which he had been coaxed into attending. None of the paintings had interested him. But a piece of alabaster sculpture, designed as a lamp base, had caught his fancy. It was in the shape of a nude woman in a classic pose.

"Did you imagine her?" he asked the artist.

"Oh no! She's real."

As if on cue, Ana had appeared next to the senator, breathtakingly sensual in a black dress. The artist introduced them. And after a few minutes chatting with her, the senator offered to take her home.

"Oh, but I came with someone," was Ana's reply.

"In that case, I will take her home," the senator countered, indicating the sculpture.

Three weeks later, the gallery manager rang the senator's office to ask where he would like the piece delivered. When this was relayed to him by his secretary, it took him a few seconds to work out what she was referring to. He had forgotten about the sculpture. He had, after all, purchased it on a whim. So it was with indifference that he instructed to have it delivered to his office.

The following day, his secretary announced that someone was waiting outside with the piece from the gallery. Without bothering to look up, the senator asked her to go ahead and have it brought in and placed at the corner table.

"Oh, but you could appreciate me better if I were on your desk," said a soft, husky voice he instantly recognized.

Looking up, the senator saw Ana standing in front of his desk wearing one of her trademark black dresses as she embraced her alabaster likeness.

And that was how it began between them.

Since then he had come to consider her as the best of his mistresses. What differentiated her from all the others was the fact the she never made any demands on him to leave his wife.

Thinking of his wife irritated him. He still remembered the look on Lorena's face when he had come home on the morning of the Loyola riot. Her slightly raised brow. Her cool gaze. If she had said something, he would not have been so disturbed. But because she remained aloof, he felt a sense of uneasiness. It was after all the first time he had broken their unspoken agreement.

To prove Lorena had no hold on him, he chose to be reckless. He had gone to the jeweler's store opening and bought his mistress the pearl pendant that now dangled between her breasts. And while he had always confined their lovemaking to Ana's town house, he now chose to defy his wife further by booking a suite at the Maharlika.

The senator reached under the table for Ana's thigh and felt the slithering smoothness of the fabric which covered her like a second skin. She crossed her thighs, capturing his hand.

He felt his blood course through his veins with greater urgency. In a voice suddenly grown husky, he said, "Let's hurry up and order. There's a suite waiting for us upstairs."

As soon as they had finished their meal, the senator handed Ana a key and she rose and made her way across the room, a vision impossible to ignore. Unknown to her and the senator, eyes followed her, and eyes searched for her escort. When a few minutes later the senator followed in his mistress's wake, everyone had the answer to their question. Among the watchers was a woman called Clarita Mendez, a society writer who had a byline in the country's leading magazine. She was also an old school friend of Lorena Zamora-Mijares.

17

The Vigil

Now I shall tell you of the night I saw my mother for the first time.

I had rung the parish church the day before, as soon as I returned from the convent to the house at Vito Cruz. I spoke to the priest I met on the day of the fire. He remembered me. I told him I wished to come and see him the following evening, on Monday, after the crowd had gone. And yes, it was regarding the woman Consuelo Lamuerta. What about? he had asked. It's personal was my reply, nothing to do with the paper. Silence followed this. Then he said yes, do come, I will see you.

I arrived at the church at seven on Monday evening, Padre Luis was waiting for me by the side door. Even from a distance, I felt his eyes studying me. I greeted him and we walked along a shadowy corridor that led to his office in the rear of the church.

Once there, he listened to what I had to say, not once interrupting me as I told him why I had returned. I decided that only the truth would serve, even if the telling of my life was something I had always been uncomfortable with. I hated being the subject of speculation. Reporting on the lives of others was far easier than reporting on myself.

When I finished my recital, all he said to me was, "Come then, I will take you there now."

"You believe me?"

His eyes on my face, he replied, "How can I not believe you, Clara?"

I look like my mother.

"Not always," Padre Luis said, "not when you are speaking or moving. But when you are still, when you're listening or watching, you have her face in repose."

I gazed into the wardrobe-door mirror. In it were reflected my face and my mother's as she lay sleeping in her bed. But the distance made it difficult for me to compare our features. So I drew nearer to her bed, contenting myself with the contemplation of her face alone. The similarities were there all right.

"When I saw you with the landlady last Monday, it was like seeing Consuelo in front of me. But only briefly. After that the resemblance disappeared and I thought I had imagined it. I can now see that the difference is in your eyes. Hers have a far-off gaze."

I stopped myself from asking him what expression mine wore. His words left me wondering whose eyes I had. I pushed this thought aside. One thing at a time, Clara.

"I will wait downstairs. Take your time. Talk to her, Clara. I believe you can bring her back."

When the door shut after him, I sat on the chair by the bed, immobilized by the weight of the moment, looking at my mother's face in the lamplight. In sleep it was of indeterminate age. Her prayers have preserved her. And I can tell you now that after going through life believing myself to be alone, it was the strangest thing to find that someone in the world wore my face. And to see it myself, the evidence of my connection. I was connected to someone, I was not alone.

I leaned closer to study her. This woman who held the answers to the mysteries of my life. Who possessed my beginning. Who was half of me. But my mother was not ready to speak yet. So I could only work on what I had. There were clues everywhere about her past. Even where she believed she had left none.

Take her bare walls.

Did you know that her walls had nothing on them? They were

unadorned. Empty. It was the first thing that struck me on entering her home. The nothingness of it. What we hang on our walls is as revealing as what we refuse to put on them. Omission speaks a language of its own.

My mother kept her home free of objects. Did this not reveal a desire to be free of all reminders? A troubled mind burdened by unpleasant memories, so that she must deny she had memories at all. My mother had wiped her mind clean. Or had desired to.

In this way she and I differed.

My room in Vita Cruz was rich in objects. Lacking an early history, I had been busy putting myself in context. Providing a multitude of reference points to ensure the moments of my life would forever be remembered. Every chair, every pencil in my pencil holder, every picture on the wall, every book on my shelf—they were all references to my life.

I was driven by an opposite need, you see, I wished for connections while my mother wished to shed hers. She shed me, did she not? I am surprised at this sudden understanding, and offended by the rejection it implies.

I sat and pondered my mother's choices, wishing to know the circumstances that had led her to this room. The road she had traveled. But I realized that whatever scenario I painted would not be based on fact but on conjecture. Only my mother knew the truth, and for that I needed her to speak to me.

The first move was mine.

I began to talk to her, gesturing at times, pacing occasionally. I was aware of the shadow shapes I made, they danced on the walls of the room, larger than life.

The first thing I said to her was this: "I am Clara. The child you gave away."

I said this close to her ear. And I imagined she heard me and that cold fear gripped her and that she willed herself to sink deeper into her sleep. But I kept her with me. In my mind I imagined my words like a giant hook embedding themselves in her, and myself as a fisherman reeling in his catch, drawing it closer and closer. I wished to draw my mother from her hiding place.

On that first night I spoke to her about choice.

"People are always making choices. Choosing consciously or choosing by default, but choosing nevertheless. Why did you choose to do this? What drove you to it? I want to know your mind at the moment of choosing.

"You see, although the possibility of finding you was never strong, I nevertheless thought of you. It wasn't so much who you were—although I will admit to having thought about that—but why you chose to do what you did that preoccupied me. What I'm saying is: the why of it matters more. Why did you choose to give me away? Did you think about me afterward? Was your situation so hopeless that giving me away was the only course open to you? Or did you hate the child so much because of what it stood for? What did I stand for?"

I left at nine. Padre Luis waited with me until a taxi came by. I told him I would return the next night. He nodded and I said good-bye.

The following evening, I spoke to my mother about her wounds.

They frightened me. There was something objectionable about them. I wished for them to cease their bleeding. They were like reproachful eyes shedding tears of blood. They repulsed me yet at the same time I was continually drawn to them. I wondered if they would ever heal and whether there would be any trace of them on her hands and feet.

I wondered, too, if I was somehow connected to them.

People hurt themselves in many ways. A grazed knee. A twisted ankle. A knife cut. There are dozens of ways to suffer. What kind of person would manifest this kind of hurt? What degree of anger did one have to harbor in one's heart for one to bleed like this?

"Mother Superior—she was still Sister Socorro when you came to the convent—she said there was so much anger in you. Have you never rid yourself of your anger? You have to let it go or you will bleed to death."

And as I spoke of her anger, I learned about my own.

While I had no reason to believe, had never expected that I would find my mother, I never dwelled on anger. What I felt was a sense of drifting. Of not being securely moored. It was easy to understand why I felt this way. But anger was an emotion I never considered. There was no one I could be angry with. But now with my mother before me, I discovered my own anger. I resented her leaving me with strangers. I resented my state of aloneness. For I had gone through life feeling a person apart, different from all the other children I went to school with, separate from others in my solitary state. While all along I could have had a mother.

On the third night, Padre Luis showed me my mother's altar room. I told him I wished to remain there for a while. He nodded and left me.

I stood in front of the statues of Our Lady and the Infant Jesus. They returned my gaze. I pondered the meaning of their presence. And when I believed I understood at last, I returned to my mother's room.

I spoke to her about guilt and escape.

"Why the two of them? Why not one without the other? Mother without Child. Is this statue of the Infant Jesus supposed to make up for my absence? Is that little statue me? Mother and Child reunited. Is this the meaning of your altar room, the reason why you light two candles day in and day out? As if all this light could fill the dark void of your life, and your prayers heal you.

"What did you pray for in that room? Forgiveness? Or did you pray to forget? Or were you punishing yourself so that you now carry your unnatural wounds? But you can't forget or escape."

I drew a breath to rest. When I continued, I said, "While there is someone in the world thinking about you, you will remain a captive of their mind, imprisoned by their thoughts. Which is why even the dead cannot die. They live on when we think of them. For as long as I am here to ask you, for as long as you do not answer me, I will give you no peace. You cannot escape your guilt unless you wake and answer me."

I leaned closer to her sleeping form, and did something I hadn't done before. I touched her face. You may say I imagined this, that in my agitated state I imagined her reaction. But I swear I felt her react to my touch. She flinched.

"Wake up! I know you can hear me," I told her, begged her,

leaning even closer so our faces touched. "You have to deal with this. Now. You cannot run away any longer. Wake up and speak to me, then you can be free. It is better than lying there, bleeding with remorse, paying the price of your cowardice."

I felt drained of everything after this and spoke no more.

Sometime later a shaft of light cut suddenly through the darkness. I swung around and rose from my seat. The light that poured through the door hurt my eyes. I squinted in its rude glare, trying to focus.

I saw the silhouette of two men. The one behind was the padre, I could tell from what he wore. The other one, the one who had pushed open the door, was taller.

They entered the room and I heard Padre Luis say, "I'm sorry, Clara, this was unexpected." I said nothing, for my attention was on the other man. An imposing man who strode into the room as though he owned it. I stepped forward to meet him, to see who this intruder was.

He stepped into the halo of light.

I found myself looking up into a pair of hostile gray eyes. His expression left me in no doubt of what he thought: what was I doing here? I returned his gaze, challenging him, and watched him as he tilted his head to see me better. I refused to let his piercing gaze intimidate me. I told myself I had a right to be here. This woman was my mother. Who was he to her?

Then I saw it. And he must have seen it on me at the same time. For he drew back the same moment I did, as though struck by some invisible force. On the right temple of this stranger, whose face I had seen before and whom I now tried to place, grew a white streak of hair. Like mine.

I, Clara Perez, who had come to Calle de Leon in search of my mother, had also found my father.

18

❦

The Don's Story

I disliked him.

An instinctive, spontaneous reaction to his undisguised disapproval of me. When I finally realized who he was, I understood why. Don Miguel Pellicer. The man whose photograph I had gazed at only a few days ago, studying it so carelessly.

No other discovery I would make in the future would ever come close to this in significance; nor would there ever be anything else with the same power to change my life: I was the don's bastard daughter. My existence kept from him by this woman who hid in the safety of sleep.

Whatever their story was, it was clear that Consuelo had, by a twist of fate, served up an unpleasant surprise for him. Me.

As he scanned my face, he wore the look of someone who had suffered an injustice. That his seed had taken root and sprouted someone like me went against his finer sensibilities. That I even looked like the woman who lay unconscious—though I believed even then that Consuelo was not oblivious to what was unfolding in her room—was a further source of anger to the don. He may have tolerated all this if fate had not rendered one final blow.

"You wear the mark," the don said in an icy voice that I would forever associate with him.

I raised my hand to my right temple, knowing he referred to the white streak of hair that grew there, feeling I was being accused of wearing what I had no right to. I thought his resentment lay in the fact that it betrayed our connection. Only later did I understand what the mark meant.

Meanwhile, the don walked to the window and opened it. A warm breeze entered the room. The heat that marked the day had not faded with darkness. The don remained standing with his back to me, his hands clasped behind him as he stared at the empty street below.

He began to speak and this is what he told me. This is the don's story.

"She was not of my world," was how he began.

To understand my world, I must tell you of the day my father took me to the top of a hill and showed me my inheritance.

We went on horseback, leaving as soon as the sun was out. It was one of those rare moments when it was just my father and me. He was a distant man who inspired awe in those around him. I was always in awe of my father.

I was five years old. And it was close to harvesttime. The land was covered with rows and rows of sugarcane standing upright in the sun. Like thousands of warriors gathered to greet me. It was a sight I have never forgotten. I said little during the ride, preferring to let my eyes roam, taking in the land and its many shapes. There was the land east of the river where the cane was planted. Then there was the land that took you into hilly country.

"Do you know where we are, Miguel?"

"No, sir."

"Do you know who owns this land we are traveling on?" We were on rising ground now.

"No, sir."

"This is our land."

"Sir?"

This was news to me. I had always thought our land ended where no sugarcane grew. I had never been that high up before, on top of that hill. I had only ever looked at that place from the flat land. But now my father, who held the reins to what even then he referred to as an empire, had revealed to me the extent of my patrimony.

The horse came to a stop and my father dismounted. I sat astride the animal, my child's legs aching from the strain of sitting on its wide body, and waited for my father to lift me. He reached up and raised me in the air, then set me on the ground. The horse snorted. As if remarking on the size of his master's heir. I must have seemed insignificant to the majestic creature who was used to carrying the imposing figure of my father.

"All this, Miguel," he said, his hand sweeping the scene before him, "all this will be yours one day. You will inherit everything before your eyes."

My father then told me the story of how, in the early 1800s, the Spanish governor of the islands had taken it upon himself to reward a loyal supporter. He had asked the man what he desired. The man could have asked for gold, but he asked for land. To him, land was the basis of real wealth: it never diminished in value and always grew in demand. That astute man was my great-great-grandfather, Diego Pellicer.

"It was on this very spot that the Governor General came with Diego Pellicer. Here, he spoke the following words: 'I grant you all the land before you for as far as the eye can see.'

"Diego Pellicer began the first sugar plantation in the archipelago. And that year he took a wife, Esperanza Prieto, after whom he named his vast land holdings. Today, Hacienda Esperanza is the jewel of the south. It is the heart of sugar country. It has sustained generations of Pellicers."

When my father told me that all that lay before me would be mine one day, I felt my heart swell with pride. That was also the moment when I learned what it meant to be a Pellicer. It meant being above the ordinary. But the child I was failed to understand the price of being different. That the happiness ordinary men can aspire to was not for me. I believe now that I paid for my specialness with the currency of ordinary happiness.

"How you manage your inheritance will determine whether your son will one day stand here with you and look at all this. They say,

Miguel, fortunes are made and lost over three generations. I am the fourth. You, the fifth. I have no intention of losing this. I will pass it on to you not only intact, but greater than when I inherited it. And you must do the same."

I will go down in our family history as the Pellicer who built the biggest sugar refinery in the world. The world! And I am also the Pellicer who possessed the foresight to find another source of wealth other than sugar. I bought tracts of swampland nobody wanted outside the old city. "Miguel, you are sinking good money into worthless land!" That was what everyone told me. I have proven them wrong. Just look at what has risen on the land I developed—a thriving new business district!

My father died in my tenth year.

How often it is that what we love kills us. Hasan, his black Arabian stallion, threw him. He was brought back to the house and laid out on the sofa in his study. I can still see him. The dirt on his riding breeches. The tear on his sleeve. The blood on his collar. He who was always immaculately dressed. He had broken his neck and died instantly. In the moment his breath was cut short and his heart stopped beating, the Pellicer fortune became my great burden.

There was no time to grieve. My mother confined her grieving to an evening of silent weeping. After that I never saw her shed another tear again.

"We must look to the future," she announced. "The dead are dead." She consigned my father to the irredeemable past.

My widowed mother rose to the challenge of running our vast holdings. She found within herself an astuteness that had lain hidden. A potential never realized, for there had been no need to hone and shape it while my father lived. Whatever tenderness she possessed, she quickly shed. She became frighteningly strong in her determination to preserve the Pellicer empire. As for me, my education began in earnest. I applied myself. The years passed. And through it all, I never questioned where my duty lay or my destiny.

Until the summer I met her.

* * *

At that time I was still based down south. Flying to the city only every other week to oversee our operations there, staying two or three days at a time.

It was on one of these visits that I first saw her. I went straight from the airport to our office downtown. It was mid-morning. I took the lift up to the third floor and as it shuddered to a stop, I stepped out just as a young woman holding a basket stepped in. We collided and the contents of her basket spilled out.

She apologized; I said nothing, irritated by the delay. But good manners dictated that I help her, so I bent down to help her pick up the things that had fallen by the lift door. She, too, was busy gathering food and sweets from the floor, her head tilted to one side.

Do you know those paintings by the old European masters? Renaissance images of the Madonna and Child? There was something of the Madonna in her, the same serenity, perhaps it was the shape of her face. She was beautiful.

I deposited a handful of cellophane-wrapped sweets into her basket, my eyes on her face, my initial irritation gone. As if sensing my gaze, she raised her eyes and, on meeting mine, smiled and said thank you. The serene Madonna was gone, in its place a lively face with a pair of smiling eyes. We both straightened up and just then the lift door opened again and she quickly got in, waved at me before it shut, saying sorry and thank you once more. I walked off, not giving her another thought. I knew many beautiful women.

The business in the city took a few days to finish. At the end of it, I flew back to the plantation. But as I said, I visited the city regularly. Sometimes I stayed the weekend, catching up with my close friend Manolo Pelaez. We would dine out on Friday evening and make the rounds of the nightclubs. Saturday we played polo. Together we often featured in the society pages. Wealth is a constant source of fascination to most people. We were also never short of female company: rich women who wanted rich husbands, and not-so-rich women who wanted to be rich.

I was twenty-six the year I met her. A man who found life in the south too limiting. My mother and I did not live on the plantation itself. The running of it was left to the *contratista*. I concerned myself with the financial side of things. So home was a sprawling house in town close to where we had an office. Only later, when I learned to seek solitude, did I build the house on the hill, the same hill my father took me to long ago.

"I have been doing this for sixteen years now, Miguel, and I am tired. Do you know that at your age, your father already had a son?" My mother made no secret of her impatience for me to marry.

"What about this Ysmael girl?" she suddenly asked.

"How—"

"I have my sources. I know her father. He comes from a good family, although his wife, well, she is of poor stock. But nevertheless the Ysmaels are not to be laughed at."

"We're just friends."

Perhaps it was my mother's hope that something would come of my friendship with Zenaida Ysmael that made her encourage me to base myself in the city. A week into the new year, I moved into the house which my father had bought some years before his death. It was a spacious old house but simply furnished. For all his wealth, my father never indulged in luxury. Once I moved in, things changed.

Zenaida saw to this. Before I knew it, she was arranging for an interior designer to meet me. And between the two of them, my house was slowly transformed before my eyes. At great cost.

"It's called the nesting instinct, Miguel. A woman who redesigns your house has designs on you." My friend Manolo had a dramatic bent, but I appreciated what he was saying. I took care not to give Zenaida the wrong idea. I enjoyed her company but knew she was not for me.

One Friday morning, I had gone to the bank and had just returned to the building when I saw her walking in front of me toward the lift. Recalling Manolo's words, I turned around and walked out of the building to avoid her company.

I got into my car and drove off, just following the flow of traffic. After a while, I took note of my surroundings. I was in the university belt. I pulled over and turned the motor off and sat watching the people go by. It was then that I saw her again, my woman with the basket, only this time she carried a bundle of books. Her hair was combed back from her face and gathered in a thick braid down her back. Even in that huge crowd of bustling people, she stood out.

There is something my father used to say to me. That when the time is right for a thing to happen, everything falls into place to hasten it happening.

I had only ever seen her once before. But from this day onward, everything conspired to throw her in my path.

The following Monday, we nearly collided once more as I stepped out of the lift. On recognizing me, she burst out laughing. I shook my head and smiled. It was a brief encounter. I figured that she studied at university and sold sweets and snacks to support herself. That she followed some sort of schedule. My interest in her at this point was due more to idle curiosity than to any specific desire to see her again.

True enough, she turned up the following Monday. As several of the staff headed for the reception area, I followed them. The morning had passed in a monotonous manner, I was in need of diversion. On seeing me, the lively chatter that filled the room faded. I pretended not to notice. I saw her then and she returned my gaze, a hint of laughter in her eyes, waiting to see if I would bark or bite.

"What do you recommend?" I asked the receptionist casually. Around me, the talk and banter gradually resumed.

"The *empanadas* are delicious, sir," the receptionist replied. Then, turning to the woman, said, "Consuelo, give Mr. Pellicer an *empanada*. Consuelo makes them herself."

Her name suited her.

Waiting for Consuelo's arrival on Mondays became something I looked forward to. So that when I was away one Monday, attending to some business down south, I thought of her. She was without artifice and symbolized for me a simple, uncomplicated life. And mine was far too enmeshed at the moment.

News of Zenaida redecorating my house had reached my mother and she read too much into it. As for Zenaida herself, I could not shake her off. It didn't seem to matter how many times I forgot to return her call or found an excuse not to go to dinner with her, she was determined to forgive me anything. She continued to drop by the office whenever she felt like it. As for my house, she had free access to it as well. I never managed to get the spare key back from her. Manolo, observing her in action, could only shake his head in admiration. He disliked her but could not help admiring her determination.

Consuelo was a welcome change. Consuelo for consolation, she was true to her name.

Soon after my return to the city, I bumped into her in the foyer of the office building. We stood there and talked. I learned that two mornings a week she visited several offices in the city selling snack foods which she prepared the night before. The rest of the time she studied at university. After this, our Monday meetings took on a more relaxed tone. We exchanged a few words whenever I bought something from her.

During these casual meetings, I further learned she was working for a teacher's diploma. She was born and raised in the city, and since her parents' death had been living with her godmother. I liked listening to her. There was a pleasant lilt to her voice and her eyes lit up whenever she spoke. A serene Madonna whose face took on a different kind of beauty when she became animated. I laughed a lot in her company. And I told her so.

"Mondays, then, you must be prepared to laugh!" she said, her eyes twinkling mischievously.

One morning, as I stood in the reception area chatting to Consuelo, Zenaida walked in. Oblivious to the conversation before her arrival, she came between us. "You must come with me this minute, Miguel, and look at this wonderful painting Paula found for the *sala*."

Before I knew it, Zenaida was leading me out to the lift. I turned back to look at Consuelo, wanting to explain to her that there was nothing between me and this woman. As for the painting, it was perfect for the lounge room but I refused to buy it, to Zenaida's great disappointment.

The next day I was unexpectedly called down south for an urgent meeting with the *contratista*. It was a relief to be out of Zenaida's reach. But it was also at this time that I began to miss Consuelo. I didn't know when things had begun to change for me, but Consuelo had taken on an importance in my life. That week away brought this to my attention. It was an unsettling fact. There was no future in it, I told myself. She was not of my world. My mother would never countenance an association with someone of her class. It would have been much wiser to have ceased all contact with Consuelo. But my sudden discovery of my feelings for her created a sense of excitement.

Being young and rash, I made up my mind to get to know her better. What harm could there be in that? I reasoned. So I returned to the city at the end of that week and found myself impatient for Monday.

She did not come that Monday or the one after. I went in search of her. I drove to the university and waited patiently outside the gates. At about one o'clock, she walked through the entrance, books clutched in her arms. I got out of the car and hurried toward her.

"Consuelo," I said as I fell in step with her.

She turned to me in surprise. I gave her no chance to protest. Just ushered her into my car. "I just want to talk to you," I said to reassure her.

She looked doubtfully at me as I drove us to the boulevard. And there we walked along the beach and I began to talk. I told her I liked her a lot. That I wanted us to be friends. Nothing more. Surely, we could be friends.

"We're too different," she told me. Three words that summed up everything. Even she saw it. But I refused to give up.

"Don't you like me?"

The troubled look on her face was answer enough.

I began to wait for her by the university gate whenever I could get away from the office. We would go to one of the crowded cafés along the university belt. Small, dingy places safe from prying eyes. The time we spent together always passed too quickly. And we always felt we were breaking some rule by seeing each other. I couldn't take her to places that I liked. I couldn't introduce her to my friends. And on her part she didn't wish to be gossiped about by her peers or questioned by her godmother. Our disparate backgrounds made many things impossible.

She lived in a dismal neighborhood whose pockmarked streets, profusion of rubbish, and dilapidated buildings became familiar to me. She didn't belong here. My Madonna. She was bright and beautiful, while all around her was nothing but drabness and squalor. I wanted to take her away from this. But I didn't know how.

One Saturday, after refusing to meet Zenaida for lunch, I left the house and picked up Consuelo at a bookshop downtown where we had agreed to meet. I drove us to the town of San Ibañez. She fell in love with it. And I finally acknowledged to myself that I loved her. How strange that it came upon me in this way. Love when I least expected it. And to the least likely person. Outside my world and my reach. And that was the cruel irony of my situation: I could have anyone I wanted in my world, but I couldn't have her. Because I had too much and she too little.

That day in San Ibañez, after exploring the town, I drove us to a promontory where we looked down at a lake. Here, we told each other stories. She had a lightness of spirit about her. Serene when in repose, but full of life in conversation. The place itself was an idyllic spot. And I rolled out a picnic rug and lay down, my head on her lap.

"You are growing old fast, Miguel," she said to me, her fingers on the white streak on my right temple.

I smiled, keeping my eyes closed. "It is not age," I said, "just something some of us have in our family." Then I told her the story about the mark.

"They call it the mark of the Pellicers. As the story goes, it first appeared on Diego Pellicer, my great-great-grandfather, who founded Hacienda Esperanza. Since his time, a Pellicer in every generation has worn the mark. It usually appears between our late teens and mid-twenties."

"What does it mean?"

"The person who wears it, they say, will achieve great things."

"Only men get it?"

"Yes, at least as far as I know."

Twirling her finger around my hair, she said, "And what will *you* achieve, Miguel Pellicer?"

I opened my eyes and smiled up at her. "A sugar central. The largest mill ever." So I told her about my dream, explaining in detail my grand plan. She was a good listener, my Consuelo. But there was one dream I dared not tell. That I wished to spend my life with her.

"Where have you been?"

I found a furious Zenaida waiting for me at home after I dropped Consuelo off just after dusk that Saturday. She accused me of being unfaithful. And I stupidly replied, "You do not own me. I am free to see anyone I wish."

"You *are* seeing someone! Who?" she demanded.

I told her it was none of her business who I saw. She stormed off.

The following morning brought a phone call from Manolo. "I know it is an unholy hour, but then your girlfriend woke me at an even earlier hour."

"Zenaida?"

"Who else? Unless you really have another woman. Are you alone, my friend?"

I assured him I was. Then, imitating Zenaida's tone, he replayed their conversation. In spite of my irritation and a growing anxiety I could not explain, I laughed. Zenaida accused him of leading me astray. Demanded that he tell her who I was seeing and where I met this woman, for I was avoiding her. She told Manolo she would not allow me to dump her.

"But I never proposed to her."

"That's irrelevant. You've gone out with her too long. As far as she's concerned, she is Mrs. Pellicer."

"I'm not marrying her."

Manolo spent the next few minutes giving me his opinion of women. Then suddenly he asked, "So is there someone else?"

I hesitated in replying. And that was all he needed.

"Aaaah . . . so the jealous Zenaida wasn't so insane after all. This must be serious, Miguel, you have never hidden anything from me."

An hour later, I sat drinking Scotch at Manolo's, finally unburdening myself of my secret.

"You have been a sly one, Miguel, keeping this from your best friend. What were you afraid of? That I would talk you out of it? And you would have been right. It is foolish to play with nice girls. They don't understand the rules."

"I love her."

He paused on hearing this, needing to recover from my embarrassing confession. When finally he spoke again, it was with an earnestness I had never encountered in Manolo before.

"Listen to me, Miguel, you will love many more times. But this one you must end now, and as brutally as you can. Make her hate you. Yes, she will suffer, especially if she is the kind of girl you say she is. But it will force her to get on with her life, and one day she'll get over it."

Then, as if reading my mind, he added, "And no, you cannot make it work. She may be able to survive Zenaida. But survive your dear mother she will not."

I was not surprised at Manolo's advice. But I could not bring myself to end things with Consuelo. To make matters worse, I made her mine.

It was an act of desperation.

Knowing that I was going to lose her, I clung on and took what I could. I didn't think of the consequences. The future. I simply wanted her. And she me. In those hours of desperate love, I saw her eyes shine with unshed tears. My violent possession of her betrayed the turmoil of my mind. But she clung to me as hard as I clung to her. No words were spoken.

Consuelo sensed something was not right in our world. That we had reached some turning point. The time for gentleness and laughter was gone. How could she not know? I who always laughed and smiled and bantered in her company was rendered speechless in my misery.

So this meeting of bodies became our new way of communicating. And we would meet and make love. So young and intense. So confused and frightened. We never touched on the why. As if by keeping silent, we would dispel or at least postpone the coming crisis. The time to talk would come soon enough.

As always, Zenaida was the catalyst.

She still had the key to my house. I found her waiting for me one night, looking cool and in command. Zenaida announced she knew all about my ambitious little provincial girl. "She is not for you, Miguel. What can you have been thinking of, dirtying yourself with that low-class woman who is just after your money! A food vendor at that!"

I sent her out of my house but not before I made her return the key. Later I learned from Manolo, to whom she could not help telling her tale, that she had been following me after work. She knew everywhere I had been and what I had been up to. But that was not the end of Zenaida. She had one more card to play.

A few days later, my mother sent for me.

Unlike Zenaida, who wasted her words attacking Consuelo, my mother used her words wisely. She spoke about duty. My duty. Had I forgotten who I was? What name I carried? Had I forgotten all this? I was a Pellicer with a Pellicer's responsibility and the Pellicer name to uphold.

"Being your father's son, you know where your duty lies." My mother knew how to talk to a Pellicer.

So the time for talking finally arrived.

I returned to the city. And the following day saw Consuelo. I drove us to the boulevard. We walked by the seawall, for once uncaring who would see us. Then, as we sat by the ledge, I told her.

I told her I could not see her anymore. I told her that it was wrong of me to have pursued her. To have allowed matters to get that far. That this thing between us had no future. That our worlds could never touch. Should never have. It was the way things have always been and will always be. That to try to change things would only cause both of us to suffer. And we would hurt many others as a result. Then I told her I was sorry to have hurt her.

My responsibilities as a Pellicer I explained to her. My inheritance, my position, and the burden I carried. The things that were expected of me. The behavior that was demanded of me. My life was not mine to live. My family and my heritage owned me. The dictates of living as a Pellicer were harsh and difficult. Could she find it in her heart to understand my situation? This I asked her.

She did not meet my eyes as I spoke, but kept looking in the distance, her head turned away from me. I would have preferred angry words to her silence, but she refused to speak. Then, slowly, she rose and began to walk away. I made to follow her but stopped myself. I thought she wanted to be alone for a while, to think. That she would return. But she kept walking. I waited but she never came back.

It was the last time I ever saw her.

I buried myself in my work.

I worked as though driven by the devil himself. I worked long hours. Starting early, working through the night. I brought forward my plans to establish a sugar central. I looked for as many things as possible to divert me from thoughts of Consuelo.

Zenaida proved useful in her renewed pursuit of me. I found myself other diversions because of her. I began squiring other women around. I knew that every photograph of me with another woman in the social pages earned her fury. With time, she got the message. And so did my mother, who stopped asking me about her.

But whatever satisfaction I got from thwarting Zenaida's plans never made up for losing Consuelo. The image of her walking away from me on the boulevard and her continued silence robbed me of peace. I read in her actions a harsh judgment. My family may have judged her as not being good enough, but it was I who felt unworthy of her. She had turned her back on me, denying me even her words of anger. She judged me as worthless because I had been a moral coward.

Time, I told myself, would numb the pain, for all things must pass. I was thankful when business required me to travel to the States. I needed to get away, to have a change of scenery. I was gone for three weeks. If I thought a change of place would blot her from my mind, I was wrong. I thought of her constantly.

As it turned out, on my return home to the south, my mother had news of Consuelo for me: she had written to me while I was away. On hearing this, my heart dared to hope, until I learned what had transpired during my absence. For a side to Consuelo I had never seen before had come to light. What I learned opened my eyes to my own blindness.

"I paid her off," my mother announced.

My mother showed me Consuelo's letter. It had been marked urgent and forwarded to the south. My mother opened it. Consuelo had written to say she wanted to see me and said I must meet her at the usual place. My mother flew to the city herself. A resourceful woman, she made discreet inquiries and got hold of Consuelo's details. She waited for her by the university gate.

"She is beautiful. I can see why you fell for her," my mother said. "But underneath that beauty is ambition. She told me the extent of your relationship. That you had been intimate with her. I understood that she was angry enough to cause a scandal. I told her I would not allow her to cast a shadow on the Pellicer name.

"I told her that if what she wanted was money, that was not a problem. I told her to name a price. She named her price. I wrote her a check and handed it to her. I saw the look on her face when she read what I had written. It was for more than she asked. But I told her there would be no more coming. That she was not to bother you again. I told her if she used the money wisely, she could start a new life."

"She is not that sort of woman!" I said in anger.

My mother laughed. "Not that sort of woman, Miguel? You have turned this woman into a saint, which she is not! Yes, she may have loved you, I am not saying she did not. But just because she couldn't have you doesn't mean she had to walk away with nothing. Even I can understand the logic behind her actions. Besides, your ending this affair of yours was enough to make her hate you!"

She thrust a rectangular sheet of paper into my hand. "Now tell me if you still think she is not that sort of woman!" It was the check which my mother had made out to Consuelo. It had been cashed.

You may think me a hypocrite, my anger unjustified, for I, too, had wronged her. But I have never been able to move beyond that point of betrayal. It has soured my life.

In anger I told my mother: "Find me a woman you approve of, and I will marry her!"

My mother wasted no time. Two months later, she presented me with Marina. The society columnists had a field day when our engagement was announced. For Marina was heiress to a vast Castilian fortune. And her family was titled, which suited my mother best of all.

I was married soon after. A marriage of convenience. It didn't matter to Marina. Love or the lack of it was not something she cared about. Name and wealth were her paramount concerns. This suited me. For I had resolved to devote my life to building my family's business empire. As for Iñigo, he is like us. The true son of heartless parents. Yet he is not the son of my choosing. How could he be?

The don turned around to face me.

"And seeing you now, I know at last the depth of her anger. You are Consuelo's revenge. She hid your existence from me, knowing the difference it would have made to my decision."

I rose from my seat, marveling at his blindness. How was it possible that with me standing before him, he still failed to see—to suspect—his mother's role? Perhaps he persisted in his warped view of Consuelo because it allowed him to judge himself less harshly. And no, I was not going to explain the situation as I saw it. He would have to figure that out himself.

Instead I said, "Why should it have made a difference, your knowing of my existence? Just because she carried me can't change the fact that your mother had to pay her off!"

"Because you are my blood!" he snapped. "I may be many things but I am not so lacking in honor as to shirk my responsibility even to a woman who deceived me!"

Then, slowly, so that each word hung in the air, he said, "And you wear the mark."

"She could not have known that," was my retort.

"But as fate would have it, it is on you." This he said accusingly, for I had stolen what he believed was his son's birthright.

Here is the don's dilemma: he suspects that his heir is but a shadow of the great Pellicers. And now, seeing the presence of the mark on me, he has final confirmation of his fears. The mark will never appear on his son to strengthen his nature. The Pellicer fortune is at risk after generations of obscene abundance.

Thinking of the unsavory alliance Iñigo Pellicer was about to make, I saw the don had cause for concern. A thought that gave me an immeasurable sense of satisfaction.

"I bet no bastard has ever worn this mark, not until I came along." If it is possible for stone to harden further, I saw it on his face. Moving closer to him, I said, "And the irony of it is, I do not care for it, because it is from you."

"There is no changing that. It seems we must suffer each other's existence."

I was about to retort that I had no intention of being within spitting distance of him. But I didn't. From somewhere in the room I heard a soft moan. He heard it, too. And together we turned. Our eyes, unbelieving, gazed into the eyes of Consuelo Lamuerta.

19

Consuelo Remembers

Two nights later, although still weak and pale from her long withdrawal from the world, Consuelo spoke.

The don, I must tell you, was with me. If you wish to verify what I am about to tell you, ask him. That is, if you can reach him. For he now lives on his island, having chosen to turn his back on the world.

But here is what I remember of Consuelo's words.

I didn't want the child.

I was all alone. There was no one to turn to. So I wrote to you. You, the cause of all my pain. I wished to forget you. And were it not for the child, I could have. But when I discovered I carried it, I knew I would never be allowed to forget.

I demanded that you see me. Urgently. I did not say why, just said you had to come. But you sent your mother; at least, that was what she told me at the time. I realize now that your mother deceived me, that she lied. But back then I told myself I never really knew you. You were a coward who did not have the courage to face me. But in case you think I have changed my mind now because I know your mother's role, I have not. The other thing you did to me, turning your back on me on the advice of others, I have never forgiven you for. For all your appearance of strength, you were no more than the weak-willed son of a vicious woman.

The moment I saw her, I knew who she was. Pride must be something one inherits. She did not speak at first but instead looked me over with a frightening intensity. A frown appeared momentarily on her face only to be quickly replaced by her haughty expression.

"I am Doña Carmela Pellicer," she announced. "I am Miguel's mother."

She said you had read my letter and had no wish to see me. She said I had to stop bothering you, for you regretted your actions and now sought to put the past behind you. Hadn't I read about you and the women you were taking out in the papers? She advised me to do the same, to get on with my life. Both of us had been rash, she said, but that was because we were young and failed to think of consequences.

As for me, she said I was wrong for you, I could never fit in. The Pellicers, she informed me, had a reputation to uphold. And I with my background could never be accepted in your world. I would only cause you embarrassment.

I had heard this all before from you. Hearing it from her, I learned at last your true nature: you were your mother's creation through and through. You had no thoughts of your own. How you disappointed me. No one had ever disillusioned me the way you did.

Then she handed me an envelope but I pushed it away. I knew what it contained.

"Do not be foolish! You can right matters with this."

I shook my head and walked away from her. But she reached out and grabbed my arm, her nails digging into my flesh. I turned to free myself, aware that people were staring at us. She did not care. She brought her face close to mine. "Get rid of it!" she said.

She knew. Your mother knew.

"Get rid of it!" she said once more, hissing at me like a snake. "I have seen many women in your condition before. I know the signs. You cannot fool me. How long . . . how many weeks?" she pressed me to tell her.

I shook my head in denial but she gripped my arm harder. I winced.

"Don't lie to me! How long?"

I told her. I felt weak yet strangely relieved that I had told someone.

She cursed under her breath and remained silent for a brief moment. Then she spoke again. "You must take this." She motioned with the envelope. "Get rid of what you are carrying. And buy yourself a new life. Don't think you can make him return because of this. I will not allow it."

She took my hand and pushed the envelope into my palm. "You are not so lacking in sense as to keep this thing you are carrying. The Pellicers will never recognize it. And it will only be a burden to you." She left me standing in the street with the envelope in my hand, her venomous words ringing in my ears.

I did not want your mother's money. Dirty Pellicer money. I felt cheapened by it. The same way I felt soiled by your child. I hated it the same way I hated you. For I grew to hate you with the same passion I once loved you. And yet I could not bring myself to do as your mother said. It went against everything I was taught. Your seed, another proud inhuman Pellicer, continued to grow inside me.

Then one day I read about your engagement. You had forgotten me so quickly, so easily. You with your inconstant heart. Like your mother's it is black.

I needed a new identity.

I cashed the check. Your mother, I am sure, feared I never would. Only after I cashed it, I imagine, did she sleep peacefully. It was the sign she was waiting for. It said I had done as she wished. There was no unwanted Pellicer in the world.

Without intending to, I had misled her. Is she still alive, your mother? Then you must tell her that the child lives. That you have seen her. That she looks like me but wears that precious mark you are so proud of.

As I said, I cashed the check. I walked away from my old life. The university, my plans, my friends, my godmother's house.

I moved here, to Calle de Leon. To this apartment. I arrived wearing black and have worn only black since that day. I was a widow who mourned the death of her husband of less than a year. In many ways, this was true. For the love I felt for you did not survive your abandonment of me. I grew to despise you. You who judged me not good enough for you, as if class and wealth were all that made up one's worth.

My parents, I said, were dead also; that at least was true. As for my dead husband, I made it clear that speaking of him caused me pain, so I never spoke of him. I made it clear, too, that he was survived by an older married brother who lived in a remote part of the south. Even then I was keeping a door open, planning for the future, for I knew that I would have to leave before I began to show.

My status as widow in mourning suited me. It not only explained my wan appearance, but gave me a reason to keep to myself.

As soon as I could, I started to bake and cook again. Not that I needed to. The check your mother gave me was for a substantial amount. If I was careful, it would see me through for a long while. But I didn't want the neighbors to wonder how I supported myself. So I resumed my business. Making sure the women saw me go to market every couple of days, buying ingredients to make the foods I prepared. And I made sure they saw me depart three mornings a week, to go out selling.

And that was how I met Charlie.

I took a tray of cassava cakes to his store one day.

"Could I leave this here to sell?" I asked him.

"Yes, yes, of course, I sell for you," he said.

I explained to him that I would give him so much for every piece he sold but he kept shaking his head, saying, "No need to do that. You leave them here, I sell for you."

Charlie, I realized, had heard about my sad story. I saw the compassion in his eyes. And the honesty. I felt ashamed to be deceiving him. I insisted that this be a business arrangement. Seeing that I meant it, that it mattered to my pride, he agreed.

He must have pushed the neighbors to buy my cakes, for by the end of that day, I heard a knock on my door. I found Charlie standing by the doorway, holding in one hand the empty tray, which he had washed clean, and in the other, the money from the sale. There was a big grin on his face. He looked so pleased that my cakes had all sold.

"You make some more," he said to me, "I sell for you again, okay?"

I smiled and nodded. Soon, I was bringing him other foodstuff. Sweets, too. And he would tell me which things sold better. As the weeks passed, we began to do more business.

I trusted him. Not just in business, but as a person. He was the only person in the neighborhood I allowed myself to grow close to. There was something so comforting about Charlie. In his presence, I felt calmer, less frightened and angry. Charlie was a good listener. Which was why people were drawn to him. There was always someone in front of his store. Someone with a story. A piece of gossip. A problem. A secret.

It was to Charlie that I told mine.

When the child moved, I knew my time was running out.

I was lying in bed when I felt the pressure of its exertion. Was it a raised fist? A foot? An elbow? It wasn't enough that it fed off me. It was making its presence felt. I held my breath until the movement stopped. And then I wept.

You see, there is nothing like the routine that filled a day to deceive one that life was normal. So during those first few weeks at Calle de Leon, the routine of cleaning and making a home for myself, the marketing, cooking, and selling of food, all this made the act of denial easy.

I didn't want to deal with my situation. Even when I noticed that the loose black frocks I wore felt tighter and I could see the signs of my body filling out, I still delayed making plans. Fear made me impractical. I knew I needed to think about moving again but couldn't face it. After all, where could I go?

The night the child moved, I was forced to face my problem. I did not sleep that night. I spent the time weeping in despair then calming myself so I could think about the future, but it was not long before I began crying again. The following morning, my eyes puffy from crying and lack of sleep, I stayed at home. I paced about my small bedroom. I climbed back into bed. I got up. Paced about again. I alternated between crying and cursing and calling you names and saying I didn't want this thing, this child that grew inside me.

Then I heard the knocking on the door. I hastily wiped my face of tears and went to open it. There stood Charlie holding two empty trays under one arm and a small envelope containing the proceeds from the previous day's sale. He had his usual grin on his face. But on seeing my face, it quickly disappeared.

"What is wrong, Consuelo?"

Hearing the kindness in his voice, I burst into tears.

Charlie lost some of his calm. "Don't cry. Don't cry. You tell Charlie the problem, I solve for you."

I shook my head and kept crying.

"Tell Charlie. I solve problem. I help you."

Finally, between sobs, I blurted out my problem. "I am pregnant."

Charlie drew a deep breath, then sighed. I knew what he was thinking. That I was carrying my dead husband's child, but I couldn't stomach continuing this deception. So I told him my true story. The only thing I kept from him was your identity. It wasn't because I wished to protect you, it was because I couldn't bear to speak your name.

He listened in silence as I poured out my sordid tale. At the end of my recital, I said to him, "I am sorry, Charlie, I deceived you."

I believed I had lost a friend. Although he was a kind man, I didn't know whether his kindness could stretch far enough to accept someone like me. So it surprised me when he took my hand and patted it gently as though I were a child, and said, "You no worry anymore. Go and rest. I go away and think."

With that, he took his leave. And I went upstairs and slept.

They were expecting me.

I arrived at the Convent of Santa Clara silent in my shame. I had left Calle de Leon with a trail of lies in my wake. I said I was leaving for the south to help care for my brother-in-law's ailing wife. I would be back in two weeks. Charlie, of course, knew I was going to be away far longer than that. We agreed that after the two weeks was over, I was to send word to the landlady saying I was going to be away longer but would continue to pay my rent. I decided, you see, that I wanted to return to Calle de Leon. There was nowhere else for me to go.

Mother Superior was waiting for me. She asked no questions, though I was aware of her measuring gaze. She told me that as Charlie's friend I was welcome at the convent. She showed me to my room. She told me what time meals were served. When mass was said in the chapel. She told me the history of the convent and who Santa Clara was. She told me what chores the nuns did. She told me about the child refuge they ran. She said I may wish to visit it one day. She told me where to find things in the convent. Where I could go for walks to get some exercise. She told me about Charlie and how he had come to live in the convent, a story I heard for the first time. She told me many things. But she did not tell me what Charlie said about me.

I told her I would do the cooking. I told her I wanted to be useful. She nodded, saying only that I was not to tax myself, avoiding any direct reference to my condition. So I cooked for the nuns. The challenge of coming up with interesting dishes kept me occupied, for the nuns' pantry reflected their simple life. The kitchen became my domain and the preparation of meals saved my sanity, for otherwise, the many quiet hours I spent would have driven me mad.

At first the nuns all seemed the same to me. When you first meet two dozen nuns, the veils and voluminous flowing habits they wear give them a deceptive sameness. But with time I learned to see the differences in them. There were the more contemplative ones who seemed to have taken a vow of silence, going about their business quietly, nodding to me as I passed them. Then there were those who liked to talk, stopping to address me every now and then. But on the whole, the nuns left me on my own.

The need to keep busy drove me to start a vegetable garden. With Mother Superior's permission, I marked out a square plot of ground near the kitchen. It did not take long before a novice and a young nun came to help me. I picked and pulled weeds and fist-sized rocks, I dug and turned with my trowel. I worked compost into the soil, conditioning it so good things would grow from it. My companions

warned me to take it easy, their eyes on my growing middle. I told
them not to worry. And continued to work on the plot for the rest
of the week. The physical exertion did much to drive my worries
away. It made sleeping easier.

And I started to visit the chapel.

Not when a mass was being said. For since I discovered my condition, I stopped going to communion.

I took a sitting in the chapel for hours, and I discovered that the
act of praying took the edge off my anger.

I did not want to face my anger. Or the future. If I had my way, I
would never have faced it. But Mother Superior, who until then had
left me alone, never pressuring me, but who kept watchful eyes on
me, chose to speak at last.

"Have you decided what to do with the child, Consuelo?"

Mother Superior asked me this one afternoon after coming upon
me in the little cemetery, where I sat on a bench, resting after raking
the leaves on the ground. I made to rise but her hand stayed me.
Then she sat next to me.

"You have been here five weeks now, Consuelo, have you considered your options? You do have them, child."

I shook my head.

"I am not telling you what to do, Consuelo, but I would like to suggest that you visit the convent's refuge center. You may wish to go and
see it on Saturday. Every Saturday is an open day when couples come
and see the children. There are many of them, Consuelo, who would
love your child. You can be sure the child will be in good hands."

I went to the refuge center two Saturdays later. I went but did
not enter. I stood by the door and looked at the cots that lined the
room. There were half a dozen or so children there when I visited. I
heard the mewling sounds they made, the whimpering of one, and
the distressed cry of another. A novice motioned for me to step
inside. But I remained where I was. Then I turned and left. Walking
as fast as I could back to the convent.

I refused to see you.

They told me I had a daughter. And when they tried to give you to me, I turned my head away. The nurse quickly left with you. Then Charlie came into the room with Mother Superior following close behind.

I told them I could not bear to set eyes on you. Or touch you.

Charlie returned the following night, with you in his arms. He said, "You look at the baby, Consuelo, she is very beautiful. You will love her."

I refused. You began to cry.

Mother Superior tried once more. "Name her, Consuelo. What you name will be yours."

I shook my head.

"She is his blood," I told her. "And though she is but a girl, I hope she wears that mark of his. I hope she steals it from his sons, steals their luck, their fortune, their everything."

Mother Superior seemed to age before my eyes in those minutes I finally revealed my anger. In the nun's sad eyes I saw the ugly thing I had become.

I was in hospital for almost two weeks. The doctors said I had lost much blood giving birth to you. In your own way, you had tried to take my life, to punish the mother who rejected you.

In the end I made my decision. Perhaps I knew all along that I could not bring myself to raise you, could not face returning to Calle de Leon with a child I needed to explain, could not face moving again. More than anything, I could not face being reminded of the past. It didn't matter that Charlie said you looked like me, half of you was still him. I did not want that part. I didn't even want the part that was me. So I did what a mother would never do. I told them to take you away.

"Find someone else who will raise her. Perhaps," I said, "perhaps away from me, she can grow up untainted."

"You have to be sure, Consuelo, that this is what you wish. Not just now but forever," Mother Superior said. "Once she is adopted out, there is no way of tracing her, we are bound by secrecy."

Charlie and Mother Superior waited another week before taking you away. They hoped I would change my mind. When it was clear I would have nothing to do with you, for I still refused to see you, they accepted my decision. Or at least I thought so then. They took you away. And I made Charlie promise never to bring the past up again.

But now I know they never lost hope. For you are here, Clara. Go and ask the nuns for the truth, they have not told you all.

As for Charlie, did he foresee this moment?

We never return the same person. Not after we have experienced pain. We are never the same.

I returned to Calle de Leon. Without the child. But its absence from my body did not erase my memory of it. I could not resume my old life. What was it about anyway? A foolish young woman who dreamed too much, loved unwisely, gambled and lost. For I loved you, you know. Or at least the twenty-two-year-old woman that I was thought she did. And right from the beginning, even when I knew how different our worlds were, I still hoped that perhaps what was not meant to be could be by sheer force of will, if not desire.

Anyway, as I was saying, I returned to Calle de Leon without the child. But I was no longer whole. There was this big emptiness in the center of me where you had once been and where your child had lived for nine months. It was an empty space, something carved out of my flesh and my spirit, a gaping wound that would not heal.

So I filled that space with prayer. I lit candles and I prayed for forgiveness and I prayed for my hatred to be removed from me and I prayed to be healed.

One day I walked to the local Catholic center and I bought a statue of Our Lady, the perfect, loving, forgiving mother. The mother I never was and never would be. But she was so alone. A mother without a child. So I went back to the center and I brought home the image of the Infant Jesus, the perfect child. And in my altar room, mother and child are together forever.

And now you are here in front of me, Clara, the way Charlie must have always believed it would be. But still we are not one. The past divides us.

But do not think I never thought of you, Clara, for not a single day went by that I did not think of the child I gave away. I prayed that you would be spared the pride of the Pellicers. I prayed that the anger I felt toward you as you grew inside me had not poisoned your spirit. That somehow you would be spared. For I thought you were a child cursed. Why else would you have parents like us?

And you have the mark of the Pellicers, as I hoped you would in a moment of foolish anger. So tell me, Clara, do you suffer from the sin of pride? If so, I fear for you.

She beckoned to me. And I went, reluctantly, to her side.

Pointing to herself then to the don, who stood impassive beside me, she asked, "When you see your mother whose name is Anger, and your father whose name is Pride, what do you see, Clara?"

I declined to answer. What could I tell her? Or him? I had too much to think about, to try to understand myself. I had heard their stories and was torn between wanting to condemn them—for their selfishness had made me grow up parentless—and needing to see things objectively, with a reporter's eye. The latter I knew would lead me to understanding quicker, but it was difficult to suppress my feeling of having been grossly wronged by these two people. I felt like an innocent pedestrian, a hit-and-run victim.

I needed to get away from them, from that room, so I could think clearly. I glanced up and met my mother's eyes. There was in them a questioning, pleading look. What was she asking of me? Understanding? Forgiveness? I couldn't tell. And I doubted if I had it in me to give what she sought. Not yet.

Then I looked at the don. And what I saw made me pause and hold my breath. In that unguarded moment, his eyes were like windows to his complex soul. Without being aware of it, as he gazed upon my mother, the woman he turned his back on many years go, he revealed his fathomless regret. For in giving her up, he had preserved his empire but had lost the world. She was the one person who loved him, not for his wealth and power, but for the man he was, and she could have taught him to love. He was full of irony, this man who could see promise in hectares of empty swampland but who failed to see the value of someone who loved him. Just as well that he was blind in that respect, for his loss, if he realized it, could well shatter him.

But all these musings of mine were useless. It was too late for both of them. The heart, after all, is not dissimilar to any other organ; it atrophies from lack of use. When it fails to love, to fulfil its purpose, it shrivels away. There was little heart left in my mother and my father. Who could save their hearts? I doubted that they could save each other.

I could see, though, that they had a lifetime to talk about. Perhaps that would chip away at some of the hardness that now encased their beings. He, I could see, had much on his mind, much that he wished to express if he could but swallow his pride. And my being there was a hindrance to any exchange between them.

So I decided to leave. Without saying a word, I turned and walked out of the room. The truth was I had no desire to see them again. What would another meeting achieve? I had found my parents but I was still alone. Standing in that room between their battling selves, I was aware that I was still Consuelo's unwanted child, and would forever be so. And as for the two of them, they would forever be two people estranged by the choices they had made.

We were ill-fated beings, the three of us. Had we never met, our lives would have been simpler. And as I made my way down the stairs, as I said good-bye to Padre Luis, who asked me to be understanding and forgiving, as I shut the door to my mother's home, I swore never to return.

The night was old and Calle de Leon asleep by the time I stepped out into the street. I passed Charlie's store, or rather, where his store once stood. I continued walking. Turning every now and then at the sound of a vehicle, thinking perhaps it was a jeepney or taxi I could hail.

By a row of town houses, I walked past a man getting into his car. In the dark, the long shadowy shape of his Mercedes caught my eye. Before driving away, the man glanced up toward the window of the town house he had just left. And I caught the shape of a woman by the window looking down.

I continued walking, wondering how long it would be before I got a ride. Finally, a jeepney pulled up in front of me along Remedios Street and I clambered up the rear steps. The driver took off as soon as I got in. And as I leaned forward to give him my fare, his foot hit the brakes and I found myself flung against the seat.

Two lorries had careered out of a narrow street, driven by maniacs who had turned into the main road without looking. What they carried was hard to see. Huge tarpaulins shrouded their load. The jeepney driver cursed with passion as I righted myself and sat down, willing him to get moving.

At that late hour, I craved for sleep. I knew sleep would restore me. So that tomorrow I could return to the Convent of Santa Clara and claim the last fragment of my missing past; after that I would let it go and be myself again. Clara Perez, no more, no less.

20

❦

An Act of Impulse

I left for the convent soon after daybreak.

My early start was precipitated by the need to be on my way before the marchers took over the streets. It was the day of the protest march. By mid-morning I knew all the major thoroughfares leading to Campo Diaz would be impassable.

I also knew that the area around the convent would swarm with marchers coming from the south side of the river. The slum dwellers of Milagros. Had I not my own story to pursue, or more to the point, had I a say at the *Chronicle*, this would be the one I would ask to write.

But I was not even going to be at the newspaper that day. Before leaving the house in Vito Cruz, I rang the paper and left a message for Torres saying I was not coming in.

As I said, I had my own business to attend to.

Mother Superior had just returned from morning prayers when I arrived. From the way she looked at me, I knew she had been expecting my return. Now that I was there, there was no reason to hurry.

I joined the nuns for breakfast around the long dining table I used to polish when I lived there. Tucking into my plate of scrambled eggs with relish, sipping a cup of black coffee. I had not realized until then just how hungry I was. I hadn't had anything to eat since lunch yesterday. The other nuns seated around the table plied me with food and questions. All of them glad to see me. What was it like at the paper? What stories had I covered since they last saw me? How had I been keeping?

In the background, an old transistor set crackled. I heard the announcer report that a large contingent of students from far-off towns had set out before dawn, torches in hand, marching toward the city. The announcer also said that thousands of office workers were also expected to join the marchers. And that there was no telling what the final numbers would be.

"Why are you not covering the protest march?" Sister Luisa asked.

Before I could even think of an answer, Mother Superior spoke for me. "I have something to discuss with Clara."

So after breakfast, I walked with Mother Superior to her office. And as I seated myself in a chair, she asked if I cared for some Chinese tea.

I told her I didn't know she liked Chinese tea.

"It's an acquired taste of mine," she explained. "Charlie always had tea when he came to visit. He was, you know, a creature of habit."

Charlie had very precise habits. So much so that the first time he failed to open his store, the residents of Calle de Leon feared something unfortunate had befallen him.

Charlie, you see, always opened his store at precisely seven in the morning. Seven days a week. Three hundred and sixty-five days a year. In the thirty years that he lived and did business at Calle de Leon, there were only two days that he failed to open at his usual time.

The first time was the day I was born.

Early that morning, the convent caretaker arrived with a message from Mother Superior saying he was to meet her at St. Paul's Hospital. Charlie understood that Consuelo's time had come. He dressed quickly and headed out, not thinking to leave a sign saying the store would be closed that morning.

When, at seven o'clock, the first of his regular customers arrived to buy her bag of *pan de sal* for breakfast and found his store window still shut, the woman thought that perhaps the Chinaman had overslept. She waited awhile but ten minutes later, the window panels remained closed. She decided to knock. But Charlie did not respond.

Soon the woman was joined by another neighbor and together they knocked on the panels then knocked on the door. Still no answer. Perhaps Charlie had gone out for a while and would be back. This early in the morning? Well, maybe it was important. The two decided to return a little later.

By eight o'clock the store still had not opened. And old man Caloy, thirsty for his morning beer, called out to Charlie in his big gruff voice. "Wake up, Charlie, I'm dying of thirst." Caloy, the neighborhood drunk, took to pounding on the door but after a while gave up. His knuckles red and sore, he stalked off, mumbling to himself about unreliable shopkeepers.

Another hour passed and still Charlie did not appear by his store window. By this time the two women had returned and were joined by several more people from the neighborhood.

"It's so unlike Charlie not to open for business. Why, I can't remember when he ever did this."

"What could he be up to?"

"Where could he have gone?"

Then someone said, "What if he's in there and something's happened to him?"

And soon the possibility that something had befallen the store owner seized the imagination of the people of Calle de Leon. The crowd grew and the discussion became more involved as the people began to argue about what course of action to take.

Someone suggested calling the police but another party said this was a job for a doctor, for surely Charlie was ill and too weak to rise or, worse, lay dead on his bed. A man suggested breaking open the door but was quickly talked out of this because the landlady would demand payment for the damage to her property. Why not bring the landlady here, then, she had a key after all. Everyone agreed to this and so one of the men volunteered and went off to find her. Meanwhile, one woman offered to fetch the doctor just in case. Then another fellow decided to summon the police anyway.

Less than an hour later, a policeman and a doctor had joined the crowd and together they watched the landlady arrive in her car. The landlady, seeing the anxious expressions of those around her as she made to open Charlie's door, feared that her worst expectations would be confirmed. That she would find the Chinaman's dead body sprawled on the floor. This, of course, would be the worst luck, for the store would then be difficult to let, what with someone having died in it.

But before she could push the door open, a woman was heard to shout: "Charlie! It's Charlie!"

All turned to look in the direction the woman was pointing, and true enough, there stood Charlie the Chinaman, waiting to cross the street on his way to his store.

In their relief to see him alive and well, they called out to him, laughed, thumped his back, and shook his hand, and even the difficult landlady greeted him with the warmest smile. What they failed to see was the tired and sad look on Charlie's face, which was soon replaced by bewilderment at his reception. When asked where he had been, Charlie explained that he had gone to see a supplier. They asked no more, simply glad that the Chinaman was back.

Ten minutes later, Charlie stood by his store window and served a throng of customers. He wore his usual smile and all felt their world was right again. But unknown to them, not all was well with Charlie. He had come home that morning with not only Consuelo's situation to ponder but also her unwanted child's fate to worry about.

The event itself became part of the street's lore and was known as the day they thought Charlie the Chinaman had died. But knowing Charlie, his neighbors said, he would never fail to open his store again. Charlie, however, surprised them.

Five weeks later, they found the store window shut once more. But this time Charlie had remembered to leave a note saying he would be late opening that morning.

And here Mother Superior paused in the telling of her tale. She hesitated for a second before saying, "It was the day he stopped your adoption."

This is what happened.

One Saturday, when I was about five weeks old and had been in the refuge for three weeks, a couple came to visit. They had been several times before but had failed to find a child they wanted.

On seeing me, the couple made their decision. They wanted to adopt me. Sister Socorro took down their details and after they left, rushed back to the convent to tell Mother Superior. The solicitors were instructed to investigate the couple and within the week they got back to Mother Superior saying that husband and wife were of a good background and capable of supporting a child. All seemed in order, so Mother Superior approved the adoption.

Mother Superior sent Charlie a note to inform him of this development. She thought he would be glad to hear that a home had been found for me.

Early that evening Charlie arrived and asked to see Mother Superior. He wished to know more about the adopting couple. Mother Superior told him all that she knew and said she was confident they would provide me with love and a good home. Charlie nodded and asked when they would return for me.

"This coming Saturday at nine. The papers will be ready for signing. They'll take her home afterward," he was told.

Before Charlie left that evening, he asked to see me one last time, and stopped by the refuge after leaving the convent.

Sister Socorro brought me to him in the small sitting room. Charlie, she knew, had hoped that Consuelo would change her mind, but now it was too late. He did not stay long, and left a sad man. But in spite of his misgivings, the nuns believed Charlie had resigned himself to the situation.

Charlie did not sleep well that night. And the next morning, as he opened his store and went about his business, he caught sight of Consuelo walking by, basket in hand, to do her regular rounds. He wanted to call out to her but stopped himself. He had promised never to discuss the child and the past with her. No. He could not bring it up. Her mind, he knew, was in a fragile state. He would not push her. No. He knew from experience that a person's calm demeanor was not necessarily a reflection of their inner state.

He shrugged away his thoughts about Consuelo and her child, and concentrated on minding his store. But that night, he once more tossed and turned in his bed. Thoughts of the child leaving kept him awake. He reasoned with himself, saying it was not for him to decide. That he was just growing sentimental with age. He told himself that it was best for the child. A child needed parents. And as for Consuelo, she needed to start a new life. After this, Charlie felt he had resolved the problem in his own mind. In the following days, his concerns seemed to fade and he trusted that this meant it was not a bad thing after all.

Until Saturday itself arrived and Charlie found himself driven by an impulse.

He arrived unexpectedly very early in the morning at the Convent of Santa Clara. Normally a calm, soft-spoken man, he could hardly contain himself that morning.

"Sister Socorro, I must see Mother Superior, please. . . . I must speak to her."

"Charlie, what is the matter?" Sister Socorro asked.

"I must stop it!"

"Stop what?"

"The baby . . ."

So Charlie was taken to see Mother Superior and there he poured out his concerns.

He said that the child must not be lost to them. For it would mean she would be lost to Consuelo. Mother Superior answered that Consuelo had made her decision. But Charlie argued that Consuelo did not know her own mind. Not now. But later, she will want the child. When? How long? Mother Superior asked. Charlie shook his head and said he could not answer that. But that the only thing he knew to be true was that a mother and her child must remain connected. So Charlie argued, reasoned, and begged. And when Mother Superior said the couple would be arriving soon and what was she to say to them, Charlie astounded her by his answer.

At nine, the excited, happy couple arrived. And an hour later they departed; the man with a scowl on his face, his wife weeping quietly.

Mother Superior called Sister Socorro into her office as soon as she got back from the refuge and she told her, "Sister Socorro, one day you will be in my position and I hope you will prove stronger than me. May you never allow yourself to be swayed by others to lie for their purposes."

Mother Superior, acting on Charlie's suggestion, had told the couple, "The mother has changed her mind. She has returned to claim her child."

And this was the agreement between Charlie and the nuns of the Convent of Santa Clara: the child would be named by Mother Superior. She would not be adopted out but would remain in the refuge until such time as was necessary for her to move to the convent. The child would be Charlie's ward but this would remain a secret.

"You must honor this agreement when you take my place, Sister Socorro," Mother Superior said.

"And what about the truth?" asked Sister Socorro.

"You will know when the time to tell the truth has come."

Sitting in Mother Superior's office, I thought about Charlie's impulsive act, which led to my being where I was at that very moment.

We had all come full circle.

I learned that while I still lived in the refuge, Charlie came to the convent every fourth Sunday of the month. Then when I moved into the convent, it was at the refuge that the nuns saw him when he visited. Which was why I never caught sight of him, was never aware of his presence.

"When you finally moved away, things changed once more. And in that chair you are sitting on, he sat and talked to me many times."

"Did he never see me?"

Mother Superior smiled wistfully. "Charlie knew everything about you, Clara. He never tired of hearing about you. In fact, when you were at the refuge, we took photographs of you and the children. There was no need to, we did it so we could give Charlie your picture. You don't remember, do you? You were very young then."

After pausing to catch her breath, Mother Superior continued. "Do you remember the toys that arrived at the refuge every now and then?" I nodded, remembering vaguely. "They were from Charlie. He would have showered you with more toys and beautiful clothes and God knows what else, but we told him it would raise too many questions."

As Mother Superior continued to speak, I listened carefully, drinking in her words, every drop of them. And I saw in my mind a simple Chinaman whose warm heart shone like gold, who watched me from a distance, who listened to the tales of what I said and what I did, who laughed and smiled with pleasure at the child that I was. And as I listened, I saw that there had been someone at least who had felt gladness in his heart that I was in this world.

But what was the meaning of all that had come to pass? Why was I there at the convent at all, at that very moment? And why had I been placed there twenty-three years ago? I found it difficult to believe that the great powers of the universe had engineered the coming together of so many people—so many coincidences, if you would like to call them that—only so that a child would find her mother and her father, and learn of the impulsive act of a well-meaning stranger. There was something I was failing to understand, and I sensed, was convinced beyond doubt, that there was more to come and that my intention to resume my old life would come to nothing. It was too late for that. For my life had taken a strange turn, gone off in a direction I still had to work out. I knew that the answer would come eventually. But it would surprise me just how soon.

21

Waiting for Rain

I can smell rain.

As a child I could tell the coming of rain. It is raining today. It will rain soon, I would announce to the nuns.

And after the punishingly hot day we had just had, I waited for its coming the way a lost desert traveler thirsts for water.

Sitting out in the cemetery, I felt the gradual drop in temperature. A breeze brushed against my face, lifting strands of my hair. The leaves on the mango tree and the bushes rustled softly in response to its passing, barely able to contain their excitement at the promise of rain. They, too, waited for the first blessed drops to fall.

I had decided to stay the night. Mother Superior understood why and helped me make my bed herself. We went up to my old room and flung the window open to take the mustiness out. It had been a while since I had stayed overnight.

I wished to be close to where it all happened. I believed this way nothing would escape my grasp. To be where decisions were made, words spoken, and actions taken seemed vital to me.

All the facts were with me now. I was waiting for understanding to come.

To tell you the truth, I was surprised that there was no automatic process of enlightenment. To think that I believed facts brought understanding. A simple equation that ruled life. The lack of facts about myself had so colored my sense of self that I expected the moment I possessed them, all things would become clear to me.

So as I sat on the bench in the middle of the night waiting for the rain to fall, I thought each drop would somehow bring me a fragment of understanding.

I heard it before I felt it. The first drops that landed on the thirsty ground, on parched leaves, and on my face. I smiled in the dark, for they were a relief from the heat that had driven me out of my room to sit under the night skies. They pitter-pattered, like the plucking of guitar strings, the sound they made magnified by the quiet of night.

Against the weak light of a night sky, I saw the drops travel a diagonal path. And in the shadows, I saw the trees bowing in welcome and homage.

The rain gathered strength and fell with greater intensity and the thin cotton nightdress I wore was soon soaking wet but I continued to sit on the bench, my legs crossed, my feet tucked under my thighs, my hair in wet strands plastered against my face. It was many years since I had stayed out in the rain.

I listened to its changing rhythms.

Looking on the ground, I glimpsed the growing puddles of water that sometimes caught streaks of light. A few more minutes passed and the rain became a peltering force. It was time to go back in. I uncrossed my legs and set my feet on the ground. The water squished under my slippers; I curled my toes, and soon my feet were covered in cool muddy water.

But before I could even take a step, a loud bang ripped through the air, reverberated, and was followed by another. I wondered what it was, this exploding sound. But in the rain all sounds arrived distorted. I thought no more of it as I pulled at my nightdress, trying to separate it from my skin.

Then from the corner of my eye I saw something move near the wall. I swung around, my insides knotting tightly. My heart pounded so hard and loud I thought it would burst from my chest. A shadow moved toward me. I panicked and took a step back, almost tripping over my own foot. The shape staggered then lunged forward. I screamed. But my scream went unheard, for just then it thundered. The figure fell to the ground, splashing mud on my legs. A flash of lightning followed, illuminating the world around me, so that for a brief moment I saw the figure in the water with its pale face, its hands clutching the wet soil. Then it was dark again.

And I ran. I ran through the rain.

PART III

22

The Protest March

From the Channel 4 chopper that flew over the city, the thousands of people advancing toward Campo Diaz resembled a series of small tributaries emptying themselves into a main stream. The group below represented the largest contingent of marchers, drawing from the universities and colleges near the palace.

Glancing at the news cameraman, the pilot shouted over the whirr of the blades. "You expecting trouble?"

"It would make a better story," the cameraman replied.

The pilot nodded. After a few more minutes he turned the chopper around and headed toward the dockside, where the marchers from Milagros poured out of the slums in an endless stream, their swelling numbers impossible to guess.

By ten-thirty in the morning, the North Diversion Road had become impassable. The section near the entrance to the city was clogged with thousands of marchers. Though the sun had climbed high in the sky, its heat failed to hinder their progress.

Coming from far-flung universities and colleges outside the city, they had been on the move since dawn. Under a still-dark sky they had converged in front of a small church, then set out, lighting their way with torches. From above, they had resembled a river of fire in the still landscape.

Now as they poured into the city, they waved their many-colored banners, raised their fists, and broke into a rousing song. Their voices lifted in the wind to announce their coming.

As the chopper veered southeast of the North Diversion Road, a third group of marchers came into view. On Remedios Street the Loyola contingent, led by Luis Bayani, who had ignored an order to appear before the Jimenez Commission, met with the fifteen-thousand-strong State University marchers.

As they turned into Generoso Street, their numbers continued to swell. First to join them were three hundred students from Santa Isabel College who chose to defy the stricture of the nuns. A round of cheers greeted the group. The nuns of Santa Isabel may have preached noninvolvement, but in a surprise move, a group of priests from the Loyola announced they were marching. It was noted by the press that the Catholic archdiocese did not comment on the matter.

All over the city, showers of confetti greeted the students. At Felix Sandoval Street, a bus driver began honking his horn as the human tide passed before him. Soon, others followed suit. There was something fiestalike about the morning. And wherever the students passed, they were joined by ordinary people. So that by the time the marchers reached Campo Diaz by midday, the initial estimate of their size had more than quadrupled.

The marchers were not the only ones on the move.

In front of Campo Diaz, the riot police disembarked from several open trucks. Moving with clocklike precision, they went to work, setting up barricades by the camp gates and along the perimeter of the camp wall facing the highway. This done, they began positioning the water cannons at regular intervals. When all was in order, they took up their positions. Standing thirty deep to a column and armed with truncheons and gripping their shields, they were, in their black uniforms and gleaming black helmets, an intimidating sight. They stood to attention, scanning the three points from which the marchers were due to emerge.

Earlier, the palace had issued a final appeal from El Presidente to call off the march. The statement also addressed the public, saying the government would be following a policy of maximum tolerance. In line with this, the military would stay behind the camp gates. The riot police would keep law and order.

The students, as expected, ignored El Presidente's plea. In an interview Luis Bayani denounced the government's refusal to allow the students to build a platform and install sound facilities in front of the camp. It was, he said, a violation of the citizens' rights.

The riot police had arrived expecting to see a platform being erected. They had orders to dismantle it. But they found no platform in the area in front of the camp.

Less than a kilometer away from the camp gates, on Santiago Avenue, which ran alongside one of the city's major shopping centers, two lorries rumbled past. Huge orange tarpaulins held down by ropes covered their load. And on the back of each lorry stood three men, hanging on to the ropes.

The lorries turned in to the shopping center and headed for the rear parking lot. After turning their engines off, the driver of the lead lorry switched on his two-way radio. It crackled to life.

He spoke into it. "Mario here . . . we've arrived."

Over the sound of static, a voice said, "I read you. We're about an hour away."

"We're illegally parked and may have to leave sooner."

"Delay as long as you can. If you get there before us, you'll have trouble. It's eleven twenty-eight now."

The driver checked his watch and adjusted the time as the other party signed off. Then, turning on the radio, he and his companion listened to the news coverage of the march.

Some minutes later, one of the men behind the lorry called out, "Mario . . . we've got trouble."

Mario looked out his window and saw a policeman hurrying toward them. "You can't park here. This is for shoppers," the man called out as he approached.

The one called Mario got out to meet him, joined by the second driver. "We've got equipment to unload."

"What equipment? I was told nothing."

The second driver said, "The sports center. There was no parking available there, so we're waiting here."

"I was told nothing," the man repeated.

"Check with Castro, the manager," the first driver added. "We're just following orders."

The policeman hesitated briefly then stalked off.

"That should buy us at least half an hour," the first driver said.

While the men in the lorries waited, a van of an indeterminate shade of green with the words PRESTIGE INTERIOR DESIGN written across its sides turned into Amelia Gonzaga Street three blocks away from the shopping complex. The driver parked the vehicle four houses from the street corner. Then sat back and waited.

Amelia Gonzaga Street was the site of several construction projects and was lined with half a dozen delivery vans, two cement mixing trucks, and an army of workmen drilling and hammering away, all raising clouds of dust. Over the last three months a row of exclusive town houses was slowly taking shape here. While across the road, a monstrous-looking mansion shaped like a castle was nearing completion.

The idle van's presence raised no curiosity. Any of the building sites could be employing Prestige Interior Design. The driver of the van rolled his window down, then reached into his shirt pocket for his cigarettes. He shook the pack and counted what remained. Three. He decided to have one and keep two for later.

"How long?" his companion asked.

The driver checked his watch. "About an hour. Depends."

"Can't see why we have to move in stages when we can just head there."

Striking a match, the driver, cigarette between his lips, said, "Orders."

"From Marquez?"

The driver nodded, then after blowing his match out, added, "You know, of course, he's taking orders himself."

His companion shot him a curious look.

Before explaining, the driver eyed the control panel next to the steering wheel. The speaker switch was in the off position. They couldn't hear him in the back. He leaned toward the other man then and said, "Ever wonder why the colonel's back?"

At precisely five past twelve, the two lorries left the shopping-complex parking lot. The lead driver turned into Zamora Street then right again until he came back out on Santiago Avenue. Close behind him followed the second driver. The lorries rumbled down the road until they reached the highway. Here they turned left and traveled along the approach to the camp.

From overhead, the Channel 4 cameraman caught sight of the lorries. A warning bell sounded in his head. He looked at the bright orange tarpaulins, following their progress with interest. Oh yes, yes, this was it.

He called to the pilot, gesturing excitedly. "Move in! Quick! See those two? Yes, yes, those two!"

The pilot, on catching sight of the two moving lorries, shook his head in disbelief. His voice was tinged with awe as he exclaimed, "My God! Who'd ever have thought they'd come up with this!" He banked the chopper to the left to bring it closer to the scene.

"Look at that, will you!" the pilot called out.

Below them, on the highway a hundred meters from the camp gates, the lead lorry came to a grinding halt. Then the second lorry, which had kept a measured distance behind it, began to move clockwise until it had completed a hundred-and-eighty-degree turn.

Across the road, by the camp gate, the riot police gaped in stunned fascination as the two lorries joined rear to rear. Suddenly, the riot police broke into a run.

"Dismantle it!" cried the officer in charge.

By this time the drivers had joined their companions in unveiling the platform they had transported, while the rest of the group rapidly assembled the sound system.

Meanwhile, a large band of reporters, video cameramen, and press photographers joined the race to the lorries.

"Keep away!" the officer shouted to them. A frantic tussle began as the riot police clambered up the back of the lorries, their movement impeded by members of the media. But all their struggles abruptly came to a halt seconds later. For suddenly the air was filled with a new sound.

The sound of singing came from different directions. A rousing sound that grew louder, gaining power, as the four groups of marchers took up the song. Along the highway near the camp, they finally met, merging to become one mighty throng. In the noonday heat, they were a shimmering vision, this sea of humanity, waving their banners like an army come to do battle.

The students had arrived.

Meanwhile, the green van left its position at Amelia Gonzaga Street. Like the two lorries, it headed for the camp. But unlike them, the van did not turn in to the highway. It went straight across, turned in to a series of backstreets, and finally emerged in the road that ran along the side of the camp. There it came to a halt. Unnoticed.

The driver switched off the ignition. Seconds later, he heard a tap on the dividing panel. He flicked the speaker switch on.

"Is it time yet?" a voice asked.

"No. Just sit tight."

The driver switched the speaker off. Turning to his companion, he said, "I wouldn't be in such a rush if I were him."

The man he referred to was a twenty-two-year-old recruit of medium height and build, who possessed no distinguishing features. This was why they had chosen him. But the young man did not know this. He believed his superiors saw some promise in him. Why, Marquez himself hinted at some reward, a promotion, most likely.

Forget the uniform. Marquez said they would give him something to wear for the day. He was disappointed at the green T-shirt they made him put on, and complained about the loose fit around the pocket area of his baggy trousers. You need room there, they told him.

Seated in the back of the van with him were three other men. He had never seen them before. They hadn't volunteered their names. Not even when he had asked.

I'll show them, he thought to himself. I'll show them. What reason did they have for acting so superior when he was the one who would do the deed? They were there only to smuggle him away, to shield him when it was done. He reached into the loose side pocket of his pants. His hand familiarizing itself with the object once more. The shape of it. The pin. He withdrew his hand.

He was impatient to be out there. Every now and then he turned to look out of the window. But the dark tint and the position of the van prevented him from seeing much. He glimpsed only a small part of the crowd. And could not hear clearly, for the men insisted on keeping the windows shut.

He drummed his fingers on the seat. His companions eyed him, but he continued his drumming. Then one of them touched him lightly on the shoulder, and said, "Relax. It'll soon be over."

By the time the first two speakers finished addressing the crowd, the shouts and cries that rang from the audience were deafening.

Standing in front of the platform, Father Salcedo, a Jesuit, looked about him with growing unease. If violence broke out, the second speaker, he thought, had a lot to answer for. The student leader from the State University was a fiery orator. An angry young man whose denunciation of the government, the military, and the palace elicited a frightening response from the crowd.

Father Salcedo hoped the final speaker could defuse the tension, because a mindless rampage against the police and the military now would achieve little. It was with relief that he watched Luis Bayani make his way up to the stage.

Had the priest's attention not been so focused on the student leader, he might have noticed the scruffy young man in the green

T-shirt who made his way to the front of the crowd next to him. But the priest took no notice of the man in green. For, at that precise moment, Luis Bayani began to speak.

He spoke of the nature of power. How power without responsibility could lead to a dictatorship. And he spoke of the responsibility of every citizen to demand reform. And how reform was creative and transformative, whereas revolution was destructive. He spoke in the intelligent, lucid manner that was his trademark.

The mood of the crowd shifted. Began to cool. Their passions gradually tempered by his words of reason. For, unlike the two speakers before him, Bayani had not come to talk about revolution and the overthrow of the government. He had come to teach control.

Then Luis Bayani asked for five minutes of silence. Voices rang out.

"What for?"

"We're not afraid!"

"We refuse to be silenced."

Unruffled by this show of dissent, Bayani said, "There is silence born of fear. And silence born of control. I ask you to observe five minutes of silence as a demonstration of strength . . . and as a way of remembering our dead."

He paused, then continued, his voice ringing through the highway packed with tens of thousands of people. "We no longer hear the voices of friends who have died as they marched with us. But in our silence we will hear them once more."

Then he looked at the crowd before him, took a deep breath, and called out the name of the first of the fallen. And paused. Then he called out the name of the second of the fallen. And so he went. Pausing after each name, giving the people time to remember a friend, recall a face, hear a familiar voice once more.

The crowd grew silent. Starting with those closest to the platform. Then like a rolling wave, the silence washed over those behind them. By the time Luis Bayani finished reciting the names of all the fallen, even the beeping and tooting horns of impatient drivers had been silenced. From the streets running off the highway, people had emerged from their cars to stand with the marchers.

As Luis Bayani predicted, each person heard a message in the eerie quiet that descended in front of the camp. They heard the protest of the dead. The cries of the disappeared. They heard the weeping of the disenfranchised. But most of all they heard the message of their own heart. And they heard something more.

A loud explosion cut through the air.

And for a brief moment, the crowd believed they were hearing fireworks. Then a second explosion followed. And now from behind the camp walls, a blaze of fire began to rise in the skies.

Many would later say that by calling out the names of the dead, Luis Bayani had brought the fallen back into the world, where they exacted their vengeance. Eight soldiers died from the grenade blast. Their lives seemingly claimed by the eight students who had died in the June 6 riot.

Meanwhile, in the confusion that followed the explosion, several things were happening all at once.

From the camp gates poured a stream of soldiers sent out to aid the riot police, while on the platform, the student leader from the State University grabbed hold of a microphone and shouted, "We've been set up!" Then the sound system went dead. The riot police advanced toward the student leaders, who stood unprotected on top of the lorries. Seeing their leaders' vulnerable state, dozens of students surged forward to meet the police.

Fighting broke out.

Later, the Jesuit priest would tell reporters about the young man in green who almost knocked him down as he burst forward to climb onto the platform. "I saw this flash of green. Suddenly he was there flinging this thing in the direction of the camp. An explosion followed. I then saw the man turn to face the crowd, as if searching for someone. While he was still looking into the crowd, the second explosion followed. He couldn't have been the one who threw the second grenade. How could he when he was facing toward me? For a brief moment, his face took on a different expression; there was a flash of recognition in his eyes. I think he saw whoever it was he was looking for. He made to jump then and that was when the shots rang out and he fell from the platform."

The police report on the attack stated that the man in the green shirt—whose identity was still unknown—had rushed the stage and thrown two grenades in a row. Causing the death of eight soldiers, the wounding of another sixteen, and the destruction of two army vehicles parked near the gate. The report also stated he was gunned down after hurling the second grenade.

The official report also contradicted the evidence recorded by the news cameraman, which showed the man in green throwing a grenade only once. What the official report did not include was what happened after the man was shot.

When the man fell, a female student ran to his aid while around her several others pressed in. She bent close to the man, whose shirtfront was now soaked in blood. With glazed eyes, he stared before him. She held his hand as he struggled to speak, gasping out the words, "They said . . . they help . . . escape . . . but shot me." Then he fell silent, the light gone from his eyes.

Her eyes bright with secret knowledge, she turned to look at the people around her. Strangers, all returning her gaze. It was wrong to be here, she thought. I shouldn't be here. She got up on her feet and made to leave but before she could take a step, three men pressed against her and two strong hands grabbed hold of her arms. She kicked and screamed then, calling to the priest who stood right behind the men.

"He was one of them! He was one—"

They dragged her away just as the priest tried to reach her. It was impossible for Father Salcedo to move closer. A news cameraman who was trying to take some footage of the dead man blocked his way. One of the strangers shoved the man away in an effort to stop the filming. He fell against the priest but kept his camera rolling. In the end, he would provide the only evidence that Sophia Ramos-Sytangco had been taken into custody by some unidentified men.

Meanwhile, powerful jets of water hit the crowd as the riot police tried to keep the students at bay. The fighting had escalated.

On the platform, Luis Bayani struggled with his attackers. Next to him, the Lyceum leader soon fell to the effects of tear gas. A few meters away, the leader from the State University exchanged blows with two men, but three cracked ribs and a dislocated shoulder would finally render him powerless. As for Luis Bayani, he became the center of a concerted and daring rescue effort.

Bulldog, the Loyola soccer team captain, charged up the platform and flung his powerful bulk at the men pinning Bayani down. Freed from his captors at last, the student leader struggled to his feet.

"Luis . . . Luis!" a familiar voice called out to him. Bayani looked down and saw Laslo at the head of the pack of students. As they charged toward the platform, Laslo shouted in a voice grown hoarse, "Jump . . . we'll cover you!"

A second later, Luis Bayani disappeared into the crowd. By the time the riot police and the soldiers reached the group, all they found were eighty unruly, abusive students. Luis Bayani was nowhere in sight. By mid-afternoon, he would become the object of the nation's largest manhunt.

23

Too Late for Misgivings

It did not take long for the Chief of Staff to realize that the news of the grenade attack on Campo Diaz was not news to El Presidente.

On delivering the information to his superior—information that had personally upset and concerned him—all the Chief of Staff elicited from El Presidente was a steady gaze followed by a quick nod.

"You knew?" he said with undisguised surprise.

"Yes, Raul. I knew. And the Defense Minister knew, too."

The Chief of Staff weighed this piece of information. Something wasn't right. Something about the nature of the plan was out of character with the Defense Minister. Then it slowly came to him. How foolish that he had not seen it sooner. Taking a deep breath, the Chief of Staff said, "Aure?"

"I am surprised it took you so long to figure it out," was El Presidente's reply.

"I believed he was here to prevent another outbreak of violence." To himself, the Chief of Staff wondered how he could have forgotten that Aure's business was the perpetuation of violence.

"That would have been a waste of his time and his talents," El Presidente said, interrupting his thoughts. "He is a strategist, one capable of executing his own plans."

"Soldiers were killed and wounded, sir."

"A necessary sacrifice."

"But from all accounts, sir, Bayani had things under control."

"Ahh . . . but he didn't, Raul. We were in control this time. We may not have been in control in the past but we are in control once more."

The Chief of Staff did not know what to say to this skewed view of the situation. He wished to contradict his superior. To say to him: you relinquished all control when you brought Aure into the picture.

He had always believed there was more truth than rumor to the things whispered about Aure. He believed, too, that one day something would set Aure off and all the blackness he harbored inside him would be released. And this was the man El Presidente had chosen to trust. He shuddered at the thought.

Unaware that he had lapsed into silence and that El Presidente was now watching him with growing irritation, the Chief of Staff remained lost in his thoughts, the furrows on his brow deepening.

"What is it, Raul?"

"It seems unnecessary, sir, that we should instigate another outbreak of violence. I mean, what have we achieved?"

El Presidente exploded. "We have discredited the students! Discredited Bayani! Surely you can see the danger he poses to me? Raul, you are not questioning my decision, are you?"

The Chief of Staff did not reply. It stunned him that El Presidente failed to see that the grenade-throwing incident was in contradiction to all he wished to achieve with the Jimenez Commission. How could he choose to implicate the military then decide to implicate the students as well? It was as though any ability to see the big picture, to make decisions consistent with an overall goal, no longer existed in the palace. And now, what was he to say? How much leeway did sixteen years of service give him, how much room for honesty? He was not sure.

El Presidente rose from his seat. He walked around and stood in front of the Chief of Staff, giving him an angry look. "You *are* questioning my decision!" he accused.

The fact that the man questioned plans he had approved, plans that had become actions too late to undo, undermined the satisfaction he had felt on hearing that things had gone according to plan. Now the taste of success was tainted. But El Presidente was not yet lost to all reason as to refuse to listen to a man he knew to be honorable, and most important of all, one whom he knew to be loyal. The Chief of Staff was someone he trusted. He was respectful but he never toadied to him, not the way the Press Secretary did. Unlike the rest of the palace staff, the Chief of Staff was not there simply because he served a purpose, but because he was trusted.

"I will allow you, Raul, to speak your mind. What is giving you concern?"

"That there will be far-reaching consequences, sir. That it was not thoroughly thought out."

"Aure is reliable. Very thorough. You are not questioning my assessment of his abilities, are you?"

"No, sir. Although I have never hidden from you my personal dislike of the man, I am aware of his abilities. I do not care for his actions. But I recognize he has done much to control the situation down south."

El Presidente settled into an armchair by the window, all the while continuing to watch the Chief of Staff.

"Then what?"

"His nature, sir. I fear he is dangerous to us."

24

A Mission for Laslo

*L*aslo stepped outside and breathed in the night air. It still smelled of smoke.

He checked the time. It was ten past eleven. He had been in the detention center at Campo Diaz since the protest march had deteriorated into yet another violent showdown. He had been arrested, repeatedly interrogated, and now allowed to go free. But Laslo was not heading home. Not yet. He had business to attend to. Business he would rather have left to someone else.

Thinking about his mission ended his inertia, at the same time that it filled him with dread. There was no time to waste and yet he didn't know how to go about the task given him. He forced himself to move. He began to walk briskly down the path a soldier had pointed out to him. He knew it would take him to one of the camp gates. Not the main entrance. That had been sealed off following the explosion that had left eight soldiers dead that afternoon.

He glanced back at the detention center. Then forced himself to push away thoughts of Sophia. He had been afraid to leave her but he had had no choice in the matter. All he could do now was make good use of his freedom. It was her only chance.

His own early release had come about only because he was the judge's son. It shamed him that he had got off lightly compared with the others. True, he had grown weary with the round of questioning. They had called him in three times. Asking the same questions over and over. Where is Luis Bayani? You engineered his escape. You must know. Who is the grenade thrower? He was one of you. Who was behind the plot to blow up the camp? Was it Bayani? Did you know about it? Who supplied the grenade?

To all this, he had shaken his head. Insisted he didn't know. That helping Bayani escape had happened on the spur of the moment. He had acted spontaneously. Secretly, he had been surprised at his own daring, his quick thinking; he had never in his life seen this aspect of himself, the part of him that could be decisive, that could lead. But his actions concerned him, for he knew they had drawn attention to him. And now, with the grenade blast, the whole situation had taken on a seriousness he had not expected.

Then he heard Sophia's tale.

He had not seen her when he was first brought to the detention center with the others. And even when the room they were confined in filled with new arrivals, Sophia had not been among them. It was only later, after his third interrogation session, that he saw her.

She was in a room on her own, which should have surprised him. But all he could think of on seeing her was his good fortune at being in the same place as her. He didn't question why he had been brought here this time instead of being returned to the big room to join the others.

She looked pale and tired. A haunted expression in her eyes. Laslo sat next to her and to comfort her said, "We'll be released soon enough."

"They will not let me go, Laslo."

"Just because you're a YRM council member? No. It's illegal to keep any of us here indefinitely . . . without charges."

"You don't understand. . . . I was a witness, Laslo."

"We all were. We all saw the explosion."

She sighed and closed her eyes. Leaning her head against the wall, she said slowly, "Listen to me, Laslo. I heard the man they gunned down. Before he died. I heard him speak. He was one of them. It was a setup."

Laslo stared at her. The meaning of what she said sinking in. And what she said next frightened him even more.

"And they know I know. The men who gunned him down were next to me when the man spoke. That was why they grabbed me." Laslo reached for Sophia's hand and squeezed it. It was clammy, like his.

In a whisper so soft he only just made out her words, she said, "I don't want to die, Laslo."

"Stop," he said urgently to her. "You must not say such things. We'll find a way. I must get to the others and tell them. The more people know, the better."

Then the door to the room was flung open. Laslo stopped talking. In stepped one of the uniformed interrogators, a burly man with a mustache who looked at Laslo and said, "Jimenez, get ready, you're being released! I'll go get your papers." The man turned to go but not before he gave Laslo a scornful look and announced, "You can thank your father for that."

As soon as the man left, Sophia grabbed his hand, saying, "Luis! You must find Luis."

He disagreed with her. "My father can protect you better."

"Laslo, Laslo . . . he has never approved of your activities. It is Luis you must find. Don't you see? This whole thing was set up to discredit us. To destroy Luis. He must clear himself and the movement. And with my story he can do this. Once he knows, and the people know I am being held here, I stand a better chance of being set free. It is my only chance, Laslo."

"I don't know where to find Luis."

"Go to Smoky Mountain."

Seeing the look on his face, she explained, "Long ago, Luis said to us, if you find yourself in a bind, go there. It is the last place people will look for you. It is easy to lose yourself there. And knowing Luis, that is where he has gone. The Milagros marchers must have left with him hidden among them. He is probably waiting for us to figure it out. To send a message to him."

It took Laslo a good twenty minutes to get a ride, because at that time of night, few vehicles were about. The jeepney he boarded would take him as far as Natividad Street downtown. From there he would have to get another ride to the dock area. Once there, he would have to go on foot toward the slum district of Milagros, where Smoky Mountain was.

The thought of searching for Bayani at Smoky Mountain occupied his thoughts as he sat in the front passenger seat next to the driver. Had he been more watchful, it may have come to his notice that behind him two cars were keeping a measured distance from the jeepney. And that when he finally got off and changed rides, one car had driven past the idling jeepney and turned into a side street while the other car continued on.

Perhaps it would have come to his attention, too, that as soon as he got on the second jeepney, which now took him to the dock area, a car emerged from a side street and followed close behind. And that as they approached the dock area, the second car appeared again.

Laslo got off at the dock gates, where all was quiet at that time of night. He looked around him. Then began walking nervously toward Milagros. A few minutes later, a battered dark blue Corolla overtook him on the road. Laslo barely gave it a glance.

He decided to take the next street, hoping it would lead him to the giant tip. As he walked, he looked at his surroundings carefully. And he kept his ears tuned for every sound. Milagros, with its high crime rate, was no place to be walking at this late hour.

Laslo had never been here before. YRM, he knew, ran a community center in the area, but he had never involved himself with the center's activities. Spending his free time in the slums did not appeal to him.

A vehicle's headlights shone behind Laslo. He could hear the crunching of pebbles under its tires. Because the street was fairly narrow, he walked closer to the side to let the car through. But the car slowed down and a gruff-sounding voice said, "*Pare*, it's not safe to be out here at this hour. Go home."

The car passed him and was now several meters ahead of him when Laslo ran after it.

"Please," he said, calling to the man, "I'm looking for Smoky Mountain."

The car slowed to a stop and the man and his companion eyed Laslo. The man spoke once more. "You don't look like a scavenger."

"I'm looking for someone."

"Who? At Smoky Mountain?"

"Umm . . . I have to see someone."

"In which street?"

"Smoky Mountain, just Smoky Mountain."

The man leaned over to the driver and spoke to him. Then he stepped out of the car. He motioned with his head and proceeded to walk. "I'll take you there before you get lost." Laslo followed. Grateful for this change of fortune.

They walked in silence, their steps muffled by the dirt-packed road. The man took out a packet of cigarettes, offered it to Laslo, who shook his head. The man lit one and began to smoke.

"It helps kill the smell."

As they neared the end of the road and turned toward an inclined walkway, Laslo understood what the man meant. Even at that distance, the smell assailed him. The smell of rotting refuse. The stench of it growing stronger as they made more progress. He reached into his pocket and pulled out the crumpled handkerchief he had used all day. It did little to mask the smell. But Laslo kept it pressed to his face. For each gasp, each quick intake of foul air, sickened him.

Then it was before him. A vision so surreal. An alien landscape of rubbish, several stories high, glistening with bits of foil, rising obscenely under the rude glare of the towering streetlights. On its slippery slope an army of scavengers busily worked. Each carrying a pail or container of some form in which they deposited their finds.

Laslo gazed at the scene before him, speechless with wonder, momentarily forgetting the smell of this world. As he looked at the figures that scaled the mountain—men, women, and children—moving in and out of the light, he wondered how he would find Luis Bayani, if he was here at all.

The sound of coughing brought his attention back to his guide. He turned to the man and thanked him.

"Do you know where you're going? I more or less know the place, so I can take you. It's not pleasant to get lost here."

Laslo shook his head as he scanned the maze of narrow streets crammed with cardboard and metal-scrap shanties. No. No he didn't quite know where to go but he would just go looking.

The man inclined his head and seemed to weigh Laslo's words. Finally, he nodded. "Well then, I shall leave you to it. Good luck. I hope you find . . . your friend."

Laslo headed for the mountain, his handkerchief over his nose. Before climbing, he glanced over his shoulder and found the man still looking his way. Then the man turned and made his way back to the walkway. Laslo gave his attention back to the mountain. He took a deep breath through his handkerchief and began his search.

He climbed the mountain. The light from the row of streetlights was insufficient, so Laslo kept to the lit areas. The squishy sound of rubbish underfoot made him cringe. But he continued to climb. Sometimes almost losing his balance. And at one point, to keep from falling, his hand touched the ground and came back reeking of whatever it was he had touched. How he wished himself gone from that repulsive place.

A band of children came charging down the mountain carrying pails filled with an assortment of discarded goods. Laslo gazed at them, wondering what value their find had. Worthless bits, mutilated parts of unidentifiable objects.

As he made his way up Smoky Mountain, he glanced about him, searching for the figure of Bayani. He cursed to himself. He didn't know whether they even knew Bayani. Whether it was safe to ask. And who he could ask. He decided to keep silent for the moment and search on his own.

Laslo was aware of the curious glances directed his way. He did not belong here. And he wondered what these people thought of his presence. He stood and watched the activity around him. At the digging scavengers. Some so old and some so young. Then a chugging noise announced the arrival of another convoy of trucks. A good number of them stopped their digging and headed out to meet it with its fresh load of rubbish.

"Dig!"

The sharp order came from an old man standing a few meters across from him. A scrawny man with a hump on his back, thin wizened arms with bony hands that scraped busily at the rubbish around him. The man pointed at Laslo.

"Don't just stand there, boy, dig!"

Lost in the unreality of this world, Laslo found himself doing as the man ordered. He bent down and began to dig. Then, realizing what he was doing, he stopped.

"Keep digging! What are you waiting for?"

Laslo wanted to shout at him and say, "What is there to dig for? Who would want any of this?"

As if hearing his thoughts, the old man cackled and broke into a coughing fit that shook his frail body. When the fit ended, bits of saliva gathered at the corners of his mouth. He wiped this with the back of his filthy hand, then reached into his pocket and pulled out an object. He showed this to Laslo.

"I have already found a nail," he announced. "While you, you still stand there empty-handed, with nothing to show for your time here. All this . . ." He made a sweeping movement. "All this and you find nothing worth picking!"

The old man pointed at a spot in front of Laslo.

"Look there, boy!"

"My name is Laslo."

"Hah! Laslo then, look at that spot before you. Tell me, what do you see?"

Laslo looked down. The ridiculousness of it all hit him. What was the point in all this, this study of refuse?

"Garbage! Useless garbage!" he told the old man.

The old man snorted with disgust.

"If that is all you see, then you have not been looking. Pluck your eyes out, they serve you not. You will not find what you are looking for!"

The old man proceeded to rummage through the spot. As he dug with his hands, he continued to speak, bringing up one object after another.

"This—here—is an old fork, bent, yes, but it is metal. It is worth something."

He kicked with his foot to uncover another layer of rubbish. A yellow plastic ice-cream container came into view. He picked it up and threw the fork in.

"Plastic, Laslo, is money. You can sell it."

Laslo watched with growing fascination. How was he to know what value to put on things he freely discarded? What was the currency of life here? He looked on wide-eyed as the old man stooped down to swoop up a crushed aluminum can, letting out a triumphant cry as he threw this into his plastic container. Then the old man flicked a finger against the can.

"There's a few *centavos* in this can. Now you better start digging before everyone else picks up all the valuable things!"

Laslo had had enough by then. "I didn't come here to look for . . . rubbish. I'm not a scavenger."

"Eh? Not one of us, are you?"

Laslo ignored the old man's sarcasm. "I came to look for someone. A friend. Maybe you know him?"

The old man straightened up and looked Laslo in the eye. "You find three things of value and you may find what you're looking for."

The old man walked off.

Laslo's first inclination was to storm off. He didn't have to put up with this. No. Not him. He didn't have to yield to the old man, agree to play his stupid games. He wasn't even sure if the old man could help him. But Laslo stayed. Leaving, he knew, would not help Sophia. He swallowed his anger. Cursing under his breath, he began to search for God knows what.

The first object he found was a clear plastic bottle with a Coke label around it. Well, maybe it was worth something. He hung on to it. With his bare hands, he kept rummaging. At first gingerly picking things up then putting them down. But it was slow work. So after a while, he suppressed his revulsion and grabbed at things, lifted them, scraped through the putrid mess. Before long, his nails became black and his fingers sticky. The odor did not lessen with time but in his effort to look for two more objects, he found himself thinking less of the smell and more about finding things. Had the situation been different, he might have laughed at himself.

His finger came in contact with a thin pointed object. He pulled it out of the heap. A coil of wire. He turned it in his hand, then threw it back on the pile. A woman swooped down and picked it up. Laslo made to protest as she pocketed the object.

"You had your chance!" she told him.

He went back to digging. After a while he found a piece of polystyrene. He picked this up and looked at it, then he looked up and caught the woman looking at it, too. He tucked it under his arm.

"You're learning fast," she said, giving him a toothless grin as she walked past.

One more object. He walked farther up the slope where the light was weaker. Perhaps there were things in the shadowy sections that the others had missed. He found a spot and kicked at it with his foot. A layer of vegetable peel came to light. Soft and mushy. As Laslo kicked once more, a rat sprang from somewhere in the shadows and bolted away. He stepped back with a start. His distaste for the whole exercise returned.

In his anger, Laslo gave the pile of rubbish another kick. His shoe dislodged a crushed aluminum can. He bent and picked it up. The old man said aluminum was worth something. As far as he was concerned, he had the three objects the old man insisted on him finding.

Laslo made his way down the slope where he had last seen the old man. He passed a group of scavengers. One of them shouted at him. *"Di mo 'to territorio."*

Clutching his finds possessively, he backed away. He had breached some unspoken territorial rule. He moved quickly back to where he had come from and in his haste to get away bumped hard against a bent figure, who grunted in protest. Laslo apologized without looking at the man, he was in a hurry to find the old man.

On realizing the old man had somehow disappeared from sight,

Laslo wanted to howl with frustration. He found an empty can of paint and sat on it. He could not begin to think of where to look for Luis Bayani. The old man had simply wasted his time. In his anger he threw the plastic bottle and aluminum can in front of him and was about to hurl the piece of polystyrene away when a familiar voice addressed him.

"Wasting the fruits of your labor, Laslo?"

He felt his heart leap. He looked up and there before him was the figure of Luis Bayani. For one moment, he wanted to rush to the student leader and hug him. Luis Bayani studying him with a hint of a smile in his eyes was the most welcome sight Laslo had seen on this, the longest day of his life.

"Really, Laslo, you learn to find such valuable things and now you throw them away."

"It was you I was really looking for, you know."

"But I was always here, Laslo. I was right next to you when you were speaking to old Mang Serio. And you bumped into me just now, but didn't stop to look, just apologized and rushed off. It's all about seeing, Laslo."

Then, motioning to Laslo to follow him, Luis Bayani made his way down the mountain. "You need to wash up I think, this place does need getting used to. You need to get some food into you, too."

"There is no time." And with that Laslo poured his tale out to Luis Bayani, who listened with a grim expression.

"There is even less time than I believed. We must leave while it is still dark."

"Were you expecting someone to show up?"

"I was hoping someone would. I was giving it till the morning. Which was why they were watching out for you—not you specifically, just for someone—to come."

"I've never been here before. But someone showed me to—"

Luis shook his head. "Someone followed you, you mean. Everyone here knows everyone. That man was a stranger. They were ready in case he caused trouble."

"They?"

"The people who live here. They are very territorial and protective of their kind."

"But you're not one of them."

Before Bayani could answer, they arrived in front of a small shanty made of planks of plywood, corrugated iron, and pieces of plasterboard. Luis gave the low-hanging door a push and it creaked open. He motioned for Laslo to enter. Laslo ducked his head and stepped inside, where he found himself in a room that was no more than three square meters in area. He also found himself staring at a familiar bent shape.

"Aaah . . . I see you have found what you have been looking for."

It was the old man from the garbage heap. And seeing the surprise in Laslo's face, he cackled, then turned his eyes to Luis Bayani. "What have you decided, my friend?"

Luis Bayani raised his hand and touched the old man's shoulder. "I must go, Mang Serio, while it is still dark." And he passed on Laslo's tale about the grenade thrower and what Sophia had heard.

"I have to act quickly for her sake and for the movement's. Besides, you can't hide me forever. Laslo was followed here."

The old man nodded; then pointing to a pail of water, he told them to wash. "There's food on the table, you two must eat before you leave." With that, he left them alone.

Over a simple meal of coarse rice and salted eggs, Luis continued their earlier conversation. "I come here a lot. I spend time with them, Laslo. I listen to them. To old man Serio, whom I call the Philosopher of the Mount. He likes that name. Earlier you said I am not one of them. You are right. But it doesn't mean I cannot listen to them.

"I first came here on one of those field trips the priests organized back in high school, in my senior year. And I never forgot those four hours we spent here. One part of me wanted to leave. The other part wanted to see more. An ambivalence of feeling not dissimilar to when you see a fatal road accident. You cringe at the blood and signs of mutilation, but you move closer to get a better look. The image haunts you. We boarded the bus and returned to the campus, but I took with me the sight and smell of this place.

"It was the memory of that visit that made me apply for a place in the economics department at the Loyola. I believed that by understanding the economics of poverty I could change things. But I soon realized this wasn't enough. I needed to know the workings of the law. For what you see here is institutionalized poverty. Our laws promote poverty.

"The problem feeds on itself. A prolonged experience of poverty convinces the poor there is no other life. That they should accept their lot. When I started YRM, one of our projects became the establishment of a community center. We use the center as a meeting place. We hand out medicine, provide free legal aid, and more importantly, we plant new ideas. Instead of silent acceptance, we encourage the people to take control of their lives, to speak out."

"I've never been to it . . . the community center."

"I now. Sophia wanted to involve you. But I said to her you would arrive at that decision in your own time."

Then Laslo asked, "Where do we go from here?"

"We will leave together but we must part ways."

"Why?"

"Laslo, I do not know what lies ahead after we leave here. There may be men waiting for me out there. It is safer for you not to be in my company. I will contact you when I need you next. Meanwhile, you must return home where you will be safe. No. Do not take offense. If I had a father who could protect me today, I would be very thankful. You look surprised, Laslo. Did you make me out to be a hero? I, too, want to live."

Luis Bayani rose and began clearing the table, but the old man came in and told him not to waste time. Five minutes later, the three of them stood by the door. "May these old eyes see you again, Luis," the old man said.

Luis Bayani held the old man's hands in his and thanked him for his kindness. The old man then turned to Laslo. "You must think of this night as the night you learned to use your eyes, eh? Go with God, both of you, and return when you can."

The old man stepped back into his shanty and in a moment the two departing figures were no more.

* * *

They kept to the shadows, away from the moonlit paths. They wove their way in and out of the narrow maze of lanes with its mishmash of shanties standing side by side in countless rows. While they made their way through this confusion of shapes, their progress was unimpeded. But both men walked with thumping hearts. The farther away they moved from the slums, the greater the danger grew. They agreed to walk together, each fearing the moment of parting, but both knowing it would be soon.

"Before we reach the main road, Laslo, we must part ways."

Luis explained that once they hit the open road where darkness could no longer hide them, the hunt, if there was to be one, would begin. So before then, they would need to take separate routes. Luis would turn left two streets before the main road. Laslo would take the opposite direction.

They walked in silence. Feeling the soft breeze which had started to blow. The night had cooled. Even the air smelled different. After a while, it began to drizzle.

"Rain. It's harder to hunt in the rain," Bayani said to himself.

As he finished speaking, thirty meters from the main road, half a dozen figures emerged from the shadows. They had come sooner than he expected. Before he could call to Laslo, Bayani found himself thrown to the ground, and as he made to rise he caught sight of Laslo a meter away from him, two men holding on to either side of him while a third came at him with a rocklike fist. Laslo would have crumpled had not the two held him up. Before the third man could come again at him, Laslo raised his leg and put all the force he could muster behind it. The man fell to the ground, groaning in pain, his hand over his groin. It was the man who had accompanied him to Smoky Mountain.

With a strength born of fear and desperation, Laslo twisted free from his two captors and flung himself against the three that grappled with the student leader. One attacker slipped on the wet ground but still the men outnumbered the two students.

Then a light in an upstairs window went on. The attackers hesitated long enough for their captives to break free.

"Run! Luis, run!"

The student leader, after a brief glance at Laslo, broke into a run. Three men gave chase while the remaining two grabbed Laslo once more. Laslo shouted as loud as he could, his voice ringing in the silent street. More lights came on but before anyone could come to his aid, his captors hauled him into a car. The door slammed shut, the engine came to life, and the car sped away into the night.

Luis Bayani, running in the rain, ran blindly—his glasses had been smashed earlier in the street scuffle. He ran across the main street, and before his pursuers could follow, a passing bus blocked their way. Once across, Luis Bayani took the first corner open to him. The rain pelted down and he could not tell from the sound of its fall what other sounds it muffled behind him. But he ran as fast as his feet could take him, staying away from the lit areas that would betray him.

He turned left then turned right then ran the length of another block, always keeping his choices random. He ran as though chased by the devil and knew not in which direction he was heading. His hopes rose as the rain fell harder, like a heavy curtain, making seeing harder. But the sound of an upturned bin rolling behind him told him his pursuers had not lost him. He glanced over his shoulder and saw the shimmering figure of a man as he passed under a street-light. They were near.

Just as he made up his mind not to look back again, just to keep running, he heard a loud bang resound through the rain. And not until he felt the sudden, searing pain in his shoulder, did he realize a bullet had found him. He clutched at the throbbing spot, while continuing to stumble through the wet streets that were now beginning to flood, the water rushing toward him, so he had to fight against its flow. The pain grew worse and his shoulder oozed a warm liquid he knew was his blood. Then another loud bang went off and this time a similar pain shot through his leg and he stumbled and fought to stay on his feet.

He heard the men moving closer now and his feet sprang into life, carrying him and his pain. He passed a group of garbage bins and kicked them with his good leg, losing his balance, for his other leg could hardly support him. He righted himself as the metal bins rolled across the street behind him and he kept running. He turned a corner and kept going. All the while his shoulder pulsed with increasing pain and his leg threatened to give way under him.

He gasped for breath and made for a shadowy wall that stretched along one side of the street. He knew he was losing precious time but the pain in his leg had taken hold. He clutched at the rough protrusions of the wall to keep himself from falling. He felt the blood draining from his face and knew any moment he would faint. Then suddenly his foot caught at the edge of a crack and he found himself slipping through. The wall fell away, and he clawed at empty space. He stumbled forward and the world around him began to spin and he saw the ground come up to meet him.

As the world faded before him, the last things he remembered were the shape of a woman standing somewhere before him and the sensation of water on his face followed by a flash of blinding white light. Then his pain finally claimed him and all was as black as night.

25

❧

The Longest Night

So it was that Luis Bayani came into my life. But I didn't know who he was then. All I knew was we needed to get him to safety, to hide him in the convent.

We carried him in the rain. The younger and stronger of the nuns and myself carried him through the soggy grounds; all of us drenched to the skin, struggling with his deadweight.

In the weak light of that wet night, I glimpsed his face as he passed in and out of the shadows. It was pale, like death, and I feared we were carrying his lifeless body. For I knew by then that the two loud bangs I heard had been the sound of guns being fired.

We carried him as far as the small room at the end of the connecting passage that led to the chapel. It was the room the chaplain used on the rare occasions he stayed at the convent. We laid the man out on the narrow cot, the springs of the cot giving under him.

Under the fluorescent light, his pallid face and the sight of his blood roused our fears once more. Then Mother Superior felt for his pulse and announced: "He is alive."

Meanwhile, I went to work. I needed to identify him. I searched his shirt pocket. It was empty. With the help of Sister Luisa, I managed to lift him slightly and quickly reach into his pants pocket. I was luckier this time, it yielded his wallet. I looked through this hoping to come across something that would identify him. I found his wet and crumpled *cedula*. As I unfolded and read it, I heard Mother Superior say, "Sister Luisa, call for an ambulance quick."

I looked up at that moment and told her, "No. No ambulance. He must stay here."

"What are you saying, Clara? This man is bleeding to death!"

I handed the man's *cedula* to Mother Superior. She read the name and I saw her start. Then she handed the document to Sister Luisa, who stared at it, taking a while to place the name before raising her eyes in recognition.

"Whoever shot him," I explained, "will still be looking for him in this area. So we can't call an ambulance. We can't take him to a hospital either, it's where they'll look next. He has to stay here."

Sister Luisa said, "But we may lose him, Clara."

I thought about what she said. And I thought about Luis Bayani's chances outside these walls. He was still safer here.

"We'll have to pack the wound. Tight. Then go and find a doctor."

"In this rain, Clara?"

"I'll go," I told her.

We worked through the next two hours. The nuns with their limited first-aid knowledge and emergency supplies, and I with my forced courage, for I hated the sight of blood no matter how many times I have seen bullet-riddled corpses or the mutilated bodies of accident victims.

So I forced myself to look at his wounds, to touch the flesh around them. He was bleeding profusely. The thin mattress drank up his blood and the air smelled of it. The fabric around his wounds was wet and sticky. As we cut around it and lifted it off his skin, he moaned softly, and all three of us froze as if keeping still could cancel his pain. But there was no time to lose. He was losing blood fast. We cleaned the angry gaping flesh quickly.

There is no sight as offensive as violated flesh. A gunshot wound leaves a hole with the flesh around it swollen and the rim turned out, daring one to look inside. Looking at Luis Bayani's wounds, I felt an anger that was almost uncontainable. What gave a person the right to do this to another? To me, those wounds represented the ultimate act of negation of another human being. I was offended by the sight of them. How the others were feeling I could not tell. All I knew was that my anger got me through those terrible hours of working with blood and violated flesh.

We made things up as we went, depending on our instincts and our prayers. And when we were done, we still could not rest. I walked to the window and stared at the rain pounding on the ground and I wondered where I could go in search of a doctor. If I or the nuns knew of any, I could simply have called one. But none of us had ever been sick enough to need one, and calling a hospital was out of the question.

Mother Superior came to stand beside me. "Clara, you cannot go out in this rain, wait for it to ease. And as you said, they could be looking for him around here, so your going out now will draw too much attention."

I said nothing, for although what Mother Superior said made much sense, I worried as to whether Luis Bayani could last the night. I went to stand by the bed and gazed down at him. His face matched the color of the sheet and gave me no reassurance whatsoever.

"I will stay and watch him," I told the nuns. "Go back to bed and I will call you if I need anything."

Before they left, Sister Luisa handed me a towel and made me change into some clean dry clothes. Then I returned to the chaplain's room, where I drew the curtains shut in case someone managed to breach the convent walls—the same way Luis Bayani had—and looked through the window. I turned on the small lamp and shut off the ceiling light. Then I drew a chair close to the bed, where I sat and watched Luis Bayani.

He was running a temperature now, perhaps from his exposure to the rain, although I suspected it was from the bullets that still lay embedded in his flesh. I hoped the bullets were not of the variety which bored through flesh then exploded once inside, causing irreparable damage to bone and tissue. I have seen the damage these do. The city morgue is full of their victims.

I shifted the ice packs Sister Luisa had prepared, setting them more securely over his wounds. As I said, we were making things up. We hoped these would help stop the bleeding. We didn't know if what we were doing was right. Hopefully, it would do him no harm.

As I sat waiting for the night that seemed to go on forever to pass, I planned what I would do come morning. I would try to get Mel at home before setting out to find a doctor. I needed to find out what was going on. Obviously the protest march had ended in disaster. All day long, I had been unaware of anything outside my own affairs. I had failed to pay attention to the news that day, not even to the evening report. But then, knowing what had happened would still not have prepared me for Luis Bayani's coming. How could it?

I had the distinct feeling that I was being drawn into the heart of a whirlpool, into something big and unpredictable, and that I had no choice and no power to fight it. I felt that any resistance on my part would be futile, for I was destined to see the whole thing through. The thought scared me at the same time that it filled me with a sense of awe. For at no time have I sensed the presence of a force, a greater intelligence, directing my life as much as I did in that moment. How else could I have explained what I had gone through in the last few hours? And if there was anything I could be certain of in those very uncertain moments, it was this: the coming of Luis Bayani had somehow determined the path I was to travel in life; and whatever else might happen, I would never again sit on that stone bench in the cemetery without recalling that night.

Laslo, too, would have memories of that night to last him a lifetime.

For many years afterward, he would find himself screaming on hearing the familiar strains of that melody, and hearing the name Rachmaninoff would be enough to send him hurtling back into his dark nightmare. For those terrible hours at the detention center would never leave him, and the face and hands of the man called Aure would continue to haunt his dreams.

On being brought back to the center very late that night, Laslo demanded to use the phone. His demands were ignored. He was immediately led away and taken deep into the building. Down where there were no windows. And where the walls were sound-proof. Where you could scream all you liked and no one would hear. Where even footfalls were muffled.

The eerie silence was the first thing Laslo noticed. It was the only thing he could hear. That is, until they led him down that last long corridor at the end of which stood a slightly open door. As they neared the room, Laslo heard music playing. Not the piece that he would forever remember, but another.

One of his captors pushed him inside the room and shut the door behind him. He stood in the center of the rectangular windowless space. There was a cot against the far wall. And in the center of the room were two chairs facing each other. Laslo slumped into the chair facing the door.

He smelled of Smoky Mountain still. And he was soaking wet. His clothes clung to his skin. And his hair had curled into tight rings. At that moment, he wished for nothing more than to be clean, dry, and warm again.

His glance returned to the cot. He thought of pulling the sheet off to wipe himself. He rose and reached for it, then drew his hand back. The sheet was stained with old blood. It suddenly felt chillier inside the room. He took a deep breath. He felt closed in.

Laslo walked back to his chair. His wet jeans heavy against his thighs. He curled his toes inside his squishy shoes. It was cold in here. Maybe it was just him. He rubbed his arms to keep warm.

He waited. His mind jumping from Sophia to Luis and back again. His only hope now was his father. How he wished he had not let Sophia persuade him, that he had gone directly home and spoken to his father. Then he would not have unwittingly betrayed Luis's whereabouts. He was glad now that Luis Bayani had not told him of his next destination. For he knew this was why he, Laslo, had been brought back to the camp. They believed he knew where Bayani had escaped to.

The music faded to its final note and Laslo heard the door open. He rose from his chair, expecting to see one of his earlier interrogators. But the man who entered was a stranger, and he was followed by a soldier who remained standing by the door after it had shut.

The man was dressed in an officer's uniform that was so neatly pressed it looked as though it had just been put on. He also noted the man's carriage. How he stood with his back straight. Very erect. How his steps were deliberate. But rigidity was not what defined him. What held Laslo spellbound was the graceful movement of his hands. They were beautiful, so fluid in motion. And Laslo was to see those hands at work throughout the coming hours.

As Laslo watched the officer, the officer, too, watched Laslo. And when the man spoke, a worm of apprehension curled in Laslo's stomach.

"Aure. My name is Colonel Santiago Aure."

It was like a cold wind. That voice. A cold wind that blew into the room. It had a detached quality to it. An otherness that was disturbing. Although the colonel's voice was soft and gentle, it made Laslo think of ice.

"I see you do not know of me. But I know of you, Laslo."

Laslo blinked and swallowed painfully, feeling the sudden constriction in his throat. He found it hard to think in the presence of this man, who elicited from him a strange and disquieting fascination.

"The music. It is no longer playing. Did you like the piece, Laslo?"

Laslo nodded in confusion. Why this talk of music? He wished to get down to the heart of it. Of his detention. He wished the night to be over.

"I had them play it for you," the colonel continued. He motioned to the chair behind Laslo. "Please sit down, Laslo."

The colonel took the chair opposite Laslo, raising his hand to summon the soldier as he sat down. "The music. Play it . . . but not too loud, as Laslo and I will be speaking. And yes," he said, waving his hand at the soldier, "you can wait outside."

The soldier disappeared behind the door and it clicked shut once more. A few seconds later, the music returned. The colonel spoke, his voice a soothing commentary over the piece.

"It's by Rachmaninoff. But it's . . . it's very different from his usual somber pieces. You know Rachmaninoff? Good. Then perhaps you know something of his nature. He was, they say, a chronically depressed man. But this composition of his is different. The explanation lies in the fact that this music is based on someone else's creation. Niccolo Paganini. Paganini wrote an étude for solo violin. Rachmaninoff then took these twenty-four measures and created one variation after another. This one we're listening to now is the seventeenth. The eighteenth, of course, is the most famous. You will recognize it, I am sure."

He lapsed into silence after this. And Laslo watched, mesmerized, as the colonel began to move his hands, seeming to draw the music from thin air, like a magician. Then he began to speak once more, his voice sitting above the melody.

"Paganini's theme was turned upside down by Rachmaninoff. From it he created gavottes, minuets, fantasias, and little marches. Quite impressive. But the light in him failed to hold out against the pull of the dark that had always resided in his soul. So he made room for it. For the darkness. Listen," the colonel said, his hand pausing in midair.

Laslo held his breath, hearing not the music but his madly beating heart.

"Listen carefully, Laslo, and you will recognize the strains of the *Dies Irae*. There! Hear that? You see, the composer took music from the Roman Catholic mass for the dead and blended it with Paganini's melody to create a masterpiece. An interesting fact, don't you agree?

"Tell me, Laslo," said the colonel, leaning closer to the student, their faces almost touching, "tell me, what kind of man could take something so dark and gloomy and fuse it with light?"

Without waiting for an answer, the colonel continued. "A genius of an artist! To be able to blend two opposite natures and arrive at something greater than its parts requires genius."

The selection ended and after a short pause the next piece began. The piece that would reside in Laslo's memory from that night onward.

"Aaaah! The eighteenth variation. I see you know this. I chose wisely."

The colonel shut his eyes and leaned against the back of his chair, his hands moving gracefully once more. Laslo watched with growing unease the man's contained madness. The music played on, soaring notes and all, and the colonel said not a word, lost in the stirring melody that filled the room.

Laslo knew this piece all right but if in the past its magic moved him, it ceased to give him pleasure from that moment onward.

Then the moment he dreaded came upon him without warning. As the piece came to a close, the colonel, in his soft, soft voice said, "Where is Luis Bayani, Laslo?"

His heart in his throat, Laslo gave the only answer possible: "I don't know."

Then as if by some secret signal, the door opened. Laslo looked up to see a soldier enter and behind the soldier came Sophia Ramos-Sytangco and behind her came six uniformed men.

Laslo's eyes locked with Sophia's. And each recognized the other's fear. Sophia, pale and silent, came to stand next to Laslo, who had risen to shield her from the men.

"Ahh . . . Sophia. Sophia who knows *many* things."

Sophia drew a sharp breath and Laslo, feeling her tense behind him, reached for her hand and clasped it tightly. An action that drew a knowing smile from the colonel.

"How rude of me not to introduce myself to you, Sophia."

Sophia shivered as the man's voice caressed her name.

"I am Aure. Colonel Santiago Aure."

She gave a start. "The butcher of the south!" Sophia blurted out.

The colonel's face beamed with pleasure. He shifted in his chair. "You have heard of me, I see, but what you hear is not true. Butcher I am not. I am an . . . artist."

Laslo found his voice then. Challenging the colonel, he told him, "Enough of this! What do you want from us? You have no right to detain us."

"Laslo . . . Laslo . . . there is no need for such an outburst. You see, there are places where rights do not matter. And shouting achieves . . . nothing."

He paused. Then continued. Looking at Sophia, he said to her, "But Laslo is right, Sophia, we must not waste time. So help me,

Sophia. Laslo here tells me he doesn't know where Luis Bayani is. Perhaps you can tell me where he is, Sophia. After all, you know many things."

The colonel waited. His eyes on Sophia. When no reply came, he lowered his eyes, then nodded. And the men in the room moved toward Laslo and Sophia.

"Get away from her!" Laslo shouted, backing Sophia against the wall as he struggled to keep the men from her.

But it was a futile fight.

Two men grabbed Laslo and strapped him to his chair. The others went for Sophia. They pushed her down onto the cot. She struggled and cursed at them. They laughed. She made to rise. One of them punched her in the stomach. Hard. She doubled over. They laughed once more. She tried to rise again. A fist sent her head snapping sideways. More. Yes. More. They liked her spirit. It excited them. They licked their lips. Eyes now bright and eager. Appetites whetted by the first bruising contact. Then one of them unbuckled his belt. The sound of ripping fabric followed. And the nightmare began.

Besides the accursed piece of music which played on and on, punctuated by Sophia's screams of anger then of pain and the obscene laughter and grunting of Aure's men, there were a thousand words and images from that night which would return to Laslo unbeckoned in the years to come.

Like the colonel's words on life.

While Laslo sat strapped to his chair, his hands tied behind him, his feet bound by a piece of rope, and his mouth stuffed with his handkerchief, the colonel, in a voice that seemed to come from outside his body, spoke of life.

"Watch, Laslo. Observe human nature. See how Sophia, even while she is robbed of her wholeness or what humans call dignity, continues to fight for self-preservation. As if it is possible to live when one is no longer whole. It is a strange human characteristic.

"I have seen it many times. In other circumstances, of course. I have seen men who have lost, say, a finger, two fingers, still beg to live. A hand, two hands, an arm, maybe a leg, still begging to live.

"It makes for an interesting case study, you know, to see how, when you slice through flesh, cutting deeper, removing bits here, parts there, the subject begs . . . yes, begs to be allowed to live.

"You can remove so much of what makes up the human body, of what defines a human being or human life—and I refer to the physical as well as the psychological—and still the subject stubbornly insists on continuing his or her existence. The subject believes it is possible to go on living in spite of a less-than-perfect state. The subject is totally lacking in the understanding that life must be lived whole for it to be lived as art. When one is no longer perfect, no longer whole in all dimensions, one makes a mockery of life.

"Which poses an interesting topic of debate: where should one draw the line between human life and a lesser form of life? And is the life of this less-than-perfect human specimen worth prolonging? An ethical and relevant question, don't you think? It is something I have pondered on many occasions.

"I have one other question: who is to make the decision of whether life should be granted or denied? The imperfect subject or another party whose vision is not marred?"

And so the colonel went on as his men continued with their business and the windowless room began to fill with the smell of sweat and of sex and of blood. And through it all the sound of Rachmaninoff's music and the sound of the colonel's musings reached Laslo, who could only howl into a piece of soiled handkerchief stuffed in his mouth.

When at last the men finished with Sophia, the colonel rose from his seat. The men drew back and watched with interest as he approached the cot with the rumpled sheet where the woman now lay whimpering, curled up like a fetus. They watched with bated breath, knowing the best, the unexpected, was yet to come. This was the colonel after all. They watched him closely as he gazed at the woman. Watched him bend close to whisper in her ear.

"Sophia . . ."

Her eyes flew open on hearing his voice. She drew a quick breath.

In a soft, gentle voice, he said to her, "Tell me your heart's desire, Sophia, tell me, do you wish to live?"

Laslo, mouth gagged, tried to speak. The colonel glanced at him, saying, "Listen carefully, Laslo, I am about to reveal the truth of my words."

He spoke to her once more. "Sophia, tell me your heart's desire."

In the silence of that room, Sophia's words came softly but clearly. "I don't . . . want . . . to die."

The colonel slowly shut his eyes, savoring her words, and a smile formed on his lips. He opened his eyes and looked across at Laslo. "How interesting, Laslo, that Sophia should define living as not dying. You see, once reduced to this imperfect state, the desire to live is nothing more than a fear of dying."

He bent over Sophia once more. His voice suddenly stern, he passed judgment on her. "You are no longer perfect, Sophia."

Then shaking his head gently, his voice filled with regret, he said to her, "I'm afraid I cannot let you live."

Hearing this, Laslo gave a violent twist of his body, the sudden movement causing his chair to topple. Lying on the floor, tied to his chair, unable to help Sophia, Laslo watched Aure's hands at work.

Gently, like a lover, he gathered Sophia's hair away from her face. As one man raised her head, and the others pinned her down, the colonel parted her long hair in equal parts, on either side of her head. With graceful movements, he combed out the tangled strands with his long fingers. Then, he carefully twined the two sections around her neck, making them cross and cross again, pulling tighter each time, until at last Sophia understood.

She tried to scream or perhaps to beg once more or to gasp for breath to last her forever, it is not clear, for the colonel, at the exact moment the music soared, pulled the ends of her hair, pulled them so tight that Sophia's eyes widened and her body for a brief moment went rigid before slowly letting go, letting go of life, as the music died.

When it was all over, Laslo remained on the floor. He recalled the door opening. But perhaps he only imagined this. Imagined that a soldier came in with a basin of water and a white towel draped over his arm. Imagined that the colonel raised his hands and dipped them into the water, then lifted them up once more. Imagined that the colonel wiped his hands dry. Perhaps he imagined this and imagined all that went on before this. He prayed he imagined it all. And prayed he could imagine himself away from here.

The judge sat up in his bed and, seeing his wife still asleep, eased himself off the bed. He put on his slippers and quietly let himself out of the room.

In the hallway, outside his room, he stood stock-still. Listening. There. There it was again. That sound. Surely, he would have heard if Laslo had come in that night. He had checked the boy's room twice in the small hours of morning but it had been empty. Laslo was probably in the camp with the other students arrested that day.

Then the sound came again. A soft keening.

He walked toward Laslo's room. He pushed the door open and entered. The curtains were half-drawn. And from the light of a street lamp he saw the empty bed. He turned to go. But he heard the keening sound once more. It came from a shadowed corner of the room.

The judge stepped closer. As his eyes adjusted to the dark, he made out the huddled shape of his son. Laslo sat on the floor with his legs drawn against his chest, his arms about them as he rocked back and forth, softly weeping.

The judge got down next to the boy and shook him by the shoulder. But Laslo's weeping only grew louder and his shoulders began to shake and his rocking grew more violent.

His keening brought his mother into the room. With her help, the judge lifted their son and guided him to his bed. There Laslo fell into a tormented sleep. In his dream he was nailed to a chair in a windowless cell where a man with beautiful hands pulled music out of thin air and a woman turned around and around so that her long hair twined about her neck as she danced the dance of death.

In his sleep, Laslo muttered fragments of a terrible tale. The tale filled the judge with revulsion and he found the very act of breathing painful. Seeing his horror mirrored in his wife's face, he sent her away. When the music played once more in Laslo's mind and he screamed out loud and thrashed in bed, the judge gathered his son in his arms and held him tight the way he used to when Laslo was a child. And in this way, he impatiently waited for morning to come.

26

Unexpected Visitors

Morning brought the unexpected.

I did not leave early as planned. Luis Bayani, on waking, caused his wounds to bleed again. The blood seeped through the bandages in no time. And its cloying smell filled the air. As we battled to stem the flow, Luis Bayani, conscious of the pain now, kept his eyes shut and seemed to turn even paler, if that was possible.

With my hands sticky from his blood, it was hard to work on the dressing. I wiped my hands on my jeans, smearing it an angry red. It was an unfortunate thing to have done, for just then a novice burst into the room, wide-eyed and breathless as she delivered her unwelcome news.

"Clara! There are men outside. They have come to search the convent."

I felt myself go cold inside. I shot Luis Bayani a look. He, too, had heard.

"Where are they? How many?" Sister Luisa asked urgently.

"Five, maybe six. I asked them to wait. Said I would go and get Mother Superior. I came here first. I must get her now. You must move him somewhere safe." Before the novice left, she said, "Clara, you must change, there's blood on your clothes."

I looked down at my jeans as the door shut after her. Sister Luisa and I exchanged looks. Then she said, "I'll get you something to wear." She left the room and I pressed the doorknob to lock it.

I shut my eyes and took some deep breaths to calm myself. One. Two. Three. Slowly. Until my heart stopped racing and my head began to clear.

He spoke then, his voice weak.

"I will . . . walk . . . if you . . . help."

I opened my eyes and met his.

"No. You're too weak and you're bleeding. You have to be carried."

This was easier said, of course, for there was no one around to help me carry him. Needing to do something, I began to pick up the towels and spare sheets, bandages, and other things that we had left in the room the night before. We couldn't afford to leave any telltale sign of Luis Bayani's presence. While I moved about the room, my hands busily grabbing at things, my mind was frantically searching for a way to move Luis Bayani himself. Just then I heard frantic knocking on the door and I felt my heart in my throat until a soft voice said, "Clara, it's me."

I breathed out to ease the pressure in my chest and quickly unlocked the door to let Sister Luisa in. She thrust some clothes into my arms. "Put this on. Quick. It's all I could find. Mother Superior's delaying as long as she can but it won't be long."

As I put on the clothes she gave me—I put the white habit straight over my shirt and bloodstained jeans, which I folded at the legs—I thought aloud. "The chapel, the altar cloth will hide him, but we'll need two of them. It is the only place, for the other end of this passageway takes us to the foyer where the men are. But we're going to need help. We can't carry him."

Sister Luisa shook her head. "There's only you and me. There's no time to get help."

We looked at each other. Then we approached the bed, both taking a deep breath to give us the strength we would need. Luis Bayani helped as best as he could. Straining to stand in spite of his wounds. But he was so weak and could barely lift his head. As for Sister Luisa and I, we only managed to support his back for a brief while before he fell back on the bed, releasing a long sigh as his strength gave out. I felt our hopes die.

The silence of despair is a palpable one. The three of us felt it. The hopelessness of our situation. I looked at Sister Luisa, whose eyes were bright with tears of frustration. At Luis Bayani, who returned my gaze with cloudy eyes. I wondered what his thoughts were as he waited for the men to come. I wanted to tell him how sorry I was to fail him. That I didn't have the strength to carry him to safety. I was angry at my inability to do more for him. Had it been left to me to determine the outcome of the moment, I would have made him disappear from that room and kept him from harm forever.

I realized in those seconds of silence that I had accepted Luis Bayani as my responsibility. Not just me, but Sister Luisa as well, and all the nuns in the convent who had carried him through the rain into this room, who had touched his blood, who had cared for him. I realized, too, the truth in something I had read long ago: we become responsible for those whose lives we save.

Then we heard the sound of approaching footsteps.

I drew a deep breath and both Sister Luisa and I stepped closer to the bed, our bodies shielding Luis Bayani. Together we turned to face the door, which I realized too late I had forgotten to lock after Sister Luisa's return. The footsteps stopped. And a second later, the door opened. The novice entered, and behind her I saw a face I never thought I would see again, or be so glad to see if I did.

I found myself face-to-face with my father.

The look on the don's face was indescribable. A mixture of disapproval, astonishment, and heaven knows what else. But I was not about to explain why I was in a nun's habit. Nor was I about to waste time asking why he was here in the room with us.

"Help us carry him," I said to him, pointing to Luis Bayani.

He looked at the figure on the bed, and I could see him taking stock of the situation, trying to make sense of it, as to who this man was and what he was doing in that room, and how I and the nuns were involved in this.

"They'll find him," I said. "They'll find him if we don't move him."

"Who is—"

I told him. And saw the shock on his face. "How on earth—"

"Later! There's no time to lose now," I said, cutting in. "Just carry him away before they find him!"

The don did not budge. Sensing my temper was about to get the better of me, Sister Luisa quickly stepped forward and in a soft, pleading voice said, "Please, sir, please . . . they will kill him." She was unaware of his identity.

The don hesitated.

"Where to?" he finally asked, his voice cold and distant.

"The chapel . . . under the altar," I told him.

If this surprised him, he did not show it. He waved us aside. The don is a tall, commanding man. And strong. He lifted Luis Bayani while Sister Luisa opened the door.

"Clara!" he called to me, indicating with a turn of his head that I was to follow him.

I shook my head, saying, "I have to clear this room." The don's eyes took in the blood-soaked sheet Luis Bayani had been sleeping on. I tugged at it and to my dismay found that the thin mattress underneath was stained as well.

"Clara, use the bedspread!" Sister Luisa said.

As I ran to the chair to pick up the old woven cover, I said, "Go! I'll follow." I looked up and saw the don still standing near the door, hesitating and looking at me with a frown on his face. "I won't be long. *Please* go now!" I begged.

Finally he moved but not before saying, "Open the window, Clara, clear the air."

With that, he left at last with Luis Bayani in his arms and Sister Luisa leading the way to the chapel. Meanwhile, I straightened the bedspread then did as the don said. I flung the curtains apart and pushed the window wide open, hoping to clear the air of the smell of blood.

The men, six of them, accompanied by Mother Superior, came into the chapel a few minutes after I joined the don and Sister Luisa.

Mother Superior addressed the don as soon as she entered the chapel.

"I am sorry not to have been able to show you around, Don Pellicer; as I explained earlier, these gentlemen here"—she paused at this point to glance at the six men who stood some distance away from our party—"these gentlemen you met at the lobby have come to search the grounds for some escaped criminal. But Sister Clara will explain the convent's project to you. She has been helping me with the plans."

The don smiled at Mother Superior. "Yes, she has. I have seen the west wing and I will be most happy to help with its renovation. As for this chapel, installing new windows is not a problem."

Then the don turned to the men, saying, "And have you searched the grounds well?"

The men smiled and shuffled on their feet, and one of them, their leader perhaps, spoke up. "We have searched everywhere, sir, only the chapel remains to be checked."

With a wave of his hand, as if dismissing the men, the don said in an intimidating and imperious manner, "The convent is safe, then. This chapel is as good as checked by me."

He turned his back on the men and faced me, making it clear to them that the matter was closed as far as he was concerned. "Now, Sister, what is this about a new altar?"

"That's right, Sister, explain the problem with the altar to the don." Then, with a conspiratorial glance at the men, Mother Superior said, "We may yet convince the don to replace it."

The men returned her smile, flattered that they were included in the discussion that involved the powerful don.

Together, the don and I walked toward the altar, where Sister Luisa was busying herself, straightening the altar cloth that reached to the ground. Which on closer inspection revealed itself to be made of two separate cloths so that all sides would be covered all the way down.

While we talked, the men kept their distance, the don with his haughty air preventing them from approaching the altar. And after a while they took their leave of us. The don nodded to them in his civil yet aloof manner. Then Mother Superior led them out.

* * *

The don glared down at me from his great height.

I sat slumped on the front pew in the chapel. Still in my nun's habit. As soon as the men had left, the don carried Luis Bayani upstairs to my room. It seemed safer there than leaving him downstairs, where anyone roaming the grounds could see him through the window. Sister Luisa and the other nuns tended to him. He was bleeding again, and was feverish and disoriented.

The don and I returned to the chapel, of all places, to have it out.

I owed him an explanation. So I told him everything that transpired from the night before. He listened in silence. When I finished telling my tale, I told him, "You must find a doctor and bring him here."

"That is a wanted man you are harboring in this convent. You cannot be so foolish as to want to be involved in this!"

I couldn't believe his words. "I didn't choose this!" I said. "You make it sound like I did. And as for being involved, I am involved. His blood is on my clothes. If I let him die, it'll be on my hands as well. I cannot uninvolve myself."

"You think you're on some crusade . . . some heroic rescue mission?"

I stood up and faced him. My voice bouncing off the walls of the chapel. "How like you to think this way . . . to consider turning your back on people, on situations that threaten your comfort!" I saw him start on hearing my words, but by then it was too late for me to stop. "But why should it surprise me? You've done it all your life."

Refusing to be silenced by his intimidating look, I continued. "In theory, it is a decision anyone could easily make. Decide not to become involved. But we are not talking about theories and hypothetical situations. In case you have forgotten, up there in my room is a man with two bullets in his body. I cannot just decide to ignore his presence and hope he'll go away. Or perhaps you would prefer that I turn him over to the palace? And that way we can all get on with our lives!"

I wondered what it would take to move this man. It made me furious that I could not find the right combination of words to move him. Could anyone truly be so heartless? So I gave up, but not before saying one last thing.

"One would think," I told him, "that you would have realized by now that your life is no more and no less than the sum total of all your decisions. What have yours been about? You ... you ... and only you!"

"Is that what you think of me?" he said slowly, his face a mask and his tone devoid of all emotion.

I didn't bother answering him, simply turned and made my way up the aisle. But before I reached the chapel door, I heard his voice ring in the vaulted ceiling of the chapel.

"Where the hell do you think you're going?"

Without looking at him, I shouted back, "To get a doctor because you won't!"

Before I knew it, he had charged up the aisle and was gripping me hard on the arm. "Stay here! And change out of that ridiculous costume!" he ordered before striding angrily away.

Standing by the chapel door, I watched him leave. The reluctant don. How he must regret the day he went in search of my mother, for in the process, he found me. And now I have placed him in a situation not to his liking.

He returned two hours later. With him was a silver-haired man of perhaps sixty, maybe older. I showed them upstairs, where the man, who I was sure was a surgeon by the look of his hands, asked for boiled water to be brought up to the room.

"I will need help," he said, looking at the nuns.

"I will help you," I said.

The don looked at me in surprise and gave me one of his censorious looks to discourage me. But I ignored it. I then repeated what I said to the doctor, who studied me with interest. After a while, I saw his eyes light up as his gaze fell on the white streak of hair on my temple. I saw him look at the don. I saw the don return his look, eyes unwavering. Then the doctor said, "Yes, I believe you can do it, young lady."

Before we started, I asked the doctor one question: could he operate under these conditions? I noted, you see, that he had brought with him what I thought were the bare essentials in terms of instruments. I recognized some of them: a scalpel, some clamps, and what looked like a very fine pincer. There was little else besides these.

"I learned surgery in the battlefields during the Japanese Occupation. After that, anything is possible."

I nodded. Satisfied with his answer. And for a brief moment, I caught what seemed like amusement in his eyes.

And so we began—the doctor, the don, Sister Luisa, and myself.

The shoulder wound was the tricky one. It had shattered some bone. It would take a long time to heal and Luis Bayani would never be right in that shoulder again. The bullet in his right leg had missed rupturing a vein by a hairline, but had nevertheless caused much loss of blood.

I watched the doctor work. His hands probing, coming up bloody, probing again, all the while I felt my stomach turning and I fought hard to keep myself from being sick. I must have turned quite green, for I caught the don and Sister Luisa looking at me. I pulled myself together then and handed the doctor another swab.

As for Luis Bayani, the doctor had to stop and administer more local anesthetic midway through the operation. Luis Bayani was never quite far from feeling pain. Through it all, he woke, moaned in agony, and passed out several times. Every once in a while, to reassure and encourage him, the doctor would say, "We're almost there, young man, just hang in there."

I can tell you now that there were many moments back then when I thought I would pass out myself. But the sense of detachment I forced myself to maintain kept me going. That and the don's presence. I felt my father's eyes on me many times through those hours, and I swore I would not show any sign of weakness before him, not after I had stubbornly insisted I could help the doctor.

There would be many attendant problems, the doctor warned us, like infection setting in. His temperature would be a telling factor. Then, of course, the loss of blood had weakened the patient greatly.

Unfortunately, a transfusion was impossible, as the doctor could not access blood from a hospital or blood bank without raising questions.

The last ordeal was watching the doctor put needle and thread through tender flesh. Each prick and each pull brought a soft cry from Luis Bayani, for the anesthetic was wearing out fast and the doctor had no more to give. I felt like screaming with the agony I imagined he was suffering. Toward the end Luis, unable to bear the pain, passed out again, for which I was very thankful. Nevertheless I mopped his head, which was beaded with perspiration. Then the doctor told us we could start cleaning up. So Sister Luisa and I gathered up the soiled swabs, towels, and sheets. And it was with great relief that I heard the doctor say we could leave while he finished up bandaging the wounds with the help of the don.

I ran to the washroom downstairs and rid myself of the bloody gloves. My hands gripping the sink, I kept my head down and took some deep breaths. When I had calmed myself somewhat, I headed for the back door and strode out into the grounds. I felt the warm breeze on my face but I didn't mind it. Anything was better than the overpowering smell of blood and sweat. It had been so hot in my small room where Luis Bayani now lay.

After a while, I heard someone approach and on looking up I found the don walking toward me, a mug in his hand. Sister Luisa must have told him where to find me.

"Drink this," he said in a voice that would brook no objection.

"What is it?" I asked, looking into the mug, at the small amount of red liquid, sniffing it with suspicion.

"Must you always be so stubborn, Clara?" he replied, a sardonic look on his face. "It's wine."

"Wine? Where did—"

"From the chapel, Clara, and with Mother Superior's blessings. Now will you drink it!" he said with exasperation.

I wrinkled my nose and drank the sweet liquid, feeling it travel down my throat and warming me. All the time thinking about this complex man whose nature, whose very substance, was made up of atoms of contradictions. The don confused me. He defied any kind of label. For as soon as I thought of him as being one thing, he would act in a way that made me question the soundness of my judgment.

To me he was a moral coward who had abandoned a woman he professed to love because of his family's bloated pride. He was someone who valued reputation far more than his heart's desire. And yet how could a coward be imbued with so much strength, enough to reassure those around him. His very presence had lessened my own fears as we fought to save Luis Bayani. Never in my life had I experienced what it was like to be able to rely on someone, until that day. And though I had thought him heartless many times since knowing him—had even heard him describe himself as such that night in Consuelo's room—he had gone off and found me the doctor Luis Bayani needed. True, he had done so reluctantly, but he had done it just the same. Behind his mantle of pride was his heart. I had caught a glimpse of it today, heard its quiet beating; some part of it had not been smothered by his innate coldness and pride.

So I thanked him at last, my words coming out stilted, for I didn't know how to speak to the don. But my gratitude embarrassed him. So he quickly said, "He is an old friend, he can be trusted," choosing to talk about the doctor instead. Of his own role he was reluctant to talk, so I let the matter rest.

We sat in awkward silence after that, until he spoke again. "I know it is too late to dissuade you from involving yourself, Clara, but I will say this just the same: you must think carefully what you intend to do from here on. You may find that it is more than you've bargained for. And in spite of your stubborn nature—yes, Clara, there is something implacable about you, even now you lift your chin in defiance of me—you are intelligent enough to see why he cannot remain here for long." What he said surprised me, for I could have used the same words to describe him.

I learned from him that he had rung the *Chronicle* yesterday and discovered that I had not been to work at all. He had spoken to someone, a woman, who had refused to give him my home address. So he had come to the convent to learn my whereabouts from the nuns, and found me.

He said he had come to tell me that he was returning south the day after tomorrow. I wondered why he was bothering to tell me this, for I was really no one to him, but I kept my thoughts to myself, remembering in time what he had done for Luis Bayani. The don then told me he would be seeing Consuelo before he left. I understood that they had some unfinished business between them. But if he thought I wanted to know what, I did not ask. My mother with her strange wounds remained absent from my life. And with all that had transpired since last night, I had had no chance to think about her or the don. But now the don was sitting next to me and had claimed my attention once more.

He gazed at the headstones around us, perhaps noticing for the first time where we were. After a while, he said, "This is where you came to play." It was a statement more than a question. It took me aback. Did he desire to know about my life here or had he spoken just to fill the silence? I looked at him for some clue to what he was thinking but his eyes were fixed on the lichen-covered stone angel.

In the end, I said, "Up that tree. I used to climb it." I waited for him to speak once more but he said nothing. Another minute passed and he rose and in a brisk tone said it was time to go. He needed to take the doctor back.

We returned to the convent, neither of us speaking. But as we walked through the quiet corridors of the place that had been my home because he had not been around to give me one, I was aware of him taking it all in. At one point his steps slowed and he paused briefly, becoming very still. I glanced at him and I could have sworn that he had been about to speak but he changed his mind and continued walking on.

I was beside him all this time. And as I made my way through the familiar place, I suddenly saw an image of myself as a child. I was alone and running up and down that same corridor. It was a game I played where I listened to the sound my footsteps made, running harder to make them ring louder. I understood at last what it was I was doing. I was striving to fill the silence, to break it. For the silence signified something I had failed to give a proper name to. "It was very quiet there," was what I told Mel on the only occasion she had dared ask about—and I had deigned to discuss—my childhood. I know now that silence was just another name for my loneliness.

For a brief moment, I allowed myself to think about how different my life would have been had he and my mother been around. Until I realized the foolishness of such thoughts. The past could not be retrieved and changed. And who knows how he would really have acted, what his decisions would have been, had he known about my existence. I would still have been the daughter of a woman not good enough for him. I still am.

We found the doctor drinking a cup of coffee in the kitchen with Sister Luisa and Mother Superior. On seeing us, he said, "I have done what I can, not it's up to the young man to pull through." He told me he would come again tomorrow to check on the patient. I looked at the don, who nodded but said nothing. Then the doctor informed me that he had given Mother Superior his private number in case an emergency should arise.

Mother Superior, the nuns, and I thanked the doctor. Then turning to the don, Mother Superior said, "I don't know what we would have done without you, sir." The don said a strange thing in reply: "It is I who owe you much." Only later would it occur to me he had been referring to the nuns caring for me.

My unpredictable father.

We walked the men to the car. The doctor got in first, all the time giving Sister Luisa and Mother Superior last-minute instructions. Meanwhile, the don reached into his pocket, took out a card, and scribbled something on it before handing it to me.

"You can reach me at this number. Whatever happens, I will get your message." Having said this, he got into the driver's seat and pulled the door shut.

Moments later, I stood by the front steps of the Convent of Santa Clara and watched my father drive away, clutching his card in my hand. I stood there for some time, gazing at the empty space before me while the dust and leaves reclaimed the ground.

I would see the don one more time after that day, before he took himself off to his distant island. The enigmatic don, my father who has the power to fill me with sadness and regret.

27

❧

Eating Fire and Drinking Water

After the don and the doctor had left, I rang the *Chronicle* and spoke to Mel. I told her I had some personal business to attend to and would not be in for a few days. I asked her to tell Torres and the others that I was ill and had gone to stay with friends. I said good-bye to Mel and hung up soon after. Then I made my way up to see Luis Bayani. Let me recount to you my time with him.

He was at the convent for six days. But I will always remember his words even if, with time, I am finding it more and more difficult to recall his features with clarity.

He was a man of impossible expectations who made me feel sad because I knew the world would disappoint him.

"You cannot ask much of people, of life and the world," I told him.

Nevertheless, he opened my eyes and my mind to his dreams. And I would later find myself carrying the burden of his vision. Trying to right the world for his approval. Such was his effect on me, this man who was only a few years older than I was and yet who lived as though there was not enough time to see the world become as he wished.

I was with him the morning he woke. It was two mornings after the doctor extracted the bullets from his shoulder and his leg. In between those times, the nuns and I took turns monitoring his temperature, watching him in his disturbed sleep, giving him water when he asked for it—he seemed incredibly thirsty in his delirious state.

Weak and feverish, he spoke in his dreams. Spoke of the need to move on before it was too late. And on the first night, I heard him say a woman's name: Sophia. I wondered if she was someone special in his life.

The doctor came to see him as promised. Arriving at midday, every day, administering shots to fight any possible infection. He also brought with him bottles of intravenous feed, and with the help of Sister Luisa and myself, he changed Luis Bayani's bandages.

"Unfortunately, he is very weak from all the blood he lost. What he has going for him is his youth. Young bodies have the ability to withstand much abuse. This, of course, goes beyond the normal, but he will weather this, if he can keep still." Saying this, he paused, realizing the impossibility of Bayani remaining where he was. The doctor had worked out his patient's identity. "Well, at least get some sustenance into him as soon as he is strong enough to eat."

Before he left, the doctor told me, "I had a call from the don. He asked after the patient. And you. I said you were still here."

I said nothing to this, just thanked the doctor for coming.

When Luis Bayani finally opened his eyes, I said to him, "You're at the Convent of Santa Clara. The men didn't find you. And a doctor has removed the bullets. You must rest, then you will be all right."

He nodded then looked about him.

"We moved you upstairs," I continued. "It's safer here."

He smiled a weak smile and I heard him say, "Glasses . . . lost them." Another weak smile. "I can't see you. . . . I'm sorry."

"We'll have to try and get you another pair. But now, I better get you some food."

We took turns feeding him.

"Your name?"

"Clara."

"Sister Clara?"

He remembered.

I laughed. "No. I'm not really a nun."

"Why are you here?"

"I started life at the refuge, then I moved here."

"Clara . . . of the Convent of Santa Clara."

I told him he had hit the nail right on the head. That I was named after the convent. Then I told him my story. More or less.

He was a good listener. He was still too weak to talk in those first days, so I did the talking. I told him about life with the nuns, my education, my writing, the *Chronicle* and Torres. But I told him none of what I had learned in the last few days.

On his fourth day at the convent, our roles changed. I listened and Luis Bayani did the talking.

"I spent a summer down south three years ago. If you think what you see in the city is poverty at its worst, you haven't seen anything until you've lived with the *sacadas*.

"We were a group of volunteers on a mission-finding trip organized by a priest. We spent two months living and working with the *sacadas* in one of the haciendas. I was not prepared for what I found in those cramped sleeping quarters nor for the work in the fields. Backbreaking work that begins early and ends late.

"In more prosperous countries, the harvesting of sugarcane is done by machines. Most of the work at the hacienda we visited was done manually. Labor is cheap. It is a vicious cycle. If machines are brought in, then there will be less work for these contractual workers. Yet when they work, they are really no better off. The longer they stay at a hacienda, working under a *contratista*, the deeper they get into debt.

"The first day I worked in the fields I came back sore and tired, my body aching and my hands full of blisters. I could not flex my fingers. Swinging an *espalding* all day made them painfully rigid. I was too shamefaced to wince. Back in the *cuartel*, I pricked the blisters and one of the women applied a special salve on my hand. The following day I went back and worked next to the men. I joined them again the day after, though I would have given the world to stay in bed and sleep my aches away. But I had come to live their life and theirs did not include rest.

"There was a boy in his late teens who worked in the fields. He lived in the second *cuartel*. A shy young man who didn't mix much. He preferred to read in a quiet corner. I never even learned his name. I left him my copy of Rizal's book to read. I hoped it would feed his hungry mind.

"They said he was a boy with ambition. A dreamer. The men shook their heads and said all the reading the boy did would not change his lot. Their acceptance of their life angered me. But I realized anger was a wasted response. These people couldn't see beyond their life, for it was all they ever experienced.

"It's like saying to a man who believes the world is flat: 'Sail on, you will not fall off the edge because the world is round.' The concept of a round world is alien to him, as much as the concept of a better life is alien to these people. It is not their reality.

"At the end of my stay, I returned to the city vowing to help change things. It was one of the reasons why I formed YRM."

When he was through telling his tale, he fell silent, shut his eyes to rest.

I asked which hacienda he had stayed in.

"Hacienda Esperanza, the one owned by the don."

Then he turned toward me, opened his eyes, and looked into mine. "That was the don who was here the morning the men came."

I nodded.

"You know him."

"He is my father."

I told Luis Bayani about my strange history. About Calle de Leon and Charlie. About Consuelo and the don. There was something about him that made me pour out my most secret thoughts and feelings. Perhaps it was the comfort one receives from a stranger that loosened my tongue.

You can bare your soul to a stranger, I think, because you trust him or her not to judge you. And the chances of your seeing the person again is small. So you can speak of the most intimate things yet maintain your distance. But somehow Luis Bayani did not seem like a stranger. So perhaps I told him about my life because I had never met someone who listened so well.

I told him about growing up in a convent and what that meant to me, and to others. I said, "Everyone in the school I went to had a family to go home to, they all lived in a proper house or apartment.

" 'Where do you live, Clara?' How I dreaded that question. Because every time someone asked me that, I would have to answer: 'In a convent.' And the questions, the same questions, would always follow. I was always made to feel someone apart, different, and I still am."

"Even now, Clara?" he asked. I knew he meant now I had found Consuelo and the don.

"Yes . . . even now, I don't belong to them even now," I replied.

"Where are they . . . your parents?"

I told him the don had returned to the south and I doubted I would see him again.

"And your mother?"

I told him I hadn't seen her since the night she told her story, that I wasn't sure we would meet again. "There seems no reason to."

He was very quiet for a while and I thought he had tired himself out speaking with me. But then he spoke again. "There's a YRM member, a few years younger than myself, probably your age, quite headstrong and very reckless. A while ago I told him off for something, and he was ready to storm off. I could have let him go, Clara, but I called him back. I don't know why but I did. What I learned from that was there's always a reason why people are in our lives. He saved mine, Clara. On the day of the protest march, when the riot police came after me, Laslo helped me escape. And he came looking for me again at Smoky Mountain, risking his life once more. I'm not even sure he's aware of what he's done or realized that there's something in him capable of the impossible. I never had the chance to thank him, you know, and I don't even know if he managed to get away."

Hearing him recount this, I thought about how he had been saved by the nuns and myself, by the doctor and even the don. How intertwined our lives were now. Why? I asked myself. If his reasoning was right, to what purpose had we come together?

But going back to the subject of my parents, I found myself shaking my head and saying, "Why now? Don't you think our meeting now is so pointless? Consuelo and the don ... there's no going back for them. It's too late. As for me, at twenty-three, I don't need them anymore; and they have no need for me. I can't see the reason for us meeting after all this time. We're better off washing our hands of each other."

Holding my gaze, Luis replied, "But, Clara, there's no such thing as washing our hands of people and situations."

The following afternoon he said something I have never forgotten. He said to me: "I didn't go looking for this, Clara."

So I learned about his doubts.

"YRM grew, and I had to grow with it. We are seldom conscious of growing into our roles, we just do it."

He paused.

"Now things are moving in a direction I can no longer foresee or plan for. I started out in control. Then the thing took on a life of its own. Now I am simply reacting. Choosing the best of the options available to me.

"The June sixth incident, the Loyola sit-in, and now the grenade explosion. We ... I didn't foresee any of them. And even after each incident, when I thought I could maintain order and discipline, things still went wrong. I no longer control the situation. It has grown bigger than me.

"When I formed YRM, I never imagined it would come to this. But now violence is a reality. No, Clara, I did not go looking for this. And the frightening thing is, there are things that still have yet to be played out."

I kept silent. What could I say to someone who felt his death lay not in some distant time but at any given moment in the immediate future?

*   *   *

"How do you think it will end, then?" I asked him the next day.

We were sitting in an alcove upstairs and the light streamed through the window. He was walking now, although still weak.

"It doesn't end," he replied. "We just see things in a linear fashion. Beginning, middle, and end. But in reality life isn't linear. Look at our history. It's filled with cycles.

"We are a strange people, Clara. We swallow so much of the injustice, hardship, and cruelty our fellow humans mete out to us. Why, we even have an expression for it: 'We can take it.' And we do. We would rather let things go and take all the wrong done to us than do something to correct the situation.

"Then we find ways to defuse the crisis. It's like putting out a fire. Only this fire is inside us. In the belly of this country.

"We can fight fire with water provided we can get it there soon enough. But often we act when it's too late. The result is splattered in the pages of our history: bloodbaths, uprisings, revolutions, you name it. And on it goes. We learn so slowly. After so many centuries, we're still a people who eat fire and drink water."

"Why bother, then?"

"Because we have to believe that one day we'll learn."

On his last night, he changed into the fresh set of clothes the nuns had managed to find for him. He was far from strong but was walking without support. The doctor saw him earlier that day and on hearing of his plan to leave advised him against it. But Luis Bayani was adamant.

"I have stayed too long."

He refused to say where he was headed for. But he told us about Sophia Ramos-Sytangco. As insurance, I think. If something happened to him, the information would not be lost.

Had I reported for work that week, or kept in touch with Mel as I had originally intended, I would have learned something about Sophia. After the detained students were released, Sophia's parents had come forward to ask after their daughter who had failed to return home. Her disappearance was now the subject of much controversy. I learned of all this much later when it was too late to delay Luis Bayani's departure.

He joined the nuns at the dining room for his last meal at the convent. We all prayed together. After dinner, Mother Superior made sure he took his medication before leaving. Sister Luisa checked his dressing one last time. And I gave him all the money I had on me. He thanked me, saying he would find a way to repay me.

"Let me take you where you wish to go, I'll get us a cab." I tried once more to convince him to let me go with him.

"It is not safe, Clara."

In the end, we accepted there was no stopping him. Mother Superior and the nuns said good-bye to him, then Sister Luisa and I walked with him toward the cemetery. Standing in the shadow of the mango tree that night, he thanked us once more. Then he held my hand, squeezed it, and said, "Who knows, Clara, you may write about this one day."

I laughed, trying to keep the moment light, though I was sick with worry. I answered him, saying, "Yes, if you promise to read it."

As he slipped through the crack in the wall, limping as he went, I called out to him softly, "Luis, take care."

My last thought was of his glasses. "He cannot see," I said to Sister Luisa. "I never found him a pair he could use. He cannot see."

She patted my hand to reassure me. "He'll be fine."

Luis Bayani's missing glasses would cause me much distress that night and the night after. I worried that he could not see clearly.

28

Revenge of the Ice Princess

The senator sat at his table at Il Mare and watched an approaching wave gather force. It surged against the craggy rock face then slapped hard against the restaurant's glass wall, leaving a trail of white foamy spray. When the glass was clear again, the senator caught sight of two tankers in the distance heading toward the open sea.

"Can I get you something else, sir?" a voice asked.

The senator looked up and saw the waiter who had showed him to his table an hour ago and who had brought him two Scotch and sodas since. He shook his head and said he'd like to use the phone instead. As he waited, he thought with irritation about the unexpected dilemma he faced.

The senator was not a man who took kindly to having his hand forced. And that was what the dean's surprise visit had done. When he received the call from the dean of the Loyola University requesting an hour of his time, the senator had been puzzled. But it was difficult to refuse him. He, after all, knew the dean personally, had in fact been his student at one time.

The business turned out to be something the senator had no desire to be involved in: the unexplained disappearance of the Loyola student Sophia Ramos-Sytangco. The dean handed him a letter cosigned by the parents of the student and the university officials. He, the senator, was being asked to take up the matter with the palace.

The senator had stared at the document and said it was really not his area of responsibility. What he held was the economics portfolio.

The dean had looked at the senator from across the desk and said, "That is the last thing I expected to hear from a Loyolan, Sixto. Have you forgotten what we taught you? That those who have the advantage of education and power are always responsible?"

Irked by this admonishment yet embarrassed by it, the senator could only say he would consider the matter. The dean had made it clear that such an answer was not good enough. He expected the senator to act on the matter immediately. Before he left, the dean's only words were: "You know there is only one correct course of action . . . this is a moral decision, Sixto, not one of political convenience."

The senator, as he sat in the restaurant thinking about his dilemma, still refused to commit himself. He had never involved himself with this end of politics. As for the students' cause, he had watched it with a kind of detached interest. What surprised him was the rumor that had circulated in the senate soon after the grenade incident. If there was truth to it—as is often the case with rumors involving the government—then the current administration was indeed on shaky ground. Personally the senator felt it was a stupid knee-jerk reaction. One that betrayed the desperate state of mind of the man in the palace.

But just because he knew of these tales and just because he was a former Loyolan did not mean he had to go charging to the palace and confronting El Presidente with the business of the missing student. He had no wish to embroil himself in what was fast turning out to be a highly sensitive issue.

His thoughts were interrupted as the waiter returned with a white portable phone which he set on the table in front of the senator. He needed to call Ana. It was unlike her to be so late.

The senator dialed the studio's number. Ana, he knew, was scheduled to work there that morning. A photo session for a fashion spread. But the photographer informed him in his whining voice that Ana had never arrived. That he tried reaching her at home but her phone was disconnected.

He tried the town house, thinking perhaps she'd mixed her appointments up. Or perhaps she'd slept in, which was just as likely, for she was like a cat when it came to sleep. A recorded message said the number he dialed had been disconnected. He tried again and heard the message play once more. There must be some mistake, he reasoned.

Another fifteen minutes, he'd give her another fifteen. The thought that he would have to leave without taking his lunch irked him. The prospect of going outside so soon did not appeal to him either. It was hot as hell out there. There had been a sudden torrential downpour the night before, but the morning had brought only more burning heat.

He had looked forward to a lazy, long lunch with Ana. Followed by a protracted session of lovemaking. He had booked a suite at the Regent Hotel, just ten minutes away on the boulevard. He decided to ring the Regent and inform them he wasn't coming. As he put the phone down, the waiter returned carrying a note.

"Message for you, sir."

He took the folded note. As expected, it was from Ana. It read: *Ana won't be coming to lunch today. Come home.*

"You were on the phone, sir, when your wife rang. So I took a message instead," the waiter explained.

The senator nodded, smiling at the man's words. Then he asked for the bill and for his car to be brought to the front.

Ten minutes later, he was on his way to Ana's. The weekday traffic was surprisingly light. Perhaps the ferocious heat had discouraged many from stepping out. It did not take long before he found himself on Remedios Street. And three minutes later, Ana's street came into view. He turned in to it. As he approached her town house, he looked for her car. It was nowhere in sight.

Puzzled, he eased the Mercedes into a spot in front of the town house. It was much easier parking the Mercedes than the Lincoln. The Lincoln was for work really. He liked being driven in it, disliked driving it himself. The times he drove the Lincoln to Ana's meant letting the chauffeur off early. The last thing he needed was for the man to know his personal business.

He locked up the Mercedes and walked to the front door of Ana's town house. He rang the doorbell and waited. He rang it once more but still no one came to the door. If Ana was in the shower, where the hell was the maid? He reached for his wallet and took out the key.

The moment he pushed the door open he knew something was amiss. Not just because Ana's hysterical Japanese spitz did not rush to greet him with her usual high-pitched yelping but because before him Ana's usually cluttered lounge room, with its pile of magazines, rows of pot plants, and painting-covered walls, now stood empty.

Everything was gone.

The senator stood absorbing the emptiness. Then he strolled through the empty dining room, the empty kitchenette. His footsteps echoing after him. He climbed the stairs to the bedroom, taking the steps two at a time. On the way up he noted the bare walls with their empty picture hooks.

The door to the master bedroom was ajar. He stepped inside. The carpet was still marked deeply where the legs of the bed, the side tables and dresser once stood. He leaned against the wall, thinking. The mystery of it all filled his mind.

The last time he saw Ana was on Monday. There was nothing about her that evening that hinted at her planned departure. She was her usual sensuous, lusty self. They had agreed to meet for lunch on Thursday. She said fine. I'll write it in my diary. Make it half-past twelve, she said. She was going to a photo shoot in the morning.

He walked into the dressing room. Slid the wardrobe doors open. No clothes there, just bare hangers. He stepped inside the bathroom. Pulled the vanity drawers out. Nothing except for a dusting of powder on the bottom of each drawer.

It was obvious this had not been a hasty departure. Had she met someone else? The possibility intrigued him. For Ana to have a good reason to leave him, the man would have to be far more generous than he was and far better in bed. He found the latter difficult to believe.

The senator let himself out of the town house. The heat greeted him once more. He looked up and down the street. Well, that was the end of that, he thought. He knew he wouldn't be coming back here. He would ring the real-estate agent and see what he could do about the lease.

Inside his car, he caught sight of the note the waiter handed him. He straightened out its creases and read it once more. He recalled the waiter's words to him.

"Your wife left a message."

He looked at the note again. At the words. *Come home.*

Senator Sixto Mijares, unwilling to believe what his mind was suggesting to him, sat back in his car, his thoughts in a jumble. Could it be? No. He pushed the possibility away. But the thought returned once more.

He started the engine and headed for home.

The gardener, who had been weeding the flower bed alongside the driveway, ran to open the gate. The senator drove through quickly, almost sideswiping the man. He left the car in the driveway, not bothering to park it in the garage. He charged into the house and raced up the stairs.

As he neared the top, he slowed down. Thinking. At the landing, he saw a maid enter Lorena's room with a glass of water on a tray. He thought of entering his wife's room but stopped himself. What was he supposed to say? Where is my mistress? What if she didn't have anything to do with it? He made for his room instead.

As soon as the door shut behind, he sat on the armchair facing the bed and bent to remove his shoes and socks. Then he got up and stripped off his shirt. He walked to the air-conditioning unit to turn it on when something caught his eye.

On the bedside table right next to where he stood was the alabaster lamp base that had been next to Ana's bed, the very same one he had bought at the exhibition months ago. His hand came up to touch it. Behind him, the door to his bedroom opened. He turned.

Lorena Zamora-Mijares, dressed for an afternoon of tennis, stood by the door gazing at the senator, whose face resembled a brewing storm. "What took you so long . . . coming home? Didn't you get my message, Sixto?"

Seeing the senator's hand on the lamp, she said, "I thought you'd miss her, so I brought her home for you. Besides, you did pay for her, so she's rightfully yours."

The senator, eyes narrowing dangerously, walked to stand in front of his wife. "Where is she, Lorena? What have you done to her?"

Lorena gave him a lazy smile before turning toward the stairs. Here she paused for a second. "I don't know. Last I saw your mistress, she was screaming . . . in pain."

In a private clinic run by the country's leading cosmetic surgeon, a young woman slept a sedated sleep in one of the six rooms in the two-story building.

It had taken a while to calm her. And understandably so. The woman had been beautiful once. He could tell from the left side of her face, which had been miraculously left undamaged by the acid that had burned the other side.

She had arrived a few days ago accompanied by the sculptor who had designed the centerpiece in the clinic's waiting room. The artist said she was a friend of his, a model he used at times. The woman was in hysterics. And the surgeon, looking at the damage to her face, thought: Who would do this? Who would be so vicious as to damage this beautiful woman? He was a man who appreciated beauty. He was, after all, devoted to creating it.

He eyed the sleeping woman once more, looking closely at the raw marks on her face. At least she had had the sense to splash water on her skin after the unfortunate "accident." But the acid had already eaten into the skin, burning a path from the right side of her face all the way down her neck, where a pearl of some size had melted on contact with the fluid.

"Shall I throw this away, doctor?" his assistant had asked as she held the half-dissolved pearl pendant in the palm of her hand, its gold chain still looped through it. He had been inclined to have her get rid of it but on second thought had her set it aside in case the woman asked for it.

The woman moaned softly. He looked at her more closely and thought about the work he needed to do to restore her face. He shook his head and sighed. He knew that no amount of expertise could restore her original beauty. The skin would always be tight, lacking the suppleness of her original skin. The cost would be astronomical. Skin grafts would need to be made. He would take that from her buttocks. Then he would have to work on the eye area. This would be tricky but not as tricky as her lips.

He explained all this to the artist on his next visit. The man listened carefully, and when the doctor finished talking, he said to him, "Just do what you need to do. And send the bill to Lorena Zamora-Mijares."

The doctor finally understood.

Before the artist left, the doctor handed him the acid-eaten pearl. He took it, placing it in his breast pocket. But on the way to his car he took the tissue-wrapped pendant from his pocket, stared at it, then threw it into the public bin.

"What a waste," he said to himself.

Had Ding Sarmiento known what had happened to the beautiful priceless pearl he had sold to Senator Sixto Mijares, he would have mourned its loss. Just as well then that he would forever remain ignorant of what had transpired between the senator's mistress and his wife.

Ding Sarmiento was having a little celebration with a friend, a precious-stone dealer who had supplied him with the pearls and diamonds that had gone into making the Sarmiento Tiara. The jeweler had spent the last half an hour recounting his palace triumph, down to the very last detail, and was pleased to see his friend looking suitably impressed.

Now, as the jeweler paused to extract an oyster from its shell, the dealer raised his glass and toasted him, saying, "To more palace commissions!"

Ding Sarmiento nodded before popping the oyster into his mouth, relishing its soft silky texture, its juiciness. Then he picked up his wineglass, took a sip of his favorite white, and repeating after his friend, said, "To more palace commissions!"

29

The Judge Acts

While the senator—who had been caught by surprise twice that day, first by the dean of the Loyola and then by his vengeful wife—was busy seeking the truth about his mistress's strange disappearance, the Hanging Judge was about to upset the palace with a surprise of his own.

In order to understand what lay behind the judge's decision, I must take you back to the moment soon after he heard Laslo's tangled tale. Needing to verify what his son had shouted in his sleep, the judge decided to visit an old friend.

The last time the judge had visited his friend's farm was four years ago. It was on the occasion of his friend's fiftieth birthday. Now as he turned in to the narrow dirt road that ran for half a kilometer and led to the farmhouse, the judge noted how the place had changed. The fruit trees were thriving. Mango and *kaymito* and what seemed like a cluster of jackfruit trees lined the road. He told himself he must remember to take some home to his wife.

His friend was waiting for him on the front steps of the farmhouse, a long single-story structure with thatch walls and roof and a bamboo floor. In his farm clothes, standing with his hands in his pockets, the judge's friend had the appearance of a gentleman farmer. Looking at him, the judge could not help comparing himself with his friend. He thought how well the other man looked.

Although now in his mid-fifties, Dante was still in excellent shape. Certainly in better shape than the judge.

"Farmwork must suit you. You look well," the judge said as they shook hands.

"Well, Romero, you should have bought a farm yourself. Sitting in court robs you of exercise. You know, I only come up here on weekends but the work and the air do me a world of good."

"Well, you've always liked the land. The army didn't knock that out of you," the judge replied, adding, "Whereas I have always liked the city."

Dante, the judge's friend, was none other than General Dante Cortez. He and the judge went back a long way. Forty-eight years to be exact. They grew up in the same northern town. Played in each other's backyards. Roamed the fields in each other's company. Fished and sold their catch for pocket money. Eyed the girls together. Even departed for the big city on the same day.

Only after high school did their companionship cease. Dante entered the nation's leading military academy and became a career soldier, while the judge enrolled at the State University and pursued a law degree. But their friendship remained intact. Each man stood as godfather to the other's son.

Their close connection was not a widely known fact, however. General Dante Cortez was the judge's secret contact in the military.

After Laslo's return home on Saturday, the judge had rung the general.

"I don't know if the boy is just raving. He is not himself at the moment."

The general promised to find out what he could. "Meet me at the farm. We can talk there. And a day out in the country will do you good."

Now the general guided the judge toward a shaded area by a rushing stream. "It's been so hot these last few weeks this had nearly dried out. But then after the sudden downpour we had, look at this, so much water."

"Laslo's caught a chill from it. I still can't get the whole story from him. His clothes were damp when I found him in his room. But from what I understood, he was locked up in the camp."

The general sat on a weather-beaten bench, the judge next to him.

"They let him out for a while. Followed him to Smoky Mountain, where Bayani was hiding. Bayani escaped and they still haven't found him. Laslo was taken back to the camp. And that was when it happened . . . the business with the woman."

And so the judge listened to the general's account of the unspeakable events of the previous night. The general spoke without looking at the judge. He looked at the trees and the skies and the birds perched on the branches of trees. As if by focusing his eyes on the natural world, he could lessen the horror of what he was now reporting.

The judge heard the name Aure many times. He heard that Luis Bayani was a prominent figure on the military blacklist. He learned of the bungled attempt to arrest Bayani at the rally, and how Laslo had been set up by Aure to lead his men to Bayani's hideout at Smoky Mountain. He heard his son's mumbled nightmare confirmed. He heard of the assault on a young woman and her eventual murder by Aure himself.

"It's true . . . it's true," whispered the judge.

"Yes. And it shames me to be a part of the army."

"And her body?"

"It's been taken somewhere, to one of the sites they use, an hour or so from the city. They'll never find her."

The two men sat in silence. The sense of outrage they felt in stark contrast to the idyllic setting of trees, stream, and clear skies. Both men had seen greed and corruption in their lifetime, each of them believing they had seen and heard the worst. But being pragmatic men, they recognized their inability to change things, and sought to serve their country to the best of their abilities, maintaining their personal integrity within its corrupt and corrupting system.

But the evil revealed to them that day made them ask whether it was right for them to continue serving the government. That a man such as Aure could commit so blatant a crime and still remain under the protection of the palace was beyond both of them. That such savage acts were employed to keep El Presidente in power disheartened them. Perhaps the students were right after all, perhaps the system was beyond salvation.

"I am sorry the boy had to witness Aure in action," the general said. "I have heard Aure say no two deaths should be alike. The monster believes murder is an art form. And his followers—oh yes, he has admirers in the army—they quote him, Romero, these men who model themselves after him, wishing they had the same talent. And in the palace is a foolish leader who thinks he can use a man like Aure and control him. To think your son was forced to see his handiwork. He will never forget last night, poor Laslo."

Sighing, the judge told his friend, "You know, Dante, I used to say Laslo needed to have his eyes opened. But not this way, my God, not in this way . . ."

The general turned to the judge. "There is something else you need to know, Romero. . . ."

"About last night?"

The general shook his head. "No. About the investigation."

For the next few minutes, the general spoke and the judge listened, the latter's expression growing more and more grim, his face darkening with anger. He took it all in, finally understanding at last. But what he thought he kept to himself.

Soon after this, both men rose from the bench and made their way back to the farmhouse.

"Take some fruit back with you and give my regards to Rosario. When this is over, bring her up here with the boy. I still think of him as a boy, my godson, but he is not that anymore."

"No . . . not anymore."

They loaded the baskets of mangoes and *kaymitos* into the back of the car. And before the judge drove off, the general said, "What will you do now, Romero? It would not be like you to do something rash."

"I will think about it carefully. But you can be sure they will never dare to manipulate me again."

* * *

After spending several days pondering the matter, the judge had arrived at what he believed was the only course of action open to him.

In a surprise move on the Thursday of the second week of the investigation, Judge Romero Jimenez summoned the soldier Rogelio Campos into his private quarters. The legal counsel representing the military made to join the soldier but were summarily dismissed by the judge. The three military advisers protested, saying this was highly irregular. That their client must at all times be spoken to in their presence. But the judge ignored their protestations. He said to them, "This is my commission. My court. And in here, I make the laws."

So Rogelio Campos, aware that the coming meeting would either spell doom or liberation, followed the judge to his chambers.

The members of the commission, the military representatives, the students, the spectators in the room, along with the representatives of the papers and the television networks broke into involved discussions about this unexpected development.

What questions did the judge have to ask in private? Why not in front of the commission members and the public? What was he up to? Surely, this did not augur well for the soldier. The soldier would definitely hang. But who was to know, others argued, this was the unpredictable Hanging Judge after all.

Half an hour later, Rogelio Campos was escorted back into the room by two guards. All eyes followed him, trying to read his face and failing. For Rogelio was himself confused and stunned by all that had transpired between him and the judge. As he took his seat, he found the members of his counsel eyeing him. One of them leaned closer to interrogate him, but before the soldier could reply, the side access door to the courtroom opened and the judge stepped into the room and took his seat.

He wasted no time.

Before the people in the room could recover from his earlier unexpected move, the judge served up another surprise. He would surprise even the members of the commission, who had not been warned of his decision.

In a clear strong voice, the Hanging Judge announced that there would be no more sessions and no more testimonies. Beginning that afternoon, the Jimenez Commission would deliberate behind closed doors. He informed the people that the commission now had all the information it needed to construct a report. And that the commission would announce its findings on Monday of the following week.

Ignoring the questions fielded by the reporters in the audience, and the sudden uproar from the gallery, the judge signaled to the commission members to rise. And together, the group left the room.

News of the judge's unexpected decision reached the palace within minutes, leaving everyone wondering just what Jimenez was up to.

"Get him on the phone!" El Presidente ordered.

El Presidente did not have long to wait.

Soon after receiving news of the judge's action, he would hear from the man himself. But the judge did not ring about the commission's business. When El Presidente questioned him on his unorthodox behavior that morning, the judge simply reminded El Presidente that the Jimenez Commission was an independent commission. And as such, was not answerable to the military or to any government body, not even to the palace. If anything, the judge said, the commission was answerable to the people, for whom its findings would be made known the following week.

El Presidente was about to explode at this insulting disregard of his authority when the judge began to speak of a matter that soon left El Presidente at a loss for words. It was a one-sided conversation that lasted twenty minutes. The Chief of Staff, who was in the room with El Presidente, looked on with interest, then with concern, as he noticed his superior's grim expression and lengthy silence, and that his face was rapidly turning gray.

"Romero"—El Presidente finally spoke—"in the interest of this government, you must leave this matter to me. And forbid your boy from speaking of what happened."

El Presidente put the phone down and leaned against the back of his chair, his posture that of a tired and defeated man. The Chief of Staff approached the desk.

"Sir?"

"You may be right, Raul, you may be right after all."

"What about, sir?"

El Presidente shook his head, too tired and unwilling to explain. "Get Aure. I want him here. Now."

A short while later, the Chief of Staff reported to El Presidente that the colonel was not at the camp and that no one knew his whereabouts. But he had left a message asking the colonel to call the palace as soon as he returned. What the Chief of Staff could not foresee was that before the message could be relayed, something important claimed the colonel's attention as he arrived back at the detention center that evening.

After a weeklong search, the colonel's men had delivered into his hands at last the quarry that had long eluded him. So while El Presidente waited for his call that night, Colonel Santiago Aure, artist of pain, was lost in his work, his hands busy on a subject called Luis Bayani.

30

Sing a Dirge for Me

They say that in the beginning the universe was shapeless. All was energy. That with the passing of time, this primal energy channeled itself into different forms. Taking on various states and shapes. Becoming identifiable. But whether it became plant or animal or something solid and immobile like rock, it remained connected to all that existed around it. Everything, after all, springs from the same source. And when the time comes for the passing of a life, for death, its passing is always felt. The loss of a life leaves all that remains diminished.

So it can be said that when Luis Bayani gave his last anguished cry, when life seeped out of him, the world shuddered and stopped for a moment. And when it resumed its turning, it did so in a diminished way, for one life had been subtracted, lost forever.

The world shuddered, too, when it heard a voice say, "Feed him to the river."

It was an unfortunate turn of events that finally led to Luis Bayani's capture. Another way of looking at it, of course, was that Aure was a man who always found his prey.

When his men came back the first time to say they had lost Luis Bayani after following him from Smoky Mountain, the colonel said, "Let me explain a very simple fact to you. People do not disappear.

Like objects, they can get misplaced, but they do not disappear. Go back to that street you claim he disappeared in. Comb every inch of it. Keep watch over the surrounding area. He is hiding there somewhere. And find out where he was staying at Smoky Mountain, who his host was."

The colonel stood and was about to step out of the room when he stopped by the doorway and, turning back, said, "Come back with answers, not excuses."

The men returned to the area. Searching patiently, speaking to the people who lived there. They searched, too, in the neighborhood clinics and in the nearby hospital. But Bayani continued to elude them. Then one of them came across the crack in the wall by the convent's cemetery. But a check of the convent turned up nothing.

However, the men continued to patrol the place. And one night, their patience was rewarded and they discovered that the colonel was right. People did not just disappear from sight.

The young man limping toward the main street caught the attention of two men who, in the past week, had taken to sitting in the local beer garden during the day and in the early evenings. They watched his slow progress with keen interest. The taller man asked for the bill, paid it quickly, and the two of them rose and casually walked across the street.

It was close to eight in the evening and the street had quietened down as the residents settled in for the night. The blare of television shows and radios could be heard from the houses that lined the street. And every now and then, the men walked past some pedestrians on their way home. The jeepneys and cars still went past this side street, so the men put off making their move.

Then the young man reached the main street.

Luis Bayani was unfamiliar with the area and didn't know the routes of the passing jeepneys. His hazy vision made it impossible to see the signs written on the front boards and the side panels of the vehicles. But just the same, he decided to hail the next one, for he could feel himself tiring, growing faint. Clara and the nuns were right. He wasn't fit enough to be on his own. But it was too late for that now. Besides, he had wasted close to a week and couldn't afford to delay any longer.

In the distance—it was hard even to judge distance—he saw the multicolored lights of an approaching jeepney. He raised his hand to wave to it. At this point, he was joined on the street by two men. One lit a cigarette while the other eyed him.

"*Pare*," Luis Bayani asked the men, "can you tell me where this one's going?"

"Can't you see?"

"Not too well," Luis replied. "I lost my glasses."

"At Milagros," said the man, looking at him with the confidence of a hunter who had cornered his prey, "you lost them at Milagros."

Before Luis Bayani could react, the other man grabbed him by the shoulder. The side that had taken the bullet. He winced at the pain, feeling the blood drain from his face. Then he felt blood spurting from the wound that opened from the pressure of the man's hand.

The jeepney pulled up just as Luis Bayani doubled over.

"You getting on or what?" called out the driver.

The man with the cigarette shouted back, "No . . . our friend here's feeling sick."

"Had too much already! It's only eight!" The driver laughed then stepped on the accelerator. As he drove off, the two men dragged Luis Bayani into a waiting car. By then, a dark patch was quickly forming on his pants and he had lost consciousness.

Forty-five minutes later, Luis Bayani would wake and see before him the waiting hands of the colonel.

Now the colonel has finished with him.

Now Luis Bayani is making his last journey. The river is still when the men arrive in the old pickup. They hear the familiar sound of its waters slapping against the sides of moored vessels and returning to lick the rubbish-strewn land. They hear, too, the sound of liquid flushing out of lengthy pipes into the giant basin that is the river. Toxic waste from the factories nearby. In the dark, they find their way. They know this place well. The secluded spot on the south bank. They have been here many times before, carrying, as they do tonight, a salvage victim rolled inside meters of hessian. They park in their usual spot. A narrow road hidden from view by an abandoned warehouse. They like using this place as a tip-off point, it is a good place from which to feed their load into the deep black waters.

There is no need to rush. The night has many more hours of darkness left. Three men get out. They walk to the low wall that serves as a barrier to the water. A bright yellow flame comes to life, blazing for the time needed for two men to share it as they light their cigarettes. In the night, the trail of the smoke they exhale is invisible. But the scent of tobacco hangs in the air. The smell is more pleasant than the smell from the river.

The third man walks around. His eyes trained to the ground. He is looking for something. Something heavy. The orders were clear. This one must be weighed down. Must never rise again. Never be seen. But there is nothing heavy, no rock, with which to do the job. The man tells this to his companions. They confer amongst themselves. They agree to throw the body in just the same. The hessian will take in water. It will add weight. And if the man was found, well, there would be difficulty identifying him. A man looks completely different, a far cry from his usual self, with two gaping holes where his eyes used to be. Besides, they reassure each other, he has been stripped of everything that could identify him. One man has his watch, another his wallet. What about dental records? one of them asks. His fingerprints? You worry too much, the other two answer. They finish their cigarettes, throwing the glowing butts into the river.

In the half hour since they arrived, the night has grown cooler. The river, too, has changed its mood. It is no longer still. The lights dance now on its rippling surface.

The two smokers join the third man, who is opening the boot of the pickup. They watch as he pulls at one end of the rolled hessian. The body slides down. The first man takes hold of one end while the second takes the other. The third man picks up the loop of rope and wraps this around the body to keep the hessian in place, silently regretting the waste of good rope. They carry the body toward the wall where the ground rises to the left. There they stand, swinging it from the elevated spot. They swing left and right and left and in one final synchronized movement, with all the strength they can muster, they fling it outward. After what seems like an eternity, they hear the splash.

The water parts and swallows the body.

In a small boat, two men making a late-night run hear the gurgling, churning sounds of the river. They laugh, believing in their drunken state that they are hearing things. The boat tilts to one side as a strong ripple passes under their vessel. The water is growing turbulent. One man almost falls over and is saved by his companion, who grabs on to his leg.

The first drops of rain fall on the faces of the men in the boat. The three men who stand looking over the river wall feel them, too. One of the men shivers, not from the cool wind, but from a queasy sensation. He looks up and notices the clouds that are traveling fast across the sky. Against the reflected light of the moon the clouds look like a piece of negative film. He calls to the others to move on. The drops of rain fall in quicker succession, like a swarm of flies landing on his face, pestering him. He gets into the pickup and waits impatiently for his companions. They follow him, then stop in their tracks. They exchange looks and one of them speaks.

"Did you hear that?"

His companion listens, thinking someone has seen them and is approaching. Then he realizes his friend is referring to a strange sound he now also hears.

"Where's it coming from?"

His friend motions to him to stop talking. Together, they listen and look around.

The man in the pickup curses, calling to his companions to hurry up. Finally he opens the creaky door on the driver's side and hops down. Then he hears it, too.

"What is it?"

They walk to where the sound is coming from. They walk and stand over the river wall where moments earlier they had flung the body of Luis Bayani. They hear the sound coming from there. A deep humming. They strain their ears to hear better. They strain their eyes to see the men responsible for the sound. There is no one there.

It is coming from the river.

They stand in awe. And suddenly they find themselves caught in some strange dreamscape. They listen to the humming. A slow and low sound, carrying a sad melody, like a dirge heard in some shared past. They recognize the sound as the world in mourning. It is the sound one makes to soothe a weeping mother who has lost a child.

This song of primeval sorrow rises from the river and is carried by the wind across the city. It breaches the walls of the heart and the mind. It is heard in the sleep of the men and women who live by the banks of the river. The poor of Smoky Mountain. The powers that sleep in the palace.

In her silk-covered bed, Madam turns on her side and mumbles in her sleep. Next to her, El Presidente wakes and hears the soft sad humming through the large window overlooking the river. He thinks it is a sound left over from his strange dream. He shuts his eyes and falls back into it. The melody continues to play in his mind.

The sleeping city hears it. Like the men who stand by the river, the sleeping citizens recognize it in the depths of their subconscious. It belongs to a world so ancient they have long forgotten it. Now it slips through a door into the land of their dreams, and the forgotten past touches them. In the morning they wake to the last strains of the river's humming. And they will whisper: the river, the river sang last night. Did you hear the river sing?

And so it came to pass. The first sign of the seer's prophecy.

I, too, heard the river sing its mournful song that night. I heard it in my sleep. But unlike the many who heard its lament, I knew why the river grieved.

It is a thinking, feeling thing, this river; it is alive and has been sad a long, long time. On the night that it sings its sad song, it does so because it knows what has been fed into its waters. It is all-knowing, for the river is the very soul of everything.

When the body of Luis Bayani descends into its depths, when its currents carry it out into the wide reckonless deep of the open sea, the river cries to the Mother of All Rivers. It says: It is time to wash away all this sin. I am sick of all that I carry. Look at me, I carry the tears, the troubles, the sorrows, the blood, the pain, the shame, the heartache, and the shattered dreams of so many. I want to be clean again, innocent once more the way I was in the beginning.

Softly, the Mother of All Rivers answers the river. But only the river hears its reply. And it sighs.

I weep in my sleep. For in my dream, Luis Bayani comes to me, not to say good-bye, but to tell me that he cannot see, he can no longer see.

Now I will tell you of the dream I had of his death at the hands of Aure.

I see Aure opening his wounds. Opening them with a scalpel, slicing through them, deftly yet tenderly, loving each stroke that he makes. Then I see him pick up an instrument with a long fine handle and a scooped end. He inspects this against the light. Then he brings it down close to Luis Bayani's eyes. With his fingers, he forces a lid open, then he inserts the instrument under the eyeball. Luis's body jerks. His mouth opens to shout but in my dream, all is silent. Still, I hear his silent scream. The colonel continues his delicate operation. He runs the instrument gently around the rim of the eyeball, meticulously severing the connecting membrane. Freeing the eye from the socket. So clean, so neatly does he do this. He moves on to the other eye and repeats the same procedure. Slowly. Always slowly. This way, his victim sees him, the executioner, at work as his sight gradually fades. Then the victim is blind at last. His final vision that of his murderer.

It surprises me how little blood there is. Perhaps Luis is surprised, too. I wonder if the amount of blood one sheds is in proportion to the amount of pain one feels. Little blood. Little pain. One hopes. But just the same, he must die because Aure will tolerate no less than the subtraction of life.

On the threshold of death, Luis Bayani takes his time dying. He is conscious of his life passing. He is savoring what remains of it, discounting his pain. For the pain is inconsequential in the face of a lifeless eternity. Aure, too, is in no rush to end things. But it is not life he savors, but the taking of it and the accompanying pain he so artfully inflicts. I see all this and I weep in my sleep, a weeping so full of grief that it brings the nuns running to my room.

In the boundary between sleep and waking, I decipher the meaning of the images of my dream, and when Mother Superior shakes me awake, I say to her, "He is dead."

"It is only a dream, Clara."

But I know with unshakable certainty that it is true. I do not remember much else of my brief waking that night, for soon I roamed the hopeless empty landscape of grief in search of my dead friend.

Later I would learn that the nuns sat and watched by my bedside in the small hours of that God-abandoned morning. And at the first sign of light, Mother Superior went down to the chapel where not so long ago we had hidden Luis Bayani under the altar, his blood staining the floor. There she prayed for his soul. For if what I dreamed was true, then Luis would need help to find his way back home.

Mother Superior prayed for me, too. It was all she could do to help me. Charlie was no longer around to advise her. The don she knew not how to reach. And as for my mother, she remained absent from my life. Although for a time I had found them all, Mother Superior realized only then what I had known all along—that I was still alone. So she trusted in her God and the power of her prayers.

When morning finally came, the doorbell to the main building rang. Sister Luisa, who had been in the foyer, heard it. Expecting to see someone with an offering of fresh eggs, she pulled the door open, and what she saw made her stand still. To this day she still says to me, "God heard us, Clara, he answered our prayers."

So she sent a silent prayer of thanks above and, with a smile of relief, welcomed the woman who stood before her. After an absence of more than twenty-three years, Consuelo Lamuerta had returned at last to the Convent of Santa Clara. And to Sister Luisa, whom she recognized, my mother announced, "I have come back for my daughter Clara."

31

Mother and Child

In my dream I felt a cool hand against my feverish brow. A welcome sensation that made me open my heavy lids briefly. What I saw was my own self looking down at me.

I asked this other self: "Why are you here?"

"Because I left something of mine in this place long ago," she replied.

Before I could ask what it was, sleep claimed me once more. That is, if you could call it sleep. That hazy world of floating images and echoing voices, where time was of a different substance, and there was no day and no night and no ticking of clocks.

In another dream I was standing at the end of a corridor in the upper story of the convent. I called out to Mother Superior and she emerged from a room at the other end. I saw her and smiled, then I walked to meet her but the corridor began to stretch longer and longer, so that each step I took failed to decrease the space between us. Then she was just a tiny figure in the distance. I called out to her, and she to me, and our voices became smaller and smaller, like our shrinking selves.

I woke up but this was a dream, too. And once more I saw myself looking at me. On some level I thought to myself that there must be many Cláras in the world. Yet how was this possible, this splitting of my self?

"Which Clara are you?" I asked the one who gazed at me with a puzzled look.

Before she could reply, my heavy lids fell and I drifted again in the dark void that I roamed.

Then I dreamed of him.

I didn't see him at first but I knew this was a dream about him. For I heard the lapping of the river. It was dark out there but I heard him coming. Staring into the shadows, I saw his lean shape emerging from the water.

The night was cool and the wind brushed against my face. I shivered. And I thought to myself he was wet and would catch cold and we would have to nurse him till he was well again. I meant to tell him this, so I walked out to meet him.

My feet touched water and it soaked through my shoes but I kept walking until I was standing in the middle of the river facing him. But before I could speak he said to me, "My eyes, you have my eyes, Clara."

"I know, Luis, I forgot to get you another pair of glasses. Can you at least see a little?"

He shook his head. And only then did I notice he had no eyes. I asked him where they were. And he replied, "Didn't the colonel give them to you?"

I shook my head.

Then he told me something that frightened me. "But you are wearing them, Clara. You have my eyes, Clara, *you* are my eyes."

"No!" I cried out. "These are mine, not yours. These are my eyes."

But he repeated his words once more, pointing to my eyes. "*You* are my eyes." The waters began to rise and gradually they swallowed him. I called out again and again, my voice sounding desperate and feeble. "No, Luis, these are my eyes. Mine!"

I covered my eyes with my hands, making sure he had not taken them from me. Then I felt a pair of cool hands over my burning ones. And I heard a voice say, "You are safe, Clara."

"My eyes. I do not want to lose my eyes."

"They are with you, Clara, open your eyes. You can see with them."

In my dream I opened my eyes and once more saw my other self.

"Who are you?"

"Don't you know who I am, Clara?"

"Me. You look like me."

"Yes, we look alike," my other self answered.

I shut my eyes and in that twilight world, the dream returned, the waters of the river parted, and I woke once more, hands over my eyes. There were many faces above me this time. My own and Mother Superior's and Sister Luisa's, they had all come into my dreamworld. And I said to them, "Tell him, please, these are my eyes and that he cannot have them."

But Luis was insistent. He returned again. Only this time, he said to me, "Come to the river, I am here, Clara, promise me that you will come."

"I promise."

When I opened my eyes next, I told my other self, "I made a promise. We will go to the river. He wants us to go to the river."

"You're not well."

"But we must go."

"When you're well, yes."

"Promise."

"I promise."

The dream did not return that night. And I stirred awake in the small hours of morning, my body no longer burning. I turned my head slowly and found myself gazing at a familiar face. Mine but not mine. And I realized that I had not dreamed this other self at all. She was real, only she wasn't me. Sitting on a chair by my bed, Consuelo Lamuerta returned my gaze.

"You don't have to stay with me."

I told Consuelo this as she spooned up some chicken soup for me. I refused to eat but she stubbornly held up the spoon. I was hungry but too weak still to feed myself. But I had no wish to have her feed me.

Mother Superior came to see me and I told her to send Consuelo away. That I was fine and that I could manage. But Mother Superior told me I was being foolish. She could be perverse sometimes, Mother Superior, and from then on, she made sure that only Consuelo remained with me in my room.

So I angrily said to her, "I didn't ask you to return."

She put the spoon down and raised her eyes to meet mine. "I gave you away and you have never forgiven me. You are still angry."

My mother forced me to look at my own anger. It struck me then that I could never escape her. I was truly Anger's daughter.

"That was twenty-three years ago. Why should you think it still matters? If guilt is what is keeping you here, then I absolve you of it. You may go!"

"It is not within your power to do so," she replied calmly.

"Who has the power, then?" I challenged her.

"I do. Only I can forgive myself." She spooned up more soup for me.

She refused to leave me.

And hunger finally won out. I knew I would never have the strength to feed myself if I didn't start eating. So I let her feed me. Grudgingly. And I let her bathe me, too. All the time I kept saying to her, "You don't have to do this. Haven't I told you that you can go?"

I must have said this a dozen times and drew nothing more than a steady gaze from her, which riled me even more. There was a stubbornness in her, and thinking this, I suddenly remembered the don's words to me. Stubbornness must be something than ran in our veins, the three of us. She also possessed a calmness that made me want to shake her. I tried doing this with words.

One morning, as I sat in bed watching her fold my nightdress away, I said, "Why are you still here? Have you no pride?"

She stopped what she was doing, weighed my words, then turned to me and said, "Pride? That is what has brought us to this point. His pride, my pride, and now yours."

It was the first time she referred to the past, to him. And she made me think of my pride. I was Pride's daughter, too.

In spite of myself I wanted to listen to her, I wished for her to say more. For Luis Bayani spoke the truth when he said to me there was no walking away from people and situations. Just take her. She has refused to leave.

She must have wanted to unburden herself. Something in me told me to stop pushing her away and to listen. So I found myself moving to make room for her on my bed. Side by side we sat, my mother and I, and my mother began to speak. But unlike that first time in her room where the don and I listened to her angry tale, this time she spoke without rancor. And as I took in her words I was surprised to find that I, too, had shed some of mine. For you see, I admit now that I had not yet forgotten her words spoken that night.

"I didn't want the child," she had said then. How was I ever to forget that?

She told me something which surprised me. "I heard you, Clara, I heard every word you spoke to me in my sleep. It was why I returned, why I woke. The child I gave away has brought me back to myself. And that is one of the reasons why I refuse to let you send me away, Clara."

She paused for a moment before continuing. "But you were wrong. I bled not so much out of anger but because I could not forgive myself even after all these years. It has taken me a while to understand the true meaning of these wounds. These are Christ's wounds. He died so that I could be free, and yet I have stubbornly refused to be free of my guilt. Now he has given me his wounds to remind me it is time to forgive myself."

I stared at her hands as she opened her palms. I had earlier noticed that the backs of her hands no longer bled, so I thought they had healed. But now I saw that the flesh of her palms still wept blood. I winced as if her hands were mine. She told me her feet still bled, too.

"But they are slowly healing, Clara, that is a good sign . . . a beginning."

She told me of what passed between her and the don.

"We spoke that night, after you had gone, and once more the day before he left. We spoke of his abandonment of me; no matter how I looked at it, I told him, it would remain the act of a coward. He said nothing, you know, he did not deny it. But I see now there is little point in harboring so much resentment. It has done nothing but make me unhappy. And what for, Clara? What for, when I had been foolish, too. I knew from the start that I was hoping for the impossible but I continued to see him. So in the end, he had to make a choice. Not an easy one to make and he has had to live with it. As for his mother's deception and the bitterness he felt toward me, what a sad waste of a life to have spent all those years living with a false sense of betrayal. I think that believing I had wronged him allowed him to erase some of his own guilt, but of course I did not tell him this.

"But I am more fortunate than Miguel. I have found you. You must believe me when I say I thought about you every single day of those twenty-three years. I may not have wanted to keep you, but I never forgot you. As I said, I am more fortunate than him. Like me, he has found you, but he can never be a part of your life, Clara, because of who he is and the ties he is about to make. And to think that you are the child after his own heart."

I started on hearing this. Seeing my reaction, she said, "Oh, you cannot be so blind as to fail to see that you are the child he would have wished for, the one he would have been proud of. It may be my face that you wear, but it is with his nature that you live your life. The same strong will ... and pride, Clara, you have the Pellicer pride. Don't look at me like that. Even he saw himself in you the moment he met you that night in my room. He told me so. Not so much because of the mark you wear, but in your very defiance of him. The way you carry yourself. Poor Miguel, all that he could have learned to love will forever be denied him. He must content himself with watching you from afar."

What could I say to this, this revelation? I kept quiet, absorbing Consuelo's words, their meaning racing through my mind as I tried to understand my father's heart.

Then Consuelo turned to me and revealed her own heart's desire.

As a steely look came over her eyes, she said to me, "I know you refuse to make room for me in your life. But I am determined, Clara, to claim back the daughter I gave away."

The following morning, I ventured out to the little cemetery, with my mother close behind. It was the first time I had been out since the harrowing night Luis Bayani came to me in my dream. In the cemetery, I told her, "I am going to the river."

Before she could say anything, I added, "I made a promise."

"When you are better, yes, and I will come with you."

I looked at her and she explained. "I promised you I would, or don't you remember?"

I remembered then.

32

Judgment Day

On Monday, I rang Torres to say I was better but would be taking the rest of the week off to recuperate. I had expected him to say something about my long absence and was taken aback when he readily agreed to give me the extra days off. He seemed distracted and in a hurry to end our conversation so I bade him good-bye before he had the chance to change his mind.

Only as I listened to the news on the radio later that morning did I realize I could not have called Torres at a more opportune time. The *Chronicle*'s news editor was in the middle of something far more important than the absence of a reporter. To be more precise, he was busy with the day's biggest story: over at the judiciary building, the unpredictable Judge Romero Jimenez had succeeded in upsetting the students, the military, and most of all, the palace. And an hour after the commission's findings were made public, the city itself was in an uproar.

When the Jimenez Commission's findings were finally announced to the public at ten in the morning on Monday, only two people derived any satisfaction from it.

The first being the soldier Rogelio Campos, who found himself cleared of all charges of instigating violence. The commission's findings stated that Rogelio had indeed fired the weapon that resulted in the death of one Chen Lu Pin alias Charlie, but had done so in self-defense. The commission drew attention to the fact that the soldier was being chased by twelve Loyola students and had fired in a moment of panic. That an innocent man, a bystander, had died was unfortunate. But the mitigating circumstances called for the acquittal of the soldier. The commission also recommended that the suspension of Rogelio Campos be lifted and that he be returned to full duty with the 22nd Infantry.

Listening to the commission's findings, Rogelio felt not so much surprise as relief. He had known of the judge's intentions since the day the judge summoned him into his chambers for a private discussion.

He had followed the judge into the room, a big high-ceilinged office with a large mahogany table, a pair of tall windows in the wall behind. The judge had seated himself in his chair and motioned to Rogelio to take the chair by the desk. Rogelio hesitated for a moment before finally taking a seat. He clasped his hands before him and rested them on his lap to stop them shaking. The judge's gaze, which Rogelio was determined to meet, did nothing to ease his nervousness. But Rogelio reminded himself that he had chosen to trust in this man's just nature and his ability to see through false-hood, and besides, it was too late to change his mind now.

So the soldier and the judge sat facing each other. And after a while, the judge picked up the folder in front of him, opened it, and took out a sheet of paper. Then he returned his gaze to Rogelio. "Can you read?" he asked.

Rogelio took a moment to respond. He nodded. The judge handed him the sheet. "Read it."

So Rogelio discovered at last just how alone he was. That what he had suspected all along about the lawyer assigned to defend him was true. His instincts had been right. And what frightened Rogelio was that the people who had betrayed him knew of his secret past.

"Is there any truth to that report, young man?"

Rogelio had a breath to decide. And with a sigh, nodded. Eyes unwavering, he told the judge, "I escaped from the Hacienda Es-peranza. I owe the *contratista* money which my brother is working to pay off. I know it was wrong to have run away but I wished for a new life. But, sir, the rest, there is no truth to the rest."

"And your friend?"

"Dario is . . . was innocent, sir."

The judge leaned back and for a long time said nothing. Rogelio waited. He consoled himself that he had told the truth and that was the most a man in his situation could do. Finally, the judge leaned forward; he placed his hands on the desk and spread his fingers wide apart, studying them, before lifting his eyes to meet Rogelio's.

"Young man, what I am about to say to you must not go any farther than the walls of this room. The army you serve is going to sacrifice you. But I will clear you of all charges. If you are wise, you will leave just the same and find some other career. The army is a dead end for you now. Besides, I will tell you now that you will not be losing much in leaving it, for it is an institution that has lost all honor. As for choosing between life as a soldier and life as a *sacada*, there is little difference. In both, you are equally lacking in freedom; you must find some other way to live freely. As for running away from the *hacienda*—the judge had paused at this point as if considering what he was about to say—"that is your business, you must live with your decisions."

Sitting in Court 2A, Rogelio wondered what the future held for him. It was now more uncertain than it had been when he left the south three summers ago. At least then he knew he was joining the army. Now he had to leave it and had nowhere to go. For he saw the truth in the judge's words. There was no future in the military for him. After today, he was no longer welcome there. The displeasure on the faces of his legal counsel was enough to make this clear. Looking at the lawyers who sat next to him and at the other military representatives in the courtroom that morning, Rogelio wondered how they were going to explain this unwelcome turn of events to their superiors.

The other party who found an enormous but secret satisfaction from the morning's announcement was, of course, the Hanging Judge himself. Though his face revealed nothing of what he was feeling.

Little would be known of what occurred in those closed-door deliberations of the members of the commission. But the truth was, during the ensuing discussions, the judge acted in his most dictatorial and domineering manner and simply took over the decision-making process. Using the sheer force of his personality, he convinced the commission members on two other crucial matters: one, that the dead soldier Dario Mariano had fired his weapon and wounded a student under extreme provocation and thus should have his name cleared just for the record. And two, the students involved in the sit-in had acted in a most irresponsible manner and should be punished for their behavior.

On hearing the punishment recommended by the commission, the students and university representatives present in the courtroom exploded in a show of temper and ill will. For the commission recommended that the five hundred students be required to each render two hundred hours of community service within the next six months.

Even before the reading of the report was completed, a chorus of insults and abuse began to fly across the room. And by the time the report was concluded, the courtroom had become a scene of acute confusion and disorder.

The judge banged his gavel once before rising, and was followed by the members of the commission. Then, without another glance at the unruly crowd gathered in the room, he departed through the side door. All around the courtroom and up in the gallery shouts could be heard, drowning the questions of the jostling reporters.

"Whitewash!"

"Setup!"

"*Tuta!*"

The judge, to the surprise of all, bore the last insult stoically. In all his years as a defender of justice, he had never before heard himself described as an obedient puppy.

Strangely enough, when he departed from the room, it appeared to some that the judge wore a self-satisfied look, which, of course, made no sense at all.

* * *

If the public received the commission's report with derision, the palace received it with trepidation. For no sooner had the announcement been made when another call for a mass demonstration was made. It was the last thing the palace needed.

"Damn Jimenez!" El Presidente shouted. Even from outside his office, his voice was heard and it soon spread through the palace that El Presidente was in a towering rage.

The judge's announcement and timing could not have been worse. Already the foreign dignitaries and international celebrities had begun arriving for the wedding to be held on the weekend.

Why was it nothing happened as it should anymore?

El Presidente paced the room. Gesticulating with frustration. How he wished the whole thing, even the damn wedding, was over, then he could think things through more carefully. Right now he felt besieged on all sides. Because too many eyes were on him, his hands were tied. He could not act as he wished.

And Madam hadn't yet heard about Jimenez's announcement. The bastard Jimenez was about to make El Presidente's life even more miserable from that quarter. He could not bare to face his wife's anger and the torrent of words which he was sure would ensue from her mouth. The difficult unpredictable Jimenez. He would have him debarred. Who did he think he was?

He suddenly remembered the way the judge had spoken to him on the phone the week before. How dare he use that tone on him? His words were not abusive, but his tone! And now he had the gall to pull this stunt. To destabilize the government. Damn him! He would hang the judge one day.

El Presidente swung around and told the Chief of Staff, "Get him on the phone! I want him to explain this . . . this act of subversion. How dare he disregard the interests of this administration!"

The Chief of Staff remained where he was, making no move to do as he was asked, which only enraged his superior more.

"What is the matter with you, didn't you hear me? I wish to speak to that damn Jimenez. I wish to make it clear to him that he is not the law. I am the law in this land. Call him now. Don't just stand there. Doesn't anyone listen anymore?"

"Sir, I do not think it is wise to cross the judge."

"Wise? Do you think I fear him? Why should I?"

"Because he knows about the other business, sir."

El Presidente lapsed into a sullen silence.

Unfortunately for El Presidente, the matter of the female student's disappearance had not gone away as he had hoped it would.
In fact, it had become a growing irritation. The student's parents
claimed that she had never returned home on the day of the protest
march. The palace had quickly dispatched a reply saying that it had
looked into the matter, had in fact checked the records at Campo
Diaz, and that nowhere was Sophia Ramos-Sytangco's name listed
among the students detained for questioning.

After that, the palace had chosen to forget the matter. Until the
letter arrived. The missing student's parents, along with the Loyola
administration members, had sent a letter petitioning El Presidente
to begin a formal investigation.

New proof had come to light. A news cameraman had on video
proof that Sophia had been dragged away by three men. The film
footage had been viewed by a Jesuit priest who claimed he had seen
it happen.

No. The business of Sophia Ramos-Sytangco's disappearance was
gaining an importance which El Presidente did not like. Why, even
Senator Mijares had come to see El Presidente regarding the matter.

Senator Sixto Mijares had finally seen the damage done to Ana's
face. He had received a call from her artist friend and had gone to
see Ana at the clinic. What he saw had shaken him to the core. He
had sought to comfort Ana but words failed him, for he did not
know how to cope with his guilt on account of his wife's actions, or
the revulsion he felt at the ugliness before him. Half beauty and half
beast. This woman who had once filled him only with desire and
given him so much pleasure.

Ana had said only one thing to him: "Restore my face."

He promised he would, promised that no cost would be spared,
promised to pay Lorena back.

The senator then returned to his office and paced angrily around the room to release his pent-up rage. He was at this point still far from understanding that the responsibility for Ana's face lay not so much with his wife Lorena but in another quarter altogether. The senator was not yet the enlightened creature he would later become. At that moment, he was simply an angry man who needed to release the anger that was building up inside him.

He found the outlet he was looking for on returning to his desk. On top of his table was a copy of a letter that Sophia Ramos-Sytangco's parents, along with the university officials, had sent El Presidente. He read it and was in the process of crumpling it when something stopped him. Without thinking about the repercussions, he reached for the phone and dialed the palace number. He asked to speak to El Presidente and insisted they meet in the palace.

So the senator became involved where he did not wish to be involved. Had he been asked to explain his decision, he would not have been able to do so. His motives were vague, if he had any at all. But although his action was not deliberate, the result was nevertheless decisive and would help change him into a different man altogether.

Needless to say, El Presidente was as upset as he was puzzled by the senator's meddling in the student's business. It was so out of character. El Presidente rightly guessed that the senator had been approached by the university and was an unwilling messenger. What he failed to judge correctly, however, was how to handle him during their meeting. El Presidente had sought to dismiss the senator and his concerns quickly, but in doing so had played his cards all wrong. Senator Sixto Mijares was in no frame of mind to be ignored. So when El Presidente had shown unwillingness to take the matter seriously, the senator had become more and more stubborn about the business at hand.

Finally, the senator brought into the open what others only whispered behind El Presidente's back. He said, "What has Aure to say about the matter, sir?"

The fact that El Presidente was taken aback by the mention of Aure's name was obvious. He was lost for an answer. The silence stretched awkwardly until El Presidente answered, "He is looking into the matter."

The senator nodded politely, confident that his serious intentions had been communicated to his superior. He rose and ended the interview himself, saying, "I trust you will inform me, sir, as soon as you have the colonel's report."

After thanking El Presidente, the senator departed. The man he left behind, though, was reminded of another problem he had yet to face. For what El Presidente failed to tell the senator was: he had no idea where Aure was.

For the truth of the matter was, since Thursday when he had tried to get hold of the colonel at Campo Diaz, and later in his home, he had had no word from him. Where was Aure? El Presidente wanted the colonel to answer for the death of Sophia Ramos-Sytangco.

"Sir, would you like me to take the call?"

El Presidente gave a slight jolt on hearing the Chief of Staff speak. He had been so lost in his thoughts he had forgotten the man was in the room with him. He turned to him then and said, "Yes, take the call, Raul, I have no wish to speak to anyone."

The Chief of Staff reached for the handpiece and as he spoke to the caller, El President walked to the balcony door and pushed it wide open. He stepped out and gazed at the river, which always had the power to clear his mind. But his moment of peace was soon interrupted, for the Chief of Staff came out to stand beside him, saying, "Sir, that was the Defense Minister; he would like a word with you."

Shaking his head, El Presidente replied, "Tell him not to waste my time. Tell him to find Aure, it's Aure I wish to speak to."

The Chief of Staff hesitated before saying, "It's about Aure, sir."

El Presidente felt the hair on his back rise and his insides turn. Without looking at the Chief of Staff, he said, "What about him, Raul?"

"Aure found Bayani, sir."

El Presidente turned to face the Chief of Staff, his eyes bright and alive. "He's finally got him, has he?"

"Bayani is . . . he's dead, sir, been dead since Thursday."

* * *

The secretary knocked on the door and quickly stepped inside. She hesitated for a second. Madam, she knew, hated to be interrupted as she attended to her day's correspondence—personalized letters requesting donations to her pet projects, letters of condolence to the family of dearly departed friends or political supporters, letters of congratulations to deserving citizens for some meaningful contribution to society, and short thank-you notes like the one she had just finished writing to the jeweler.

Each morning, an hour was set aside for these bothersome but necessary matters. It was all part of the job and she attacked it with the same discipline she applied to all the other areas of her life as wife of El Presidente.

The secretary hovered behind her. Madam was in the process of signing her name with her trademark ornate signature on the perfumed parchment paper she always used. She finished and lifted the sheet to check whether the ink had dried. When she was sure it was safe to fold the sheet, she did so with care, then slipped it into a matching parchment envelope and wrote the recipient's name.

She turned to her secretary then and handed her the small pile of correspondence she had finished that morning. The secretary would take care of affixing Madam's official seal to each envelope.

But the secretary had not come for the letters this morning. She had come to summon Madam on an urgent matter requiring her attention.

"El Presidente has been taken to his room, Madam." She imparted her message quickly. "I think he fainted or fell ill, I'm not sure. The doctor has been called."

Madam rose from her seat. Even in an emergency, she moved in a regal fashion. She was composed. But irritated. How inconvenient for El Presidente to have fallen ill at this time. The wedding being so close at hand. She had urged him repeatedly to take it easy, but as usual, he had turned a deaf ear to her scolding.

"Have these hand-delivered. For the Santoses, send some white lilies. And make sure Sarmiento receives my note today. And, one more thing, have a dozen eggs delivered to the convent."

The secretary followed close behind, making a mental note of all the things she needed to do as Madam made her way along the corridor leading to the private quarters.

By the door to the presidential chambers was the Chief of Staff, the Press Secretary, and a whole group of staff members.

"He has regained consciousness, Madam," said the simpering Press Secretary, "but I am most concerned and insist the doctor stay close at hand for the rest of the day."

Madam ignored them all, waved them away, and entered the room. El Presidente lay on the enormous silk-covered bed—two queen-size beds positioned side by side in an elevated section of the room. The room itself was richly furnished with antiques. And on the walls were the works of the masters, local and European, borrowed from—and still to be returned to—the National Art Gallery.

As he watched his wife approach, El Presidente reassured her that he was fine and this was just a passing problem. He was intent on pacifying her, for he saw from the frown on her face that his sudden illness was an inconvenience she could have done without. Illness, if it had to happen, had better wait until after the wedding. He decided to put off telling her about the unfortunate events of the morning. And as for the Aure business, he would keep that for last.

But in the same way that the judge and the business with Aure had upset El Presidente's plans, turning his world suddenly chaotic, Madam, too, was about to experience her share of unwelcome complications.

Before sundown, news would reach her regarding some madman up north who was at that very moment planting fear in the minds of the people, prophesying the coming of an earthquake in the next few days. The man, later identified as the head of the Seismological Study Center who had apparently gone AWOL, was calling on the people to evacuate their towns and leave the north. He predicted that the earthquake's fault line would run right through the center of Salinas, El Presidente's hometown, where the bridal party would pass on the way to the Cathedral of the North.

On hearing this, Madam's usually composed face was marred by deep furrows, her lips curled in fury as she said, "How dare this man say these things! Put a stop to all these stories at once. Have him arrested."

Then she summoned her secretary, saying, "I will not have anything bad happen on the day. I will not allow it. Make it a hundred eggs, not just a dozen. Deliver a hundred eggs to the Convent of Santa Clara at once."

33

A Thank-you Note

Valle de Oro, nestling between two picturesque hills in the municipality of Libertad, is a little paradise. Its name was inspired by the golden hue the valley took on at sundown. The place itself is the residence of many of the city's affluent citizens. It boasts of sprawling homes with generous gardens, high walls, high security, and most important of all, unlike the rest of the busy congested city, peace and quiet.

On the day I am writing of, its customary silence was shattered by the screaming of an ambulance siren.

The maid found the jeweler facedown on a plate that had, when she served him an hour ago, contained an assortment of cheese, crackers, and crispbread whose names she could not pronounce. She would tell the reporters from the various newspapers that he had woken up late that Monday morning and announced he would go and check on one of his shops after lunch. He had informed her that he would be lunching out but wouldn't mind something light in the meantime.

"Some cheese, Norma," he said, telling her which ones he wanted by describing them to her. "And a half . . . just a half glass of white wine."

She had brought him the smelly tray as he sat on his favorite chair in the study. All the while she wondered how he could manage to eat the stuff; why some of them even had mold growing on them. The maid left Ding Sarmiento to his light snack and returned to the kitchen to await his next command, which always came through on the intercom installed on the kitchen wall. As she waited, she flicked through *Super Star* magazine for the latest gossip. Her favorite stars, Czar Villegas and Cecilia Zalamea, were on the center spread.

The back door opened and shut. She looked up and saw the house-boy wiping his slippers on the rubber doormat. Good. She hated the dirt he always brought into the house from the garden. The boy handed her an envelope. Its fragment perfume undisguised even by the odor of the boy's heavy sweat. She knew who it was from, even before the houseboy said, "It's for sir, the palace car arrived and the driver handed it to me."

The maid took the envelope and inspected the writing. The letters were rendered with great flourish. How she loved their orna-mental loops and curves. She turned the envelope over and ran her fingers lightly over the gold seal, feeling its embossed surface. She recognized it. Had seen this several times before. But the thrill she felt on handling an envelope containing a letter from the palace, from Madam herself, had not diminished. The novelty remained.

She took out a small silver tray and rubbed her apron on its sur-face, polishing away smudges until the tray mirrored her face. With much ceremony, she placed the envelope on it and left the kitchen, the houseboy staring after her enviously.

She knocked on the door and entered the study. The jeweler, she saw, was chewing a piece of cheese with relish. All the crackers were gone from the plate. He glanced up as she approached him with the tray. And seeing the manner in which she carried it, knew at once it was something of great importance. He looked at the envelope. His heart gave an excited lurch. He ran his tongue over his lips the way he always did when anticipating a treat, then he wiped his hand hastily on the napkin draped over his lap before reaching for the envelope.

The maid retreated, knowing she was not wanted, wishing just the same that she could stay while he read it and thus learn its contents. She shut the door behind her, unaware that she had been the bringer of unwelcome and devastating news.

Ding Sarmiento carefully picked at the seal, wishing to keep it intact even after opening the envelope. Reverently, he pulled out Madam's note, catching a whiff of her perfume as he unfolded the stationery. The words rendered in the most ornate strokes took some time to sink into his mind. He read the note once, then read it again before finally comprehending its meaning. His eyes widened and his breath caught somewhere in his chest.

His mind raced back to his last meeting with Madam, and as he did so, the words he spoke to her returned to him with a blow. Oh no, how could she have misunderstood him! The honor is enough, he had said. But he had said this to flatter her. He had not expected her to take his words literally. He had to explain things to her. The tiara, which cost a fortune in pearls and diamonds, was a commissioned piece. Not a gift. He would be ruined if this was the case. He had to make this clear without losing face or, worse, earning her displeasure.

The jeweler took a deep breath but found breathing itself painful. He opened his mouth this time to try to get in more air. He felt his whole being tighten. He reached for some cheese. Some comforting soul food. But a pain ripped through his chest and he clenched his teeth before pitching forward, his face landing on the plate in front of him.

This was how the maid found him some ten or fifteen minutes later. She had returned on the pretext of asking him if he would like some more wine.

The houseboy, the chauffeur, along with the rest of the servants heard her hysterical shouts. "*Dios ko . . . Dios mio . . .*" she kept repeating to herself when seconds later, they joined her in the study. By then she had lifted her employer's head and seen his gray pallor.

A neighbor called for an ambulance and soon it pulled up in front of the jeweler's house. The two paramedics rushed in, carrying the stretcher into the study. But on seeing the size of the man they had to lift, they stopped in their tracks. They both looked at the jeweler's houseboy and the chauffeur. Yes, they would need help. It was a mammoth task requiring gargantuan strength. After much heaving and struggling, the four men finally moved the jeweler from the chair to the stretcher. He was still breathing. But only just. That much was clear. And when the necessary procedures to increase his chances of survival were made, he was quickly taken away.

By the time the stretcher was loaded into the ambulance, a dozen or more people had gathered outside to watch it depart. Within minutes, news of the famous jeweler's heart attack had spread all over Valle de Oro.

That night, the jeweler's heart failed him. When news of his untimely demise reached the palace soon after, Madam was heard to say with regret, "He never listened to his doctor, you know."

Then, proving once more her generosity of spirit and her unfailing concern for those close to her, she instructed that a special mass be given for the jeweler's soul at the city's great cathedral.

It is worth mentioning, though, that soon after the jeweler was taken to the hospital, his maid returned to his study and found the letter from the palace on the floor. It had been trampled on by the servants and the paramedics. She picked up the note and tried brushing the dirt marks off the parchment paper. But the marks stayed. With illicit delight, she looked at Madam's beautiful writing and was saddened by the thought that it had not been enough to stop the jeweler from suffering a heart attack.

Because the maid, being illiterate, could not read the note, she took it next door to show to the jeweler's neighbor, the one who had called for the ambulance earlier. On seeing the note, the woman's eyes lit up. For she had found cause to think that perhaps it was not gluttony that killed the jeweler after all. What the note said was this: *To Ding, my generous and talented friend, thank you for the beautiful tiara you have given to me, which I shall proudly wear on the occasion of my daughter's wedding. It is a gift I will cherish forever. Your admirer and patron, Madam.*

So was born another rumor to keep tongues wagging all over the city.

As for the unfortunate jeweler's servant, the poor woman, on hearing Madam's message read out loud, wept with deep regret. Oh, poor, poor Mr. Sarmiento, he would never make it to the grand wedding now.

PART IV

34

❦

Wedding Bells

Morning brought a golden light and an unblemished sky. It was made-to-order weather for a wedding. And with the exception of only a few people—like myself—it can be said that the nation's attention was focused on the town of Salinas.

As light from the new day bathed El Presidente's hometown, its streets appeared to be paved with gold. From the windows of the houses that lined the main road, a soft light glowed. The little squares of *capiz* shell that made up the panes had all been cleaned of the dust of years, so that, with their natural luster revealed once more, their surfaces mirrored back the morning light.

The whole town had been turned upside down, inside out for the event. In the little town plaza, the stone statues of El Presidente and Madam, which had stood in the open, covered with grime and bird droppings, had been steam-cleaned just the day before. Now they gleamed in the sun. At the base of the statues, plants in terra-cotta pots added a country touch.

There were flowers everywhere. Red, orange, pink, yellow, and white blossoms lined the streets and cascaded from the windowsills of every home.

At measured intervals along the main road, little girls in white satin dresses with yellow sashes around their waists stood at attention, each holding a basket filled with the velvety-soft petals of yellow roses. With their neatly combed hair, dainty outfits, and polished new shoes, they made a pretty picture as they watched attentively for the signal they knew would soon come.

As the time for the bridal journey to the cathedral drew near, the wedding guests slid the windows wide open, peering expectantly into the distance. How the guests came to be in these houses was an interesting story in itself. The people who lived in them had simply moved out for the duration of the wedding celebration. They were handsomely paid for the use of their homes, which had been superficially refurbished on the outside, and comfortably refurnished on the inside.

The bridal party finally arrived.

The first to come into view were the four white limousines carrying the eight flower girls, three bridesmaids, the maid of honor, and Madam. They advanced at a leisurely pace, allowing the crowd to view them, to cheer, to clap, and to wave. In the background, music wafted gently from the PA system mounted on colorfully festooned electric poles.

Now only the bridal car was left to be seen.

Suddenly, at the top of the street, a loud "Oh!" was heard and onlookers craned their necks to see better. There was a tinkling of bells and the sound of hooves, then an open silver carriage with a royal crest on its door drawn by six white Arabian stallions came into view. Holding the reins, which had been strung with miniature bells, was a regally uniformed driver of foreign appearance.

The carriage, it was soon learned, had come all the way from Vienna and had been loaned to Madam by a count. The horses had traveled from Rabat with their trainer, courtesy of a wealthy oil sheikh, who at that moment stood gazing at the bridal party from one of the windows fronting the road.

As for the bride herself, she was a vision to behold. A princess in a fairy-tale wedding. Her hair was pulled back off her face and gathered by a bead-encrusted band that matched the intricate beadwork on her bodice. Only later, when she marched down the aisle of the cathedral, would the two thousand guests see what those beads were made of.

The little girls who lined the road threw thousands of fresh yellow rose petals in the wind as the carriage passed. Their sweet scent filled the air. From her carriage, Maia, the princess bride, smiled and waved to the well-wishers. And sitting next to her, El Presidente, too, waved at the crowd. But the smile he wore failed to reach his eyes.

The horses began to move at a smart pace as soon as they cleared the town. At this point, the guests swiftly made for the waiting air-conditioned double-decker buses. These would take them to the cathedral via a quicker, alternative route. The route had been carefully worked out to ensure they would arrive before the bridal carriage, and thus be able to join the other fifteen hundred guests already there in welcoming the bride. The guests, it must be mentioned, had been flown in by the national carrier, which had put on twenty-four additional flights over the last two days.

Half an hour later, the bridal carriage drew up in front of the cathedral. Soon after, the wedding march began. Singing a madrigal, the choir's voices filled the interior as the country's revered cardinal led the march. Behind him were the four priests who would assist him, and they were followed by six altar boys.

The interior of the cathedral was illuminated that morning by six hundred candles. On either side of the central aisle was a profusion of angel's trumpets in stone vases. The aisle itself was covered with a white silk runner on which the ring bearer, followed by the eight flower girls, now walked.

Soon the three bridesmaids came into view, and close behind them the maid of honor. Then in pairs, the three sets of secondary sponsors for the candle, the veil, and the cord, and behind them the three sets of major sponsors.

Now the mother of the groom, in an elegant silk gown, was escorted down the aisle by the Senate Speaker, Emilio Zamora, who was one of the wedding godparents. And a few paces behind, resplendent in a yellow hand-embroidered *terno*, came the tall and regal figure of Madam, and next to her the imposing and aristocratic Don Miguel Pellicer.

At last, the moment the late Ding Sarmiento had dreamed of finally came to pass. The Sarmiento Tiara held the attention of every woman present; they gazed at it admiringly and enviously while their husbands secretly wondered what price to put on this latest object of extravagance, and how much it had added to the national deficit.

The central piece was a luminous pearl the size of a quail egg. On either side of it evenly matched pearls, with gradations in size, were set in a curve. And between each pearl was a perfect diamond. It was apparent to all that the stones had been painstakingly chosen. Everyone agreed that Ding Sarmiento had created a masterpiece. It was so unfortunate that he had died before savoring this moment of triumph.

If the Sarmiento Tiara drew much attention, nothing could compare with the reaction of the crowd at the entrance of the bride. For only now, up close, did they see that her gown and headgear were studded with pearls from her mother's famed South Sea pearl collection. Later, Madam herself would reveal that a total of five hundred and twenty-eight pearls had gone into the making of the bridal gown.

Then the moment finally arrived for El Presidente to give his daughter's hand to the groom. Standing by the front pew, Iñigo Pellicer was a handsome young man of a slighter build than his father. His face bore a strong resemblance to his mother's, with its high cheekbones and sharp features.

Many were seeing father and son together for the first time. And this provided a rare opportunity to compare the two. Quite a number of the guests secretly thought that the son had not the father's commanding presence, and very likely lacked the father's vision, acumen, and legendary drive.

The guests also had the rare opportunity to study the seldom-seen matriarch of the Pellicer family. Because she lived down south and rarely visited the city, Doña Carmela Pellicer, now in her seventies, was a source of interest for many gathered in the cathedral. She was much admired for the way in which she had kept the Pellicer empire going after the death of her husband, while her son grew into his role. But she was not a woman one warmed to. Her expression had grown more forbidding with the years, many noted.

Sitting on the groom's side of the cathedral, her back rigid, she wore a severe expression bordering on displeasure. And why shouldn't she? Her mind, after all, still replayed the unpleasant words that had passed between herself and the don.

"There is another Pellicer out there, Mother." The don had spoken these words to her, without so much as a preamble, on his return from the city.

He had come to her part of the house—the north wing—the moment he arrived. He still wore his traveling clothes, and she had looked up and was about to acknowledge him when he strode straight into the room, then stopped in front of her, to speak those words. It had taken her a while to make sense of them. And only after he spoke again did she understand.

He said, "You never imagined I would find out, did you? My child whom you believed you had got rid of . . . lives."

She knew then. And her first thought had been how he had found out. Surely he had not spoken to that woman after all these years. His anger, too, appeared unreasonable to her. It was a thing of the past, which had lost all importance with time. So what if she had kept the matter from him? Why, she had done it for the good of the family. And had she not found him a proper wife in Marina? A woman of their own class, the right blood, the right upbringing, one worthy of a Pellicer—unlike that other one, that cheap, deceitful woman who had obviously disobeyed her wishes even after having taken the money. That she should have had the child was an outrage.

But her curiosity had to be satisfied. And the don watched with interest the play of expression on his mother's face. He waited for her to speak. Finally, she said, "A boy?"

With a smile like a sneer, he said to her softly, "A *true* Pellicer, Mother."

The don's mother flinched. And the don felt a sense of cruel satisfaction. "A *true* one, Mother, one who wears this mark that I wear. With a strength of character and courage that would impress even you. Not like that one who carries our name, born to fortune, yes, but not likely to make anything of what he has been given. One whose claim to fame will be his association with the most disreputable family this country has ever seen. You threw away gold, Mother, and must settle for dust, and I cannot say you did not deserve this!"

The don had purposely misled his mother, letting her think his bastard child was male. He had done it to punish her, for like him, he knew his mother looked at Iñigo with concern. Like him, she found Iñigo wanting.

He had also misled his mother for another reason. He now had her true measure and did not trust her not to do something destructive. Perhaps he had said too much already. But it was too late to take back his words.

"Surely, you cannot be thinking of acknowledging this . . . this . . ."

"My other child? What makes you think he would wish it? It would shame him to be called a Pellicer."

Seeing the astonishment on his mother's face, he laughed. "Not everyone, Mother, values our name as much as us. I am beginning to think it a curse myself."

With that, the don strode out of the room, leaving his mother to ponder the past and the uncertain future.

Like his mother, the don sat in the cathedral with an expression impossible to read. His mother, glancing at him, could only guess in vain what was going through her son's mind. Had she known his thoughts, she would have found little comfort in them. For the don, that very moment, had arrived at a decision that would give his mother much cause for concern.

The don had decided to leave his empire behind.

He was a man who had at last seen his life for what it was. It had taken him twenty-four years to arrive at the realization that he had never lived his life as he wished. Never followed the dictates of his heart. He had sacrificed his own wishes for the sake of his family fortune. For all his wealth and possessions, he had never known true happiness.

Assessing his life, he saw that he had for a mother someone who valued reputation above his personal happiness. In fact, everything and everyone was expendable as long as the Pellicers kept their august position. As for his wife and son, well, they left him cold. He had for a wife a woman he had never loved. And a son he could never be proud of.

And all this was his reward for having given up his life for his family. How worthless it was in the end. All his effort and all his sacrifice would be rendered useless at the conclusion of this ceremony. Iñigo, through this ambitious marriage, would taint the Pellicer name and the Pellicer blood. And soon that blood would mix with that of a woman whose family he could only look at with distaste.

So the don made the decision to turn his back on everything he once valued. On Iñigo's return from his honeymoon, he would initiate him into the business. He would give him more and more responsibility while he, the don, would increasingly withdraw from the running of the vast Pellicer business interests. He would be there to guide his son for the next five years, after which Iñigo would have to stand on his own. And if the empire should be lost, so be it. The don was too disillusioned to care. He decided, too, that on returning south, he would call his real-estate agent. If the island he had said no to some months ago was still on the market, he would purchase it. And there he would live.

Of his mother's opinion, the don did not spare a single thought. For the first time in his life, he would ignore her wishes. Their interests no longer coincided. From now on, he swore to live for himself and by himself.

In the cathedral, as the choir sang another hymn, their heavenly voices reaching up toward the sky, the don thought of the future and of the time he would no longer need to be among this family of his whom he cared nothing for and who cared nothing for him. He wished this part of his life over.

The bride's father, too, could find no pleasure in what should have been a joyful occasion. After sixteen years in power, he had finally acknowledged that all that he held would soon be lost to him, slipping through his fingers like fine sand. It was just a matter of time now.

As the secondary sponsors came up in pairs—the first to light the candles, the second to pin the veil over the bride and groom's shoulders, and the third to slip a silk cord over their heads—El Presidente thought of Aure. He acknowledged to himself that in using the colonel, he had done himself a disservice. The colonel's actions were guaranteed to hasten El Presidente's downfall.

He was chilled by the memory of his last meeting with the monster.

El Presidente had expected to see a nervous unsure Aure. But the man who entered his office was a self-contained being who exuded nothing but calm. Aure's air of command enraged him but it also showed him the truth behind the Chief of Staff's warnings. Aure was a different sort of creature and had to be handled with care and cunning.

Suppressing his desire to abuse the colonel, he greeted him instead with a detached courtesy. El Presidente had decided to play a different game. He told Aure that the impression he had wished to create with the grenade explosion had been achieved. And that being the case, his task was now complete. "You have got rid of a big thorn for me. The controversy will eventually die down. As for the students, well, they are leaderless now, which is what I wanted all along. Now I wish you to return south, where you are urgently needed. And I expect you to do as good a job there as you have done here."

If the colonel felt anything was amiss, he showed no sign of it, which reassured El Presidente. Oh yes, he had the cunning of a fox still. He would outsmart this monster. He told himself that he would make him pay.

"You will depart as soon as arrangements can be made. And since I shall not be seeing you again before you go, as I myself leave for the north tonight, you must drink to my daughter's happiness before you leave."

Champagne was brought in and El Presidente himself poured the bubbling liquid into two long-stemmed crystal glasses He gave one to Aure and took the other. Then he motioned for the colonel to join him out on the balcony.

The two men stepped outside and stood in silence, looking out toward the river. Together they watched a man in a punt go past, the water lilies parting to make way for him. And in the distance, they listened to a ferry chugging through the water.

Without glancing at his companion, El Presidente asked, "By the way, where did you dump his body?"

Aure, his eyes on the water, replied softly, "Why, right here, sir . . . in the river."

It was just as well that the colonel was looking out toward the river when he said this, for he missed the look of shock on his superior's face, which quickly gave way to distaste. El Presidente struggled to mask his feelings, although his sense of revulsion would remain with him long after Aure had gone.

Not trusting himself to comment, El Presidente simply nodded. And Aure with his twisted mind took this as a sign of approval and appreciation of what he himself considered a nice imaginative touch.

It would have astounded the colonel to know how his revelation had shaken El Presidente to the core, for from that moment onward El Presidente could never again look at the river without seeing the image of Bayani, and feeling his presence so threateningly close to the palace.

After Aure departed, El Presidente summoned the Defense Minister to his office. Two hours later, the man was ushered in by one of the presidential aides. The minister immediately noted the darkness of the room. Only on seeing the curtains drawn across the balcony door did he realize why. But before he could remark on this, El Presidente spoke. "I want you to arrange for Aure's return to the south."

So Aure was to be exiled for his actions after all.

"I'll brief him before he leaves," said the Defense Minister.

El Presidente interrupted the man; leaning forward, he told him, "You don't understand, my friend, I do not want him . . . to arrive."

So El Presidente had sealed Aure's fate, at the same time sensing that his own—the end of his regime—could not be too far behind.

But having come this far, having held on to his power this long, he was not in a hurry to relinquish it without a fight. Aure had to be done away with because he knew too much. It was a desperate measure but then these were desperate times.

The cardinal intoned the final blessing and soon the customary taking of photographs began. El Presidente and Madam stood next to Maia; the don and his wife next to Iñigo. And gradually they were joined by the sponsors and other guests until the whole altar area was filled with people. An hour later, the organist played the final march and the choir sang another glorious song as the wedding party emerged out into the sunlight, where the bride and groom were greeted by a shower of rice grains and confetti for good luck.

The cathedral bells rang loud and clear, their clanging joined by bells from all the neighboring towns. And for the next five minutes, their collective pealing filled the air and was heard a great distance away.

Then the two thousand guests—the women decked in their finery and priceless jewelry, the men in their elegant formal wear—made for the giant canopies that had been erected within sight of the church ruins. It was a magical setting. The crumbling walls with their vine-covered arches gave the guests the impression that they had stepped back in time, and that the celebration that was about to commence was of historic importance.

As the guests took their seats by the long linen-covered tables, the eighty-six members of the National Philharmonic Orchestra—flown in the day before—played their first piece for what was to be a noon-till-midnight feast.

At the table nearest the principal party, close to a fountain that spouted French champagne, Lorena Zamora-Mijares sat with her brooding handsome husband, the notorious Senator Sixto Mijares, who could no longer bear to be near her.

The senator was at last in the process of realizing his responsibility for what had befallen Ana. His philandering ways, he saw now, had turned his wife into a vengeful creature. Feeling slighted by him for so long, she had finally lashed out at his mistress. He realized, too, that she must have been angry with him all these years but had shown no sign of it. For her action, he knew, was not consistent with her nature. Lorena was a woman who displayed only good breeding.

It is important to note, however, that although the senator was finally able to see much of what was once hidden from him, like many of his gender he still failed to see into a woman's heart. He remained blind to the fact that at the core of his wife's action was her disappointment at having failed to win his love. Nevertheless, this newfound awareness would have an effect on his character. And an unexpected and distressing development would finally complete the change in his nature.

After seeing Ana's face, the senator had done two very rash things. The first, as we know, was to confront El Presidente on the matter of the missing student. And the second was to try to pay his wife back by taking up with a well-known actress. He had wined and dined her, and on the third day of his seduction scheme had booked a room at the Regent, the same one he had chosen for his aborted tryst with Ana.

The evening, which had begun so promisingly, ended in disaster. For the first time in his life, the virile and sexually gifted Senator Sixto "El Toro" Mijares failed to perform. No matter how hard he tried and how much he willed it, his body failed him. For at the crucial moment, the woman's face was transformed into Ana's damaged face. And this would be the cause of El Toro's lasting impotence: every woman he attempted to make love to would, in the final moment, take on his mistress's half-beautiful, half-ugly face.

This failure would, in the end, hasten his transformation from a man driven by carnal pursuits to one who lived a life of asceticism. He would maintain his magnetism, but with no way to release his drive, he would channel his energies not only into the formulation of brilliant economic policies, but also in just causes. And so gradually his reputation as a womanizer would be eclipsed by his contribution to the nation.

As for Lorena Zamora-Mijares, her success in punishing her

wayward husband brought her no pleasure. A momentary satisfaction, yes, but this was quickly replaced with a sense of horror of herself. The act of throwing acid on her husband's mistress had revealed to her a side of her self she had not been aware of. Lying in bed at night, she could still hear Ana's screams as the acid burned into her flesh.

It did not help either that a rumor soon circulated in the city's papers regarding the matter—beginning, I can tell you now, at the rumor mill called the Press Club—so that one gossip columnist would maliciously write: *The Ice Princess has turned into an Acid Queen.* On reading this, Lorena stayed home for two weeks. Then her father, the senate speaker, had come to see her. And told her the thing could not be undone, that she must face the world no matter what. So Lorena put on a show of courage. She left her room and stepped out of her house. She threw herself into charitable causes and became known for the good work she did, and with time would be considered the exemplary wife of a rising political figure.

As for her relationship with the senator, I wish I had better things to report. But only the truth will do in these pages. The senator would never transfer his amorous attention to his wife—it had become impossible for him to do so anyway—so her bed remained cold, but she took comfort in the knowledge that at least no other woman could have him either.

Sitting side by side but showing little interest in each other and little interest in the celebration itself, the senator and his wife were in danger of being the gloomiest guests at the wedding banquet. But their indifference was to be shaken, if only momentarily, for even they with their unhappy hearts could not help but be moved by the spectacle that was about to unfold.

A multitude of little girls in floral frocks walked toward the surrounding trees, and as the orchestra played a joyous piece specially composed for this moment, the girls reached out for the long satin sashes that dangled from giant bell-shaped cages hanging from hundreds of tree branches. As the violins soared and the cymbals clanged, the little girls gave the satin sashes a light tug, releasing into the air a thousand white doves. From where they sat, the guests heard the flapping of a thousand pairs of wings, beating harder and faster as the doves launched themselves skyward, joyous in their freedom, flying higher and higher in a formation resembling a giant heart.

On seeing this, all the guests, including the surly senator, rose to their feet and broke into a round of happy, spontaneous applause. For how many could say they had ever seen a sight to match this, or been to a celebration as wondrous as this wedding banquet by the majestic Cathedral of the North, on a day that shone so clear one could say the gods were indeed smiling.

As the doves winged their way heavenward, becoming but tiny dots in the clear blue sky, Madam was heard to say to those around her, "What did I tell you? Today would be a perfect day!"

35

✹

To the Mountain, to the River

On the morning of the wedding, as the rest of the country was waking up with a sense of excitement and turning on their television sets to watch the coverage of the event, Laslo was perhaps the only person in the whole archipelago who was unaware of what day it was.

Unlike the previous week of sedated sleep and blurred waking, today he opened his eyes and looked at the world with an alert mind. He rose from his bed, feeling slightly giddy and unsure on his feet. He opened the door and stepped out into the hall. No one was about. He made his way to the bathroom, where he cleaned his teeth and splashed water on his face. Then, without bothering to shower, he returned to his room and dressed.

On his way downstairs, he heard the sound of the television set. He wondered who could be watching it at this time of morning, and what there was that was worth watching. Then he met the maid, who froze at the sight of him.

After a shocked silence, she exclaimed, Ay *salamat sa Dios!* and proceeded to make the sign of the cross. But before she could express her joy at seeing him up and about, Laslo had reached the bottom of the stairs.

She turned to follow him, saying she would make him something to eat. He kept walking. She ran down after him and saw him head toward the front door. She asked where he was going. Laslo did not stop to reply. He opened the door and shut it behind him. The maid stood immobile with indecision. Should she chase after him or run to warn her mistress?

Either way, she was too late.

The jeepney driver pulled up by the curb, the engine idling as Laslo boarded it. He paid his fare and sat back, gazing at the traffic scene.

Smoky Mountain in the glare of sunlight was no longer surreal. Without the play of light and shadow which gave it a sense of mystery, it was simply an ugly monument to poverty. One thing remained constant. It reeked to the high heavens. Its ability to turn Laslo's stomach had not diminished by day.

Laslo, standing on the inclined walkway, surveyed the area about him. He realized he was still ignorant of its terrain. Places seen at night appear different by day. He felt lost. But he couldn't remain standing here. He walked the last few meters to the end of the walkway, scanning the confusion of shanties around him.

Hands in his pockets—his pants felt loose, as though they belonged to someone else—he took the first street to the right. As he walked, he was aware of the curious glances directed his way. He refrained from meeting anyone's eyes, just kept his gaze fixed on the shanties built with pieces of plywood, scraps of metal, and old plasterboard, all fitted together by necessity. Most of the homes were no bigger than his bedroom. It occurred to him that poverty took on many forms. What he saw here was a poverty of space. You needed money to buy space. And fresh air.

A scrawny dog, ribs sticking out, raised a leg and pissed on the base of a streetlight. Laslo wondered where humans went to relieve themselves in this place. The shanties on this street were too small to house a toilet. He turned a corner and for the next hour walked about the narrow and congested lanes of Smoky Mountain.

His stomach rumbled. He was hungry. But even if he found food here, he wouldn't dare eat it. Then he remembered the meal he had at the old man's place on the night he had come in search of Luis Bayani.

Was that why he had come back here? To search for Luis? Laslo
wondered if he was safe. Since the night he returned home from the
camp, he had been paralyzed by his grief over Sophia's murder.
Sophia. Laslo shook his head to clear his mind of the memory.

A dog growled and a cat hissed and three children scampered by.
A short distance away, a group of boys played with marbles and two
girls played hopscotch. He wondered what it was like to be born in
this place, and to die here never knowing another life. He slowed to
a stop. Eyed the ramshackle homes, trying to understand how life
could be sustained within their narrow, dark, and suffocating con-
fines. What made up the minimum requirements of human life?
Suddenly, the colonel came to mind. Laslo shuddered.

He moved on. At the end of the street he paused. Left or right?
He turned right once more. He didn't know where he was. But there
was something familiar about the place. Perhaps he and Luis Bayani
had walked through this street that night. He slowed down. And
oblivious to the curious looks of the women and children that
passed him in the street, he studied the shanty in front of him with
its low-hung door.

No. It couldn't be, he said to himself. He looked at the doors
of the other shanties. All of them were hung low. He turned to go.
Just then, the door creaked open and he heard a woman's voice.

"Dahan-dahan, Mang Serio! Huwag mong bibiglain."

The woman came out first, then, behind her, an old man. The
hunchback from the mountain.

Laslo stood frozen. His gaze never leaving the old man whose
hump he would have recognized anywhere in this city. The man
looked frail. And the woman kept admonishing him to take it easy,
not to rush it. She heard him say it was after all the first time the old
man had risen, so he simply had to slow down.

The old man looked up at Laslo, who blocked his way. A look of
recognition spread over his crinkled face.

"Aha!" he cried. "What brings you here again, Laslo boy?"

Then before Laslo could think of something to say, the old man
coughed and clutched at his ribs and Laslo reached out to stop him
falling over. The women close by gathered around to help old Mang

Serio. One of them quickly placed a stool behind the old man. When the coughing fit had passed, he took a deep breath and sat down. After a while he said to Laslo, "They nearly killed me, boy, but it wasn't my time yet."

Laslo learned how a group of men had come for old Mang Serio the night after his escape with Bayani.

"Where is Bayani heading?' they wanted to know.

"Well, I figured I had lived seventy long years and anything more would be sheer greediness. So I didn't really care what else happened. As they held me down and one of them asked me again, at knifepoint, where Bayani was, I spat at him. Hah! I can still see the look on the bastard's face! It was worth dying for. He raised his knife but just then the Santos boys rushed in."

The old man paused to catch his breath. "You see, Tonio next door heard all this noise coming from my place. Walls are thin in these shanties. He called for help. Since Luis left we had been expecting trouble, you know, because it was no secret that the Loyola students ran a community center here. Oh, the men were prepared all right. The Santos boys—all six of them—came running with their bits of chains, their *balisongs* and *bolos*. I don't know how they all fitted in that box of mine, well, you've seen the inside yourself. The men were outnumbered and let me go. The boys would have killed them but Tonio stopped them in time. We didn't want more trouble than we already had. They ran, those cowards, like dogs with their tails between their legs."

Old Serio spat on the ground in disgust. An act that caused him to wince in pain. He clutched his side again. Then looked at Laslo and said, "They broke my ribs. Four of them. *Putang ina!* Now, Laslo boy, what news have you?"

Laslo shook his head. Tired of crouching on the ground, he rose to stretch his legs.

"Not talking, eh?"

"Have you had news?" Laslo asked.

The old man did not answer, just looked away. Then he motioned to Laslo to come and help him rise. He wished to go back inside. Laslo let him use his arm as support. The old man stood and slowly made his way back.

"Kicked this door in, they did, huh!" he mumbled to himself. "What are you standing out there for, boy, come inside."

Laslo went in after the old man. And the door shut behind them.

That morning of the wedding, I kept my promise to Luis Bayani at last. I left the Convent of Santa Clara accompanied by my mother. We headed for the river.

I had never walked along its banks before. Like many city dwellers, I never paid much attention to it. It was just there. A body of foul water I crossed every day on my way to the *Chronicle*. The jeepney I rode always traveled across one of the seven bridges that spanned the river. I would give it a passing glance, looking without seeing, smelling more than I saw, my mind always on something else.

Now on the south bank—the poor side—my mother and I walked along the low concrete wall. She didn't say much. Just followed behind me. I didn't know where I was going. All I knew was I needed to come here. It had featured so vividly in my dreams.

There was not much worth looking at. The south bank wore an ugliness that spoke of poverty. At the foot of the bridge there was a worn path that led to that barren world. The earth failed to sustain even weeds. Here and there were discarded old tires, rusty metal containers and pipes, and all kinds of industrial throwaways to break the monotony of nothingness.

Overhead, I could see the tall exhaust stack of the coconut-oil refinery. Like a giant fat cigar sending a whorl of black smoke into the sky. The smell was thick, rich, and cloying. Hinting at sweetness. It masked the smell of the river.

I trudged on, uncaring of the heat. Behind me I heard my mother following, shadowing my every move. I turned to look at her, thinking about her still-bleeding feet, which made walking a punishment. There was a dreamy quality to her face. This perplexing woman who was called to my side by my nightmare, who fed me and gave me water to drink and wiped the tears from my face in those nights of my restless sleep. She had not left me since, continuing to follow where I went.

"You don't have to come with me today," I told her as I dressed to go out. "You can't walk far."

"I will come," was her reply. So I let her decide. But I wondered what she would do afterward. I was to return to work on Monday and would be going home to Vito Cruz again.

"Where will you go?" I had asked her as we waited for a ride to the bridge.

She told me that Mother Superior had said she could stay on until she made up her mind. One thing was sure, though, she would never go back to live in Calle de Leon. The uproar caused by her wounds had made it impossible for her to return. Her neighbors, she told me, looked at her strangely at the same time that they fussed over her. She could not bear the attention, she said.

When I told her I would be returning to the house in Vito Cruz, she had accepted my news silently, but I saw her stiffen. And feeling I had to say something, I said, "I will see you at the convent, I visit there, you know." She said nothing.

I heard the tooting of a ferry in the distance and returned my attention to the land before me. Then I saw it. It was nothing worth looking at. Only an empty warehouse with no signage to identify its past purpose. But I knew this place. The shape of it was somehow imprinted in the film of my memory. I walked around it while behind me I heard my mother's slow, careful steps on the hard ground.

Then I found myself climbing a mound. As I started from its base, it was high enough to block the river wall from view. When I finally stood on top of it and gazed down at the water, my skin tingled, and the hairs on my arms and the back of my neck rose. I felt myself sucked back into the dark vortex of that night. I felt once more its soft breeze, heard again its water lapping back and forth. Perhaps I heard all this in the present. Perhaps I was hearing this in my dream. Then I heard the water part as a weight dropped into it. Finally, I heard the water swallowing.

"Clara . . ." my mother called to me, her voice pulling me back to the present. I took my eyes off the dark waters of the river. I looked at

her. The dreamy quality gone from her face. In its place was an awareness that embraced the whole world. I wondered if she, too, knew.

"Here . . . they fed him to the river from here," I told her.

But she spoke at the same time, and I realized it was something
else that occupied her mind. Eyes wide, she said to me, "The world
is moving . . . can you feel it, Clara?"

36

Watery Secrets

Mel and the boys let out a loud whoop as I walked into the newsroom at eight-thirty on Monday morning. I had been gone two and a half weeks. But before they could ask me how I was feeling—they still believed, except for Mel, that I had been sick and staying with friends—Torres strode into the room, information sheets and assignment pad in hand, a pencil wedged behind his right ear, which through the years, they say, had angled out more than his left. He caught sight of me. Paused.

"You're back." It was more a statement than a question. I was relieved.

"In that case," he said, taking the pencil from behind his ear and scribbling on his pad, "take this one. Waterways Department. You won't have to go out. Just rewrite their information." He searched for the relevant sheet.

I almost smiled. I caught Joey Lapus's eyes, which were twinkling with delight. But I didn't roll my eyes at him the way I used to every time Torres gave me one of these throwaway stories.

Torres handed me a sheet with the Waterways Department logo. "There's some massive river-dredging operation near the palace." My heart missed a beat. He looked up from his pad. "Find an angle. Environmental, beautification, even sanitation and hygiene, I don't know. Just think of something other than that boring drivel they sent us."

I nodded, barely able to contain my excitement. It must have shown on my face, for Joey looked at me with interest, cocking his brow as if to say, "You like this, do you?"

I did. And I couldn't wait to get out of the office. I read through the information sheet. I noted which part of the river was being dredged. Then I told Torres I was going to the site to watch the operation in progress. He looked up in surprise.

"It's not necessary, not if you don't feel up to it."

I reassured him I was fine. It occurred to me the man might have a heart after all. I got my pen and pad and stuffed them into my bag. Then I ran out of the building into the street. I couldn't wait to be outside. I almost felt sorry for Torres, who never left the newsroom. His life was run by the telephone and fax machine. He was never out where things happened. Stories came to him after the fact. The tragedies enacted, blood shed, joys shared. The energy of life never reached him in its raw form. It was distilled into news articles by people like me. He saw and heard and felt things secondhand. Poor Torres. I wondered if he envied me my river-dredging story.

The river was a beehive of activity. The dredging operation covered a wide area, beginning from the Lacson Bridge just before the palace all the way to the open sea. The Waterways Department press release said it was the biggest and most thorough operation ever set into motion. Not only would the river be cleared of the water lilies, but the debris of ages which had collected at its bottom would finally be removed. You can imagine how this piece of information affected me.

I watched the operation from the south bank, where I had been just the day before. The work was slow and not much happened during the hour I stood by the wall.

With a mind to make better use of my time, I made my way back up to the bridge, where I hailed a cab to the city's Crime Prevention Bureau. I asked to see the research-department head, whom I had dealt with in the past. I was after some statistics. I stayed for an hour, asking questions, taking notes.

I had an hour and a half to spare before the men by the river stopped for lunch. This is a country where mealtimes are religiously observed. I intended to be back there when they were free to talk. Meanwhile, I headed for the city morgue. As I entered the building and made my way to what we reporters called "the freezer," I tried to recall the number of times I had been here over the last eighteen months.

The first time was the worst. There was another junior reporter with me from one of the rival papers; I did better than he did—he was sick all over the floor. I prided myself on having been only green in the face. The smell was indescribable because the body, unzipped for viewing, was in a state of advanced decomposition. The flesh was mush and teeming with life. Hundreds of wriggling white maggots feeding on dead flesh. A form of symbiosis I did not care to see again.

"You here for the latest finds?" the attendant asked.

He described the twenty-three bodies which had arrived in the past week. None of them was the one I was looking for. I asked if anyone had been fished out of the river recently. The attendant did not have to think for long.

"A woman. Not in one piece, though. Just the upper torso. No arms. No legs. Police are checking if it's linked to the head, the one they found in the garbage bin two weeks ago at a chemical dump site."

I asked him a couple more questions, then asked if I could quote him.

"Sure," he said, eyes lighting up. "When's the story coming out?"

I told him. Then I checked my watch, thanked the man, and left the building. The change in temperature always provided a brief shock to the system. The room I had just left wasn't called the freezer for no reason. Standing outside the building, I felt I was melting.

A cab pulled up in front of me. I waited for its passenger to disembark, a reporter I recognized. We nodded to each other. I got in and asked the driver to take me to the Lacson Bridge.

*　*　*

The crew from the Waterways Department ate in the meager shade provided by a group of *ipil-ipil* trees, with their elongated seed pods dipping with the wind.

I introduced myself. Showed my ID to the man in charge. I told him to please finish his lunch. I was happy to wait. But he insisted he would eat later, eager for the interview to begin. I guess if you spent your time dredging muck from rivers and lakes and canals for a living, talking to a reporter was a novelty.

No. They hadn't found anything of much importance. Just old tires, empty bottles, metal drums, all the usual stuff that got thrown over the wall into the river. Of course, he said, they've found odd things in the past. Like cars marked with bullet holes. And on several occasions, dead bodies even.

"Well, what about the bodies?" I wanted to know. "Where do you take them?"

"Usually they get sent to the morgue."

"Usually?"

"Yes. But not this time. I'm to call a Colonel Oroso at Campo Diaz if we find one. They told us the military is helping crack down on crime." People will believe anything. It was easy to see why he fell for that one.

I gave the man my card and asked him to call me if he found anything interesting. Bodies especially. I told him I was a young reporter trying to make my mark. I could see he liked the thought of giving me a break, especially if I wrote him into the story. He promised to call.

An hour later, I returned to the *Chronicle* and wrote my piece.

DREDGING THE RIVER:
WHAT SECRETS WILL IT REVEAL?

The river's long-kept secrets may soon be revealed with the Waterways Department's massive river-dredging project which began yesterday.

The operation is of a magnitude that can only be described as ambitious.

According to Operations Manager Graciano Lagman, who was interviewed on the site yesterday, the project involves a crew of sixty men, which is three times what has normally been used in the past. And the work itself will take eight weeks to complete.

When asked if he expected to find anything unusual hidden in the bottom of the river, Lagman said, "We've had many surprises in the past. Once we found a dead body weighed down by a big rock, and another time a bullet-ridden car."

If the operation had begun just a week earlier, the crew would have discovered the upper torso of a woman which now lies in the city morgue awaiting identification. It's just the latest in a series of gruesome finds from the river.

Lorenzo Magalona, an attendant from the City Morgue on Salazar Street, said, "So far this year we've received eight bodies from the river. Who knows how many more they'll fish out when they clean the bottom out?"

Last year, sixteen bodies were found in the area between the Lacson Bridge and the Mendez end of the river, where the water flows into the sea—the same segment covered by the river-dredging project. The palace, which lies on the northern bank of this affected area, will also benefit from the operation.

The proliferation of chemical and human waste, household rubbish, and the occasional dead body gives rise to the worst possible stench. The dredging will, according to a Waterways Department study, "reduce unpleasant odors caused by atmospheric factors by at least sixty percent."

The Health and Sanitation Department sees the project as a means of lowering health risks for the people living in the slums along the south bank—the polluted river is a source of water for many of the poor.

Dredging the river could also shed light on the whereabouts of certain missing individuals. The Crime Prevention Bureau, in the last twelve months, listed as missing 469 people in the city alone.

In view of the fact that the river has been repeatedly used as a dumping site for victims of gang wars and "salvage" operations, it will be interesting to observe what the river coughs up over the next eight weeks. At the end of the operation, it may well be that certain missing persons will cease to be classified as missing, their fates finally known. And their spirits allowed to rest at last.

I handed it to Torres and returned to my desk. Not much else happened for the rest of the afternoon and I left soon after five.

I would read my story in the following day's papers. Printed word for word as I had written it. And the best part of all, it had my name on it. That had never happened before. Torres himself said nothing, but I didn't let this detract from the pleasure it brought me. And much as I would have liked to dwell on what I considered my first piece of good reporting, something of greater significance drew my attention.

It was with—I am ashamed to say—almost uncontainable excitement that I heard the news of a tragedy that had occurred just an hour before up north.

In the town of Salinas, where just two days ago the grand wedding had been celebrated and witnessed by two thousand guests and thousands of locals, and on which the nation's eyes had been focused, an earthquake had destroyed the town and its neighboring areas. But the most interesting thing about the quake was what happened to the Cathedral of the North. And no one could have summed up the event better than Mel, who, as she grabbed my arm, said, "Clara, can't you see? It's the second sign of prophecy! It has happened, Clara!"

37

The Cathedral Is No More

The town of Salinas woke up that Tuesday morning still feeling a sense of euphoria. A festive air continued to hang over the place. And many, in fact, believed it would never disappear. For the grand wedding held in their church—now elevated to the status of a cathedral—had brought fame to their town. They saw it as a turning point and believed that from then on, the place would be destined for greater things. None of the usual sense of deflation, of anticlimax, which often comes after much excitement, had set in. Perhaps the reason for this delayed return to reality lay in the fact that some of the wedding guests still remained, giving the locals a false sense of continuing celebration.

There were a good two hundred of them. And in a small, quiet town such as Salinas, they were highly conspicuous. They stayed on at the hotel by the sea, coming into Salinas for a few hours the day after the wedding and on that Tuesday to take in the rustic atmosphere, loving the attention and the warm welcome extended to them by the locals. They were rich city people and foreign guests to whom Salinas was a refreshing change. They spoke of visiting the neighboring areas.

Their plans, though, would come to nothing. For nature had other things in store for Salinas and its surrounds. At three o'clock that Tuesday, a tremor was felt in the town's streets. At first, some thought they imagined it. But it did not take long for everyone to realize that the earth itself was moving.

A loud, ripping sound was soon heard. Screams followed as right in the middle of the road where the royal carriage drawn by six Arabian stallions had passed just last Sunday, the ground began to gape as a fissure formed. It widened then began to lengthen rapidly, moving like a slithering snake, traveling northward.

In the center of the town plaza, the children watched with wide-mouthed horror as the statues of El Presidente and Madam, newly steam-cleaned for the wedding, tilted from their pedestal, first to one side then the other, before toppling to the ground. It happened just as a distant clang of bells was heard. The pealing grew louder as the earth shook harder. All the bells of the north were ringing.

The tremor reached far and wide. Out in the north's wide-open spaces where men worked the fields, the ground, they said, undulated, rising two meters, like waves cresting then subsiding then cresting and falling again. The terrain itself, they swore, had changed.

Along a three-kilometer stretch between the towns of Balay and San Tobias, a row of power lines and telephone poles leaned precariously across the main road. And in the towns within an eighty-five-kilometer radius of Salinas the power supply was abruptly cut.

In the main street of Mateo a three-story concrete building collapsed. The number of casualties would not be determined for another week, but the initial estimate put the figure at a hundred and sixty. Even the children were not spared. In Dagonoy, some ninety kilometers northeast of Mateo, the new hollow-block school fell within seconds of the quake commencing. From its rubble, the broken bodies of sixty-two primary students would be retrieved over the next couple of days.

In the tobacco fields, millions of dollars' worth of crops were lost as the towering concrete wall of the Great Northern Dam cracked and water poured out of the reservoir, flooding the surrounding plantation areas in no time. Because services were disrupted and would remain so for an indefinite period, the farmers and plantation owners could only look on helplessly, resigned to their loss.

As the quake wrought its damage, the country's seismographs

recorded its progress. The Seismological Study Center would later report than an earthquake measuring a magnitude of 6.3 on the Richter scale had occurred. And that it had lasted thirty-eight seconds, a brief moment in human terms but an eternity in the destructive world of tremors. Experts would reveal that the quake released energy equivalent to a one-megaton nuclear bomb. In relative terms, this was fifty times larger than the bomb dropped on Hiroshima. Just as well that the epicenter of the earthquake was located in a sparsely populated region, for the damage it would have wrought in a heavily built-up area would have been extensive.

Nevertheless, the quake was felt a great distance away from its epicenter. In the big city, which lay some five hundred and fifty kilometers south of Salinas, many claimed they felt the world turn, quite a number complained of dizzy spells and nausea, others heard their windows rattling, while several church bells scattered all over the metropolis were said to have rung of their own accord.

With the disruption of communication up north, news of the extent of devastation there would take over an hour to reach the palace. And when it did, it seemed as though the palace itself was experiencing a tremor of immeasurable magnitude.

Madam shook with anger. It was a personal affront that this had happened at all. Her first concern was to get the remaining guests out of the devastated north. She could not afford the bad international publicity that would come as a result of their experiences. Orders were thus quickly given to send a plane to the nearest functioning airport—a good hundred and twenty kilometers from Salinas—to evacuate the guests back to safety.

This done, a meeting was held to discuss in detail the necessary emergency measures. And two hours later, the palace issued a brief statement saying that a relief operation was under way. Food drops would be made while crews would be flown in by the air force to help restore essential services. Power would be restored to the major towns as soon as possible. Medical teams would be flown in within the hour. And engineers and construction workers would repair the damage to the roads immediately.

Just when it seemed Madam's anger had abated, strange news

arrived at the palace. Madam's secretary came rushing into the meeting room, flustered and breathless.

"The cathedral," she announced. "Madam, the cathedral is no more."

The first to discover that the cathedral was missing was the Dominican priest who said mass in it every Sunday. The priest had been in town when the quake occurred. He had remained there to help calm the people whose homes had been destroyed. Just before dusk he took leave of the family he had been sitting with. He wished to return to the cathedral to check whether it had sustained any damage, for news from the neighboring towns had been grim. On passing the plaza, he caught sight of a group of men struggling to raise the fallen statues of the first couple. He noted that the nose of El Presidente was missing while Madam was intact, save for a slight crack in the head.

The priest continued on his way. And he would have walked on had not a kind *kutsero* offered to take him in his horse-drawn vehicle. Together they traveled north, discussing the earthquake and how it had happened just when things were beginning to look up for the area. Now the towns had been reduced to rubble, the roads badly damaged; there was nothing to entice the tourists to visit. On they talked until at last they came to the vicinity of the cathedral. And there, the sight that greeted the priest and his companion rendered them speechless.

The land itself was scarred deeply, as though raked by giant steel claws. A kilometer-long jagged line led toward the direction of the cathedral, with rocks and boulders jutting out of what had once been flat land. But of the cathedral itself, nothing remained. The only thing that had been left standing was its bell tower, looking forlorn as it leaned precariously to the right.

The priest recalled the ringing of the bells when the quake first struck, and now understood that the bells of the north must have rung simultaneously, pealing their alarm at the destruction of the cathedral. Looking at the barren land, the priest could only imagine that it had been swallowed whole. The ground must have yawned wide and taken it all in. Walls, dome, windows, beams, cross, and altar—all swallowed in one great gulp.

It wasn't so much the loss of the cathedral that sent Madam into another fit of rage. It was the meaning of it. For, being superstitious by nature, she had not forgotten the words of the seer. And she knew without a doubt that those who would hear of this phenomenon would read it in the same light: the second sign of the prophecy had come to pass.

There was no preventing word from leaking out. There was no hiding the disappearance of the cathedral. The people would see this as a bad omen for the palace.

Madam's problems didn't end there.

The first of the aftershocks hit the north two hours after the initial tremor. With its arrival, many structures that had withstood the main shock now fell to ruin. The first aftershock registered 5.3 on the Richter scale. Three days later, a second aftershock would occur at a magnitude of 3.2. More aftershocks, in diminishing magnitude, occurred over the following week.

Another startling aftereffect of the quake came some five hours after the initial shock. The tsunami finally arrived. This giant wave, imperceptible on the ocean floor, grew in height as it approached the northern coastline. In the vicinity of the hotel Madam had built for the wedding, the wave, several stories high, crashed onto the shore, reached inland, and clawed away the pristine white sand that had been flown in from faraway Queensland in Australia. As all seventy tons of it was swallowed up by the sea, the dark sand that lay underneath reclaimed its rightful place once more.

Miraculously, the hotel itself remained standing. But the palms which had been transported across great distances, and transplanted on the hotel grounds, now leaned across each other, as if struck by the hand of God.

Unlike Madam, El Presidente did not lose control on hearing the news of the quake. Perhaps it was because he had not the energy to waste in a fit of anger. He had returned to the city mid-morning on Monday, for there was much to attend to. The hectic pace of the weekend had drained him of what little energy he had left.

The Chief of Staff was on another call when the news arrived. So it was the beady-eyed, simpering Press Secretary who delivered it. El Presidente listened without uttering a word, and with a wave of a hand signaled that he wished to be left alone. The Press Secretary, although miffed by this lack of response from El Presidente, took care not to show his feelings. He departed quickly, the model of efficiency.

When the door shut behind the Press Secretary, El Presidente remained seated in his chair for another minute or two. Then he slowly rose from his seat, and headed toward the heavy drapes that he now kept drawn even during the day. He tugged at the cord. The drapes parted and light entered through the glass doors. He pushed the doors open and stepped out onto the balcony. He stood there and stared at the river, engaging an invisible foe in battle. Since the day Aure told him of Bayani's whereabouts, the river had become a malevolent thing in El Presidente's mind.

The door to the office opened and the Chief of Staff, seeing El Presidente standing out on the balcony, joined him there. He coughed to make his presence known but El Presidente did not bother turning.

Keeping his voice even, the Chief of Staff said, "Sir, the Defense Minister rang and left this message: the chopper carrying Colonel Santiago Aure has gone down in the Batalban Mountains down south. Witnesses say an explosion occurred in midair."

The Chief of Staff waited for El Presidente's reaction. But none came, which made him think perhaps his superior had not heard him at all. Nevertheless, he relayed the rest of the message. "The good news, sir, is the colonel survived."

Slowly, El Presidente turned, a look of disbelief on his face. "What did you say?"

"I said the colonel survived, sir. He was found by some farmers and taken to the nearest hospital. He has suffered second-degree burns to his chest, his hands were badly damaged, and he has some broken ribs, but his condition is stable, sir. I thought you'd be relieved to hear this."

El Presidente continued to stare at his man. Then cursing to himself, he said, "The bastard! The devil's bastard refuses to die!"

"Sir?"

"The bastard can't be killed. You're staring at me as if I were a madman. I am not raving, Raul, I intended for him to die, do you hear me, Raul? But that son of a bitch lives on to spite me."

A look of horror appeared on the Chief of Staff's face as he watched El Presidente pace about the balcony. His horror was magnified on hearing El Presidente say, "He is no fool, that Aure, he sees my hand in this. I want him killed. Now."

"Sir, no, not now! The time is wrong."

"What do you mean 'not now,' Raul? Can't you see that Aure has become a danger to me, more so now that he knows I wanted him salvaged?"

"Sir, he must be made to think you had no hand in this. That it was an accident. Send in your best doctors to heal him, fly him back to the city and give him the best care. You must be above suspicion. The last thing he should think is that you planned this. You have seen how unpredictable he is. Who knows what he will think of doing. You must leave him with no doubt of your concern for his well-being. There will be a better time to deal with him."

Reason won in the end and El Presidente abandoned what the Chief of Staff considered his mad scheme. But nevertheless it appalled the Chief of Staff to see yet another act that attested to his superior's loosening grip on power and reason. If only El Presidente had consulted with him before ordering the Defense Minister to arrange Aure's death. Not that the Chief of Staff wished to protect the colonel. He, more than anyone perhaps, could see the advantage of disposing of Aure.

Meanwhile, El Presidente's attention returned to the river. And his words did little to reassure the Chief of Staff that all was well.

"He's out there," he said in a flat voice, more to himself than to his aide.

"Sir?"

"He's out there, watching and waiting, and all this is his doing. . . ."

The puzzled Chief of Staff listened to his superior's strange words. It was a while before he realized that El Presidente was speaking of Luis Bayani, whose body lay somewhere in the waters of the river that flowed past the palace.

"He's down there somewhere, poisoning the water, yes, poisoning it, slowly undermining me, protecting even his own murderer in order to thwart me."

El Presidente turned to his aide and said, "I want them to step up the river-dredging project, Raul. These men are not doing a proper job!"

"Sir, the operation is going as planned."

"It hasn't turned up his body! I want the river cleaned . . . cleaned of Bayani's body and spirit." With that, El Presidente stepped back into his office. The Chief of Staff watched him go, noting the slow movements of the man, sadly recalling him in better times.

While Aure and Bayani occupied El President's mind, back at the *Chronicle*, it was the seismologist Armando Cruz who obsessed Mel. On hearing about the cathedral's strange disappearance, she rushed to the phone, frantically trying to get hold of the seismologist who a few weeks ago she had been forced to interview. But Mel failed to get hold of him. And the Seismological Study Center refused to divulge his whereabouts. A few more phone calls revealed that the seismologist had been arrested up north the week before and on his return to the city had quickly resigned from his post. No one knew where he was now.

I left her still on the phone. It was close to six o'clock and I longed for the quiet of my room in Vito Cruz. I stepped out of the *Chronicle* building and instantly felt hot and sticky. I fanned myself with my hand as I walked to the end of the block, but just as I made to cross the road, a car slowed down in front of me, blocking my way. I scowled at the driver but couldn't see through the heavily tinted glass. The window came down just then and, to my surprise, revealed the face of my father.

38

In My Father's House

As soon as I saw the don, I knew that the quiet night I wished for wasn't going to happen. The look my father shot me through the car window said I had somehow done something to displease him.

His face was a mask of displeasure. And although it occurred to me that I didn't have to fall in with his wishes, I understood his nature too well. And I had no desire to have it out with him in the middle of a busy city street, especially one where I was a familiar face.

So when he said in his cold voice, "Get in!", I got in.

He drove in silence, which suited me just fine. I sat back and said nothing. I did wonder, though, what could have brought this change of attitude when the last time we were together we had arrived at a civil way of dealing with each other. What had I done now?

The answer was staring me in the face.

On the dashboard of his car was that day's issue of the *Chronicle*. The paper was turned to the page of my river-dredging story and folded to a size that drew attention to that piece alone. Surely, I thought, he could not have flown all the way back to the city because of my little story. As I thought this, I felt the don's eyes on me and I returned his gaze. For someone who has never had to answer to anyone, it was strange being made to feel that I had to account for my every action, and at the age of twenty-three at that.

But no words came from his mouth. He did not mention the

article. Yet. A sure sign that he had much to say. He was a strategist of the first grade, the don, one whom I would hate to sit and negotiate with across a table. He knew the power of silence as much as he knew the power of words. So silence it was for the next forty-five minutes that it took to negotiate the distance between the *Chronicle* and the house in the municipality of San Juan.

Welcome to my father's house.

It surprised me some that the house was where it was, as I expected someone like the don to live in a more exclusive suburb instead of this middle-class enclave. As for the house itself, I couldn't make it out clearly in the weak light of dusk. But with the help of the streetlights I could see part of it as we pulled up by its front gate. Looking through the iron grille, I saw a good-sized front garden and beyond it, a single-story bungalow. What I couldn't see was why he had brought me here. I was full of questions but refused to give him any satisfaction by asking them. I, too, knew how to play the game.

At this point, the don got out and opened the gate while I waited in the car. Then he got in behind the wheel again and drove up the short driveway, stopping the car by the front steps. He switched off the engine and, before opening his door, reached for the copy of the *Chronicle* on the dashboard. Yes, we would eventually get to that tonight. Then he signaled for me to follow him, so I, too, stepped out of the car and headed toward the steps.

I watched him as he drew the key from his pocket and inserted it into the lock. I heard it click and waited as he pushed the door open. I followed him inside. We walked through a small foyer lit by a wall light. I stayed a few paces behind him as he turned into the living room. What I saw made me pause.

In the sparsely furnished room sat my mother.

Finally, the don turned around to face me and announced: "You will live here."

It took a while for me to get over my disbelief and give voice to my sense of outrage that he should be so presumptuous as to think I would accept this from him. My anger finally loosened my tongue and I told him what I felt and exactly what he could do with this house of his. But the don only stood looking down at me, unmoved, while I spewed out all the words I could string together.

Of the things I told him, I remember most clearly my saying, "You don't have to buy my forgiveness."

To which he replied, "I never asked for it."

Then he continued to speak, making nothing of my earlier interruption. "You will move here as soon as you get it furnished," he told me, before going on to explain the financial arrangements he had made for me, and the separate arrangements he had made for my mother, and how he hoped that with time she and I would resolve our differences, for it was not Consuelo who was at fault in this matter. As he spoke, his voice echoing in the near-empty room, I paced about, waiting for him to finish.

"Did you understand what I just said, Clara?"

I turned around and walked up to him. "I understood everything. But what you have failed to understand is I am staying where I am. I am not moving into your house."

"No Pellicer is going to live in a room in a decrepit old house."

"Is that your only problem? Then you must cease to worry."

I told him then of Charlie's will. It was the first he had heard of it and from the frown on his face I knew it displeased him. I told him I had been amply provided for and would be secure all my life, but the frown only deepened.

Finally he spoke, his voice full of reproach. "You would rather receive from a stranger than from me."

I didn't know what to say to that. For he was more of a stranger than Charlie. I found myself feeling protective of Charlie, whom I had never known but who at least had cared about me. While to the don—I realized now what angered me about his gift of a house—I believed I was someone he felt he had an obligation to. So I told him, "You owe me nothing. I don't need or want your charity."

He gave me one those sardonic looks that I had come to expect from him. "I am not known for being charitable, Clara. I never give unnecessarily."

"So what makes this necessary? I am nothing to you."

Softly, more to himself than to me, he said, "You are my daughter."

Sliding the glass door open, I made my way out into the garden. Only after a few seconds did I realize that Consuelo, who had spoken not a word while the don and I battled it out, had followed me outside. I turned to watch her approach, her steps still slow with her pain but, compared with a few days ago, she was walking better.

"You knew about this?" I asked her.

She shook her head. "He came to see me at the convent this morning. That was when he told me about it."

"And you said yes," I told her accusingly, not bothering to hide my disapproval.

"My first instinct was to throw it back at him, Clara. Like you, I wanted to refuse." She paused, her eyes on her palms, the wounds still visible. "But a small voice told me to hold my tongue, to think before speaking. You see, Clara, I talk of forgiveness, pray for it, but I don't quite understand what it is about. The nature of forgiveness. I had to think awhile to see that by refusing to let him make amends, I would be continuing to punish him. There is a part of me that resists forgiving him, but I am fighting that part."

I told Consuelo, "He doesn't have to make amends, I don't expect it and don't want it. And certainly not in this way, surely, this is like . . . like buying someone!"

"Yes, it would seem so to you . . . and to me, but not to him. To him, he abandoned me, and you in the process. To right that wrong, he must do the opposite. He must provide us with a home. It is the only thing, Clara, that would satisfy his sense of justice. Do not look at me like that. For it is true, he is just in his own way."

"Well, I do not need him. I have a job, you know. And even had Charlie not provided for me, I would have managed well enough."

"Proud, proud Clara, you are truly his daughter."

I glared at her but she continued. "You fear it is pity that drives him. Have you not heard or understood anything I have said to you? You are his daughter, the child he would have been proud of."

When I made to protest, Consuelo waved her hand to stop me.

"No, please do not tell me you are Clara Perez, and not a Pellicer, nothing will change your blood and your character."

I stuffed my hands in my pockets and paced about, thinking about what my mother said, and of my father's words to me before I walked out of the house.

You are my daughter.

All my life, I had been Clara, convent waif, no one's child yet everyone's responsibility. The shared responsibility of two dozen nuns and novices, and of an invisible self-appointed guardian now dead. I had been all this but I had never been someone's daughter. Not until my mother returned for me. Not until my father called me his and opened the door of his house to me.

"It is a modest place which I myself chose," the don began on my return to the house, making no mention of my earlier angry departure.

"It is in your name, Clara, but I wish you to live here with your mother. It is too dangerous to have Consuelo's name on it. My mother knows her and should she decide to search for the two of you, all she needs to do is search for anything associated with Consuelo. In your case, Clara, you can explain it away easily enough as a legacy from . . . from Charlie." He paused at this point, as if saying the name and acknowledging what Charlie had done for me were a source of discomfort for him. He continued after a while, saying, "It is not that I begrudge you a better home. But it is better not to draw too much attention to yourself."

Then he came to stand in front of me. "Especially in view of what you seem hell-bent on pursuing."

And with that my father finally arrived at what he called my dangerous crusade.

He held the copy of the *Chronicle* in front of me.

I learned that he now made it a point to read the *Chronicle*. And that on arriving in the city that morning had bought a copy at the airport and so come upon my story. As he launched into his attack of my actions, my mother took the paper from him and began reading what I had, in my father's opinion, so recklessly written.

My pride in the story was not shared by him. "Do not think," he warned, "that your words will go unnoticed forever. The palace has farseeing eyes and far-reaching arms. If I can watch you from a distance, think how much better they'll be at it, Clara. You look shocked. So you should be. I want you to think, to be disturbed, and to be watchful."

He told me that he knew about Luis Bayani's fate. And on his mentioning Luis, I felt my loss once more. "He is somewhere in this river that you have written about so cleverly, and I know that is why you chose to write what you did. Well, leave him there before you are sent to join him."

Then the don gave me a glimpse of his secret thoughts and wishes. "This is a dying regime, Clara, be patient, for it will go by its own hand. But just because it has become weak doesn't mean it is impotent to act. Hasn't your friend's fate taught you this?"

Stunned by his disloyal sentiments, I said, "You are related to them now."

He did not comment on this or deny it, but a look of distaste flickered briefly over his face.

"My pride springs from my name and my heritage. Yours is pride of a different nature. You are gifted and strong-willed, like the best and the worst of the Pellicers. You cannot deny that part of your parentage, much as you dislike it and all that comes from me. Your arrogance lies in your moral righteousness. You believe you are ensured victory in this mad crusade you have embarked on. And your youth gives you a false sense of invincibility. But just ask yourself this: how can you take on the palace on your own?"

I chose not to answer this last question of my father's. It would have been unwise—and he would have found more cause to hound me, and my mother would have found reason to worry—for me to tell him that he had it all wrong. That as of yesterday, I was no longer alone.

I have found the others.

39

An Encounter by the River

I finally realized why Luis Bayani wanted me to come to the river. He wished for me to meet someone and, in the process, find the others.

Let me go back to the afternoon when I wrote the story about the dredging of the river. After I left the *Chronicle* that day, I did not return at once to the house in Vito Cruz.

I made my way back to the river.

By the time I got there, the men were gone. I didn't know why I felt compelled to see it one more time. But there I was once more. I decided to go for a walk along its bank. This is not a scenic area, as I mentioned before. My first visit here with my mother had revealed to me the extent of its ugliness.

It was close to six o'clock. The bright orange sun had half disappeared into the horizon. The clouds over it were tinged by its fiery rays. A million-dollar sunset in a barren landscape. I made for the mound where I had stood the first time I visited the place. Where I sensed—with unshakable certainty—Luis Bayani had made his way to his watery grave.

The figure of the young man came into view as I was a third of the way up the mound. He was sitting on the wall where I had thought to sit myself. His presence was an unwelcome intrusion, for I had come to think of this spot as my own. I wished for him to go away, for I wanted to be alone. But there he was.

I could have left, of course, but I had walked all this way. So I sat a few meters away from him, hoping he would take the hint and depart. From the corner of my eye I saw him glance at me but he said nothing, returning his attention to the river.

At least he had not sought to engage me in conversation. I was in no mood to talk. I, too, sat and gazed at the water. Peering into its black and oily depths. Trying to glimpse the face of the friend lost to me. There was so much I wished to tell him.

A pebble landed on the water, rippling its surface. I shot the young man a look and noticed for the first time his look of quiet despair. Whatever it was I saw in his face, I found myself thinking this man was in mourning. What I didn't discern yet was that he mirrored my own pain.

We are drawn to those who are like us.

He glanced at me shortly, giving me what looked like a tentative smile, then he spoke for the first time. "Are you from around here?" he asked, then after looking at me curiously and concluding that I did not look like I belonged in the wasteland, added, "You must be new here."

I thought about his question. I had been here once before today, but had returned three times this day alone. How to answer?

He turned away, thinking I had snubbed him. Somehow it seemed important to me to change this impression. He looked so alone. And just then I, too, felt the need for someone to talk to. So I said, "Not really. Last week was the first time."

Surprised that I had answered him, he looked at me, suddenly at a loss for words. So I told him my name.

"I'm Clara . . . Clara Perez."

And he told me his.

"I am Laslo Jimenez."

Sometime later, I came to stand with Laslo in front of a tiny shanty in a narrow street that stood in the shadow of Smoky Mountain.

When the door opened and I stepped inside a room the size of a box, with a ceiling so low you could reach out and touch it, I found myself staring at a wizened-faced hunchback who smelled of the mountain. The man looked as though his bones would break. But Laslo assured me the old man was tough.

Under the light of the single bulb in what passed for his living area, the old man's face was sharp and shadowy. If I met this creature in some street even in broad daylight, I would not have spoken to him. But here I was in his home, his eyes eagle-bright, measuring, seeing through my soul. Then he wheezed out these words: "Eh, Laslo boy, see what you find when I send you out for a walk?"

I felt I had passed some test.

It would be many hours before I was to leave that shanty. For ahead of us were long hours of talking. We took turns telling of our time with Luis. And in finally hearing him spoken of by others, I found myself piecing together those parts of his existence I had failed to learn in my brief time with him. And they, too, learned of his time with me in the Convent of Santa Clara.

There were many other things I would hear that night, many of them new to Laslo as well, for the old man knew Luis far better than the two of us. As we listened to him, I finally felt I could let some of my grief go. The thing was, when someone simply disappears from your life, accepting their permanent absence is difficult. But that evening we laid Luis to rest with our shared memories and found comfort in each other's presence.

So this is how I met Laslo and the Philosopher of the Mount at Smoky Mountain when I went in search of the spirit of Luis Bayani on the south bank of the river.

And you must know this: that evening was the beginning of it all.

40

❧

The Writing on the Wall

The phantom figures moved in the night along the deserted boulevard with its winking neon signs. Not a vehicle was in sight, for the city lay in sleep, its citizens dreaming their long dreams. There were thirteen of them. All garbed in black, their faces smudged with soot so that they melded into the deceptive dark. That section of the boulevard with its long wall had been specially chosen. Situated a good distance from the streetlights, it lay hidden in shadows.

Silence prevailed as the figures worked. No one uttered a word. The only sound came from their breathing and the swishing of their brushes against the surface of the wall. Their strokes fluid and bold. They had painted this on the canvas of their imagination a thousand times, so that now their hands moved surely. There is no hesitation when one is finally living a dream.

The spaces between each letter had been carefully measured in paces. Seven human paces to a letter. This was the distance that separated each writer standing before the wall. The message was short. Three words consisting of thirteen letters. One writer for each letter. They worked with precision. So that twenty-seven minutes after they began, they were gone.

The only evidence of their visit the writing on the wall.

* * *

With his meager belongings stuffed in his old army bag, Rogelio Campos got on a jeepney and headed for the northern pier where he was due in two and a half hours to board a ship for the south.

Soon after being cleared by the Jimenez Commission, Rogelio had informed Commander Reyes he was leaving the army. The commander was not surprised by Rogelio's announcement, although he regretted the thought of losing one of the few men under his command who showed some promise. God knows how few there were who displayed any aptitude for military work. He had asked Rogelio to reconsider.

"Come back to me in a few months if you still feel the same way."

Rogelio, out of respect for his old commander, had postponed his departure for many weeks, during which he gave the matter careful consideration. But the judge was right. There was no point in remaining. He was quick to note how his fellow soldiers looked at him. There was no warm welcome extended to him. It was as though he had committed a crime in being acquitted by the Jimenez Commission. It was ironic, really, how they made him feel he had betrayed them when in fact it was the army who had been quick to sacrifice him. Finally, Rogelio went to see Commander Reyes and told him of his decision. That he believed his future lay some-where else.

"What are your plans, Rogelio?"

"I am going home."

And that indeed was what Rogelio had decided to do. He was not returning to resume his work in the cane fields of Hacienda Esper-anza. No. He was not as foolish as that. He had thought carefully about his status as an escaped *sacada* and whether he owed it to Don Miguel Pellicer to return and work for him. He asked himself whether he had done a cowardly thing in escaping. But Rogelio remained convinced that he had in no way cheated anyone. By his years of labor he had more than paid off his debts to the don and to the hateful *contratista*. He owed them nothing. In fact, none of the workers should be in the pathetic state of debt they were in.

Rogelio felt the need to go home and tell those he had left behind the truth about their situation. Yes, they needed work and so should continue working for the *hacienda*. But they didn't need to put up with the unjust conditions imposed on them. They had every right to demand better terms.

So Rogelio, who had escaped three years ago from Hacienda Esperanza, was now returning to right the wrongs he had endured there. He had learned an important lesson during his time away: escaping was not the answer, it failed to solve the problem. What he wished to do on his return was to find a solution, so that no other plantation worker need ever feel he had to escape again.

A quick look into the future will reveal Rogelio's fate. He would become a labor agitator, hated by every *contratista*, labeled a troublemaker by every plantation owner. His life he would devote to the workers' cause and, in the end, he would sacrifice it in his fight for their rights. You may think this is a sad end for the former soldier Rogelio Campos, but he himself would consider his life well lived. For like Luis Bayani, whom he so admired, and like Rizal, whose book Bayani had given him, Rogelio succeeded in opening the eyes of many to their strength as individuals. But all this lies in the future. Right now his only concern is to make his way home.

As the jeepney made its way through the city streets to the docks, Rogelio gazed out the window at the passing scene. He was hoarding all the little details. The congested streets, the houses, the buildings, the fountain in the rotunda, the cinema billboards filled with the faces of movie stars, the cafés that lined the roads, the shops that went on for several blocks. He committed all this to memory, for he was not sure he would ever return to this city again.

Of all the things he tried to remember on the morning of his exodus, what stayed with him forever were the three words he saw in the distance—words that lifted his heart and filled him with hope—as the jeepney traveled along the boulevard past a concrete wall that stretched across a whole block.

In bold red letters were written the memorable words: BAYANI IS ALIVE.

* * *

The palace had been the first to make this claim.

When the student leader mysteriously disappeared after the grenade attack on Campo Diaz, it was whispered that the military had done away with him. But the palace issued an official announcement to the contrary. For a start, there was no body. Therefore, where was the proof of death and of foul play? To bolster their claim the palace offered a reward for information of his whereabouts.

But Bayani was still missing many weeks after the protest march. The public outcry grew. Bayani's parents demanded an investigation. And they were joined by the parents of the still-missing Sophia. The Loyola University administration demanded an explanation for the absence of two of its students, this time backed by the church. And various student organizations collected the signatures of over sixty thousand citizens petitioning the government to launch another investigation.

The dean of the Loyola paid the senator another visit. And this time he found the senator more receptive. Later he would tell the associate dean how the former Loyolan seemed more subdued and serious, although he could not explain what had caused this change. What was important, though, was that Senator Sixto Mijares agreed to call on El Presidente a second time to again take up the matter of the missing Sophia, along with the business of Bayani's whereabouts.

Then something unexpected happened. Splashed across the government-owned daily *National Times* was the headline: BAYANI JOINS REBELS, WITNESS REPORTS. The article claimed that Bayani had been seen in the company of a woman with long hair. Both were traveling south with two men who were known in the town of Lamarosa to be part of the insurgent movement.

Never had a news article received so much public attention. The remaining members of the YRM Council issued a statement denying any links with the rebels. YRM and Bayani were never about revolution. Bayani expounded reform. Once more they accused the military and the palace of the murder of Bayani. And all over the city, people were heard to say, "They're making it up. It's a cover-up. Bayani is dead."

To which the palace gave what has become its standard reply: "Prove it. Where is his body?"

The river never yielded Luis Bayani's body.

Laslo believed this was because Luis did not wish to be found. So late one night, he told the group gathered at Mang Serio's place, "Let us oblige the palace."

The others stared at him, unclear as to what he meant. He explained. "Luis alive is of better use to us."

"But they killed him and we need to prove it."

No. Laslo disagreed. Slowly he explained his plan. They looked at him doubtfully; the madness of it frightened them at the same time that it left their blood stirring the way it had not stirred since the disastrous protest march. Laslo had the gift of the gods that night. His words sparked a flame in the hearts of all. Oh yes, this wild, mad, daring, and grandiose plan was possible. And oh yes, they felt up to it. After weeks of being directionless, they were hungry to be doing something, something that would shake up the palace and stir the people.

Huddled together in that small shanty, they whispered into the early hours of the morning. Thirteen of them. Scheming and plotting and vowing to carry out the job. And so thirteen phantom figures set out one night many weeks after Luis Bayani's disappearance and brought him back to life.

Their message of life, of resurrection, sent a ripple of disbelief, then of excitement and of hope across the city as the morning brought the people into the streets on their way to work. And those that traveled the route that took them along the boulevard would see, splashed in red across a long concrete wall, the message that Bayani, who they thought had died, had risen and might one day come again.

The *Chronicle*, like all its competitors, ran a story—coupled with a photograph—about this mysterious giant graffito that appeared overnight on a major thoroughfare of the city.

And soon the rumor of his death was replaced by the rumor of his life. And this would give rise to another rumor, one that rapidly traveled beyond the city to the rest of the islands.

El Presidente is ill.

He lost consciousness, it is rumored, on hearing about the writing on the wall. Rumor has it that he is but a shadow of his former self. That he spends his time gazing into the river, where men continue to work, cleaning the waters of centuries of accumulated dirt and debris. And when he is not out there, he sits in a darkened office, the curtains drawn, fearful of the light, mumbling to himself.

As he grows more pale and wan and listless, Madam—they whisper—is busy planning for the succession. She sits by his side, learning his business, abandoning her own. Set aside are the beautification projects, the construction of a basilica to rival St. Peter's, the new glass concert hall in the mountains designed to reveal the valley beyond, the creation of Embassy Row with every foreign consulate in a building inspired by its country; forgotten, too, are the various festivals and celebrations and fetes that mark her calendar every year.

The business at hand is a matter of life and death.

Even the bride and her groom have returned home early from the waters of the Caribbean. Their golden-brown skin in stark contrast to the pallid color of El Presidente's face.

Rumor has it, too, that what ails him is not something that will pass, for it resides in his liver. That part of the human anatomy in which all our dark secrets and resentments, anger and anxiety reside. It was also whispered that El Presidente's liver has been the subject of much attention by specialists flown in from across the Pacific.

In a moment of desperation Madam sends for the woman from Calle de Leon, but the woman cannot be found. Madam is told that soon after Consuelo Lamuerta regained consciousness, she moved away. No one knows her exact whereabouts, only that she had returned south to live with her husband's family. A search is made down south but yields nothing.

There is much talk, too, about the closing of the bridge.

I do not need Mel to tell me why the palace has ordered the closing of the Lacson Bridge to traffic. I have never been one to believe in superstitions, but this one I subscribe to with all my heart.

Has not the river sung and has not the cathedral disappeared?

I am willing this one to happen, the third sign of the seer's prophecy, the crossing of a bridge. Madam, I believe, now understands its meaning. The bridge is the Lacson Bridge, which leads to the street that takes you to the gates of the palace.

Sometimes I close my eyes and imagine a throng of people crossing it, pouring out into the street below. I hear their cries in my mind, I see their raised fists, and I see the gates flung wide open, and the multitude descending on the palace by the river where Luis Bayani lies.

Although I can no longer cross it on my way to the *Chronicle*, I see the bridge clearly in my mind. And I swear I will be one of those to cross it one day.

The message that Bayani is alive appears more and more often now. There is no pattern. It appears at random. There is no telling who is doing the writing, no predicting where it will appear next.

Others, not known to us, have taken to writing this same message: BAYANI IS ALIVE. One night, it even appeared on the bridge leading to the palace.

And it is not just the writing on the wall that the people watch for.

Luis Bayani, from his hideout in the south, has begun sending messages to the people. In pamphlets and letters, he addresses the nation and its citizens. He calls on them to make their grievances known. He asks them to speak out. To demand changes. To participate. To take responsibility. And most of all, he asks them to bear witness.

Luis Bayani has revealed a truth that has sent the people back into the streets in even greater numbers. That Sophia Ramos-Sytangco is not with him.

Ask the palace where she is, he says.

And now it is rumored that a dark shadow has taken hold of El Presidente's liver. A shadow the size and shape of a small stone. It is growing, they say, growing inside him, eating him up little by little.

But tales like this must not be taken as truth. You must remind yourself that it is hard to tell where truth ends and a lie begins. So listen all you like, but disbelieve all you hear.

You are in the city of lies.

What about the judge? What does he believe?

The judge keeps his own counsel these days. He watches his son Laslo closely—with equal measures of concern and of interest. He is not blind to Laslo's nocturnal writings. The judge knows the hand—he is not aware that there are thirteen of them—behind the writing on the walls of the city. And he suspects—the thought fills him with a sense of pride—that the mind behind it also belongs to his son.

This is a different Laslo before him. How can one be so transformed? The carefree, irresponsible and rebellious Laslo died with the woman called Sophia. This Laslo is a quiet being who rarely smiles. One who thinks secret thoughts, plans and executes the impossible. Is the soul of discretion. The judge is not unhappy with the change. But nevertheless, it fills him with concern. Should Laslo's activities become known to the palace, the judge is no longer sure he can protect him. Times have changed, and across the river, in the palace of confusion, reason has fled.

The judge is no longer the man he was at the beginning of this tale. Like his son, he has learned silence, preferring to observe than to speak in anger. Certainty, which was inbred in him, has made room for tolerance. It can be said then that, to the relief of the judge's wife, peace has finally come to the Jimenez home. The war between father and son has ceased at last.

41

A Tale with No End

See, I have written the tale Luis Bayani jokingly said I might write on the night I saw him last. I wanted to set it in words. This cautionary tale about a people who eat fire and drink water.

Although these are frightening and unsure times, I sense we are on the brink of change. I can smell it in the air, the way I can smell the coming of rain.

Since the night he disappeared, never to be seen again, Luis Bayani claimed my eyes. I, Clara Perez, now measure the world in the terms he envisioned for it in his short life. I do this with my words. For all those pamphlets and letters that carry his messages come not from some impregnable mountain where he supposedly hides these days. They are penned here, in the city, by me.

No. I am not alone in this. There are the others. Like Mang Serio of Smoky Mountain, who sits and listens and mediates between the sometimes conflicting minds of the thirteen of us who work together. He is a sobering influence, cautioning us against our reckless tendencies. I welcome his presence, although at times he can be painfully philosophical. Luis named him well.

And there is Laslo. Witness and survivor.

I didn't know Laslo until the afternoon we met by the river. But those that knew him before tell me he has shed his old self, that he has grown quiet, older, serious.

Lost in thought, he often wears a haunted look. Then I say his name and the look quickly disappears to be replaced by eyes that glint with a searing intensity. He reminds me of Luis Bayani during these moments.

Now let me tell you something that happened a few weeks ago.

I arrived at Smoky Mountain early. And Laslo, too, had come before the others. We went for a walk down to the river which bordered one side of the slum district of Milagros. He and I often come here to sit on the wall near the abandoned warehouse. To think, to clear our heads. There is something about the place that drives away our insecurities. Perhaps because here we both feel closest to Luis Bayani. It is where Luis drew us on the day Laslo and I found each other. That, I know, was no accident.

For you mustn't think we are so fearless of what we do. That we are heroes. We do things in spite of our fears. We are often scared. Waking in the middle of the night, heart thumping, body damp with sweat. I dream often of being caught. My writing hand mercilessly chopped off, so that I must write with the blood that pours from its open stump. Such is my nightmare. Then morning comes and I feel whole again. And I remind myself of what Luis Bayani said to me one night in the Convent of Santa Clara: "We grow into our roles."

Sometimes I wish for my old life back. The simplicity of it. When I could sleep in peace and wake in peace and complain of boredom. All the cares of the past are nothing compared with what besets my mind these days. But there is no turning back, no walking away from people and situations.

Of the day I speak of, I had had one of those nightmares the night before. So Laslo—who knows what makes up his dreams, he keeps much to himself—agreed to go for a walk with me.

We sat on the river wall, like the first time we met. Not speaking. Just watching the water flow and the barges and ferries and *bancas* go by. The sound of water calming my mind. The river flowed freely. The water lilies were gone. The water, though, was still dark and murky, for the factories along the river continue to hemorrhage oil, toxic waste and sewage.

The dredging operation finished months ago. No body found. Though I had hoped they would find the body of a man whose eyes had been plucked out so that justice could be done, I have since contented myself with the thought that Luis, because of his continued absence, will live forever.

Just before the skies darkened as dusk set in, Laslo said it was time to head back. We got off the wall and began to retrace our steps. Not long after this, Laslo bent down and picked up an object. With it in his palm, he moved his hand, tilting it here and there as he studied it.

"What is it?" I asked.

"Look. It glows red."

He brought his hand in front of me and I saw the small stone, the size of a twenty-five-*centavo* coin. It was a dull gray. I told him so.

"Here," he said, angling the stone so I could see it better. "Can't you see it? There, it just glimmered."

I shook my head. He gave up trying to make me see, puzzled at my blindness. We continued to walk.

Some days later, he still had the stone.

"What are you keeping it for?" I asked.

He shrugged.

Then I recalled all the tales about the stone, all the rumors and all the old stories that Mel used to tell me.

Now I watch Laslo closely. For telltale signs. I have been keeping company with Mel too long, I think. But nevertheless I keep an eye on Laslo. There is much comfort to be derived from the thought that nothing is lost in this life. One life goes only to bring into the world a new life. A stone is lost, a stone is found.

Who knows? I may write about that, too, one day.

Now I shall tell you about my mother.

She no longer wears black. I saw her for the first time in color the day we buried Charlie. Oh, how long ago it all feels now. She wore a blue dress as we gathered to lay Charlie to rest in the little cemetery that lies at the beginning and end of this tale.

We stood side by side, all of us, the nuns, myself, and my mother, and the lawyer Pepito Mariano. We stood and watched as the coffin containing Charlie the Chinaman's remains was lowered into the ground.

Mother Superior chose a spot near the mango tree where long ago Charlie slept when he first found the cemetery through a crack in the west wall.

The wall itself had been repaired.

My mother and I were to learn later from Mother Superior that the don had arranged for the old stone wall to be sealed, and for the refurbishment of the chapel.

"He did that? What for? That was all an act!" I exclaimed in surprise. I was referring to the day the men had come in search of Luis Bayani and the don had carried him to the chapel and hid him under the altar.

"He is a proud man, Clara, and honorable in his own way, which is why he felt he needed to do something for the convent in return for the years we cared for you."

"He told you this?" I asked, thinking that they had spoken.

"No, Clara, it is what I read in his actions." Touching my arm lightly, Mother Superior said, "Learn to see him with your heart, Clara, not with your mind."

My mother, on hearing what the don had done, seemed not surprised at all, perhaps because with every day, she forgave herself and him more. My mother craved for peace.

As the first clump of earth fell that day, I looked at Charlie's grave. I knelt and picked up some moist soil, its rich smell reaching me. I sprinkled this onto his coffin, and said a silent thank you to this man whom I never met, but who watched me from a distance when my parents' eyes were focused inward on their tormented selves.

I regret never meeting Charlie, and learning of him only after he was gone. As is often the case in life, we missed each other on the road and I wonder how different things might have been had we met somehow. And standing there by his open grave, it amazed me how we had come full circle. Here, in the Convent of Santa Clara where Charlie's journey began so long ago, it had come to an end at last.

But his end marked many beginnings. For as Luis Bayani said long ago, time is not linear. There is no beginning and no end, only a cycle that repeats itself. Take this tale that I have written, it has not finished and never will.

One of the beginnings I speak of is the journey my father and I are making toward each other.

Today I received a letter from the don.

He has been on his island for over a year now. And until six months ago, I had not heard from him. But I thought of him much in his absence. Away from his domineering presence, when the dust of our skirmishes had settled, I could see and think of him with more objectivity. And given enough time, I came to realize an important thing.

Do you remember that night in my mother's room when she told us her story? When at the end of it I stood looking at her and the don and I asked myself who could save their weak, damaged hearts?

I, Clara Perez, am the protector of their hearts. I can make them feel again.

At last I understood why I had been returned to my mother, and my presence made known to my father.

So I began to write to the don. Swallowing my pride, I wrote to him. He did not reply for some time and there were times when I cursed his silence. How many times must I be kept out of his life? But I kept writing just the same, encouraged by Consuelo. Letter after letter telling him of my life and how my mother was keeping. Her hands have healed, I told him. Her feet no longer bleed, I wrote next. I told him, too, of my assignments at the *Chronicle*—but never of my other business. Sometimes I felt I was talking to a deaf, dumb, and blind person. But I persisted. He was right when he called me stubborn. What stopped me from losing hope was realizing at last that the don was a heartsick man who lived under the misconception that by turning his back on the world he could live without pain at last. In his island fortress he guarded his heart. But each letter that I penned was a knock on his door. I stormed his fortress with my words, refusing to be ignored, until at last he let me in.

Six months ago, he sent me his first reply. I will not tell you what he wrote, for the don would hate to have his life made public. But I will tell you that his first letter was brief and his words gave nothing away. How like him. But with time, his letters have grown longer. Slowly, he has opened the window to his life, so that from where I am I can see him clearly.

I see him early in the morning going down the steps of his house by the sea, onto the sandy stretch below. I see him strolling, traversing the perimeter of his island, feeling the wind on his face, watching the gulls take wing as the palms sway overhead. Then I see him by the small jetty, waiting for the arrival of the boat. The man hands him a packet. Letters and business papers and the major dailies, including a copy of the *Chronicle*. The packet under his arms, he walks back to his house. While he sits and has breakfast, he goes through the day's correspondence. And when at night, I sit at my desk by my bedroom window, I know my father, too, is sitting by his desk in a little study off his *lanai*. And as he begins to write, I imagine it is for me that he puts pen to paper.

His heart is thawing and so is mine. And I see our words building a bridge on which we will walk toward each other one day. I imagine that we will see him again. My mother and I. The future is a place full of possibilities.

My mother and I live in my father's house. The house we could have chosen to keep empty to punish him, but have chosen to fill with our presence. It still surprises me that I have agreed to live with her, but it feels right. And that is enough for me.

These days, Consuelo no longer spends all her time praying. Her statues are with Padre Luis in his parish church. Now much of her time is spent in the kitchen where she cooks and bakes with passion, setting plates of delicacies in front of me when I come home from work. I build bridges with my writing, my mother with her cooking. When we sit across from each other at the dinner table, it often occurs to me that even from his remote island, my father has the ability to see his wishes come true. My mother and I are together.

And yes, this was Charlie's dream, too.

She tells me her many dreams. Consuelo, who for many, many

years had difficulty recalling her nocturnal imaginings, now remembers them clearly on waking.

"Sometimes, Clara, I dream six dreams a night. Sometimes I wake in the middle of a dream and when I fall back to sleep, the dream continues."

Last night, my mother dreamed of the river.

"Clara," she said to me, "it was early morning in my dream, and the river was making a bubbling noise that sounded like singing. I rushed outside to look at it, for strangely enough, this house that we now live in stood right next to the river, separated only by a low wall. As I gazed down, I discovered the river had changed. Its waters were clear, so clear I could see to the very bottom.

"The river kept humming this song. It was calling me. So I climbed over the wall, and the water rose some, lapping at my feet, receding then coming back like a hand beckoning to me. I knelt before the river. I cupped my hands and scooped up some water. I drank it. It was sweet, Clara, the water was so sweet, and it smelled clean and pure, and I thought the world, the whole world was new again. I woke up then, feeling refreshed. I felt reborn."

I believe in dreams.

San Juan
31 March 1996

© Greg Parsons

Arlene J. Chai was born and educated in Manila. In 1982, she migrated to Australia with her parents and sisters, and now lives in Sydney's northern beaches area. Her first novel, *The Last Time I Saw Mother*, was an Australian bestseller and has just been published in the US and the UK.